DON'T BANK ON IT

ON IT

GW00778077

HUGH PRYOR

STA BOOKS

www.spencerthomasassociates.com

Cover design – Oscar Viney

Also by Hugh Pryor

RUN AND BREAK (ebook)

POINT OF NO RETURN

Acknowledgements

I really owe this book to my agent 'Rottie', without whom it may never have been published.

I also owe an enormous debt of gratitude to all the great friends and colleagues with whom I have worked over the years and without whose shared experiences the book would never have been written in the first place. They know who they are and they also know who is buying the next round when we meet up!

Chapter 1

"Good morning, Sir. Can I help you?"

"Good morning. I would like to see the Manager please."

"Do you have an appointment?"

"No, but I am here rather unexpectedly and I need to see him on some fairly important business."

"I see, sir. And what might that be?"

"Well, that's why I want to see the Manager."

"Yes sir, I appreciate that, but I'm sure that you also appreciate that the Manager is a very busy man."

"I see. Well, is he available, or not?"

There was already an atmosphere. Alex felt he was facing a grey-haired female stonewall between him and the 'very busy man' who was holding his money. His money had been handed to the bank for them to look after, a service for which he paid. That's how they earned their salaries. Part of the service a client would normally expect therefore, was access to somebody who could offer advice on problems that might crop up during the course of the bank's guardianship of their funds. Certain aspects of that guardianship required sensitive and sometimes confidential handling. The open forum of a banking hall was not the setting of preference for discussions of this nature.

"Well maybe I can help to sort out your problem for you, sir." The lady said, brightly persistent. "The Manager is not always available to passing account holders. He is, as I said, a very busy man." She looked up at Alex, "Or perhaps you would like to make an appointment?" She shuffled through some pages of a diary. "He's pretty booked up, actually. Let's see now... three o'clock next Tuesday? Would that be good for you?"

"At three o'clock, next Tuesday, I shall be in the Sudan. I leave tonight."

"Oh, I'm so sorry, sir. When are you coming back?"

"I will be away for three months."

"Oh well, that should give you a chance to make an appointment to see the Manager when you get back."

"I don't think that you understand my problem, madam."

"So, what is your problem, Mr... er ...?"

"Stewart. I want to take all my money out of your bank."

Alex Stewart's account stood at just over a million Swiss Francs a fact of which she was unaware at that point.

"You wish to take all your money out of the account? But why, Mr Stewart? Why do you want to remove your money? Are you unhappy with our service?"

"That is why I need to speak to the Manager."

"Oh, Very well, Sir!" said the woman with a dismissive shake of the head, as though she didn't wish to waste her time with matters of so little import. "In that case you had better talk to the Manager!"

"Precisely."

Prior to this incident, when Alex had been at the beginning of his flying career, he had served with the military and flown fixed wing aircraft in the deserts of the Middle East. While he was on duty, his mother had had a severe stroke and he returned to the UK on compassionate leave. He arrived four hours after she had passed away.

He was the seventh child in a family of four brothers and three sisters. They were a close-knit unit so the division of the spoils was carried out without rancour. The effects left behind by a mother who had been close to canonisation in Alex's eyes included a 'Deposit Account Passport' in the name of Alexander Selwyn Stewart. There was only one entry in it. A sum of £3,000 had been deposited in the account on the 7th of October 1967. This was, in fact, money bequeathed to him by an aunt when she died. Alex, being overseas at the time, was totally unaware of the bequest until he found the Deposit Passport on his return to England, many years after her death.

The bank, meanwhile, merged with another in the early seventies and the management of the new company so formed decided to invest a considerable sum of money in computerising their accounting system. The job was undertaken by a large firm of management consultants and took three months to complete. In order to streamline the operation, management adopted a new method of numbering the accounts. All clients were advised of the new system and were requested to acknowledge receipt of their revised account numbers. Alex, being out of touch with civilisation at the time, received no news of his windfall and obviously could not comply with this request, so his account remained untouched for almost thirty years.

In 1975, the old account numbers were all abandoned and, since Alex had failed to acknowledge receipt of the new account details, the bank applied the five-year Statute of Limitations. Alex's three thousand pounds effectively became anonymous and the account officially declared dormant. The bank's management no longer considered that it came within their realm of responsibility. At the same time, payment of interest on the deposit account also ceased. Alex calculated that, had it accrued over the intervening years, the fund would now have topped twenty thousand pounds sterling.

When he went to claim what he considered to be his rightful ownership of the principal £3,000, a clearly worried young lady member of the bank's staff referred him to the duty manager who immediately got on to his superiors in London. They said that they considered that Alex's claim, after all these years, was insupportable and referred him to the Banking Ombudsman. He, in turn, confirmed his support for the bank's opinion and advised Alex that 'regretfully' he considered the case to be closed. Alex fumed, but could achieve little.

On yet another occasion, Alex happened upon an opportunity to buy a property in the middle of the town where he and his wife Margie, kept an apartment in the south of England. It consisted of close to one acre of land with a large crumbling 1920s house on it. The old lady who owned it was equally crumbling and, in fact, duly died. Since she had no progeny, the executors put the place up for sale. Because of the dilapidated state of the house, the price was surprisingly reasonable and Alex decided to make further investigations.

He went to his bank in town and made an appointment to see the Customer Care Manager. At the appointed time, he entered the Manager's office. The name 'J.D. Stidwell Customer Care Manager' was printed on the door.

"Good morning Mr Stewart, and how can we be of assistance this morning." Mr Stidwell rose to his feet as a secretary showed Alex in.

"Well, as a matter of fact, I have come to see you about a loan."

"Oh yes, Mr Stewart, and may I enquire what the loan would be for?"

Alex removed an Estate Agent's brochure from his flight bag and presented it to Mr Stidwell.

"There is a property on the corner of Church Street and Amblehurst Road", he said, pointing at the house in the photograph. "The owner died recently and the house has come on the market. As you can see, it is in a poor state of repair, therefore the price is very attractive. My plan would be to demolish the house and build a block of twenty luxury apartments on the land. I was looking at taking out a loan of £700,000, which would cover the property and the demolition as well as the construction of the first ten apartments. At £200,000 per unit, the revenue would be £2,000,000. A substantial profit, I think you will agree. The next ten would bring in another two million."

The manager started to tap away on his computer.

"Excuse me just a moment please, Mr Stewart," he said and Alex sat back awaiting the verdict with some optimism. The manager stabbed a final key and looked up.

"I'm very sorry, Mr Stewart," Mr Stidwell raised his hands defensively, "the bank cannot enter into a loan agreement with you."

"And why is that please?" Alex responded with some surprise.

"According to our records, you have never taken out a loan."

"That is correct, yes. This is the first time I could justify the expenditure."

"Well, Mr Stewart, we cannot give you a loan if you do not have a credit rating and if you have never taken out a loan, you have no credit rating. You see, you have no record of being a reliable repayer. I'm sorry to say, Mr Stewart, but the good old days of manager/client trust have been seriously eroded by a rising mountain of bad debt. We at the bank provide a service, not a charity."

Alex was stuck for words. He rose to his feet and picked up his flight bag. Then the words came back to him.
"I have difficulty believing what I am hearing," he said.

"We could probably establish a credit rating for you, Mr Stewart, but that could take a little while. We would need to research your financial background, of course."

"Well I suppose you had better go ahead and do that then."

"There will, of course, be some small charges for this service but, seeing the length of time that you have been with us, I'm sure they will be minimal."

The search extended over a period of two weeks by which time the property on the corner of Amblehurst Road and Church Street had been sold. The new owner, according to the estate agent's books, was a certain Mr J.D. Stidwell. Alex fumed, but there was little action he could take against the man who had, effectively, only stolen his idea.

All these experiences did nothing to improve Alex's opinion of banks in general and their staff in particular. So, when he was contacted by an old schoolfriend who worked in banking, his sympathies were already blunted by what he saw as the innate arrogance of bankers and the industry as a whole. It wasn't until the friend revealed the full gravity of the situation confronting them that he realised how deep was the chasm opening up before them.

Richard Tarrant had always been well-heeled. Even at school he flaunted his obvious wealth among the more impressionable pupils. He was right on the edge of being a bully but not malicious enough to qualify. He just expected things to go his way because he was larger and richer than most of his peers.

Alex Stewart's upbringing in the rough and tumble of East Africa's ex-British colonies had given him an independent spirit. He was immune to the social barging of people like Tarrant, and Tarrant in turn, was intrigued by the challenge presented by Alex. He decided to test this calm, confident colonial to see just how far he could push him before he reacted. Alex's initials provided an appropriate goad. Alexander Selwyn Stewart. Tarrant almost immediately regretted the plan and his respect for Alex Stewart endured for many years after the broken nose had healed and the missing tooth had been replaced. An ironical friendship grew from this encounter and continued on through their careers in military aviation, which led the two men to some of the more remote and inhospitable corners of the earth together.

When their ways parted, Alex belatedly started a new career in commercial aviation and Dick Tarrant followed his father's footsteps into the pin-striped world of high finance in the City of London.

It was while delving into the ramifications of a failed financial deal one evening that his suspicions were aroused. It involved the finance and development of oil and gas fields in Russia. Europe depended, to a large extent, on reliable supplies of both in order to feed its economies. On the face of it, the deal was pretty straightforward. The negotiators on the European side were experienced in international trade, though hardly any of them had dealt with the more obscure aspects of trading in Russia. In this particular case, there was something much bigger going on than a simple financial deal. There was definitely something deliberate about the collapse of Dnepr Exchange, one of the Russian banks involved.

Then the Chief Executive of Mersey Strand, the prime lending bank, was found dead in his car parked in his garage. There was evidence of orally administered barbiturates discovered during the autopsy but the cause of death was carbon monoxide poisoning from exhaust fumes in the car whose engine was still running when he was found. He had come from a long line of merchant bankers and Melvyn Strand was an icon of the City. He was in constant contact with, not only the British financial aristocracy, but also those who were on the other side of the financial scene. The coroner declared the death to be suicide, possibly brought on by the failure of the other bank in the deal. The thing which raised Tarrant's suspicions was the fact that the entire senior management team of Dnepr Exchange, which was mostly of Russian origin, disappeared before the collapse. They left one very confused young middle management Englishman to take the rap.

When he first started in the City, George Penney had survived much ribaldry about his name but he was still one of those who appeared to be going to the top. To nobody's great surprise, the young man, when confronted by the prospect of a ruined career and the possibility of a long jail sentence, decided to take the easier option offered by a simple, painless overdose of sleeping pills. His body was not found for nearly a week.

The lending bank had taken out cover to insure against currency fluctuations for the deal. Re-payment of the loan was to be guaranteed by oil at $140 a barrel. The price of oil, influenced by the promised availability of massive excesses of Russian hydrocarbons, then fell to below $80 a barrel and continued its plunge to below $50. The Russians chose this opportunity to default on payments. The European financiers tried to claim from the insurance companies who pointed out that the cover was only against currency fluctuations, not fluctuations in the price of oil. The banks were faced with massive losses and had to approach the finance houses of the City as well as the government to bail them out. Dick Tarrant realised it was going to be a long night.

Towards dawn his brain was in turmoil. Whichever way he turned there seemed to be another can of worms. It almost looked as though there was someone planning to complicate things behind the scenes. Finally, it was the uncomplicated, straightforward nature of Alex Stewart's character which led Tarrant to seek his advice, as the full horror of the situation burst upon him.

They arranged to meet at The Checkers, a country pub at Roehook in West Sussex. It was buried in the countryside; an ancient hostelry with worn flagstone floors and head-height beamed timber, seasoned dark by centuries of smoke and ale. Its cosy interior had discreet alcoves for diners who had more confidential conversations to share without disturbance.

" 'Morning Alex." Dick Tarrant held his hand out to greet his friend. "Come and grab a seat." He indicated an old Windsor chair at a table for two by the lattice window. The table was dwarfed by Tarrant's large frame. "What will you have?"

"I'll just have a tomato juice, thanks Dick. Got to drive to my sister's this afternoon. Family gathering."

"With all the trimmings, ice and Worcester sauce, that sort of thing?" Alex nodded with a smile and Tarrant ordered the drinks.

"So what did you want to see me about, Dick?"

"Well, Alex," he looked up and Alex caught the look of concern, bordering on fear, which widened his eyes and raised the thick shaggy eyebrows of his friend. "I think I have stumbled on something which is so big that it threatens the whole economic structure of the western world."

Chapter 2

The trading floor of the New York Stock Exchange was chaos. From a distance it looked as though a civil disturbance was in full swing. The aroma of sweat overcame the powerful air conditioning. There was constant, urgent movement, but the predominant feature of the scene was the noise. It was almost impossible to work out how verbal communication could continue in such a high level of ambient sound. The desperate violence of swirling humanity conveyed an impression of panic. To the casual observer it almost seemed that a police presence might soon be required. Occasionally a stationary figure, with head in hands, an icon of despair, would stand out in the thrashing tangle of people.

Flickering digital signboards flashed news of further financial collapse in an ever-changing stream of multi-coloured announcements that seemed to be whipping up the atmosphere of alarm.

To Samuel J. Jackson Jr. the scene was thrilling. The tumbling prices of stocks offered mouth-watering opportunities for anyone with a sharp eye and money to spend. Sam, as he was known to his colleagues, originated from Trinidad. His father had been a converted Rastafarian and so Sam had never cut his hair in his life. As a result, he sported a grey, Afro-style cloud around his head. His face was the colour of old mahogany with an unobtrusive wisp of grey beard. A thick pair of chipped, rimless glasses made his eyes look as wise as those of an old owl.

Sam's earlier years had been spent among computers in the infancy of information technology. Many of the household names in the industry were on first name terms with him and he had godfathered many a young entrepreneur over the hurdles on their way to unbridled riches.

One of Sam's abiding qualities was his modesty. For a man who had piggy-backed many to the heights of international fame and fortune, he lived frugally. Due to his rural upbringing among the sugar and banana plantations of his native Trinidad, his demands on luxury were small. The quiet wisdom in his conversation hid a razor sharp mind and it was to this mind that many of the more senior members of the financial world came for advice in times of fiscal insecurity.

He and Alex had first met in the heart of the Sahara desert. Alex was company pilot for a seismic exploration team that was seeking to unravel the mysteries of the substrata. Below the dunes were vast reserves of gas which were destined for export to Europe. Sam was the information technology expert who gathered the data, then waved his magic wand and turned figures into intricate three-dimensional maps of the subterranean world beneath them. Alex found this man from the Caribbean absolutely fascinating and they struck up a relationship of mutual respect, built on an exchange of knowledge, laced with humour. In spite of the fact that Sam was almost twenty years older than Alex, their age difference had little effect on their interaction. If anything, it strengthened the bond between them, as each explored the envelope of the other's experience, in a strange kind of way.

It was Sam's expertise which led him, via a rather circuitous route, to the world of finance. During his university studies in England, he had always been fascinated by what drove computer hackers to satisfy the demands of their obsession and he had come to know quite a few of them through the opaque windows of the internet.

He focussed his prodigious mental skills on studying their habits intimately, in an effort to understand what motivated them and, in so doing, became a supreme hacker in his own right. He was known to his friends as 'Jack the Hack' or 'Hacker Jack'. During the course of his studies he stumbled upon a challenge that has titillated many a hacker. It is, in fact, the holy grail of hackers world-wide. The Pentagon.

The ingenious thing about Sam's approach was that, without their knowledge he worked his way up through quite lowly operatives in the US Defence Department, befriending, befuddling and finally breaking into the more sensitive parts of their computers via the internet. He would learn their access codes by algorithmic synchrophasing and use them to break into the next computer up the ladder. With infinite patience, he slithered quietly, snakelike, past all the firewalls and filters, into the holy of holies and deposited a visiting card there, in a top secret file in an extremely closely guarded folder. He then slid back out again, without waking up any of the security systems. He e-mailed the American Ambassador in Grosvenor Square, London, from an anonymous internet café in Warwick Avenue, West London, with the news of the break-in. He mentioned that this was simply an academic exercise and that he would be happy to furnish the American Government with details of the route he had taken to gain access. A simple advertisement for 'dandelion vinegar' in the columns of the London Evening Standard would indicate American Government interest and Sam would then proceed to make further contact.

The advertisement appeared that very evening so Sam e-mailed the routing of his attack on the Pentagon computers to the Ambassador from a different internet café in Ladbroke Grove, as promised. The answer came back immediately, almost as though they had been waiting for his message.

'We must meet. Need your services. Security guaranteed.' Uncle Sam wanted more.
'Suggest Victoria Station at the 'Crusty Roll' by platform 13 this p.m. 1800 GMT. I have Afro hair. Answer to name of 'Hacker," was Sam's reply. See you there.'

Sam was dressed in an old pair of jeans, a denim shirt and a green roll-neck sweater. He wore a woolly hat to contain his hair and a brand new pair of Reeboks on his feet. An old leather satchel hung from his right shoulder. In it was a small notebook, the novel he was reading, his driver's licence, a small computer notepad in a leather pouch, an AtoZ map of London, a small packet of tissues, reading glasses, a spare pen and a pair of clean underpants. He called the contents of his satchel his 'essentials'.

There was a public bench across the main hall from the Crusty Roll and Sam assumed a position with a clear view of the kiosk between the crowds of passing passengers. The odd pigeon fearlessly dodged the flying feet in its quest for nourishing titbits. Unintelligible announcements bounced and echoed around the high, curved roof girders, adding to the sense of transience. Sam was reading a copy of The London Evening Standard.

At 17:50 he noticed a middle aged man and an attractive blonde lady in her early thirties, standing almost half way between the barrier of Platform 13 and the Crusty Roll. The first thing that caught Sam's attention was the fact they both wore sunglasses, despite it being completely dark outside. Also, they both appeared to be deaf, judging by the discreet hearing aids they each wore in their right ears. The other thing that was a little unusual was the fact

18

that they were speaking to each other, in spite of the fact that they were standing back-to-back. The male wore a dark grey suit, which might have fitted him some years previously. He was unmistakably a prime example of an agent of the 'Men in Black' service. The woman was dressed in a conservative grey flannel trouser suit. A paisley pattern silk scarf was tossed loosely around her neck. Her shoes looked as though they were designed for speed, rather than style.

At precisely 18:00, Sam folded his newspaper, stood up and tucked it under his arm. He walked over to the Crusty Roll, removing his woolly hat releasing an explosion of grey, tightly-curled hair. When he reached the counter he ordered a hot dog, adding "... and put plenty of mustard in it please." As he turned to retrieve money from his back pocket, the dark-suited man brushed past him.

"Hacker?" he muttered as he passed. The voice had an American twang.
"Oh, Hi!" said Sam, holding out his hand, as though greeting a long lost buddy. "Long time!" he smiled.

For a moment, the American seemed nonplussed by the openness of the greeting, then, in awkward recognition of Sam's move, he grabbed the proffered hand and shook it. They were joined by the lady and Sam offered them both a roll from the menu behind the counter. The Man In Black seemed unused to civility from someone he had been told was his target and when Sam turned to the woman, she raised her hand and shook her head with a guilty smile, as though she had been offered a condom in St. Peter's Rome instead of a hot dog in Victoria Station.

"I'll just get my hot dog then and we can catch up over on that bench. Give me a second." Sam's accent was almost

'Oxbridge', with a tiny lilt to it, betraying his Caribbean roots.

They moved across to the bench and sat down. Sam positioned himself at one end and the agent sat in the middle, next to him. The lady adopted the role of observer on the other side.

"So, how can I help you?"

"We are here to make you an offer," said the agent, attempting to conceal the conversation by appearing to speak to the wall. "The Department of Defence is prepared to pay for your services."

"Tell me more."

"They will pay you to hack into the Pentagon and Langley computers, as long as you let us know your findings. You must keep this deal completely confidential. If you do not, the consequences will be most severe."

"And, if I don't agree? Then, what?"

"The agreement will be terminated." The way the agent spat out the last word implied that rather more than just an agreement would be 'terminated'.

"OK," said Sam, "let's give it a go then."

Very soon, Sam's reputation spread to the banking and insurance industries as various financial institutions requested his services to winkle out the weaknesses in their own security systems. That is how he had come to be sitting, overlooking the New York Stock Exchange at the frantic close of business after a panic-stricken day of manic trading.

Alex had contacted the Trinidadian after his conversation with Dick Tarrant. The mayhem in the New York Stock Exchange was further evidence of the malaise that had suddenly overtaken the Western finance houses. The biggest ones sold off their bad debts and mortgages to the up and coming new banks. These thrusting little enterprises bought in to the mortgage market with relish, because the older members presented the new buyers with an irresistible honey trap. So what if the client defaulted on his mortgage? The bank would still have his property and it was prestigious to own property in the States. It looked like a cast iron investment until the US housing market collapsed. Then the banks began to tumble like ninepins as more and more chancy deals were transacted.

The disease quickly spread across the water to Europe, where many of the banks had been conned into buying bad mortgages and loans from the American market. Governments suddenly found themselves in a position where they had to bail out loan sharks who had burned their fingers to the tune of billions. There were so many members of the public clamouring for their money that a run on world currencies looked increasingly likely. Only three per cent of global finance actually comes in the shape of money. The rest is simply stored in computers as figures. This is one of the great scams of the capitalist system. Money is really one big con trick. The only reason that it has any value at all is because we want it to. Senior politicians circulated gloomy predictions of recession on a bigger scale than the great depression of the late nineteen twenties. It got to the stage that the value of Sterling started to fall. In a matter of days it lost more than ten per cent of its value against the Dollar and the Euro.

Dick Tarrant looked into Alex Stewart's eyes. "If what you and I suspect is true, then we should get somebody on board who knows what to do."

"I'm going to get in touch with a friend of mine. He's in the States right now. His name is Samuel J. Jackson, known to his friends as Jack the Hack."

Chapter 3

One of the great successes of Vladimir Chernorgin, head of Sluzhba Vneshney Razvedki or SVR, the Russian successor to the old Soviet KGB, was the introduction of compulsory identity cards for all Russian citizens. Now records of each and every citizen could be monitored. Each citizen's location would be known. Terrorists would have no hiding place because to travel without an ID card was to invite a long sentence in the Gulag. In fact, a life sentence was frequently mercifully brief, since many of those convicted succumbed to the harsh conditions after a comparatively short time. For some, a grave was considered more comfortable than the accommodation offered by the Gulag.

In Great Britain a passport is about as close as you can get to an identity card at the moment. The difference between that and an ID card is that to a Briton a passport is a privilege for which he must pay for with money. In Russia, by contrast, to be caught without your ID card is a criminal offence, punishable by lengthy terms of imprisonment, while the authorities attempt to 'authenticate' your identity. The process can take many months. In Britain privacy is a right. In Russia it is a privilege shared only by the very rich and even then, it is not a right.

For the authorities, the ID card system had obvious advantages. The crime rate fell dramatically with the introduction of the cards. So successful was it, in fact, that left-leaning governments and dictatorships in other parts of the world started to introduce it. Even members of the British Parliament began to campaign for its introduction.

Now the UK, which was the nation with the highest number of CCTVs per capita in the world, would be monitored by a whole new layer of bureaucracy. Privacy, far from being a right would become something vaguely illegal, almost perverted. 'People who need privacy have something to hide' was the way one senior politician put it. The government presented the case for IDs which previous governments had considered introducing, by pointing out the advantages for its citizens.

The new ID cards would be identifiable to the Galileo Terrestrial positioning and tracking system, so old ladies and small children would never get lost again. Accident victims could have their blood groups and allergies identified even before they regained consciousness. Terrorists could not hide. The public would be protected from paedophiles and perverts. Known criminals would have their records indelibly inscribed on their ID cards. The authorities would be able to identify illegal immigrants instantly. Taken to its logical conclusion, a driving licence would become a thing of the past, as would car keys, TV licences and social security numbers. One little chip would contain the life details of every human being. Salaries would be electronically added to the chip on the card in the form of credits. Shopping would be done electronically. Tax would be deducted by a simple swipe of the card. Everything would be included on the chip. Life would be so much easier with the card. 'The ID card gives everyone an identity' was the jingle used by its promoters.

This was something of deep interest to two Russian gentlemen who sat smoking Camel cigarettes and sipping choice Pshenichnaya Ukrainian vodka in a luxurious dacha some thirty kilometres to the east of Moscow. For these two people, the card system could be used to control the

West. At last they would reap revenge on the capitalists for the fall of the Russian Empire; the Union of Soviet Socialist Republics. But first they would have to get rid of money. This would involve some fairly heavy investment initially, before the economies of the capitalist world could be brought to their knees.

"You contacted Borden in London, did you?"

"I did, Boris. He said that he has managed to make more than twenty thousand transactions so far. He said that the fools are handing out loans to any idiot who gives them a call. The fact that we have the resources to make the down payments provides irresistible bait for the lenders."

"Good, good!" said the man Boris Belnikov and took another large shot of vodka. "Now, Ivan Ilyich, we can sit back and watch capitalism thrash itself to pieces, before we implement the plan."

The plan which Belnikov mentioned was intricate and Machiavellian in concept. It would utilise one of the oldest of human urges, namely greed on a grand scale, to bring down the entire financial structure of Western civilisation. It was frighteningly simple in concept and would require the services of a very few people, but it would take the West for a ride of such violence that it would never recover. Then the Rodina, Mother Russia, would assume her rightful place as the leader of the civilised world.

The first evidence of the plan came in the form of the sudden bankruptcy of Barnard's Bank. Barnard's had been part of the city of London's financial furniture since time immemorial. It was one of those grey-headed institutions which were so well entrenched that its partners had their own dining rooms in some of the aged local eating houses

25

in the City. The building housing the offices of the bank was so well known Countryco, that it appeared on the new ten pound notes as a symbol of solidity, trustworthiness and reliability. So it was particularly shocking for the city's establishment when Barnard's Bank stumbled and crashed, overnight.

The collapse was rapidly blamed on a young trader named Brian Borden. He was one of Barnard's 'Younger Generation', the new blood which was to regenerate the ancient edifice. He had made big loans to various enterprises in the old Eastern Bloc countries. Barnard's had a reputation for letting their traders do their own thing as long as they kept the grey-heads in the loop. This policy allowed the partners to enjoy their private dining rooms without being bothered by the general running of the establishment. 'The young people nowadays know all about those new-fangled computer thingies, don't you know' was an easy excuse for sitting back in one's London Club and enjoying the fruits of a lifetime in commerce. Sadly this attitude, instead of keeping them in the loop, now put them into a noose.

Unbeknown to the senior partners, Borden had given out billions of pounds' worth of loans to establishments that were not all they appeared to be. When pay-back time came round, only two of the borrowers were able to raise any funds and even these were only a fraction of the amount required. The others just defaulted and then filed for bankruptcy. The economies of the old Warsaw Pact countries appeared to be headed for free fall.

Barnard's, for many years, had been involved in the purchase of mortgages and trading loans from their colleagues across the water in the United States. This was done very much on an 'old boy' network. Senior directors of many of the older American financial institutions were on social terms with partners in British commerce and industry. It was like a trans-Atlantic club. Its members would often meet on neutral ground, in places like St. Kitts or Kitzbühel, Antigua or Aspen, in fact anywhere where there was a bit of exclusivity away from the prying eyes of the media. It was all very chummy and relaxed, until the bottom fell out of the US housing market. Then suddenly, Barnard's found that the mortgages they had acquired from the other side of the Atlantic, had become liabilities of gigantic proportions which compounded the massive debts incurred by Borden. Within days, after frantic secret meetings behind closed boardroom doors, members of the board realised that the unthinkable had happened and the proud name of Barnard's Bank was proud no more. It was too late to leave the sinking ship. The lifeboats had already gone. The calls for help went unheeded.

The next victim was SAFI, La Société Anonyme de Finance Industrielle. This collapse caused as much shock as that of Barnard's, in the corridors of financial power in France, but with even wider implications. SAFI was the primary financier behind the development and building of the biggest airliner the world had ever seen. The French government realised that if SAFI were to fall, then, in all likelihood, so would L'Industrie pour la Navigation Aérienne, the company responsible for the construction of the airliner. The loss of jobs would probably bring down the government. Relations between France and the other countries involved in the manufacture of the aircraft, like Germany, Spain and the United Kingdom, would be strained to breaking point. France would be seen as the sick man of Europe. The implications were unthinkable. It was essential to bring about a rescue scheme. The government would have to bail out SAFI if it was to survive. The President of the republic became involved.

He called Jean-Paul Bombard, the Chief Executive of SAFI.

"Bonjour Jean," he rubbed his eyes as he spoke over the secure line, "ici Jacques Boulanger."

His greeting was duly acknowledged by the CEO. "What is the bottom line on the damage?"

"The damage, Monsieur le President, is enormous. We are looking at tens of billions of Euros."

"Sacré Bleu, Jean! How on earth did the situation get this far out of control?"

"As you know, Monsieur le President, we have been investing heavily in the American insurance and loan market. One of the biggest loan companies in the States is called Dandy Lion. They were deeply involved in the mortgage and loan business and we, for many years, were partners in the business with them."

The President nodded thoughtfully as he took on board the gravity of the situation.

"They specialised in loans to overseas investors. At the time, there was a lot of interest from the burgeoning new Russian market. They were particularly interested in property over here and in the States. The problem arose because many of the Eastern Bloc borrowers were unable to support the interest on their loans and they simply defaulted. Then the housing market in the States collapsed due to the deterioration of consumer credit repayments. A credit crunch developed which reduced the supply of money still further. That hit the housing market, causing a further slump in the price of property. People who had taken out mortgages found themselves in a negative equity situation and were unable even to pay the interest on their mortgages. The banks were forced to foreclose as debts mounted."

The President's face sank into his hands as he struggled to think of a way out of a depression to beat all depressions.

"This hit the consumer market as the money ran out" Jean-Paul Bombard continued. "The motor industry, which was anyway in a weak position due to international competition, was hit hard by the credit squeeze. Sales fell and jobs had to go. Soon thousands were out of work. The bailiffs were busy. Then Dandy Lion went into receivership with no warning at all. Suddenly we found ourselves saddled with a mountain of defaulted mortgages that we had traded in good faith with Dandy Lion. To make the nightmare complete, we discovered that one of our traders, a certain Jean Pierre Baccarat, had made loans worth billions of Euros to finance a Russian gas extraction project which was to supply, among other countries, France. When the product came on stream, the price of gas dropped and the Russians are now unable to repay their debts. We, Monsieur le President, are technically bankrupt. Our outgoings exceed our assets by around a hundred billion Euros."

The end of this peroration was followed by a prolonged silence, then, the President heaved a sigh. "This is disastrous!" he breathed. "I will have to call a meeting of the Cabinet. The country will not stand for this. The government will fall if we cannot find funds to keep SAFI afloat."

Chapter 4

Alex called Jack the Hack in New York. "Sam, it's Alex Stewart here. Do you remember? In Libya, I used to fly the seismic 'plane."

"'Course I remember you, Alex. Where are you calling from?"

"I'm in London, Sam. There is something a friend of mine has stumbled on and we need some expert advice on how to handle it. Is there any chance that we could meet up for a discussion? It is extremely important."

"I am most honoured that you would think to turn to me for advice Alex. In fact I have to come to London for a meeting at the LSE next week. It seems that the world of stocks and shares is going through a bit of a rough patch, doesn't it?"

"Indeed it does, Sam, indeed it does, and that is why we want to see you. I don't suppose that there would be any chance of you coming over a day or two early, would there? It really is important that we see you, before something extremely serious develops."

"Well, Alex, if you put it that way, I suppose I could try and get over there tomorrow. Let me just call the office and find out what they can do for me. I'll get back to you."

"Thanks Sam. You're a great help!"

It can hardly have been five minutes later that Alex's phone rang. It was Sam.

"I'll be on Continental. It gets in to Gatwick at 23:00 tonight."

"Fantastic, Sam. I'll meet you and you can stay at the flat. Fairly humble, I'm afraid, but we have ample supplies in the way of liquid and solid refreshment and I want you to meet this friend of mine. I think you will be intrigued."

"I look forward to meeting him, Alex. We'll see each other this evening, the Lord permitting."

Gatwick was so busy that the Continental Boeing 767 had to take remote parking and the passengers were ferried to the North Terminal by bus. Alex was waiting at arrivals when Sam's craggy features appeared among the crowd of arriving passengers. It had taken so long for him to get through that Alex was afraid he had missed the flight. An enormous grin spread across his face as he strode forward to greet the man from Trinidad. Suddenly a ray of hope pierced the gloom and Alex felt a wave of inexplicable optimism break over him with the arrival of the grey Afro cloud. It had been almost four years since they had met. A hug seemed to be the appropriate way to express his feelings upon meeting this pillar of strength from the past and the pillar of strength appeared to agree.

"Great to see you, you old bugger!" Alex shouted above the general hubbub of greetings.

"... and great to see you, you young whippersnapper!" Sam replied. "Now what have you got for me? Knowing you, it's something interesting."

"Let's get back to the flat and I will reveal all. A mate of mine has unearthed something which has boggled both our minds and he's waiting for us there."

They drove down the M23 motorway against a continuous stream of headlights. Drizzly rain raised a mist of spray around the rushing vehicles. It was a miserable November night with the temperature not far above freezing. Alex could appreciate why he chose to live in East Africa and Sam wondered why he was not back in Trinidad.

They reached the flat and parked the car. Alex shouldered Sam's bag and led the way up two flights of stairs to the second floor. Upon reaching No 20, Alex pressed the doorbell. Moments later there was a clatter of locks and chains and the door opened. The doorway was now filled with the imposing frame of a large-boned man.

"Hello Dick, here's Jack the Hack."

Sam held out his hand, which was grasped by the man who had opened the door.

"Come along in out of the cold," he said, hauling Sam in through the door, "and let's take a look at each other."

The big man led Sam down the corridor into a comfortable sitting room, while Alex shut out the cold. Green velvet curtains were drawn across the windows, keeping the warmth in. The dining room led off from it with a door into the kitchen. The walls of the sitting room were hung with what looked like original paintings, some oils and some watercolours. An intricately detailed Cotman drawing of a church interior lit by a finely carved standard lamp, decorated the wall above the sofa. The end wall was filled by a fitted shelving unit housed quantities of old and new books except for one shelf that contained an exotic collection of model ships. An old brass carriage clock ticked away on a shelf in the corner unit above the television. Sam reflected on how the TV seemed to have replaced the fireplace as the focal point in modern-day sitting rooms. He had fed a programme through the television in his own apartment in New York, which produced a lifelike imitation of an old-fashioned log fire. Several times he had caught himself studying it to see if there was a regular pattern to the flicker of the computer-generated flames, something he would never have thought of doing with a real fire.

"Now," Alex went through to the dining room, "what can I get you, Sam?"

"Would you have a drop of Scotch?"

"Indeed I have. Will Grouse do you?"

"That would be very nice, thank you, Alex, with just a drop of water please. No ice."

"There we are, Sam." Alex handed a generous measure to his new guest. "Dick? Same for you?" Tarrant nodded his head.

"Thanks Alex."

Drinks served, Alex returned to the sitting room. "Just before we settle down, let me show you your room, Sam." He grabbed his bag and led the way back down the corridor. "Here we go, Sam. I've put you in the haunted West Wing," he grinned. "Make yourself at home and join us when you're ready."

The room was compact but comfortable with a small shower room in one corner. Sam washed the journey out of his eyes, dumped his coat on the chair and returned to the sitting room.

Dick Tarrant had a laptop computer open on the coffee table. "Look at this. Musgraves have gone for Chapter Eleven protection." He looked up at Alex. "That's going to kick the hell out of the New York Stock Exchange."

Sam leaned over and examined the screen stroking his chin. "They were involved in that big pipeline project into Europe from Russia, as well as the mortgage and loan business. Interesting. Do you see any trends in all this?"

"Well that's why I got on to you, Sam. Dick and I thought that we were imagining things, but there does seem to be a Russian thread running through many of these collapses."

"Oh, you spotted that, did you?"

"You mean you agree?"

"Oh yes, definitely. But I hardly dare mention it in polite company. I had my head bitten off by Jack Raudermaker when I suggested a Russian connection to him. He told me to stop rocking the boat." Jack Raudermaker was the US Secretary of the Treasury and a great sparring partner of Sam's.

"So, without trying to start any conspiracy theories, what do you think is the truth?"

"Well, why don't we try starting a few conspiracy theories ourselves? We are going to look like right dummies if they prove to be true, aren't we?"

"I suppose you are right. So where do we start?"

"Well, I just want to put you in the position of the Russian President, Boris Belnikov." Sam leaned forward as though imparting confidential information. "His aircraft industry is frustrated at every turn by the likes of the Americans and the Europeans and even the South Americans. Nobody buys Russian cars, because there is a world glut created by the Americans, the Europeans and the Japanese. Nobody buys Russian televisions because the ones made in Japan and China are cheaper and more reliable."

He sat back in his comfortable armchair and looked at the two English men taking a sip from his glass. "Would you buy a camera from Russia?" The other men shook their heads. "Would you buy Vodka?" Both the others nodded enthusiastically. "Well I wouldn't. You can get Smirnoff here for half the price of imported Russian stuff. I wouldn't even buy a Kalashnikov AK 47 from Russia. The Chinese version of exactly the same weapon is half the price."

Alex stared at Sam as though he was listening to some fantastic theatrical performance. "So what would you buy from Russia?" He looked from the one to the other. Neither wanted to venture a reply. "Well what about oil? Would you buy oil and gas from Russia?"

Alex and Dick Tarrant nodded their heads more slowly this time, as though there might be some hidden reason why they would be stupid to buy oil and gas from the Russians.

"Yes you would." said Sam in a quieter tone. "But hydrogen is now set to take on the oil industry. Already Iceland has cut imports of hydrocarbons by seventy per cent and Western Australia is following close behind. The American motor industry is serious about developing hydrogen-fuel-cell-powered vehicles and the infrastructure for the hydrogen economy is rapidly coming together." he paused for a moment, to let the significance of his argument sink in. "So, if the world swings over to hydrogen, what happens to the Russian or, perhaps more significantly, the Russian Mafia economy? You have just told me what you would and would not buy from Russia and you have narrowed down your purchases to just oil and gas. If you move over to hydrogen and you don't need the oil and gas any more, where does Russia get her money from?"

Alex and Dick both shrugged their shoulders and Sam almost whispered, "She doesn't."

Chapter 5

Jean-Pierre Baccarat was the target of a massive police hunt. Financial crime was taken more seriously than rape or murder in Europe, and the crimes which Baccarat had committed threatened the whole economy of the country.

They went to his apartment, a recently renovated nineteenth century property in a good area overlooking the city of Paris on the hill in Montmartre, It was the kind of area where the 'nouveau riche' could establish their middle class credentials by living, cheek by jowl, with the artisan community.

French police lacked the tactful approach of their British counterparts so, when there was no answer to the doorbell, the big-boot-man was brought forward and shown the problem. It was as if he had been especially programmed just for this kind of situation. With his eyes half-closed as though focussing on the job, with a blur of speed he raised his great hoof and smashed the door down, ripping it off its hinges.

The apartment reeked of the foul odour of death, causing some of the officers to cover their noses and mouths. A man was lying face down on the floor, in the kitchen. His head was surrounded by a dark stain on the tiled floor. There was an old German Luger pistol in his right hand. The sergeant in charge of the raiding party immediately called the station and they dispatched a scene of crime team. Upon arrival the scene the SOCO who was wearing a surgical mask, took in the surroundings, including the fact that there was a typed sheet of paper in the out-tray of the printer. On closer inspection he established that the primary cause of death was a small hole in the back of the dead man's cranium. He also noted with interest that there was a nicotine-stained mound on the middle finger of the left hand of the corpse. It was the kind of callus normally found on the finger that supported a pen or pencil and the nicotine stain would indicate that the victim was a smoker. People who write and smoke with their left hand very seldom shoot with their right.

The sheet of paper in the printer was written in French and read simply 'Assez c'est assez. Le monde que j'ai connu, c'est finis. J-P.B.' "Enough is enough. The world as I knew it is ended. J-P.B."

Masked-up police photographers took shots of the scene, one concentrating on the corpse and the other recording every nook and cranny of the room. The SOCO muttered continuously into a small recorder, recording details that could not be noted on camera, such as smells and the fact that one plate of the cooker was too hot to touch, as well as the anomaly of the callas. He noted that there was a coffee percolator standing on a work surface near the hot plate. It appeared that M. Baccarat had been intending to have a cup of coffee before he met his maker. Another interesting point was the almost total lack of traffic noise. This building was very solidly built and well insulated, which would account for the fact that none of the neighbours had reported hearing any unusual noises in the flat, for example, a gunshot. The case began to look less and less like suicide and more and more like a murder enquiry.

In the Kremlin, The President of the Commonwealth of Independent States sat in his office that was surprisingly poky for someone who was one of the most powerful men in the world. The view from the window would have been of a red brick wall, if there had been a window. As it was, the office was sealed from the outside world; a security measure adopted to protect the Head of State against threats from Chechen terrorists and other insurgents.

Belnikov's computer chirped a short musical alarm to alert him to an inbound e-mail awaiting his attention. He opened up his Inbox. There was one very short communication. The message simply read 'Delivered'. This indicated that the SVR had taken care of the Frenchman Baccarat. So far there had been muted reaction to the deaths from the press. It appeared that the plan was working.

There was one other operative to use and eliminate in London, then they could turn their attention to America. He was a young man who was familiar to Dick Tarrant. His name was Freddie Barnes. He was a trader for a merchant banker whose name reflected several generations of banking experience. Sutcliffe Morgan Osmond Grant, otherwise known as SMOG, occupied offices on the ground floor of a new block in Paternoster Row, right next to St. Paul's Cathedral, in the heart of the City of London. When asked at a news conference, why he preferred offices on the ground floor James Sutcliffe had replied that he considered it to be his public duty.

"It may have escaped your notice, Ladies and Gentlemen," he said, with a severe tone to his voice, "that the streets of the City of London are some of the most dangerous in the world. Quite apart from the traffic there is the constant threat posed by senior members of management, should they decide to jump out of their office windows. If at any stage I suddenly feel the urge to jump, I would be less of a threat to passing members of the public in the street below." This raised a laugh amongst the assembled reporters but not from a certain young trader who worked for the same outfit. Young Freddie Barnes was a worried man.

He had been approached by a gentleman with a Slavic accent who had made him an impossibly rewarding offer. It involved giving loans, at improbably high interest rates, to a shipyard in the Black Sea. The loans would cover payment for four oil drilling platforms which were to be the largest and most sophisticated in the world. They would be designed for drilling operations in the waters of the Black Sea. Each platform would support four complete drilling rigs and provide accommodation for their crews. They would be self-propelled and fully stabilised, enabling them to maintain station within an area of four square metres. This capability would allow drilling operations to continue in sea states with wave heights of up to three metres and winds up to force seven on the Beaufort scale. Each would be provided with a purpose built, 1,500 tonne work boat. Sealed, fire resistant, invertible lifeboats would offer an escape route in the event of an emergency. The Slavic man was very convincing. He showed hi computer-generated pictures of the design. It was very impressive indeed and provided facilities for the crew that would have been unimaginable twenty years earlier. The name on his business card was Nikolai Sergei Petrov, Vice President (Finance) for BSO Odessa, the Black Sea Oil company of Odessa.

Freddie was very tempted simply to go ahead with negotiations before anyone else got their oar in. Only one thing held him back. Mr Petrov seemed to be in an inordinate hurry. He wanted the money yesterday. That was presumably why he was prepared to accept such mountainous interest rates. In order to allay his suspicions, Freddie went to the International Companies Register on the internet and searched for BSO. It was listed under 'Oil

Distributors'. It was not listed under 'Oil Producers' or 'Oil Prospectors' and there was, in fact, no mention of BSO Odessa at all, only Black Sea Oil. Far from allaying his suspicions, this raised them further.

Not wishing to go to his own bosses for advice, he decided to consult an acquaintance of his named Dick Tarrant. For Tarrant, the contact with Freddie Barnes opened a completely new avenue of investigation. Suddenly the enemy had an identity. Mr Petrov of BSO existed. He had made contact with Freddie Barnes. Now it might be possible to dig up a thread, which would lead to the powers behind the plot. He felt the thrill of the chase stirring. If he, Alex and Sam were on the right trail, he anticipated exciting times ahead. He called them for a meeting at a small pub called the Willows on an island in the river Thames, within sight of the great stone coronet of Windsor Castle's keep. The reason for choosing this particular venue was its discretion and the fact that it was not far from the house where Freddie Barnes lived.

They drove to the pub in a chauffeur-driven MPV, picking Freddie up on the way. Sam was impressed with how young the new arrival was. It appeared that the traditional grey hair of the banker was a thing of the past. Experience seemed to have been dropped as one of the requirements of international finance. The young man had a hurried confidence which Alex found vaguely unsettling. It was as though the pursuit of wealth had extinguished the art of personal interaction. He did not have time to offer, only to take. Probably the only reason why he remembered Dick Tarrant's name was that Dick had given him access to a deal which had paid handsomely enough to finance his 5-series BMW. Where the well had produced wine on one occasion it might produce again, which was worth remembering.

41

"So, Freddie, I would like to introduce you to a couple of my friends here." Dick indicated Sam. "This is Dr Sam Jackson. He is a computer specialist, with an accent on the financial aspects of the computing game."

Freddie Barnes glanced over at Sam without taking the offered hand. He was in the process of breaking off a square of chocolate and putting it in his mouth. It was as though his mind was on other things.

"And this is Alex Stewart. We were in the Military together. He's a pilot."

"A pilot? eh? That's what I'll be doing if this deal comes off. Buy my own 'plane, like John Travolta."

The accent was Cockney, sounding as though it had been influenced by the criminal fraternity of East London. In fact it was an affectation adopted by Barnes to increase his street cred. Hiding in the shallows of this youth's personality there was a vulnerable, inexperienced kid trying to prove to the world that he was a financial thug. Alex almost felt sympathy. This kind of inferiority complex sometimes reacted well to kindness. In other cases the only treatment was to ignore it. Alex decided to try the first method to begin with. A good entrée in these circumstances was to ask for advice. For an older person to request help from someone younger was an approach employed by the airline industry in Crew Resource Management. It was practiced in order to increase understanding and to avoid conflict among crews on the flight deck of an aircraft.

"So what made you suspicious of this Mr Petrov fellow, Freddie?"

"Yeah well, he wanted his money chop-chop didn't he and he was offering crazy interest rates in order to speed things up, wasn't he. I mean you don't run into those sort of rates in a lifetime! I mean, what's twenty-five per cent of two billion? Half a billion ain't it. And that's all paid back over two years. Mind you I suppose with the oil prices as they is at the moment, anyfink's possible."

"So Mr Petrov is looking for two billion, is he? Is that Euros or Dollars?"

Sam's glasses had slipped to the end of his nose and he pushed them back into place. Freddie Barnes cast a furtive glance in Sam's direction as though he had said too much.

"Pounds," he said, reluctantly and then, as though committing himself, "he says he wants pounds."

Alex sensed that they were making headway. Freddie Barnes was allowing them to see behind the screen.

"Wow!" said Sam. "That's a tidy sum! Did he offer any collateral?"

"Oh yeah," said Barnes, " 'course he did. He said that the company would back the loan with oil. It's just that they needed the capital to get the rigs in place. The oil reserves 'is guaranteed'. He showed me the field report. 'They reckons there's more than a hundred billion barrels of proven oil reserves there." He pulled a bar of fruit and nut chocolate out of his pocket and proceeded to eat two squares.

Sam glanced across at Alex. "Sounds familiar?"

"Indeed it does," Dick murmured, rubbing his chin. "Indeed it does."

"Whatcha mean?" Barnes suddenly shied away as though Sam and Alex had accused him of lying. "I'm no bloody fool. I knows when to show my cards." His eyes flicked nervously from Dick to Alex to Sam. "That's why I come to see you, Mr Tarrant." He took another couple of squares of chocolate.

"Very interesting, Freddie." said Dick Tarrant. "Any chance of meeting your Mr Petrov?"

"I don't want no trouble Mr Tarrant. If Petrov finds out I've gaffed on him I'll lose the loan."

"Don't worry, Freddie, I and my friends will be models of discretion. The thing is that if this Mr Petrov is connected to the people we are interested in, we would very much like to have a few words with him. Maybe we could act as financial consultants, if you could set up a meeting."

"I suppose I could try, Mr Tarrant, if you're prepared to pick up the expenses."

"You give me the chitties, Freddie and we'll come up with the boodle. We might even consider reimbursing you for your services. A little something to keep you in chocolate."

Freddie Barnes's eyebrows twitched in surprise.

"Her Majesty's Government can be very generous when they want to be, you know."

"Well, Mr Tarrant, if you put it like that, then I'm your man. I just give up smoking. That's why I took up the chocolate." Judging by the nicotine stains on his fingers, young Freddie Barnes was fighting a losing battle with the weed.

Dick Tarrant was not comfortable. The boy had street cred. He didn't have City cred, so Dick decided to go for some confirmation on the financial history of BSO. He went on the internet. Very interesting. BSO (Odessa) did not exist. So then what? So then, hold on to the tail of the Freddie Barnes tiger and see where it led them.

Chapter 6

Freddie Barnes made contact with Nikolai Petrov by calling the mobile number on his business card. It was answered with surprising rapidity.

"Mr Petrov, Fred Barnes here."

"Good morning Mr Barnes. Do you have good news for me?"

"That's right, Mr Petrov. I want you to meet a couple of friends of mine from the City. They specialise in fast money, in particular for the oil industry. They are especially interested in your project because of the high returns they would be making from a relatively low risk investment."

"And where are these friends of yours, Mr Barnes?"

"I am meeting them for lunch at the Angus Steakhouse near Shaftesbury Avenue at twelve o'clock."

"I will be there."

Alex, Sam and Dick Tarrant were sitting at a table near the window. One of the new-generation Routemasters, known as the New Bus for London, or NB4L, which replaced the 'bendy' or 'free' buses, slid past in the rain after dropping off Freddie Barnes and a large, balding gentleman who wore a grey three-piece suit and a grey tie. What identified him as a Russian were the unlikely orange leather shoes with pointed toes that would have been more suited to a court jester. He protected a computer case from the rain by hiding it under his jacket for the quick dash to the door of the restaurant.

They came in and Freddie spotted Dick Tarrant after a brief glance around the tables. He led the large Russian to where they were sitting and introduced him to the other three. A young girl, with short blonde hair was standing by the window in intimate conversation on her mobile phone. She moved away as the new arrivals took their places. Dick stood to shake hands with the Russian, thus indicating that he was the senior negotiator. He introduced Alex and Sam who did not stand up, thus implying that they were interested observers but not instrumental in the coming discussions. Dick showed the two newcomers to their seats.

"Can I get you something to drink, Mr Petrov?"

"I will take water, please."

"And for you Freddie?"

"I'll have a coke please, Mr Tarrant."

Dick ordered the water and the coke and sat down.

"So, Mr Petrov," Dick started the ball rolling. "Our friend here tells us that you have a very interesting project for which you might need a bit of financial liquidity. We may be in a position to offer you some of the services you require. Can you show us what you are planning?"

Petrov removed his laptop from its case and set it on the table. He opened the screen and turned it on. After dabbing some keys, he turned the computer to face his audience. The screen was filled with a gigantic piece of machinery with four latticework towers. There was a large structure supporting it, which looked like a Picasso impression of a ship, drawn during his cubist period. It floated on a calm sea. The graphics were impressive, including a skyscape with sunbeams shining down through threatening clouds on to the grey surface of the sea.

"This, gentlemen, is a computer-generated image of BSO 1" he pronounced the name 'BeeSoo.' He then proceeded to give a very professional-sounding presentation of the development of the BSO concession in the Black Sea. He included a scanned copy of the field report for the proposed oil field. It stated that reserves, proven by magnetometer, seismic and exploration drilling surveys, had established that there were in excess of one hundred billion barrels of hydrocarbons recoverable within the area surveyed. In order to exploit these reserves it would be necessary to engage the use of financial backing which was not currently available in the Commonwealth of Independent States. In order to finance the research and development necessary to take advantage of the current price of oil, it was felt by his principals that the capital needed at such short notice was only available from Western sources. Petrov adopted an almost coy expression as he admitted that Russia was not able to supply the necessary funding.

"For this reason, Gentlemen, I was asked to come to London, in search of interested parties."

"And do you have any guarantees for repayment of any loans which we might be able to provide, Mr Petrov" Dick Tarrant leaned forward.

"My principals feel that one hundred billion barrels of recoverable reserves should amply satisfy your requirements for collateral, Mr Tarrant."

Dick and Alex had to admit that the project, failing some political debacle, looked bullet-proof. In the event of default, the massive reserves would easily cover any shortfall in repayments. Petrov's presentation had been made in a most professional manner. The details were knowledgeably laid out. This man definitely knew what he was talking about. Even his English was exceptionally colloquial and almost accent-free. There was only a slightly guttural Russian inflection to the pronunciation of the 'H's'. Only Sam appeared to reserve judgement.

The meal of 'Fast Steak' was palatable, if not memorable. A glass of the new house wine was thrown in with the meal although, maybe, it would have been better thrown out. As the party broke up, Dick and Alex could not make up their minds about the veracity of Mr Nikolai Petrov.

Petrov paid the bill and he and Freddie Barnes caught another Routemaster leaving Alex, Sam and Dick Tarrant to hail a taxi. The rain had eased off.

As the men left, a petite blonde girl who appeared to be still in her teens, stood in a bus shelter on the other side of Shaftesbury Avenue. She was plainly dressed in a blue anorak with a fake fur collar. Her jeans were tucked into a pair of thick moon boots. She had been there for the duration of the lunch, apparently sheltering from the rain and had spent long periods speaking into a mobile phone. Even from close up, a casual observer would have sworn that she was using one of the ubiquitous Nokia N73s, one of the commonest mobiles around. What the observer probably would not have noticed was that the normal

49

lenses of the phone's camera had been replaced by new ones, crafted by Karl Zeiss, a very reputable German manufacturer, to a much higher specification than the original. These gave the camera an optical zoom capability of three magnifications on a twenty megapixel digital camera. The lenses had been made to a special order from a certain Russian electronics technician of East German origin, named Pyotr Doenitz, who had carried out many jobs for Spetsnaz GRU in previous years.

The telephone girl's name was Ludmilla. Apart from listening to another N73 placed on a windowsill by the table where her targets had been sitting in the Angus Steakhouse, she had taken high definition, digital photographs of the men involved in the BeeSoo deal.

Later that evening, back in Alex's apartment, the three of them sat down over a much more memorable glass of Glenlivet.

"So, Sam," said Alex, "You didn't seem convinced. What did you see that I didn't?"

Sam bowed his head and scratched it through the grey cloud.

"Well, to my mind, there was one thing which didn't add up." He leaned forward and pulled his fingers through his hair, as though extricating thoughts from his brain through the grey filter.

"Petrov is a Ukrainian name, okay, but the guy speaks with a Russian accent. Only a small one, but it's there."

"So what's your problem with that, Sam?" Alex raised his hands in a gesture of enquiry.

"If Petrov is a Russian, his 'Principals' will not be needing a two billion pound loan."

"How so, Sam?" Dick chimed in. "That's quite a big project."

"I have worked in the stock market. I have done the casinos. I have seen the whore houses of Las Vegas." He looked up through the chipped spectacles at his two friends. "I have seen plenty of Russians in my time, but I've never seen a poor one outside of Russia."

The other two looked at him with some scepticism. The popular Western conception of the general public in Russia was of a population of queues and limited resources, surviving on hard work, low pay and vodka.

"The Russian oligarchs are trying to invest their ill-gotten gains in the West." Sam's eyebrows were raised above his glasses, to accentuate his point. "Why borrow money, at exorbitant rates of interest in London when you are flush with your own. It just doesn't make sense."

Dick and Alex nodded their heads in thought. True enough, it didn't make sense to borrow money at astronomical rates, when you were trying to get people to borrow yours.

"So, what are you suggesting, Sam?"

"I am suggesting that we should do quite a bit more research into Mr Petrov's background. If we can string him along for a bit, I have a feeling that he may lead us to his controller. We could even try putting the frighteners on him."

"Alex knows about that sort of thing, don't you Alex." Alex nodded his head sideways, as though reluctant to divulge his past. "Oh go on Alex. Tell us about that time in the Dhofar war."

"Well, if you insist." he opened his hands in a show of reluctance.

"During the Dhofar war we used to blindfold three prisoners and interrogate them. If they were reluctant to open up, we would take them up in a helicopter, still blindfolded and after some minutes of flight we would throw one of them out the door. He would yell as he went and we would then climb away, and, upon reaching a respectable altitude we would remove the blindfolds from the other two. I tell you, after that, you couldn't stop these boys talking. What we hadn't told them, of course, was that we were only a foot off the ground when we tossed their friend out and our lads were down there to catch him. Very often the skydiver would join the Frontier Regiment on our team, when he saw the funny side of what we had done. Tough little people, those Al-Maharah. Good fighters too."

Sam was visibly shocked by the story and said so. "Only the bloody British could be capable of such barbaric acts!"

"Oh come along Sam!" said Dick. "Nobody got hurt and if you can't take a joke you shouldn't have joined!"

"My feeling is, Dick, that we are now entering territory where people might get very seriously indeed." Sam peered over his glasses.

"Why do you say that, Sam? I mean nobody has suffered so far."

"You conveniently forget that Melvyn Strand, George Penney and Jean-Pierre Baccarat have left the scene under well-explained but nevertheless, mysterious circumstances."

Dick noticed that Sam's glasses were slipping down his nose again and he was looking directly into the wise old eyes.

"I would suggest to you that there is more behind the scenes that we should look at. This is not a simple loan scam. This is much bigger. I have seen these boys bring large, old-established institutions and even countries, to their knees. When we talk billions, we are at a level above many companies and, sometimes, above national budgets. This is big money."

"So, what do we do, Sam? At the moment we have a big investor who wishes to feed money into our economy. What's wrong with that? That's what Western capitalism is all about. We lend you money. We charge you interest. We make money. Everybody is happy."

"Everybody is happy, if I pay back my loan... with interest." Sam's glasses were slipping again. "I have already failed to find this company on the internet. Be careful Gentlemen. Be very careful. I sense that there are some very big gamblers around the table at this moment."

"So how can we find out who the boss is, apart from sticking a gun to Mr Petrov's head?"

Dick Tarrant was beginning to wonder whether this was all going in the direction in which he wanted it to go.

"If I know the Russian Mafia at all," Alex chipped in, speaking from experience, "Mr Petrov is only a pawn. He probably does not even realise that he is part of the plot, if, indeed, there is a plot. We could be barking up the wrong tree all together. Maybe Mr Petrov is actually here with a kosher deal." He raised his eyebrows, as if to ask whether they had considered that possibility. "Somehow we need to let the opposition know we are on to them. Then if there is, in fact, an opposition, they will start making moves. A stationary object is difficult to see in the bush. It's when it moves that you spot it. Let's see if we can get them to move."

"And how would you do that, Alex, without letting them know who you are? Sticking a gun to Mr Petrov's head will definitely let them know that you are suspicious, but it will also tell them who you are. The Russian Mafia are not known for their diplomatic skills. Ask Alexander Litvinenko. Oh no, sorry, he died of polonium poisoning in a London hospital, in front of the TV cameras, didn't he?"

Alex smiled at Dick's heavy irony.

"How about telling the media that there is an enormous Mafia scam coming down to try and bust the London Stock Exchange? I mean, isn't that what we all suspect anyway?" he paused while Dick and Sam studied the floor, searching for reasons why such a scheme would not work. "We don't have to tell the press who we are, we just get them sufficiently interested to let their bloodhounds out. That would rattle the crockery enough to get the bear out of bed. Why don't we try it?"

"Go on, then, Alex. Give us an idea how you would do it."

"Well somebody could lose some relevant documents possibly, then let the press know where they are? That's happened before. Remember the 'Dear Bill' letters between Dennis Thatcher and Bill Deedes?"

"So how do we get hold of 'relevant documents'?"

"Well we could manufacture some. Freddie Barnes has the details. All we need to do is write out some official proposals, leave them in a litter bin on Hampstead Heath and tell the Sun newspaper. I believe that's the normal way of spreading embarrassing news isn't it?"

Both Sam and Dick smiled. Looking back on it, this method of dissemination was so obviously faked that it was difficult to accept that people believed it but, as they say in the funfair, 'Every time a coconut!' "You're the whiz-kid on the computer, Sam. Could you generate a couple of artist's impressions of that presentation which Petrov gave?"

"Better than that, I can hack into Petrov's computer and lift the presentation, lock, stock and barrel, right out from under his nose. He won't feel a thing."

"Brilliant, Sam! They don't call you 'Jack the Hack' for nothing!"

Chapter 7

It was snowing heavily. Boris Belnikov sat in the back of his private Mercedes S 500. The body armour had been supplied, ironically, by a company in the United Kingdom who specialised in securing VIP transport against bomb and small arms attack. Edward Schevardnadze spoke very highly of them, having survived two attempts on his life which had, in both cases, destroyed the vehicles in which he was travelling. The President had four identical black S 500s, all of which bore the same number on their registration plates. The cars came from the Mercedes plant in East London, South Africa, which had a reputation for quite exceptional leatherwork but Belnikov had turned down the ceremonial livery offered as a free option. After the armour protection, the second most important requirement for the vehicles was anonymity.

Sitting next to Belnikov was his Prime Minister, Ivan Ilyich, a member of the old school whose parents had both been swept away with the millions who disappeared during the Great Patriotic War. They had both known each other long enough for Belnikov to be comfortable with the use, by the older man, of his first name.

"I received these photographs from London this morning." He took a sheaf of colour prints out of his briefcase. "It appears that the man Petrov is out fishing and a couple of fish are nibbling at the bait. This one," he said, pointing to the largest guest, who was entering the Angus Steakhouse, "Is a financier in the City of London. His name is Richard Charles Borecombe Tarrant. He was a military helicopter pilot, operating in the Middle East. This next one" he said, pointing at the second man in the picture, "is well known to us. His name is Alexander Selwyn Stewart. He is also an ex-military pilot. We have a score to settle with him," Belnikov tapped the photograph with a long slender index finger, "... and this last one, the black man, we do not have any records on him except that SVR believe he is with the UN in some capacity. We have them all under surveillance. The black man is staying at accommodation which belongs to Stewart."

Belnikov shuffled through some of the other photos and selected another from the pack. "And here is the Barnes kid, with Petrov. They arrived by bus." He put the photographs back in their envelope and into his briefcase. "The conversation, during the meal, consisted of Petrov's presentation followed by some discussions about collateral and other points for negotiation. It all sounded quite genuine. What makes me highly suspicious is the presence of this Stewart character. He has worked with some very well connected people, including William Farrar Kearns, the President of the United States. He was involved in the team which very nearly succeeded in foiling the Icelandic exercise. He and a retired Austrian Air Force Colonel stole an aircraft from Standard Petroleum Enterprises, a British branch of PrimaGas, and used it to hunt down our operatives in Libya. They caught two of them but the other one got away with the 'product'. The other members of Stewart's gang are thought to be serving officers in British Army Special Forces but, so far, they remain unidentified. The man Tarrant has access to large quantities of finance. It was largely due to his contacts that the Hwang Ho Dam in China was constructed. He organised the procedures and protocols by which the contracts were drawn up. He fits into the picture very well. It is just the presence of the man Stewart which makes me uncomfortable. We may have to consider pre-emptive action in his case. We don't want to stir things up too much, before the plan is in place, of course. If they get suspicious they might not take the bait, but if the man Stewart poses a threat, he will have to be eliminated."

Ivan Ilyich looked out of the tinted windows at the passing scene of grey and white. A heavy mantle of snow cloaked every horizontal surface. The multi-coloured towers and onion domes of Saint Basil's Cathedral stuck out like a funfair attraction on the south-eastern corner of the great square. The riotous clown of a building was set against the grim red ramparts of the Kremlin and the sombre grey edifices which made up the rest of the Moscow. The cathedral had been commissioned nearly five hundred years earlier by Czar Ivan IV, 'The Terrible'. He had lived up to his name by blinding the architect, Postnik Yakovlev, to prevent him from creating a more beautiful cathedral for anyone else. Ilyich reflected on this strangely Russian method of expressing gratitude. He also reflected that Yakovlev was probably grateful to have survived with his life. The World would soon experience the Russian way of doing things. Limp-wristed, ill-disciplined, liberalism would very soon be past history and the human race would, at last, be back under control with Russia at the helm.

Kenya is one of the world's most highly prized tourist havens. It is rich in agriculture, geothermal energy and wildlife. Geographically it has everything from tropical palm-fringed beaches to lush temperate forests and high alpine glaciers. It is also blessed with a people who have a lot to be proud of. The population of Kenya is, by and large, hardworking, well-educated and entrepreneurial. Many of the top jobs in the world's service industries are held by Kenyans. The Chef de Cuisine of one of London's top hotels is from Kenya. Kenyan barristers have passed through the British law courts. Kenyan soldiers have served with distinction in the British Army. A man with a Kenyan father had even become President of the United States of America. The links between Kenya and its former colonial rulers are close, more like those of an uncle and a nephew.

One difference between the two countries is in the ID card system. In order to exercise their voting rights in Kenya, it is necessary for Kenyan voters to go to the place where they were registered and produce their voting card, backed up by an official ID card. The acquisition of an ID card was fraught with opportunities for corruption and this, together with the availability of indistinguishable, cloned copies had brought the Identity Card system into disrepute. Generally speaking, the electoral system in Kenya is antiquated, unreliable and open to corruption. Reforms are in the pipeline and, for the time being, it serves as a skeleton on which to build a viable democracy.

The ID card system has been around for many years for the citizens of Kenya. In theory, it is the law that every citizen must carry an ID card at all times. In practice it is almost impossible to implement this law. Kenya has vast open spaces where the sparse population rarely encounters the authorities and the rule of law is the rule of the tribe or clan. ID cards have very little relevance to life on a camel in the Chalbi Desert.

Mr Odihambo had invited Alex to a reception at the Kenya High Commission in Portland Place. It had been laid on to welcome him as the new Kenyan High Commissioner. Christopher Odihambo had been appointed as a direct result of a recommendation from the President himself. Although he and the President were from different and competing tribes, they had both studied law together at

Edinburgh University and both had married Scottish girls. Each had been best man to the other at their respective wedding ceremonies and the friendship had transcended tribal differences.

The out-going High Commissioner had been delighted by the appointment. Being a cousin of the present Prime Minister of Kenya, he came from the same tribe as the new appointee and for him to have earned such powerful recommendations from the leader of the nation, spoke volumes for the future stability of the country.

Major Freddie Kinyanjui was military attaché to the High Commission. Having received his training in England at the Royal Military Academy at Sandhurst, he had many connections in the British armed forces. He had served, on secondment, with British army Special Forces and was one of the few overseas officers to have passed selection for 'the Regiment', as the SAS is known to its members. He had been badly injured in Nairobi in an anti-terrorist incident a couple of years previously in a suspected Al-Qaeda attempt to assassinate many of the world's leaders, including the President of the United States and the Secretary General of the United Nations. Kinyanjui was shot twice, in the chest, while trying to detain a terror suspect. His injuries very nearly killed him and threatened to force the authorities to issue him with a medical discharge. It was his distinguished career and diplomatic connections which led the Foreign Minister to ask for him to be retained in his rank in the Kenya Army and to take up the post of Military Attaché in London.

Since it was a formal reception, Alex wore an ancient dinner jacket that had been handed down to him when his father had died. Strangely enough, it fitted him like a comfortable glove. The dark green silk facings on the collar gave it an unusually retro feel, which set off the sun-bleached thatch of unruly hair which framed his face. Margie, Alex's wife, liked the dinner jacket. She said, looking at her husband's hair, that green always complimented gold.

He paid off the taxi driver and stepped up to the main door of the High Commission. Portland Place was in raw, cold darkness. A heavy drizzle drifted past the streetlights and the High Commission beckoned like an oasis of warmth and light.

The door was opened by a doorman and Alex thanked him in Swahili as he entered. He went in to the function room where Freddie Kinyanjui spotted him and strode over to welcome him. He was in full military uniform with a string of medal ribbons and a set of parachute wings on his left chest.

"Alex!" they shook hands warmly, "I'm so glad you made it!" The smile, too, was warm and genuine. "I've got someone I want you to meet." he said and led the way across the room, through the throng of guests.

The gentleman's face was familiar and suddenly Alex realised why. This was the Prime Minister of Kenya, Harrison Omolo. He wore the archetypal charcoal pinstripe suit, with a red rose in the button hole, an Old Etonian tie round his fashionably cut back collar and a richly coloured silk handkerchief in the top pocket of his jacket. A gold Half-Hunter fob watch was linked to a framed miniature of his wife by a gold chain which extended from one pocket to the other across the generous expanse of his waistcoat. The watch had been discreetly presented to him by a grateful Israeli President, in appreciation of his assistance during the Entebbe raid.

They shook hands. The dark face, under the thick grey hair, was lined with wisdom and humour. The voice was deep and resonant, with no hint of an accent. He reminded Alex of one of his uncles who had served for more than thirty years in the Indian Civil Service

"An honour to meet you, at last, sir." Alex was a great admirer of this icon of the new Kenya. He combined an old-fashioned conservatism with an entrepreneurial approach to the nation's problems. His stands on political corruption were well documented and had put him in serious danger on several occasions during his career. Having served as Attorney General for ten years, he had supervised the overhaul of the judicial system. He had rooted out a dozen corrupt judges and was in the process of dismantling the Identity Card system which, as far as he was concerned, was corruption served up on a plate.

"A great pleasure to meet you, too, Captain Stewart. I hope that you are fully recovered." Omolo was referring to a gunshot wound which Alex had received during the same anti-terrorist action with Freddie.

"Oh mine was nothing, compared to Freddie's. I was hiding behind a door"

"That's not the way I heard the story." The Prime Minister gave Alex a theatrically suspicious look, under arched eyebrows.

"Nor me!" Freddie added with a chuckle.

"Well, if you insist then, I was actually hiding in front of a door."

Freddie chuckled again.

"As I heard it, you were trying to get in through the door, but anyway, you put yourself in harm's way and the people of Kenya are grateful to you for your bravery."

"Maybe they should be more grateful for my stupidity!" he said with a grin turning to the Prime Minister. "Excuse me asking, sir, but am I correct in understanding that you are intending to abandon ID cards in Kenya?" The abrupt change of subject demonstrated Alex's embarrassment about the gunshot wound.

"You understand correctly, Captain."

"May I be nosey and ask why? It's just that in the UK they seem to be hell-bent on introducing ID cards."

"Yes, I noticed that but, in my opinion, there are more cons than pros to the ID card. True enough, under ideal circumstances, you can keep tabs on the criminal fraternity and identify miscreants such as illegal immigrants and the like, but the system is wide open to fraud and corruption and we found that almost twenty per cent of the cards, checked at random by the police, turned out to be forgeries. From a personal point of view I was brought up to respect the individual's freedom. To my way of thinking, compulsory identification is an infringement of civil liberties and the first step towards the Police State."

"Fascinating to hear you say that, sir. And very refreshing, if I may say so."

Alex had not heard such forthright speaking from a politician in years. His heart warmed to this cornucopia of old values and straight talk.

"But what do you put in its place?"

"Imposing a system raises peoples' hackles. As you very well know, since you are married, the best way to get somebody to do something is to make them think that it was their idea in the first place. If you want people to identify themselves, you should make identification something desirable, make them want to be identified."

The sense in Harrison Omolo's words came from a lifetime of experiences, keenly observed, filtered and stored. It was like listening to an instruction manual for living. Alex was fascinated.

"You probably know these so-called 'social networking' websites on the internet," he continued, "like Facebook or Myspace, for example." Alex nodded his head. "There is a lot of evidence that some of them were formed as intelligence gathering tools. The point is that the intelligence is freely given and is therefore more detailed and intimate than intelligence gathered under duress. Do you agree?"

"I had just quite simply not thought along those lines before, sir."

"Oh, okay then." he looked up at Alex. "There are many ways to trawl personal information out of the general public, Captain. You know that attractive young lady who comes up to you in the street, bearing a clipboard. 'Good morning, sir,' she says, smiling sweetly. 'We are carrying out a survey on peoples' eating habits. Could I take a moment of your time to ask you a few questions?' Then she asks you a whole bunch of questions which bear no relevance to eating habits whatsoever." Alex laughed in recognition of the ubiquitous survey girl. "The mere fact that she chose you to ask in the first place, tends to mean you take it as a compliment and you open up. You feel

64

flattered. You want to give her information. You probably want to give her a whole lot more but let's just start with the information!"

Alex once again found himself laughing with a complete stranger who was turning out to be a surprisingly familiar person. He began to feel comfortable with this senior politician, which was a very unusual feeling, particularly for Alex, who was not generally known for his liking of such people.

"So how could you apply this to ID cards then?"

"Well you make the ID card an attractive thing to have, a social symbol, membership of a privileged class. 'Have you seen that Harrison Omolo? He's got an ID card already! He must know somebody.' Do you remember when mobile phones first came in? Everybody had to have a mobile phone. So much so that there was a rattling trade in fake ones!"

Once again Alex Stewart found himself grinning in recognition of something he had experienced himself. Once again he was surprised. He had always treated politicians with the kind of contempt reserved for parasites. As far as Alex was concerned, politicians were leeches who preyed on society, liars who would say anything in order to curry votes. They were people whom Alex found easy to despise. This man, however, was different. He was the perfect example of the difference between a politician and a statesman.

"And how do you reverse the process then?"

"Oh, to reverse the process you just discredit them. You make them into something which you wouldn't be seen dead with. 'Have you seen that Harrison Omolo? He still hangs on to his old Identity Card. He really is so 'last year'. When is he going to join his fellow human beings in the twenty-first century?' You make it something to be ashamed of."

"What about if it has the force of the law behind it?"

"There are many people who guard their individuality with passion. They consider enforced identification as an unacceptable imposition, a corrosion of their civil liberties. I happen to be one of those people. The argument against my stand is that I should accept the democratic decision of the majority of the people. I accept that, but it does not mean that I have to agree with it. I am still entitled to argue against the decision of the people. Otherwise there would be no debate. No debate. No democracy."

Unbeknown to either the Prime Minister or Major Kinyanjui, or Alex Stewart, there was a group of people planning a strategic campaign that would use the IDC as a weapon to bring the capitalist world to its knees. They too were familiar with the psychology governing the masses.

Chapter 8

The collapse of the world banking system continued apace. Symbols of the capitalist domination of the financial world tumbled with frightening ease. Inter-bank lending virtually ground to a halt as the credit squeeze forced the interest rates to levels not seen since the 'great depression'. Recession loomed over the horizon like a dark storm cloud. The price of gold and platinum spiralled through the roof, whereas the price of oil plummeted to levels not seen for years as the depth of the recession made itself apparent. Investors withheld their millions from an economy which not only looked sick, but close to death's door. As it slowed down, the value of money fell. People suddenly realised that money is only valuable as long as its users think it is. The demand for precious metals and gemstones climbed inexorably as the rich poured gold, platinum and gems into their coffers. The demand for oil dropped even further as industry slowed down production in response to the drop in demand for its products. It was Richard Nixon who took the USA off the Gold Standard in 1971 by removing the fixed price of gold and floating it on the open market in order to pay for his Vietnam adventure. Now the value of gold knew no limits and as the price of precious metals mounted as the value of money fell.

The ranks of the unemployed grew to levels not seen for scores of years. Despair brought desperate measures for survival and the breakdown of law and order threatened to plunge the capitalist world into chaos. The situation called for stern measures from those in the corridors of power

Lawlessness is a product of loss of control. When a government loses control over its plebiscite, it loses communication with the people. It is very important that a

67

government knows the people whom it is governing. If the people know their rulers, they can survive hard times in good order. Witness the effect of Winston Churchill on a population being bombed and threatened with invasion on a daily basis and whose food supplies hardly supported life. Not only did they survive, but they went on to defeat an enemy which, logistically, was more powerful and better trained.

Now the situation was different. The enemy was not some foreigner, easy to identify and vilify. Now the enemy was within. Captains of industry were seen to be hiding away their ill-gotten gains before closing up shop and leaving for some distant Caribbean tax haven. Their departure was perceived as a betrayal by those left jobless at home. A new subculture was developing, not a part of traditional society and invisible to the lawmakers. The only evidence of its development was the rising crime rate and the lower conviction rate of the criminals responsible. It was time to take steps to reverse this trend.

Harry 'Fightin' Crighton, the Prime Minister of Great Britain and Northern Ireland, obtained his name when, in his younger days, he took a swing at a news hound who had 'unintentionally' pushed a microphone into his face, shouting "Lollipops, Lollipops!" The pressman had tried to sue Crighton for assault but the incident had been faithfully recorded on camera and the judge dismissed the case, awarding costs against the reporter.

Crighton called an extraordinary meeting of his cabinet. The ministers took their seats in the cabinet room at Number 10 Downing Street. There was a murmur of conversation around the room which ceased as the door was swept open for the Prime Minister, accompanied by Marilyn Walters, the Home Secretary, to enter. She brought a faintly spicy and aromatic perfume with her. It was one of her trademarks. They walked quickly to two empty seats, halfway down the length of the conference table, and sat down, each placing a sheaf of papers in front of them. The Prime Minister opened a bottle of mineral water and poured some into his glass. He took a sip.

"Good morning, all of you." He glanced around the attentive faces at the table. "I have called you here this morning to discuss measures which we must take in order to maintain control over this country in the coming months and years. As you are all well aware, there is a growing threat to the country's stability, posed by certain elements of the population who like to maintain a profile low enough not to appear on police radar screens. I intend to bring these elements to the surface and expose them to the limelight. The way I intend to do this is by the introduction of an identity card system. We have discussed this many times before in parliament, but the opposition has managed to procrastinate and filibuster in the House, preventing its introduction. They maintain that it is an infringement of civil liberties. I put it to you, ladies and gentlemen, that we are one of the few countries in this world which does not insist on the carrying of identity cards by its citizens." He looked long and hard at the faces of his colleagues. He was well aware that some of them were not wholly convinced as to the moral aspects of enforced identification. "The technology is now in place" he emphasised by slamming his fist on the table, causing the glasses to jingle and the Home Secretary to flinch. "I am advised that Loughborough University is pressing ahead with the development of a revolutionary concept which will not only provide us with a reliable identity verification tool, but much, much more. Tax dodging and car theft will be a thing of the past. Money will be a thing of the past. Illegal immigration will be a thing of the past."

Crighton glared at two of the less convinced ministers. If they insisted on continuing in their doubting frame of mind, they would have to be replaced by people whose eyes had been opened. "We, ladies and gentlemen, have fallen behind the rest of the world. We are out of date and this is now threatening the very fabric of the nation. Let us therefore confront our responsibilities and implement the one programme which will put us on course to restore control over the unruly elements. I need not remind you that they are hell-bent on destroying a way of life which has taken generations to perfect and must now be nurtured and protected from their insidious influence." He once again stared into the eyes of his colleagues, particularly the waverers. Some of them looked away as the stare bored into their minds. They knew their jobs were up for grabs if they didn't follow the leader.

"So, Ladies and Gentlemen, I need your support. Do I have any dissenters?"

There was a pause while each member of the cabinet absorbed the implications of his speech and then the Secretary of State for Health, Paul Strong, raised his hand.

"You know my opinion, Prime Minister. I cannot support you in this policy, so therefore I will step aside." He rose to his feet and gathered up his papers. The doorman gave him access to the outside world and closed the door behind him.

Then the Minister for Trade and Industry, Stan Mumford, stood and fed his papers into his briefcase. "I also, Prime Minister, will have to make way for somebody more of your political persuasion," and he left the table.

The tension was tangible as the remaining members of the cabinet watched to see if there were any more surprises. Nobody else stood up.

"Very well," said the Prime Minister allowing some relief to show, "We will need a select committee to deal with the details of implementation. We need to work out the physical aspects of the implementation too and how we are going to present it to the media. I would emphasise that speed is of the essence. This country needs a bit of shock treatment right now and I intend to administer it!"

The Minister for Education, Mark Dewhurst, could not help feeling uncomfortable with this attitude. He came from a long line of liberal minded socialists. The philosophy of 'shock treatment' was so far away from his own philanthropic approach to education that it suffocated the freedoms which were an ingrained part of his psyche. He could not live with suppression of individual freedom, however 'good' it might be for the individual. He stood up. Several of his colleagues were deeply disappointed to see his departure. He had acted as an emollient foil for the more autocratic aspects of the Prime Minister's approach to government. Without his mellowing influence, the Prime Minister would have free rein to introduce some of the more radical curbs on individual freedom which he had proposed as a solution to the nation's problems.

"I am afraid, Prime Minister, that you will have to find somebody with more reactionary views than mine to support you in your shock programme."

Crighton had never liked Dewhurst's liberal attitude to education. In fact he laid the slide in national educational standards very much at his door. He would not miss the Minister for Education. What the country needed was a jolt to shake out the dead wood and encourage tough new growth. The swing of the pendulum was long overdue. In order to restore the nation's backbone, a programme of disciplinary measures would have to be introduced. If the country went into the looming recession equipped with an ill-disciplined, lackadaisical, drug and alcohol numbed youth and weighed down by State sponsored single parents with more and more citizens being paid not to work, then Britain would no longer be 'Great'. It would join the other sick men of Europe on the slide into oblivion.

The reintroduction of military service was one such measure. When Crighton left school, national military service had ended so he had volunteered. He did two years in the Royal Air Force Regiment and got to see the world. In his opinion a good slap on the bottom, administered in a controlled environment, did young children a power of good and a bit of swearing from an irascible Sergeant Major on a parade ground, did the same. Military Service would be a great tool to whip a bit of sense into the nation's youth. It was one of Crighton's great goals in the rescue of British society from decadence. Winston Churchill had been heard to say that, in spite of his mother being an American, he was glad to have been born British, since he considered that the United States of America was the only nation which had gone from barbarism to decadence, without the intervening period of civilisation. Crighton considered that Great Britain was still civilised and he intended to keep it that way. National Service would be the catalyst.

This was something that the Secretary of State for Defence, Charles Macullum, did not want to handle. His budget had been eaten away over the years of Socialist government to such an extent that the thought of having to pay for food and accommodation for half a million extra bodies, let alone uniforms and equipment and, of course, salaries, was anathema to him. He preferred to leave that to someone more unfortunate than himself.

"I'm sorry, Prime Minister, I'm afraid that you will have to find somebody else to fill my shoes. You well know my problems with the re-introduction of National Service. You must find someone more qualified than I to carry out this policy." He stood up.

"Charles!" The Prime Minister almost shouted. Marilyn Walters, the Home Secretary, flinched again. "I do not accept your resignation! The country needs you, Charles. The country needs National Service. In your heart of hearts, Charles, you know that that is one of the best tools we have to beat a bit of sense into today's youth. You have to admit that. It's the only thing they understand. Or do you want us to descend into a morass of drug-fuelled anarchy? What about the Sentrycorps heist? £27,000,000 and an expensive helicopter vanish into thin air! No trace of any of it has surfaced. It is almost as though nobody cares. What's twenty-seven million these days, anyway? What we need is a bit more discipline. These criminals could do with a good thrashing. It never did me any harm!"

"Corporal punishment was abolished while I was still at school, Prime Minister." Charles Macullum had not served in the armed services and, in certain quarters, this cast some doubt on his eligibility to take over as Secretary of State for Defence. "We are no longer at war. We do not need to train our young people to kill. That is why we have a professional, volunteer army. Today's youngsters need freedom of expression. They need leadership. They need motivation. They need inspiration. They will not get much of that on a parade ground."

His departure was accompanied by a profound silence then, after the door had closed on another member of the Cabinet, Jim Price, the Minister for Science and Technology, raised his hand. He was one of the older-generation. He had been a member of the National Union of Mine Workers which had been defeated by a woman, namely Margaret Thatcher. He knew how to recognise defeat and he knew how to use it. In fact he became a great admirer of the woman with whom he had fought, even though he was diametrically opposed to her politics. Because of his quiet guidance Mr Scargill had not been allowed to fight to the finish and the resurgent union was now proof of the success of that policy.

"Not you, too, Jim." The PM's voice was subdued. The words came out as if spoken by a dying Julius Caesar, 'Et tu, Brute?'

"All I will suggest, Prime Minister, is that we sit back and take stock, otherwise you will end up with no Cabinet at all." He looked over his half-rim glasses at the pouting face of the much younger head of government. "No Cabinet, no government" he said.

There was a very strong warning there from one of the senior politicians and Crighton could not ignore it. He could not afford to lose Jimmy Price. If he allowed him to leave then the collective boldness of the others might increase to the point where the general public might notice. At the moment, the four resignations could be spun into a healthy cabinet reshuffle with the Prime Minister showing his government who was running the country. Behind the scenes he would start the ball rolling with the identity cards.

There was an unlikely lead in Germany. The town of Braunschweig is situated on the Oker River, approximately half way between Berlin and Bremen, not far from the massive Volkswagen facility at Wolfsberg. Braunschweig was heavily damaged during the Second World War had been progressively rebuilt and restored. One tribute to the determination of the people of Braunschweig is that the Romanesque/Gothic church of St. Andrew, all-but destroyed during the war, had been restored to its original splendour, a task that took sixty years to complete.

During the post-war chaos the British Army took over the Volkswagen plant in Wolfsberg and ran it until private investors could be found. Braunschweig had to wait longer for its renaissance. It became a centre for scientific research and now spends upwards of seven per cent of its gross domestic product on this research and is now recognised as the centre for this research in Europe.

The city was virtually destroyed as the tattered German army retreated from the Russians during the final days of the Second World War. It was for this reason that a small company grew out of the rubble, financed by a Russian Infantry Major by the name of Igor Lutov. The twenty-three year old had been promoted in the field as a result of the horrific casualties suffered by his unit at the battle of Stalingrad. Despite being shot in the arm, he had personally recovered four wounded comrades and taken them to a dressing station, saving them from certain death from a German machine gun emplacement during the mindless violence of that titanic battle.

During the sacking of Braunschweig, Lutov ran for cover into what had once been the cellar of a rich Jewish merchant's house before Hitler had almost destroyed the

Jewish population of the city. As he waited for the shelling to stop, he became aware that he was not alone. In the dust and gloom, he picked out the terrified features of a girl. Her face was covered with dust and her clothes obviously had not seen a laundry since the fighting for the city had started. Numbed by the brutality and stress of house-to-house and hand-to-hand fighting, the Major's immediate reaction was to kill this unrecognised target. He reached for his NR-40 combat knife in a blur of movement and the girl's face sank into her hands in submission to the inevitable. Then something snapped in Lutov's brain. He returned the blade to its scabbard and instead, reached into his ammunition pouch where there was a packet that had been given to him by a British soldier when they had met across the Oder River. Lutov took the bag and held it out for the girl. Her head still rested in her hands, awaiting death, or worse. He reached across and touched her shoulder. She recoiled and looked up as though expecting the blade to thrust into her flesh. All she saw in the gloom was a hand holding a clear plastic bag with the words Fox's Glacier Mints written on it. Lutov shook it and reached across to the girl. Timidly, hesitantly, she took the bag and clutched it against her dress, as if to say that, at least she had one possession before she died.

Lutov leaned down and patted the girl on the shoulder. He thought of his little niece, back home. Marina would be about the same age as the little girl in front of him, maybe fourteen or fifteen years of age. He could not help pondering on how he would have felt if he had run her through with the combat knife. Communism had endeavoured to kill Christianity but orthodoxy had survived in many parts of the Union and Lutov thanked his God for staying his hand from this particular killing.

After the fall of Braunschweig a large detachment of Russian troops was left to occupy the ruined city with Lutov among them. The Glacier Mint girl followed him everywhere. She cleaned the primitive billet which he inhabited near the remains of the Cathedral and went to get water for him every day. She cooked for him on a fireplace she had built out of crumbled masonry in what had once been a cloister. She washed his clothing and brought it back, ironed and in better condition than when it had been issued to him though how she managed this was a mystery. After the brutalising experiences through which Igor had lived in the preceding years, this young girl restored a sense of humanity to his world. When he left, after two months of occupation, he promised himself that he would return to Braunschweig and see little Glacier.

In the immediate post-war chaos, many of the people of central Europe had been split up from their families. Children walked hundreds of miles in search of their parents. Newly demobilised soldiers trudged vast distances in search of their wives and children among the ruins of what had once been a pillar of civilisation and infrastructure. It was not for almost a year that Lutov was able to revisit Braunschweig. The Russians withdrew and demobilised large numbers of the troops who had served without leave, some of them for more than two years. Lutov was among them.

There were violent purges in the Russian Army at that time. The Great Pogrom was instigated by Joseph Stalin while he consolidated his position as the undisputed ruler of the vast new Russian Empire, the Union of Soviet Socialist Republics. Lutov was glad to be out of the political maelstrom which thundered through Russia after the Great Patriotic War. He seized the opportunity to return to Braunschweig very soon after he had been released from active service.

The infrastructure of the city had been systematically destroyed from the air and again from the ground. It lay in, often unrecognisable, tatters. The shattered teeth of bombed out buildings lined empty streets where the rubble had been bulldozed onto the sidewalks in order to allow access for military traffic. An ornate, gilded lamppost stood incongruously in the middle of a jumbled pile of bricks and masonry as a symbol of what had once been. It was almost impossible to imagine these streets filled with rich and fashionable citizens, promenading from shop to shop, enjoying drinks with friends at the coffee houses before visiting the theatre.

To Lutov's war-weary eyes, Braunschweig had ceased to exist. The people had left. Only the odd vehicle passed through these dead streets now, on its way to somewhere else, anywhere else. The only reason to come to Braunschweig was to get to the other side. Lutov walked over the broken streets, scarred by the scorched metal carcasses of German tanks in which desperate crews had met their final thunderous, claustrophobic moments. They sat like memorials, at many of the street corners. Nobody had touched them since the end of hostilities. Some even contained the charred remains of those whom their loved ones at home would never see again.

He eventually reached the ruins of the cathedral. It was almost exactly as it had been when he had last seen it, except that the smoke and dust of war had been swept away. Now there was no distant thunder of gunfire. There was just an eerie silence. He heard the flutter of wings as a dove launched from a gaping window, high up on the only standing wall of a blasted apartment block opposite the

Cathedral. Then he heard footsteps. They were running. Their echoes clattered off the gaunt remnants of ecclesiastical buildings near the Cathedral. Lutov turned, searching for the source of the noise and thought he must have fallen into a dream. The blonde wavy hair was flying in all directions as she ran. She was crying great sobs of affection as she leapt into his arms.

"Glacier! Oh Glacier!" Lutov could not contain his emotions as he felt the hot tears flooding down his cheeks. The two of them clung to each other, as if afraid that the dream would evaporate if they let go. Suddenly, after all these brutal years of mayhem, misery and murder, a shaft of blinding sunlight had pierced the darkness. Once again, Lutov thanked his God.

It took two years to set up the shop. The first job was for them to learn to communicate with each other. Both Igor and Glacier had a smattering of English and this became a rather rudimentary lingua franca for them.

One of the biggest requirements of a population wrenched apart by war, is communications and in the days after the surrender of Nazi Germany one of the first services to be restored to working order, with Teutonic efficiency, was the postal service. Postal services transport mail and mail needs writing paper, envelopes, stamps and something to write with. Therefore Lutov and Glacier set up a stationery shop. They started by converting the arch of a railway bridge near the station, into living accommodation. The neighbouring arch would serve as the shop. Searching all the bombed sites around the station, they collected piles of old office stationery, which had been abandoned as the workers retreated before the Russian onslaught. Soon Glacier had sorted paper and envelopes into recognisable piles. Lutov managed to sequester a slightly damaged set of office filing cabinets from the ruins of a bank opposite the railway station. Chairs and a table soon joined them and Igor managed to borrow some mattresses from the blitzed storerooms of the shattered Fürstenhof Hotel in Campestrasse, not far from the Bahnhof. Soon the railway arch resembled a small apartment. He gained access to the railway yards and laid his hands on some diesel fuel. A couple of old lamps from a locomotive which had been bombed and then dragged into the yard for repair, provided light. Coal dust from the tender of the same locomotive provided fire for cooking and heating. Lutov had constructed a rudimentary chimney out of some war-expired ventilation trunking from the hotel kitchens and, what had started life as a dank repository for a mountain of garbage, became a surprisingly cosy den. Drainage from the railway track flowed down large culverts from the bridge, into the city's sewage system and Lutov contrived to take advantage of that for Glacier and himself. Bathing was performed initially at the public conveniences in the nearby railway station

With the train services once again in limited operation, the people of Braunschweig began to filter back in dribs and drabs. Lost souls searched for reminders of lost memories. It was heart-rending to see the tears and the despair but, where there were people, there was hope and where there was hope there were more people. Soon they wanted to communicate with the outside world. They needed to restore a sense of order after their ordeals and demand for writing materials grew, so Lutov and Glacier prospered. Having started with nothing, they soon reached the point where they could bring in new copy paper, new pens and inks, new accounts books, receipt books, invoice books, all the office equipment required by a renascent bureaucracy. Soon renovated typewriters appeared in the shop. A name appeared above the door; The Arches, Stationery and Office Supplies. Business boomed.

IBM had close links with Germany, some they had cause not to be particularly proud of. Lutov was quick to see the potential of computers and The Arches became the prime agents for IBM in Braunschweig. From providing office supplies, he developed a side-line in the production of business cards, a natural progression from which was the design and manufacture of identity cards. Lutov's designs were innovative and entrepreneurial.

Anybody could make an ID card, but could they make one which was difficult or even impossible to forge? Eventually forgers can develop the technology to clone any document. Counterfeiting had been around since the advent of currency. Lutov was one of the first manufacturers to introduce embedded holograms into his cards and when the forgers came up with an indistinguishable copy of that design, which took them all of six months, Lutov introduced the embedded microchip. Even this was open to cloning, so he invented the Implanted Interface Chip. The IIC was implanted under the skin of the subject and, for it to carry out many of its duties, the wearer had to present the card to the IIC for the verification which activated the card for a transaction. The IICs were pulse sensitive so that they would automatically be de-activated in the event that the wearer's heart ceased to beat. The cards had many more functions, other than simply identifying the wearer. The new cards could be identified and located by satellites of the Galileo terrestrial positioning system. They could perform duties far above what was required of normal everyday ID cards. They could act as credit cards. They could replace car keys. A simple swipe of the card in the ignition would start the next generation of vehicles. No thief could steal your car unless he had your card, plus the IIC. Vehicle theft would be a thing of the past. Lutov was very excited by its potential.

It was at this stage that he suddenly realised that he had spent the last ten years with a girl whom he had very nearly killed in cold blood, a girl who had devoted herself totally and selflessly to him in gratitude for not being killed by him. He cursed himself for being so blind. He had missed ten years of marriage, simply because the demands of survival had blinded him.

"Marry me, Glacier," he said in a perfectly normal voice while they were sorting out pro-forma invoices for submission to Customs. Glacier looked round at her trusted companion of the last decade.

"You are still young Igor. Maybe there is someone better than me still over the horizon."

Igor Lutov laughed long and loud, until his sides ached. "Glacier!" he cried. "Everything you see here was either done by you or for you by me. You are my sanity. You are the reason why I came back to Braunschweig. It was just so natural that I, that I forgot to ask you the most important question of all." He grasped her hands in his and looked into those fiery blue eyes he had so nearly extinguished with a blade. "What do you say?"

"I cannot imagine life without you, Igor."

"Is that a 'Yes'?"

"It is," she said, closing her eyes and searching for his lips with hers.

It was nearly two years later that Glacier gave a baby girl to the world. She was the prettiest little thing that Igor Lutov had ever set eyes on. They named her Irina and Lutov doted on her. She was the apple of her father's eye. Just over a year later she was joined by a brother, Georg. Glacier adored him. Where Irina had been given Glacier's blonde hair and blue eyes, Georg, on the other hand, had much harder features. Even at the age of twelve his face was solemn, powerful, almost humourless. The two children grew up as middle class Germans but gained a more cosmopolitan outlook by being sent abroad for their university education. Irina studied Renaissance, Baroque and Rococo architecture at the University of Graz in Austria while Georg went to Loughborough University in the UK for a degree in Information Science which focussed on the relationship between digital technology and society.

One of the main reasons why he chose this particular course was to further his research into the identity industry, in particular, the smart identity card, which he was developing with his father Igor and which they had named the 'IDC'. His thesis revealed a whole new world being opened up by the ID technology. When it was published it caught the eye of, not only Mr Crighton, the British Prime Minister and proponent of the ID card system in Britain, but also the Executive Secretary of the Commonwealth of Independent States, Mr Boris Belnikov, who also happened to be President of the Russian Federation.

Chapter 9

The grey-suited doorman of the cabinet room at 10 Downing Street had, in a previous life, been a Royal Marine. Sergeant Duncan Hughes had followed his father into the service and had risen rapidly through the ranks, making Sergeant before the age of twenty-seven. This made his newly retired father immensely proud.

At the start of the Falklands campaign in 1982, Duncan Hughes embarked on the graceful, twin-funnelled ship Canberra which had been hurriedly converted from a cruise liner into a troop ship. After its arrival in San Carlos Water he had disembarked to join the other members of his squadron for the long tab over the moors to Stanley. Their arrival was not welcomed by the Argentinians.

During the attack many missiles were fired, their guide wires lying like a web all over the battlefield. It was dark and Sergeant Hughes did not see the trap into which he was about to fall. There was a low rocky outcrop above the inlet and spent guide wires criss-crossed the area. Hughes did not see the void into which he plunged over the side of the low cliff and, in fact, it was the wires which saved him from death. They became entangled round his right leg as he went over, cutting through the flesh of his left leg below the knee. He let out an involuntary cry of pain as he hung, suspended upside down, by the snare, the blood running down his upturned body. His oppos heard the cry and thought the sergeant had been ambushed so their approach assumed a tactical caution which meant they did not find him for almost half an hour. Although his leg was still attached to the rest of the sergeant when they finally got him down, it had to be amputated later as it was only the shattered bone that had held him suspended. He was evacuated after a paramedic had performed trauma first aid to reduce the loss of blood. His medical discharge came almost nine months after he left hospital with a disability pension and a remarkably effective prosthesis. He then applied for a job as a security officer at 10 Downing Street. His reputation had preceded him by the recommendation of a Parachute Regiment Sergeant called Jack Wise.

Wise was a large and powerfully built individual. He had turned down a commission in the Parachute Regiment, in spite of his privileged upbringing, because he wanted to remain among the men who had earned his deep respect in training and later in action. After leaving the army, Jack Wise had taken up various appointments advising Chief Executive Officers and senior politicians on security issues. He had become a highly valued éminence grise behind the scenes in politics and industry. He had unrivalled connections both nationally and internationally.

His fiancée had been killed in a car crash. The driver was his brother who was not totally sober at the time but was completely uninjured in the accident. Since then Jack had not looked at another woman and had temporarily withdrawn from his family to nurse his grief. He lived with a very affectionate female Dachshund who had presented him with three puppies so far in an apartment in Lowndes Street, just off Sloane Square.

He and Duncan Hughes were in constant touch and he gleaned most of his inside information about what was going on in the cabinet, from this contact. It was therefore with more than normal interest that he withdrew his mobile from his pocket and saw that there was a call from none other than Duncan Hughes.

"Duncan," he said, after pressing the answer button. "What can I do for you?"

Hughes wanted to arrange a meeting so Jack suggested a dram at 'Aunties', a pub in Eaton Square, much frequented by serving and retired military types. Jock, the barman there, was a Scot and a former Sergeant Major who had lost an eye in a highly confidential operation in the Balkans. His background and the generosity of his measures made him popular with the pub's regulars.

Jack bustled into the bar like a galleon under a full suit of tweed sails. He peeled off his mackintosh and hat and handed them to Jock as though it was a well-rehearsed ritual. The thick shock of grey hair had recently been shorn. Jack would have been almost unrecognisable without it, had he not possessed such a massive frame. His sheer size had contributed to some heavier than expected landings when he was attached to a parachute. The hair would grow back in the near future, bringing one of Jack's familiar attributes with it.

"Your usual, Mr Wise?" said Jock.
"Do you still have some of that KWV Fleur du Cap, Jock?"
"Indeed we do, sir."
"That would be perfect. Have you seen Duncan at all?"
Jock knew all the clients like a directory.
"Yes, Mr Wise. He's waiting for you by the fire in the old library."

There was a bar which had served as a library in a previous life, when the house had provided a luxurious London bolt-hole for Lord Alborough of Clune, a well known entrepreneur and philanderer in early Victorian times. Jack found Duncan sitting by the log fire in a comfortable wing chair in the book-lined, high-ceilinged room, reading the Court Circular in The Times newspaper.

"Hello Duncan. Has your knighthood come through yet?" Jack was alluding to the scandalous award of a peerage to a lady who was quite obviously having an affair with a previous British Prime Minister.

"No, I'm afraid I'm not sexy enough!" he grinned. "Can I no get you a wee dram, Jack?"

"Jock's bringing me some of that Fleur du Cap, thanks Duncan. Now why did you want to see me?"

"Well, I was doing the door at Cabinet this morning and I thought that you would like to know that four ministers resigned over this ID card issue and the re-introduction of National Service."

"Four! Wow! What did Fightin' Crighton do to cause that?"

"It looks as though he wants to bulldoze the legislation through and introduce ID cards before anybody has a chance to object. He has a big majority in the house, so he could do it, as long as he doesn't have a revolt on his hands. He also mentioned that Loughborough University is involved in the development of the cards. I took the liberty of checking with them and they confirmed that a young German has just published a paper on the subject. They e-mailed it to me. I thought you might like to take a shufti at it."

"Excellent work Duncan! Have you got a copy with you?"

"As a matter of fact I have, Jack."

He reached into the attaché case beside his chair and produced a large manila envelope which he handed to Jack. Jack opened it and drew out a spiral-bound volume consisting of A-4 pages, typed up on both sides of the paper. There were three pages of illustrations halfway through. The distinctive blue shield emblem with the shade of violet specifically called African Violet, sinister chief, of the Loughborough University coat of arms, was the main feature of the cover. The title of the work was 'Public Identity, Challenge and Response A dissertation on the rights and wrongs, the advantages and disadvantages of enforced public identification'. There was a bibliography at the back and the rest of the thesis occupied around twenty-five double-sided pages, making it about twenty thousand words in length.

"This will make interesting bedtime reading! May I take a copy from you?"

"Take that one, Jack. I made two."

"Excellent, Duncan... now... er... are you secure at Number 10? No chance of you being compromised when we meet?"

"As far as I am aware, security is happy with me and I know that you have an irreproachable reputation with them. There is no reason why I should not have obtained copies of this work and I don't see any reason why I should not be seen discussing it with you. Do you?"

"None at all, Duncan, unless I was trying to bulldoze dodgy legislation through parliament, in order to force a reluctant population to adopt a system they do not want." Jack smiled ambiguously. "Then I might be on the lookout for enemies conspiring to defeat my cunning plans."

Neither of the two men sitting by the fire had, as yet, had any inkling of the expanse of the plan which they would be confronting in the near future.

Chapter 10

Ivan Ilyich celebrated his sixty-eighth birthday with a visit to his dacha, sixty kilometres to the east of Moscow, deep in a forest of birch and conifer. The dacha was of modest proportions when compared to the palatial residences of some of the oligarchs of the Russian Mafia. It was built of timber and suited his life-style well. There were few pictures in the house but those in his study were of old-school communists like Lenin and Trotski, both of which stood on the Steinway that filled one corner of the sitting room. Karl Marx occupied a position of honour on the shelf over the door. It was strange that the founding father of communism should be buried in England. That was another anomaly that would be straightened out when Russia assumed its rightful leadership of the world. There was one curiously unlikely hero hanging with the rest. Lavrentiy Beria, had been responsible for millions of imprisonments and deaths during the Great Purge. Too late, he saw the error of his ways and, while attempting to liberalise the country, he was assassinated by his political opponents.

Ivan Ilyich had been married to the same woman for forty-one years. She was seven years his senior and having been a heavy smoker since her mid-teens, she had succumbed to lung cancer at the age of seventy-one, leaving no issue. During the Great Patriotic War, the lack of tailor-made cigarettes had forced her to use a Meerschaum pipe, in order to satisfy her tobacco craving. This had not improved the state of her teeth and finally, she had taken the radical step of having them extracted, which did nothing to improve her sex appeal. Ilyich, being childless, could then pursue limitless political ambitions without fear of patricide. He could concentrate wholeheartedly on the destruction of the system that had destroyed the Soviet Union for which he had fought, as a child and to which he had lost all his family, during The Great Patriotic War.

The suddenness of the collapse of the Soviet Union had even taken its enemies by surprise. For Ilyich it was a disaster of such gigantic proportions that he had difficulty in thinking of a reason to stay alive. Twice he had attempted to end his life and on both occasions success was foiled by his babushka. On the first she cut the rope, just as Ilyich was expire from hanging himself and on the second, she caught his leg as he tipped himself out of the window of their twelfth floor apartment on the outskirts of Moscow.

Then Belnikov had contacted him with the magnificently simple plan of revenge which he was now putting into effect and which had given him a new reason to live. No his goal in life was to survive long enough to witness the collapse of capitalism and already it was happening. The hated American Imperialists who had, by deviousness, dishonesty, bribery and brute force, suffocated the Soviet world would see what suffering they had imposed on the population of Greater Russia. The beauty of the plan was that they would be responsible for their own destruction. That same deviousness, dishonesty, bribery and brute force would be turned around and used against the very perpetrators of the crime against the Rodina. The plan was poetic in its simplicity.

It was Sam on the line and Alex greeted him warmly.

" Good morning Sam. Nice to hear you. How's tricks?"

"The trick worked."

"Which trick was that, Sam? You have so many up your sleeve!"

"I got Petrov's presentation. I have it on my external hard drive."

"You wicked little thief, Sam! I didn't believe that you would do such a thing!"

"Better than that, I also borrowed his address book. It makes quite interesting reading. I was thinking that Jack Wise might be able to dig something out of it."

"My word Sam! You have been busy! Let me give Jack a call. He'll be chuffed to Naafi-breaks! When are you going to be available? Maybe we could meet up at Aunties?"

"Sounds good, to me, Alex. What time?"

"Well, what about six this evening?"

"Sounds good to me."

"I suggest we meet up in the Library Bar. It's a bit quieter in there. Are you familiar?"

"Oh yes, Aunties used to be my local when I was living at Alborough Mews."

"Alborough Mews? I never knew you lived there, Sam. When was that?"

"Oh that was a long time ago when I was doing some computer work for the MOD. We'll talk about it another time. Rather a long story."

Alex detected a certain reticence in Sam's tone and he didn't push him. "Okay then, see you at six at Aunties." Alex ended the call and scrolled down his list of contacts until he reached Jack's name and then called him.

"Hello Alex," the Oxbridge accent was amplified by the mobile phone. The ex-Parachute Regiment Sergeant sounded more like Royal Family. "What can I do you for?"

"Are you available this evening, Jack? I thought we might meet up at Aunties for a couple of cold ones. Would you be free?"

"You know me, Alex. I'm never free but there again, I'm not that expensive either! What's on?"

"Sam has some very interesting news."

"Oh, I see." said Jack, "OK, I'll see you there. Around six-ish?"

"Yes. I'll see if I can get Dick to come as well."

Dick accepted the offer with enthusiasm. "It'll be a relief to get out of this madhouse!" he said with feeling. "I think the whole thing is going to implode, if we can't put a stop to all the banks falling flat on their faces. Did you hear about the NUB in Leeds?"

"Is that Northern Union?"

"Yes, that's the one. They had a run on the bank yesterday, which cleaned them out, so they called for more money and the Sentrycorps truck delivering it got hijacked. Three guards shot dead, one critical in ICU and £27,000,000 stolen." Alex had not seen the news since breakfast time the day before, so he had missed this particularly dramatic breaking news item.

"They used a Super Puma helicopter for the heist. They hijacked it on its way out to a North Sea oil platform. The heli and crew have still not been found. Apparently it headed west after the raid. They've got a Nimrod out looking for it. Whoever these guys are, they obviously mean business. They made the police look like amateurs."

"You can say that again!"

"Okay, Alex, I'll see you at Aunties at six."

"See you Dick." Alex closed his mobile phone and slipped it back into his pocket.

That evening was bitterly cold and raw. There was a hint of coal smoke and diesel fumes in the air, combined with a whisper of snow which made the heavily polished panelling, crowded bookshelves and warm fire in the Library Bar all the more inviting.

Sam and Alex were the first to arrive. They came up by train to Victoria station and took a bus through the busy, darkened streets to Eaton Square. Premature Christmas greetings and decorations were beginning to appear in shop windows and pubs were exhorting customers to book early for 'Traditional Christmas Fayre'. Some of the more entrepreneurial Indian establishments were in the process of changing from Diwali greetings for customers who celebrated the Festival of Lights, to Christmas greetings for others. The nativity illuminations which once brought a bit of Christmas cheer to brighten the long curve of Regent Street had been banned as politically incorrect and replaced with commercial images provided by sponsors. The veto on council-funded Christmas decorations also saved a large sum of money which contributed to the financing of an access road to The London Markaz at Abbey Mills, the vast new mosque that had sprung up in the old East End of London.

It was a short walk from the bus stop to the welcoming door of Aunties.

"Mr Jackson! What a pleasure to see you back, sir. It has been far too long." Jock had an encyclopaedic memory for names. "Come away in out of the cold." he said, the Glaswegian brogue adding a certain welcoming charm to his voice. "It's a Bacardi and Coke, if I'm no mistaken Mr Jackson." He never forgot the requirements of his regulars either.

"Amazing!" said Sam as Jock took their coats and hurried away to hang them in a pantry behind the door.

There was a mixed group of middle-aged customers at the bar and Alex recognised one of them as an old friend called Frank Dawlish. Alex had been through some serious adventures with the Major.

"Evening Frank." he said, as they passed the bar on their way to the Library.

"Evening, Alex. Looks like you are on a mission."

"I'll let you know, Frank... Early days, yet." They walked through to the Library.

Jack Wise was the next to arrive, closely followed by Dick Tarrant. "Sorry I'm late, chaps! Frightful pile-up on the North Circular." He was out of breath from running. Tarrant hated being late.

"What are you having, Dick? A dram?"

"That would be great, Alex. Do they have the Aberlour?"

"Jock assures me they do. Large, or small?"

"Oh make it a large one to kick out the cold!"

Alex caught Jock's eye and nodded his head, rubbing the crown with the flat of his hand, to indicate a large measure. The drink was delivered minutes later.

"So, Sam, Alex tells me you have some news for us." Jack held his glass out to chime with Sam and Sam responded.

"Indeed I have. I managed to copy Mr Petrov's presentation and borrow his address book. I have them here with me." He held up a memory stick. "What do you want me to do with them?"

"May I make a suggestion?" Dick Tarrant took the floor, "If I may say so, I consider Alex's idea of rattling the crockery a little to be an excellent one. As Sam says, you only see things in the forest when they move. So let's get them moving. We could drop a copy of Petrov's presentation in the Hampstead Heath delivery bin one evening and tell the Evening Standard, the BBC and the Sun Newspaper, 'pour encourager les autres'. We could let them know that BSO Odessa does not exist and the size of the loan requested. That should put the cat among the pigeons."

"We could call the media on our way home." said Alex, "Sam and I are taking the train and we can call from a phone box in the station."

"Good thinking, Alex. How will you let them know?"

"I'll just tell them that a financial disaster is about to hit the City. Details will be found in a garbage bin outside Spaniards Inn on Hampstead Heath. Have you got a copy of the presentation, Sam?"

Sam opened his ancient leather satchel and pulled out a folder. The presentation was in the form of a spiral-bound book. The full colour representations of the platforms and their amenities were shown in remarkable detail. The suggested means of financing the project was contained in its own chapter at the end. This was the perfect bait for the bloodhounds.

Dick Tarrant reached for the book. "Perfect!" he said. "I can drop it off on my way home. I only live just up the road in Bishops Avenue." The fact that Dick lived in Bishops Avenue hinted at a man of considerable wealth. The hint was no lie.

The three men finished their drinks and the party broke up. Tarrant ordered a cab from Jock, while Alex and Sam decided to walk to Victoria in order to give Dick time to bait the litter bin. He would phone Alex upon delivery. The night had become cold but dry and the twenty-minute walk up Lower Belgrave Street was bracing and refreshing after the warmth of the bar.

Alex's phone chirped just after they had entered the station. The lure was in place. It was time to call the bloodhounds. Alex and Sam went over to the row of booths, one of which contained the crumpled form of a young man who had chosen it as a shelter to sleep off the effects of his overindulgence. There was a strong smell of urine. Alex entered the last in the line. He lifted the receiver and inserted the required coins into the unit before stabbing in the number for the Evening Standard. He got through to the recorded information lady.

"You are connected with the Evening Standard press service. For general information about the Evening Standard and its history, Press One. If you want information about subscription rates, Press Two. If you want the News Desk, Press Three." Alex pressed three. The phone rang five times and a male voice came on the line. "Good evening. Evening Standard Newsdesk, Steve Grant speaking." The patter was well-practiced, almost bored.

"A major financial scandal will hit the City of London's financial institutions within the next days. Evidence of this event may be found in a litterbin outside the Spaniard's Inn Public House on Hampstead Heath. The principal player in the scandal is the Black Sea Oil Company of Odessa. This company does not exist. The deal that they are endeavouring to make concerns multiple billions of pounds sterling. That is all."

Alex heard the sudden urgency of the reporter at the other end of the line as he struggled to obtain the caller's identity and he grinned as he replaced the receiver. He moved to the next kiosk and repeated the operation for the BBC and the Sun Newspaper and then he and Sam caught the train. They reached the flat and Alex threw together some sandwiches in place of dinner.

The following morning the BBC news carried nothing about the BSO project. They had obviously got to the bin too late after it had already been raided. Or perhaps they just thought that it was a hoax. Alex then got on to the Evening Standard web site and there it was.

'BREAKING NEWS. A mystery caller last night alerted our news staff to a massive new financial scandal about to unfold in the City of London. Evidence of this scandal was found in a litter bin outside the Spaniard's Inn public house on Hampstead Heath. Our reporters are investigating the background and will keep you informed as the story unfolds and the players are revealed.'

"Great stuff!" Alex smacked his fist into his hand. "That should shake them up a bit!"

News of the revelations reached the Moscow Kremlin before Boris Belnikov was out of bed and he was an early riser.

There had been a serious breakdown in security. Heads would have to roll. If the plan were to be compromised at this early stage, there could be no guarantee of success. It was essential to staunch the flow of information before it became general knowledge and the only way to do that was to choke off the sources.

Belnikov reached for the secure phone and dabbed one digit on the dialling pad before raising the handset to his ear. "My office, now." was all he said. Minutes later a small, thin-haired man entered the room. His head was disproportionately large for the spare, bony body. The face had small, pinched features assembled around a sharply pointed nose that supported a pair of glasses with unlikely pink rims. The lips were curiously deformed, as though the face had been slashed open with a saw. But it was the eyes which revealed the true character of the man. They were hard and vicious and the palest shade of ice blue, the blue of an iceberg which hid hideous secrets out of sight. He stood in silence. This was Vladimir Chernorgin, the feared supremo of the SVR. Even the President feared this man. There was nobody in Russia, nobody in all the world, who could escape his attentions. The SVR was like a sinister octopus with millions of tentacles, each one of them armed with a deadly sting. The President spoke.

"Alex Selwyn Stewart, Nikolai Dimitri Petrov and Frederick Paul Barnes... You have them on file?"

"We have them, Mr President."

"They are to be eliminated."

Without a word Chernorgin turned and left the office. He was the only other link between Belnikov, Ilyich and the Lutov IDC system.

Chapter 11

Freddie Barnes had always fancied himself as a bit of a ladies' man. He had a weakness for proving to his friends how irresistible he was to blondes. Recently the clubs in Soho had seen an invasion of stunning girls, seeking partners in England. They were almost all blonde, young, lithe and playful. They came from Russia and the old Soviet bloc, searching innocently for a new life, the 'capitalist dream' and a gullible, rich husband who would pander to their every need, in exchange for sexual favours.

Some were not quite as innocent as they seemed. Ludmilla was one such girl.

It was Friday and Freddy decided to start the weekend off in style. He would take in a couple of nightclubs and see what luck came his way. He had a white tuxedo which had allowed him to score many goals between the silken goal posts. He was relatively well known in and around Soho and the bouncers had benefitted from his generosity on occasions when he celebrated a particularly profitable deal. He would kick off with a visit to Borodin's. It was a comparatively new establishment belonging to a Lebanese gentleman known simply by the name of Sabih. The décor of the club was over-the-top-Roman, with Corinthian columns supporting the heavy purple velvet drapes which framed the stage. Anatomically correct, naked statues of nubile young men and women disported themselves in arched niches around the walls. The bar itself was a colonnade with an architrave bearing the inscription 'With alcohol in plant and tree, it must be nature's plan that there should be alcohol in man' engraved on it.

Sabih catered for all colours in the sexual spectrum but his speciality was the new Russian influence. They were keen to earn English pounds, having suffered from the Russian rouble's buying power, and London's male population welcomed them with open arms.

Ludmilla had been tracking Freddy Barnes for almost a week now. She adopted an array of different wigs in order to avoid detection. She had observed his timetable. She had watched his diet and noticed his passion for chocolate. She had noted the fact that he bought bars of Bournville Fruit and Nut. Many times when he sneaked out for an illicit smoke during office hours, he would dip into the chocolate as well. He got through two or three bars a day. A plan formed in her mind.

Borodin's was humming. The music alternated between live traditional jazz and disco with the disc jockey sometimes playing classical Russian music.

Ludmilla spotted the white tux as soon as Freddy walked in through the heavily curtained door. She moved closer to the bar and positioned herself halfway along it. She had an apple juice with ice in her hand. It was in a whisky glass and looked like the real thing. She had an arrangement with the barmen to replenish her glass with apple juice and charge the donor for whisky. This deal suited them both, since the apple juice was considerably cheaper than a large whisky. Freddy noticed the girl standing on her own at the bar. She was petite and delicate with blonde hair that came down to a point at the nape of her neck. She looked very young and he wondered vaguely if her mother knew that she had a daughter in a nightclub in Soho, London. He went and stood next to her. She did not look up. He ordered a whisky on the rocks and turned to her holding his glass out for a toast. "Cheers" he said. Ludmilla looked up coyly, raised her glass and said "Cheers" in a voice he could hardly hear against the music.

"English?"

"Ukrainian." she replied.

Freddy took a bar of chocolate out of his pocket and broke two squares off, keeping them in the foil. He offered them to her and she took one and put it in her mouth. The nuts in the chocolate were almonds, the lips on the girl looked as though they were made out of rose petals.

"You speak English?"

"I speak little."

"You want a dance?"

"I finish the drink, then, maybe?"

"Okay. No rush." Freddy raised his glass to his mouth and sipped the whisky. "What are you doing in London? On holiday?"

"No, I work in travel agency."

Her glass was nearly finished and Freddy offered to refill it. The girl politely demurred so he threw the last half of his drink down his throat and held out his arm to usher her to the dance floor.

It has been said that dancing is a vertical expression of a horizontal intention and Ludmilla was very expressive. Freddy could feel himself rising to the bait. His right hand slid gradually lower until he felt the soft roundness of her behind. There was no sign of underclothes. He was not hiding his attraction and she was not resisting his advances. In fact she pressed herself closer as though she wanted to hide him from the jealous glances of possible suitors.

They danced for half an hour before Ludmilla said that she needed a drink. They left the dance floor and took a table not far from the stage. The Trad Jazz team started to emulate Louis Armstrong. Freddy bought the drinks and the barman paid attention to Ludmilla's apple juice-for-whisky arrangement. Freddy reached into his pocket for the restorative Fruit & Nut chocolate. There were two squares left.

"Oh man!" he said. "Chocolate's finished!"

Ludmilla excused herself. "No problem." she said. "I have to go girls' room. I bring chocolate back."

'Big bonus.' thought Freddy. 'These birds normally don't buy. They only sell. This one must be keen.'

When Ludmilla returned she held up a bar of chocolate and slipped it into the pocket of Freddy's jacket. He produced the last two squares of the bar and shared them with the girl. She ate one of the squares and stood up.

"You very kind man." she said. "Maybe we see us tomorrow?"

Freddy had not anticipated this early denouement and applied for an encore, but Ludmilla was firm. "Maybe you here tomorrow?"

"What time?" he pleaded.

"Same time, same place."

"What's your name?"

"Natasha," she laughed, because she knew that she would be many kilometres away from London by the next rendezvous time.

After Ludmilla had left, Freddy decided that this one was worth waiting for, so he swung his Tuxedo over his shoulder and left the club. He was fairly sure that tomorrow would bring Paradise, with the girl with blonde hair to the nape of her neck. Paradise it might bring indeed but the blonde hair and the nape of the neck would be far away. He left the Borodin, laughingly slipped a hundred quid to the bouncers and got a taxi home to his flat in Islington. He was riding on a pink cloud of anticipation. The softness of the girl filled his imagination. This could definitely be the one.

It was only when he closed the door to his apartment that he realised how hungry he was and remembered chocolate that the stunning little Ukrainian had bought him. It was in eager anticipation of the girl's future generosity that he consumed the bar as he watched the Sky News bulletin at ten o'clock, little realizing that he would feature on that same channel, a couple of days later.

As he sat, he suddenly felt as though he were running out of breath. He began to struggle to suck air into his lungs but the urge to cough overcame even the instinct to breathe. The coughing increased until he felt as though his lungs would burst out between his teeth. He grappled for his phone and desperately dialled Tarrant's number but the power of speech was denied him. Coughing was all that was allowed now and that reduced him to a powerless twitching imitation of a human being. He did not hear Dick Tarrant's increasingly urgent questions in reply to his call. Finally, all Tarrant could hear was a throttled gasping and then, in about 90 seconds, there was silence. The phone dropped out of Freddy Barnes's nerveless grasp and lay on the floor. A tiny metallic voice continued to shout for his attention but all in vain. His lips had turned a mauvish-blue colour, as had his fingernails. The eyes stared, unmoving, at the ceiling and the convulsions eased, as life slipped away from Frederick Paul Barnes.

"Yes Dick. What can I do for you?" Alex had been fast asleep when Bach's Toccata and Fugue in D minor had woken him. It took a moment for him to realise that it was coming from the phone.

"Hello Alex. I'm afraid something terrible has happened to Freddy Barnes." He was breathing fast, as though the drama of events had exhausted him. "He phoned me, but never got a word out. I just heard coughing and then a kind of gurgling and then nothing. He wouldn't answer me. Maybe he couldn't. I was wondering what you suggested I do."

"Call the cops, Dick, 999, straight away. Tell them exactly what happened. It's important. If he has OD'd, they will need to get to him right away if they're going to save him."

"Okay, Alex. I'll get on to that right now. I'll let you know what develops.

Alex signed off and then tried Freddy's number. It was engaged.

It was the second call-out for Police Constable Ollie Walpole and his oppo, P.C. Dutton. The first had been to a domestic disturbance in Marylebone. That ended up with an ambulance call and it took the two paramedics and P.C. Walpole to control the woman and stop her beating her already senseless husband. By the time they reached Islington, Freddy Barnes had long since passed away. The smell of almonds pervading his apartment was too strong to have originated in the chocolate wrapper that lay on the floor beside the mobile phone. This looked like another job for scene of crime officers from the Met.

Freddy's remains were removed and taken to the St. Marylebone Crime Lab. The coroner carried out an autopsy to establish the cause of death and the aroma of almonds gave it to him. Cyanide had killed Freddy Barnes. The police would only establish the method of administration after the scene of crime officers had produced the wrapper of the chocolate bar which had been the last thing to pass Freddy's lips before he died. In the forensics lab, investigators examined the wrapper minutely and found a circular hole in the silver foil which looked as though it had been made by a pin. Upon closer examination, they found traces of cyanide around the hole. It appeared that someone had injected the poison into the chocolate bar. What had started as a possible drugs overdose had now become a full murder enquiry.

President Belnikov's e-mail alert sounded in his office in the Moscow Kremlin. He opened up the new letter. The succinct contents simply read "FPB delivered", indicating that Frederick Paul Barnes had ceased to be a factor in the plan.

Now it was Nikolai Petrov's turn. That was comparatively easily achieved.

Suicide is the commonest cause of fatality on the London Underground. It is particularly traumatic for the driver of the train selected as the instrument of death. In this particular case, a girl appeared to try and prevent the man from jumping in front of the train. All the onlookers would swear blind that she had grasped him as he lunged forward. She even injured her hand in the attempt. A nasty bruise appeared where the train had hit her, as she struggled to restrain the man. She was flung back into the crowd of commuters by the impact. Petrov's skull was smashed against the windscreen pillar. He hung there for a moment, like some grotesque figurehead, before the deceleration threw him off, to be decapitated by the slowing train.

So common was this cause of death that it was only reported on the last page of the Evening Standard. It was the name that caught Alex's attention, 'Nikolai Sergei Petrov, a Vice President of the Black Sea Oil Company of Odessa'. Now, there was just one more to go from Belnikov's list. Alex Selwyn Stewart.

When he had finished reading the report, Alex immediately opened his mobile phone and called Dick Tarrant.

"Hello Dick I'm on my way back to the flat and I read a report in the Standard that Nikolai Petrov jumped under a tube train in the morning rush hour. Some woman tried to stop him but wasn't strong enough to hold him. What the hell is going on, Dick? First Freddy Barnes, and now Petrov. That looks a little bit too coincidental to me. I have a feeling that we may be seeing the results of rattling the cage. What do you think?"

"Yes, Alex. I don't like this one bit. Have a word with Sam when you get home. He's very clued-up on situations like this."

"I'll do that, Dick and let you know what we come up with. 'Bye."

Alex closed his mobile as the train came into the station. He handed in his ticket as he went through the barrier and walked out into the night. A mist of drizzle floated down in the dim light shed by the street lamps. There were a number of cars waiting in the car park. One was a new generation Mini. It was red and had a black roof. Alex had been tempted to buy one, but Margie had argued that there would not be enough room in it for the tots and the luggage. But he was still tempted. Judging by its number plate this one was less than a year old.

The walk back to the apartment usually took about twelve minutes but because of the miserable night, Alex pushed ahead at a brisk trot. It was as he turned into Amblehurst Road that he heard the racing engine. He spun around in time to see the red Mini mount the pavement and head straight for him as he searched for a way to avoid it. His only hope lay in the overhanging branch of a sycamore tree. At the last second he leapt for his life, grabbing at the branch. He found it, just as the car hit him. In the nanosecond before impact, the beam from a streetlight caught the features of the girl who was driving. She looked almost too young to hold a licence. His last thought before the crunch was, "This is no joyrider. This one means business."

Alex did not feel any pain as the car crashed into him. There was a heavy thump as he cartwheeled over the top of the car and fell on the pavement behind. His parachute training didn't have time to save him. He fell on his left shoulder and his head took the secondary collision with the paving stones. For some moments he lost consciousness, which probably saved his life because his motionless form, seen in the rear view mirror, convinced the young killer that he was dead. The car sped off into the night.

Slowly his senses returned and, with them, the pain. At first he was loath to move a muscle for fear of discovering some irreparable damage. Then he realised he needed help. Tentatively he moved the fingers of his right hand. They responded, so he went on to the right arm. It too seemed to be functioning. Slowly and with massive concentration, he reached into his jacket pocket and extracted his mobile. He scrolled down through the list of numbers until he found Sam. His call was answered promptly. Sam was like that. He hated to keep people waiting.

"Sam!" Alex's voice was more like a groan, "I have been hurt in a hit-and-run. I'm in Amblehurst Road. I'm fairly broken up. I can't move. Could you come... and... give... me ... " the voice trailed off.

"Alex! Alex! Are you still there, Alex?"

"Please... hurry..." Alex's voice trailed off.

Sam hung up and dialled the emergency services and gave them Alex's location. He told them he was in the road and was going to look for him

Sam was racing down Elm Tree Drive, now devoid of trees since Dutch elm disease had decimated their population. He crossed the Horley Road, dodging homecoming commuter traffic and attracting the angry flashing of headlights as he ran. For a sixty-eight-year-old,

110

he was fit. He swung into Amblehurst Road, just as an ambulance entered at the far end. It stopped almost as soon as it had turned in, the blue strobes flashing on its roof and the hazard lights blinking at its corners. Men in reflective yellow vests ran to the huddled figure lying on the pavement. Sam slowed his pace to a fast trot and reached the scene just as the kneeling paramedic stood up. For a moment, Sam thought that this was a sign of finality.

"Is he okay?" he asked, nervously, expecting the worst.

"Vital signs are good. Luckily he was in good shape physically before the incident but it looks like he took quite a panel-beating from the joy-rider."

Alex stirred. "Sam!" he whispered and Sam leaned down to listen. "Sam, that was no joyrider. It was a young girl and she meant business," the whisper died away.

The paramedic touched Sam on the sleeve. "Excuse me, sir. I would like to keep the patient as quiet and stress-free as possible until we can get him to casualty. Are you a friend?"

"I am indeed. It was me who called you guys."

"Maybe you would like to accompany us to the hospital then, sir. You may be able to help fill us in with his ID details, in case he becomes incapacitated."

"Certainly," said Sam. "Only too happy."

The driver and the paramedic then took out a plasticised canvas sheet and laid it on the pavement beside Alex's body. Very carefully they worked it in underneath him until he was lying on it in exactly the same position as he had assumed when he first hit the ground. There were handles at all four corners of the sheet and halfway down the sides. When he was safely in position, they placed a vacuum stretcher down beside him. This piece of equipment is basically a bag full of expanded polystyrene beans. Patients are placed on the bag that moulds itself around them. A small pump then extracts the air from the bag and it holds the patient rigidly in place until the vacuum is released.

While they were doing this, Sam opened his phone and called Dick Tarrant.

"Hello Dick, I'm calling to tell you that Alex has been seriously injured in a hit-and-run incident. He managed to inform me that he is under the impression that this was not a random joy-riding accident. It appears that the incident was an attempt on his life."

"Oh my God! Is Alex going to be okay?"

"Initial diagnosis of the paramedics is that he will survive but his injuries are serious. I would appreciate it if you could contact Jack and get down here as soon as you can. I think it is time for a council of war. The other side are obviously changing the pace now and I feel that it could be time for us to get more people involved."

The ambulance only used the siren once to warn other vehicles as they approached the station roundabout. Fortunately the hospital was very close and the ambulance team were impressive in their well-rehearsed efficiency as they took Alex from the ambulance in to Casualty. He disappeared into the triage room and the hands of the trauma team on duty. An analgesic drip was quickly inserted into his arm and initial diagnosis confirmed a fractured skull, a broken left collarbone, four broken ribs, a punctured left lung, a broken left femur and right tibia. Doctor Ravinder Singh had never seen such extensive injuries on a live patient, even though he had assisted in the recovery of survivors of the London Underground bombings. Alex was very lucky to be alive.

Sam went out of the main entrance of the casualty department and opened up his phone again. He contacted Dick Tarrant and told him the news about Alex's injuries. Dick replied that he was already in a taxi on the way to Victoria Station and that he would arrive before midnight. He had contacted Jack Wise who said that he would be driving down by car.

"Any chance of a bed for the night?"

"There are three bedrooms in Alex's flat. We can make up a couple of beds. I suggest that you come to the hospital first though because the flat is locked and I have the key. The hospital is only five minutes' walk from the station. Could you tell Jack, too, I don't have his number."

"I'll do that Sam and we'll meet up in casualty."

Dick Tarrant and Jack Wise arrived almost simultaneously. Dick came into casualty as Jack walked in through the main entrance having parked his car in front of the hospital. He asked a lady at reception for the whereabouts of the casualty department. Following her directions, he eventually met up with Sam and Dick. Sam took them aside.

"I have an idea I want to discuss with you," he said, confidentially and the other two gathered round him as if to prevent the idea from escaping.

113

"What's your idea, Sam?" said Jack

"Okay," Sam continued, "If this was indeed an attempt on Alex's life, then what is to stop them doing it again?"

"What indeed?" said Jack. "So what's your idea?"

"Would Alex not be safer, dead?"

"It depends what you mean by 'safer'. He would be out of further harm's way, for sure, but he would not be much use to us, would he?"

"What about, if the killers were to be under the impression that he was dead?"

"Aha! I see what you are getting at," said Dick. "So how can we achieve that?"

"I've done it before." Jack intervened. "We had an SAS sergeant who killed three IRA men. The IRA targeted him and he got shot in the head while walking down a street in Manchester. He survived and we took him to a very exclusive clinic in London, where he officially died. He must be one of the few people to have been a mourner at his own funeral. He was 'buried' with full military honours and his obituary appeared in The Telegraph. He continued in the service until he retired a couple of years ago. His name was Rob Berry, known to his friends as 'Daylight'."

"Wow!" said Dick. "Just imagine watching yourself being buried. Spooky! So how do we actually get things moving?"

"I'll have to speak to my lords and masters," said Jack, sliding a finger up and down his nose in mock secrecy. They have ways and means."

Alex was on powerful sedation for several days before he was considered stable enough to move. When he came round there was a white-coated doctor at the foot of his bed, studying a clipboard. He was of Asian appearance and wore a tightly wound turban on his head. He noticed the name Dr Ravinder Singh was a badge pinned to his coat pocket.

"Welcome back Mr Stewart," said the doctor. "You are very lucky to be alive. We nearly lost you that first night."

Alex opened his mouth to speak but no sound came out. It seemed as though his vocal chords had been coated with some kind of mastic, so he whispered. "Thank you for saving my life, Doctor. I am most grateful."

"It was not us who saved your life, Mr Stewart. It was the Almighty. We only assisted him."

"Well I am very glad that you were there to assist him." He attempted to laugh. The simple effort of expressing air from his lungs, sufficient to whisper, caused him considerable discomfort and felt as though he was being stabbed in the ribs. A look of deep pain crossed his features which made the doctor lunge forward in concern.

"Are you all right, Mr Stewart?" he said.

"I'm okay. It's just that I didn't realise how sore it was going to be to laugh."

"Broken ribs are always sore." said the doctor. "Oh, by the way, I have some visitors who would like to see you. Are you feeling up to seeing them?"

"As long as they are not from the Inland Revenue" he whispered, wincing again.

The doctor laughed. "Oh no! These are friends of yours. Shall I bring them to you?"

"That would be very kind, Doctor."

The doctor left and, minutes later, he returned with Jack, Sam and Dick Tarrant.

"My God!" said Sam, as he walked through the door, "You look as though somebody has been practising their bandaging techniques on you!" Alex grinned and avoided laughing. "No, but seriously, it's great to see you back in the land of the living." He patted the foot of the bed and smiled.

"Jack has a plan," he said, waving a hand in Jack's direction.

"That's right, Alex, we think that you would be better off... er... dead."

"Charming!" For the first time, Alex's vocal chords came back to life. "... and the good news?"

"We want to move you out of here if you are fit to go. We want to take you out tonight, while it's still dark."

"And where are you taking me? The mortuary?"

All three of them laughed. It was good to see Alex in such good spirits, despite his injuries.

"Not if you behave yourself," said Jack. "There is a nice little clinic in London."

Chapter 12

The Wellesley is a very exclusive private hospital in north-west London. Its facilities, including its kitchens and not to mention its cellars, are among the best equipped in the world. It caters for the extremely rich and guests of Her Majesty's Government. Its exclusivity denies access to the media. Security is very tight indeed, to the point that a small and very discreet armoury is concealed in the office of the chief of security. All members of the security staff are ex-military and some of them are armed. Jack Wise had connections up to the very top and it was these which gave him access to the clinic. Alex was impressed.

News of Alex's death spread through the newspapers and Independent television ran an obituary on him, which he watched with considerable amusement from his bed.

The news also reached Moscow. Ludmilla was quietly rewarded in dollars by a grateful nation.

The effect on Margie, Alex's wife, was traumatic. She had not been included in the plan so, when she arrived at London Heathrow with the two children in floods of tears, the press were quick to jump on the story of the tragic widow and family of yet another joyriding victim. When Jack Wise saw the story, he suddenly realised that they had all forgotten to tell her.

This was confirmed when Sam heard keys rattling in the front door of Alex's flat. He was preparing to settle in for the night. His immediate reaction was suspicion, so he armed himself with a meat cleaver from the kitchen. He heard the front door open and the cry of a child calling. "Dad... Dad... are you there Dad?" Sam crept up to the sitting room door. He opened it and saw a girl and two children silhouetted in the front doorway. When they saw him they screamed, a fairly natural reaction when confronted by a large grey-haired man wielding a meat cleaver. Margie was the first to speak.

"Who are you?" she said in a surprisingly firm tone, "and what are you doing in my home?"

"I'm most terribly sorry!" Sam replied. "You must be Mrs Stewart. I am a friend of your husband. My name is Sam Jackson and I am afraid there has been a bit of a cock-up." The two children clung, whimpering, to their mother.

"I've heard Alex speak about you. You're the computer geek aren't you?"

"Indeed I am, Ma'am."

"Well, put that meat cleaver back where it belongs." Margie pointed at the lethal looking blade in Sam's right hand.

He obediently walked through to the kitchen and replaced the cleaver in its wooden scabbard. When he returned, the mother and her two children were still standing in the doorway where they had been joined by another couple.

"Now, what are you doing in my home?"

"When your husband was injured, I came down to see if I could help. There were another two of his friends staying here, but they have gone to London with your husband."
"Why have they gone to London? My husband should be buried here at St John's Churchyard. That was his church when he lived here in England and that is where he would

119

wish to be buried." The two children started to whimper again at the mention of their father's funeral.

"Could you come inside and I will explain everything."

Margie turned to her two neighbours. "Tom, would you look after Jessie and Robbie for a moment. I'll knock on your door once I get this sorted out."

The two children were loath to leave their mother's side but she led them to the neighbours and handed them over. "Thanks so much Tom, I'm so lucky to have neighbours like you. We won't be a minute, Darlings." She stroked the two children as she turned back to Sam. They walked down the corridor into the sitting room, closing the front door behind her on the latch.

"Please, Mrs Stewart, you will need to take a seat. Can I get you anything?"

"Let's just get on with the story, shall we?"

"Okay then. The first thing I should tell you is that your husband, Alex, is still alive. He was badly injured but he should make a full recovery."

Margie looked up, her face a picture of shocked realisation, then scepticism, then disbelief.

"What do you mean, he is still alive? The whole world knows that he was killed in a hit-and-run. It's all over the papers."

Sam leaned forward and his glasses fell to the floor. He picked them up and thrust then on to his nose.

"He was indeed involved in a hit-and-run incident but we have reason to believe that it was not an accident. Because of this, we felt it would be better if our adversaries were under the impression that Alex was out of the game on a permanent basis."

" 'Our adversaries'? Who the hell are they?"

"We are not precisely sure yet."

"And who's 'we'?"

"There is a Mr Dick Tarrant."

"Yes I know Dick."

"Then there is a Mr Jack Wise."

"Yes I know him too."

"And then there's me."

"And where is my husband?"

"He is at The Wellesley Clinic in St John's Wood in north west London."

"Why there? There's a perfectly good hospital here in town."

"Yes, but The Wellesley is much more discreet and the government has used it before for certain operations which require, shall we say, er, more discretion."

"Oh, I see. So Alex is up to his tricks again, is he? He makes me sick with worry every time he goes on one of these things. He's always getting himself hurt too."

"That's because he's always in the thick of things. There are far too few like him around these days. You should be very proud of him, Mrs Stewart."

"Oh, I am, more than you could know. I just don't want to lose him."

"Well I think that what we have done is the best course of action to keep him around until we find out who is behind this whole story. The fact that you arrived in the full glare of publicity will have done wonders for the authenticity of the story. I'm just sorry that we had to put you through it."

Sam pushed his glasses back on his nose and suddenly noticed that she had her face buried in her hands and was sobbing. He reached forward and laid a hand on her shoulder, strangely moved by the sight.

"I'm so sorry, my dear. I really am."

"Sorry.," Margie sniffed, "it's just..., it's just... at moments like this I realise how much I love the boy... My Darling Boy."

"Your husband is very privileged to have someone like you, Mrs Stewart. Very privileged indeed."

Margie laid her hand on top of Sam's, on her shoulder. "Thank you." she sniffed again. "Thank you very much." She looked up into the kindly face framed by the cloud of grey hair. "It's Margie, by the way."

"Margie," said Sam, savouring the name. "Nice name."

Margie put her hand to her lips. "You gave us such a fright!"

"Well, as you probably noticed, you scared the living daylights out of me too! I don't know what I would have done with the meat cleaver! I don't do martial arts at all. I would have probably ended up chopping my fingers off." They both laughed... an explosion of relief.

"Are you staying the night?"

"Well I have been up to now but I can easily find other accommodation."

"Did he put you in the Haunted West Wing?"

"Indeed he did."

"Well, you are welcome to stay. You've got all you need there, have you?"

"More than enough, thank you."

"Okay then, I'll go and get Jessie and Robbie. It will be nice to have a man with a meat cleaver around the house, with all this skulduggery going on." Sam roared with laughter.

While Margie went to recover her children from the neighbours, Sam called Dick to tell him what had happened.

"Do you think she would be prepared to play along with us?"

"She got involved in the Nairobi affair. Her computer graphics skills contributed big time to solving that little problem. I think it would be worth a try."

"I'll ask her. Maybe she has other computer skills which would come in handy."

"I reckon you've forgotten more than she has ever learned, Sam!"

"I've never done the graphics side of computing. Anyway, I'll see what she says."

"Go for it."

When Margie returned with the children, Sam sat down opposite her in an easy chair. The children sat on the floor next their mother. They did not want to make eye contact with the knifeman and they wondered where he had hidden the meat cleaver.

Sam looked down at the two children and his glasses fell off. He laughed and the boy couldn't help grinning as the ogre replaced the errant spectacles. The girl hid her laughter in her mother's skirt.

"Margie," he said, "I understand you are a computer wizard. Am I right?"

"Well, I know a bit about computer graphics and computer enhancement but I wouldn't say that I'm a wizard. Who told you, anyway?"

"Dick Tarrant said that you were involved in the Nairobi affair."

"Well Alex was involved. I was only on the periphery. I did a bit of enhancement for them, to help identify some of the opposition. I altered some of the characters' features in order to help identify them. You can do amazing things with the modern tools; fake peoples' signatures, clone credit cards, alter peoples' ID cards. Great fun, but scary!"

"ID cards?"

"Oh yes. You can create clones of ID cards which are indistinguishable from the real thing. It is amazing what you can do with today's graphics programs. With digital cloning, you can even duplicate the chip in modern credit cards. Scary stuff! After all, these things are designed and made by computers and, what is designed and made by one computer can be copied by another. It's just a matter of telling it what to do. But I thought that you knew all about this sort of thing."

"My specialities are programming and hacking. I initially made a living out of setting up programmes, then I went into hacking in a big way and offered my services to the financial institutions, which is what I do now."

"Weren't you involved in setting up Byterroute?"

"Yes, I was Jim's primary programmer."

"What, Jimmy Broster."

"That's the one. Jim and I go back a long way. When we first met everyone was using DOS and a megabyte was something only found on a Kray mainframe computer. I remember when the first memory sticks came out. I thought that I would retire long before I could fill all thirty-two kilobytes. Man went to the moon with less

125

memory capacity than that. Today's Petabytes, Terabytes and gigabytes were not even dreamt of in science fiction in my day!"

"Incredible!" said Margie. "Now I can say that I know somebody who knows Jimmy Broster! Fame at last!"

"Now you can say that you know the great Jack the Hack too!"

"Of course! What an honour!" Margie looked at Sam and they laughed again. She was glad that she had made this ebullient new addition to her list of friends, even though the initial circumstances could have been more congenial.

All was not so merry in the outside world, however. Merchant Transfer and North Atlantic Corp were the next on the list of banks to fail and they had both benefitted from a massive government bail-out scheme, which had proved frighteningly unsuccessful. Now Prime Minister "Fightin' Crighton" assumed a new nickname, "Bitin' Crighton", after he had been filmed biting his fingernails during Prime Minister's Question Time in the House of Commons. The economic situation was becoming critical. The collapse in confidence in the banking system, caused by their failure to retrieve the massive unsecured loans, had leaked down through the money chain and caused several more runs on far flung banks throughout the capitalist world. It was infecting the economies of North and South America, as well as the Far East. Japan's economy, volatile at the best of times, faced imminent collapse.

The enormous bailouts of the major banks and industrial establishments had drained the government coffers. More money had to be printed in order to keep up with the mounting queues of people clamouring to withdraw their funds from the banks in cash. As the reserves were depleted, more notes had to be churned out to satisfy demand. Money was losing its value.

The general public suddenly began to understand the great sham of the capitalist system. With this piece of paper, worth virtually nothing intrinsically, a person could buy a house, simply because the seller believed that the piece of paper he had been given by the buyer was worth the house. Once he stopped believing that, the capitalist system would collapse.

The question now was, what is there which could possibly take its place? The British Government had sold off enormous quantities of their gold reserves, as the price of gold plunged down through $180 per ounce to resupply the interest on their monstrous loans from the World Bank and to finance their fantastic deals.

Suddenly platinum was the metal of choice but the British Government only held enough platinum to supply the jewellery industry and not enough gold to buy into the platinum market.

The barter system depends on the exchange of goods, without the transfer of money. It is difficult to run, in practice. Going to the gas station for fifty litres of diesel, at three kilos of potatoes a litre, raises all kinds of practical problems. Would you, for example, be prepared to take your change in French fries? Or, 'I'm sorry, madam, we only take payment in peas this week. You'll have to try Petrogas, in Market Street. I think they are still taking potatoes. Or, how many potatoes would you have to pay for two hundred thousand tons of crude oil? Oh, and Spenders, the super market, only take Russett potatoes this week. They won't accept King Edwards.' The list of problems with the barter system is endless.

The speed with which the economies were collapsing forced an urgency on the situation, bringing governments to the brink of panic. At the best of times, governments are not famous for their wisdom, when it comes to matters fiscal, which was well illustrated when it came to building The Scottish Parliament. Its construction went over budget by more than ten times. Any Chief Executive in private industry who under-budgeted by that much, would stand a good chance of serving a term in jail for incompetence. Not so with governments. Political decisions are above the law. So the world was tumbling into the abyss with only imbeciles to hold it back. Suddenly, with the collapse of the Bank of Credit and Finance International, the world was looking into a chasm that threatened to swallow up the human race and spit it out in an altogether different financial format.

From Dick Tarrant's viewpoint it would probably mean the end of his residence in Bishops Avenue. London's gentlemen's clubs were anticipating a wholesale loss of members as the great fortunes evaporated. Industry suffered massive losses and some of the iconic names disappeared into the archives. Cutlers of Sheffield, the designers of the internationally recognised Royal Pattern cutlery, silver and gold versions of which had adorned the tables of the rich and famous worldwide for the last two centuries, reduced its workforce to just twenty-three. There was a determined effort to reinvigorate the dying name but the company was finally bought out by an Indian producer of tableware. The name survived with a line of surprisingly high quality stainless steel cutlery presented in fine wooden canteens manufactured in Bangalore. It closely resembled the Royal Pattern of earlier years but, in some way, the ancient pattern was debased by the availability of a cheaper stainless steel imitation.

This debasement was reflected in the crumbling of 'high society'. As the value of money dissolved, so the prices at exclusive, up-market establishments spiralled. 'Spondulicks', one of the most fashionable of restaurants for paparazzi-fodder in London's West End, remained closed without warning one Friday evening, normally the busiest in the week. There was no announcement in the press. There was no 'Moved to new premises' notice on the door, no forwarding address, no contact number, just closed doors and curtains. The ornate gilded door handles were adorned with a very undecorative length of steel chain fastened by an old Squires padlock. The Christmas tree fairy had fallen sideways and the fairy lights were off. In fact, all the lights were off. It looked as though the owner had very possibly thrown away the key. Rubbish was gathering in the street outside where the feet of the fabulously wealthy had only last week paraded for the cameras. It gathered in the dark corners of the entrance where a famous royal kiss had once led to an even more famous royal divorce. It was hard to believe that, only days ago, the rich and celebrated had queued to find a table here. It looked like it was going to be a Christmas of cold nights and tightened belts. Marks and Spencer's were reporting the lowest Christmas sales figures for more than forty years.

Bitin' Crighton was sleeping badly. The country was making its feelings obvious. There were demonstrations against the fat cats of industry, insurance and the banks.

The name of Barry Makepeace, the CEO and founder of Homes & Life Insurance, did not protect his London home from the mob. Demonstrators chose his house on Primrose

Hill to vent their fury on the rich. The police were unable to contain the violence and the crowd surged through the hurriedly-assembled police cordon to smash windows and torch the premises. A car parked at the side of the house suffered the same fate. They then proceeded to attack the rescue services who arrived on the scene within three minutes of the blaze being set. Twenty-one police officers, thirteen firemen and two paramedics were hospitalised as a result of the viciousness of the attack. The housekeeper was in a critical condition in the burns unit of Guys Hospital. There was clear evidence that the violence had been orchestrated by a hard core of rioters whose features were concealed by balaclavas and motorbike helmets. They had choreographed events from the rear after setting the scene, then faded away into the darkness and the crowd of spectators who had gathered to watch the fun. Twelve arrests were made. Two of the miscreants were known rent-a-thugs. The rest were made up of down-and-outs and radical students, who accepted the small financial inducement to take part in the unrest. One of the down-and-outs, known as Kev to his friends, lived in a single room with communal facilities, south of the River Thames in Battersea. He would later be released with a caution from Hampstead Police Station, only to reappear in a similar incident involving the Prime Minster less than a week later.

Under police interrogation, one of the thugs admitted that the demonstration had been pay-rolled by a man with a foreign accent.

"It was his fault that things got out of control. God knows what he had against the owner of the house. He just told us to do a good job and we would get the rest of the payment on completion." He looked down at his hands dejectedly. "That's not going to help me much, is it?"

The Police Inspector, in charge of the interview, slowly shook his head.

"Not unless you can assist us further with our inquiries, lad. Lead us to the guy who paid you and we could be very lenient indeed. Otherwise we may have to consider a charge of attempted murder for you and manslaughter for your mate. You had better just pray that the housekeeper doesn't die of her injuries."

A look of horror crossed the thug's face. "The housekeeper?" the lad gasped in disbelief. "But he promised the house was empty. He told us there was no-one in there, I swear!"

"Well he was lying, wasn't he?"

The Inspector rose from his seat. He urgently needed to relay that information to Organised Crime. It was of paramount importance that they knew that there was some loony going around paying people to commit acts of arson.

"Let me know if you decide to remember. The longer you wait, the less likely we are going to be able to catch him."

"He didn't give us no name. He just said that we would get the top-up after the job was done."

The information very soon lay on the desk of the Deputy Commissioner of the Metropolitan Police Service, John Trenchard Jason. Through him, Jack Wise became the wiser.

It was then that the grim reaper started to scythe his way through the street people of London. Death visited eleven of them in one night. All had overdosed on amphetamines, a common cause of death among this layer of society. The authorities, generally speaking, turned a blind eye to the activities of those who chose to live without housing, as long as they did not get in the way or cause a public nuisance. The strange thing about these cases, however, was that each one of them had been detained and cautioned after the Makepeace arson attack.

Mr Barry Makepeace, meanwhile, continued his Caribbean holiday undisturbed. His London home was insured for ten million pounds, sterling with Countryco, a rival of Homes & Life. They would be incensed when they discovered to whom the house belonged and that it was also insured against acts of terrorism. Even insurance companies sometimes failed to read the fine print! Barry Makepeace quietly smiled, after the initial shock had passed.

What he had not taken into account was the fact that Countryco was so close to the edge that the loss incurred by the destruction of the Makepeace property was the straw which would break the camel's back. It was not until the following morning that the implications of that hit home. When Barry Makepeace turned on his radio while drinking coffee on the terrace by the pool, the pips sounded for the top of the hour. Next came the BBC World News. The third item was the announcement that Countryco, the third largest insurance company in the UK, had gone into receivership, as of midnight the previous night. Only a fraction of the insured value of his property would now be paid out, if anything. Mr Makepeace would have to join the queue of hungry creditors. What made a chill of insecurity grind around in his belly was the fact that a company of the size and solidity of Countryco had succumbed without a whisper of warning. Where Countryco had gone, others would soon follow. He packed his overnight bag and the driver took him to the airport.

The three night layover had suddenly become one for the crew of the 'plane.

The Falcon 2000 executive jet had been chartered specifically for the three days that Barry Makepeace had calculated he would need to unwind in his Caribbean retreat. The crew had been put up at the Ocean Reef hotel on 24-hours-a-day stand-by. The hotel also accommodated many of the flight and cabin crews of visiting international airlines. Sitting in an hotel for three days without partaking of the, sometimes, very tempting delights available in those Caribbean climes is hardly human. Tempting delights come in all shapes and sizes, genders and flavours. It is difficult to give in to one temptation, without giving in to several. Luckily, the co-pilot was not involved. He came from a religious background and had never touched alcohol in his twenty-two years of life. The captain, on the other hand, was old school. A commission in the Royal Air Force had taught him how to be one of the lads and he brought his thirst for entertainment with him into civilian life. Expecting to be on the ground in the Caribbean for three days, he had not obeyed the rules to the letter so, when the call came, only the co-pilot was strictly within limits as far as consumption of alcohol was concerned.

The Captain cursed as he put away his phone and sent the first officer to pay the bills and order a taxi. Then he quickly finished his 'Traditional English Breakfast' and called the cabin attendant. He raced to his room, packed his bag and met the others in reception.

"Come on guys, we've got to step on it. Freda, did you pick up catering?"

"It's in the taxi." Freda was a new flight attendant with the company. Her origins were central European but her qualifications were impeccable. Flight Operations had hired her to stand in for Laura Ashleigh who had been injured in a road accident two days before the flight to the Caribbean.

"John, did you get trans-Atlantic clearance and the Met and Notams?"

"I called the FBO and they said that the FMS update will be waiting for us at the aircraft with the Met and Notams. They have filed for flight level three nine zero and Trans-Atlantic is cleared. We are fuelled. I have filled out the passenger and crew manifests and a General Declaration. All we need to do is clear customs and immigration formalities. Slot time is 02:00 Zulu."

"Good. Okay, let's hit it."

The Falcon 2000 and its crew and passenger never made it to Fairoaks, a business airport south-west of London. Satellites had only identified a small area in the mid-Atlantic where the waters were calmed by a release of a volatile known as Jet A1. It was in the vicinity of the last data-link transmissions from the Falcon 2000. The search would continue but only some small pieces of honeycomb structure and the tattered remnants of a life raft would ever be found. Freda's two children, having been promised handsome rewards for their mother's sacrifice, would quietly disappear. Mr Makepeace and the crew of the Falcon 2000 would receive a 'Burial at Sea'.

Chapter 13

Sergei Novgorod was a Second Secretary on the Cultural Desk in the Russian Embassy in London. It was he who sent the e-mail to a coded address in Moscow. The message simply read 'Hot Property', which indicated to the recipient that the property of Mr Barry Makepeace had been destroyed.

The recipient was Mr Boris Belnikov, President of the Russian Federation. He dialled in a number and pressed the 'Talk' button on his office intercom in order to call the Prime Minister.

"Ivan Ilyich," he murmured. "Good news... 'Hot Property'." The Prime Minister responded by clearing his throat and saying, "Excellent. Who is next?"

"The next target is the British Prime Minister's private house in a village called Warningham, an hour's drive south of London. It is comparatively isolated and should be a soft target. The attack should be carried out on Thursday."

The attack referred to by Mr Belnikov would occur on the 5th of November. It is on this night that the British public celebrates the disruption of a plot to blow up the Houses of Parliament by a famous Catholic dissident known as Guy Fawkes in 1605. After the failure of what became known as 'the Gunpowder Plot' it was declared in Parliament that Britons would celebrate the foiling of the conspiracy every year, in perpetuity, by giving thanks to Almighty God. This thanksgiving has taken the form of bonfire parties accompanied by a display of fireworks to remind the citizens of the United Kingdom what would have happened if the plot had not been discovered in time.

Every year there are injuries and the more health and safety-minded mount new crusades against the displays, and every year the displays get bigger.

It was a cold, clear night. The villagers assembled in a field lent for the occasion by a local farmer who had a lot of old brashings to burn from a piece of forested land on his estate. The field was close to the private residence of the Prime Minister. His cottage was modest in size, a cosy little country retreat with a typical West Sussex stone roof, with heavy stones at the eaves leading up to smaller, lighter ones at the apex. The house had once been a blacksmith's forge. It contained four bedrooms and had recently been restored from the ramshackle state into which it had fallen, under the ownership of two aged twin sisters, Helen and Ethel Brundy. 'The Twins', as they were known locally, had been very popular in the area for their good works in looking after the families of some of the disadvantaged, around Warningham. They had remained spinsters all their lives and devoted their motherly qualities to relieving suffering among their neighbours. Everyone knew the Brundy Twins and loved and revered them. They even did the laundry for a family with eleven children who lived in an old railway carriage. Originally it had provided accommodation for a family of London Eastenders who had lost their home to German bombs during the war.

The carriage had remained on an old siding of the North Downs Light Railway that linked the villages of the green belt, south of London, with the railway junction at Horsham. The line had been decommissioned during the restructuring of the railway system that had killed off most of the small branch lines in the United Kingdom under the so-called 'Beeching cuts'. However the carriage had remained in place, marooned by the removal of the tracks.

The children's father had been medically discharged from the Royal Air Force and put into a mental institution after a nervous breakdown had destroyed his rational brain. The mother, in desperation, fell into prostitution as her only means of supporting the family. The eldest daughter at sixteen had a daughter of her own and was left to run the home by herself. It proved an impossible task, until the Twins appeared on the scene. They restored life, cleanliness and hope to the railway carriage.

They were what was called 'Low Church' in their religious beliefs and would sit, disapprovingly, right at the back of the Anglican Parish Church at Matins on Sundays. The vicar was what was known as 'Anglo Catholic', or 'High Church'. If the vicar's sermon was too Catholic for their tastes, they would get up noisily and leave. The next Sunday they would be found among the small congregation at the Methodist chapel. They were accepted and loved by both congregations.

The Twins had a brother who was the great bane of their lives. He had fathered an illegitimate son and spent more than one third of his life behind bars for killing the mother's husband. The son, whose name was Kevin, had nurtured a grudge against life ever since his father had been put away. He had withdrawn into himself and become a recluse. If the world didn't want to talk to Kevin Brundy, then he would not talk to the world. He became a layabout on the streets of London, surviving on shoplifting, pickpocketing and other petty crime. He was a natural recruit for the professional rabble-rousers or rent-a-mob.

When the Twins moved out of 'The Smithy', into sheltered accommodation and the Prime Minister had taken over, Kevin had a brilliant idea to wreak revenge on the establishment and Guy Fawkes Night provided the ideal occasion. All that was needed was appropriate ammunition. Fireworks were not cheap.

Eventually news of Kevin's plan filtered through, via the rabble-rousers, to Sergei Novgorod and he came up with an answer. Funds were allocated and Novgorod contacted Kevin. A meeting was arranged at a Russian safe house in Abbey Road in north-west London. An unusual feature of the house was a very large cellar which had been converted into a twenty-five metre rifle range. When Kevin entered, the first thing that caught his attention was the complete lack of weapons. The only object he could see on the firing line was a large thick-walled cardboard tube about four feet long. It was supported on a wooden tripod and pointed down range from the firing line. The tripod had a short builder's spirit level attached to its table and there was a school kid's plastic protractor mounted along the upper surface of the tube. A thin metal plate was glued to the spirit level, which projected until it nearly touched the protractor. It was plain to see that this simple mechanism was designed to give information about the angle of the tube, relative to the level. It was a ranging tool, a very simple one but effective. Kevin was fascinated. The tripod itself was a model of simplicity. Made out of cheap pinewood, the elevation of the tube was achieved by the movement, backwards and forwards, of a wooden wedge. The only visible target was a large white sheet with a patch, about a metre square, cut out of the middle of it. The lower side of the hole was about four feet off the ground.

"What's that?" Brundy, hands in pockets, nodded at the contraption.

"This is mortar," replied the range officer in heavily accented English. "Big firework." He grinned. "You like try?"

He indicated that Kevin should take a look at what had now transformed itself from a cardboard tube into a deadly weapon. Kevin squatted beside the little cannon and inspected the ranging device. It was brilliantly simple and robust. The range officer handed Kevin a ball about the size of a cricket ball, bound tightly with masking tape. There was a small box taped to the ball, making it look something like a hot air balloon. It had a thin piece of copper wire leading from it. The wire was about eight feet long.

"You put ball in pipe, this way." He indicated that the little box should lead the way. Kevin dropped the ball into the tube.

"You check eighteen degrees elevation," said the RO, pointing at the protractor.

Kevin inched the wedge back until the thin metal plate was lined up precisely with the eighteen degree mark.

"Now you stand back." Kevin sneered at the range officer as if to say 'I'm not scared of a little fire cracker!'

The RO shrugged and told him, with hand signals to carry on, if he thought he was ready. Then he swung away and covered his ears. Kevin pressed the button at the end of the piece of copper wire and the next thing he was aware of was being assisted to his feet by a laughing RO. He was completely deaf and very confused. The little firecracker had proved to be a lot bigger than he had bargained for!

The range officer then presented Kevin with three mortars, one to do the job and two back-ups with the appropriate charges. He dismantled the tripod and ranging instrument and put them in a box. The three mortars he bound together with duct tape, handed them to Kevin and sent the boy on his way.

It was an ideal night, clear and frosty with no moon and no wind. Kevin Brundy had placed the equipment in a secluded spot in a spinney close to the pyrotechnic line, on the opposite side of the field from the great bonfire and the crowd. Just as the fire was about to be lit, he crept over from his hide and positioned his mortar next to the line of its brothers which had been put in place earlier in the day, by a contractor hired by the Parish Council. They were secured to a metal frame, pointing vertically upwards towards the cold twinkling canopy of stars overhead.

The fire was now growing and its light made Kevin's work easier. He hid from its glow behind the ranks of fireworks, as he carefully aimed the cardboard tube and meticulously checked that its elevation corresponded with the figure calculated by the Russian range officer. He then felt for the copper wire which would carry the message to fire to the last mortar in the line, and attached the thin wire from his own weapon to it. Now everything was in place and Brundy crept away from the scene, back into the spinney at the edge of the field.

At precisely eight o'clock, the contractors activated their computer to set off the display. Soft fire fountains rose into the air, to rapturous applause from the crowd. They were followed by some small flash-bangs that hurled airborne Catherine Wheels whistling into the air. They made modest popping sounds at the apex of their trajectory, which did not even disturb the resident dogs. It was the mortars which drove the dogs, shivering, to find a bed under which they could hide, until the heavens became normal again. One of the mortars fired a beautiful round canister, containing three sequenced, exploding colours, straight through the sitting-room window of the Prime Minister's country retreat.

Nobody observed the trajectory of Kevin's pyrotechnic. It left a smoke trail in the dark but no sparks. The 'ooohs!' and 'aaahs!' elicited by the multi-coloured starbursts overhead kept the crowd in rapt concentration. ONE! TWO! THREE! Colours of the starbursts blossomed in the sky and as the sparkles fell, the Old Smithy was seen to erupt in flames. The first bloom of fire was a brilliant red. It was then followed by blinding white and a shining blue; the colours of the Union Flag of the United Kingdom. Coincidentally, they were also the colours of the flag of the Federation of Russian States.

The eruption was greeted initially with shock. The fire caught so quickly that the fire service volunteers who were attending the bonfire night were taken by surprise. One of them grabbed a fire extinguisher from a rack positioned close to the pyrotechnic line to combat unforeseen accidental discharges. He shouted to a colleague.

"Tom! Come and give us a hand!"

"I'll be right behind you, Eddie!" his friend replied, running over to the extinguisher rack.

Another salvo of mortars thumped into the air as he released an extinguisher and lifted it clear of its neighbours. The contractors had not realised the seriousness of the situation, until the vicar rushed over to tell them to stop the display. Eddie raced off towards the burning house, his aim to rescue anybody who might be inside, rather than to save the building. Saving The Smithy looked increasingly like a lost cause the closer he got. The crackle and roar of burning wattle and daub and old dry timber nearly drowned out the high-pitched scream. Eddie rushed towards where he had heard the panic-stricken voice. Then he saw where it originated. There was a small, frosted glass window on the ground floor towards the left-hand end of the building and a fist was hammering against it from the inside.

"Stand clear of the window!" he shouted. "Stand clear!"

The fist disappeared. The fireman took the extinguisher and rammed it through the glass. He then ran it around the frame to remove any jagged remnants of glass from the frame. A cloud of smoke belched out of the hole where the glass had been. Eddie shouted for the owner of the fist to come out. There was no response. The rescuer reached up, grasped the lower frame of the window and hauled himself up. Glass splinters slashed him as he forced himself through the window. A flicker of flame was licking the toilet door. There was not much time left. The girl was lying on the floor under the window by the lavatory. The smoke was billowing in round the door, which looked as though it was now well alight. Eddie reached down and took hold of an arm and a leg. He raised the prostrate form up over his shoulders in a fireman's lift and stood up. The smoke was insinuating itself into his lungs. He tried desperately not to take a breath but he had to shout for his mate.

"Tom, are you there? I've got one for you! She's unconscious. I'll put her through the window."

142

He offered the girl's legs to the window. He was coughing continuously now. He felt the girl being lifted away from him. He stood on the toilet seat and hauled himself up out through the window frame. It was when he was halfway out that the roof caved in. Tom grabbed his arms and dragged with all his might. He felt the strength leaking away from Eddie's grip.

"Come on man! Come on!" he shouted through gritted teeth.

Suddenly it was as though the person hanging on to Eddie's legs had decided to let go and he launched outwards, bowling Tom over. His legs were on fire. One foot seemed to have disappeared. Another volunteer raced up with one of the fire extinguishers.

"Cover your faces," he shouted, "and his too!" He then released the contents of the cylinder over the three of them.

Tom hugged Eddie's face to his chest as he felt the cold liquid extinguish the fire, which had now spread to his own clothes. He could hear sirens. The emergency services had arrived and soon paramedics were carrying out first aid on the three victims of Kevin Brundy's little prank.

The next morning, the newspapers were alive with dramatic eyewitness accounts and on-the-spot photographs of the Prime Minister's house being consumed by the raging inferno. There was even one picture of the blue part of the explosion that had started the blaze. The heroic rescue of the girl was described in lurid detail, including the fact that the hero of the rescue, Fire Officer Eddie Jarvis, had lost a foot and received horrific burns to his lower legs as a result of his brave action. The girl, who was expected to remain hospitalised for a day or two, turned out to be the Prime Minister's niece. Tom was of a retiring nature and managed to avoid the media until Eddie was interviewed, some weeks later. There were rumours that he had been put forward for the award of the Queen's Gallantry Medal.

The first people to be blamed for the incident were, understandably, the firework contractors. Police investigated the set-up of the display and it was only during that investigation that Kevin Brundy's ingenious device was discovered.

When reports of this leaked out, the more conservative newspapers started to question the state of the nation's security. It seemed that even the Prime Minister was no longer safe from the depredations of the lawless underworld. Was the house burning incident a symptom of something far deeper? Only one Prime Minister in British history, Spencer Perceval, had ever been assassinated, although Margaret Thatcher had come pretty close. Was it now time to rein in the lawless community, to restore a sense of discipline, a sense of responsibility to the younger generation? Life had been too easy for too long. Liberalism had leached the marrow out of the British backbone.

The Prime Minister, when he read the papers over breakfast, saw a golden opportunity to go forward with his plans for National Service and the introduction of the ID card system. He called his private secretary.

"Linda?"

"Yes, Prime Minister."

"Can you put me in touch with the Head of the Department of Information Science, at Loughborough University? I need to speak to him."

"Certainly, Prime Minister"

It took five minutes for his Private Secretary to come back to him.

"I'm sorry, Prime Minister, Professor Blok is in Russia on a business trip. Would you speak to Professor Tremlet? She is his locum while he is away."

"That sounds good to me Linda. If she has a moment, put her on."

There was a pause and a clicking sound as the connection was made, then a small, high-pitched voice came through the receiver.

"Good afternoon Prime Minister. Patricia Tremlet speaking."

"Good afternoon Professor." The Professor had heard about the Prime Minster and his short fuse.

"What can I do for you?"

"I was wondering if I could meet up with one of your students. He wrote a fascinating thesis on the subject of IDCs and the application of modern technology to the science of identification and I happened to come across it the other day."

"Oh yes, Prime Minister. I think you must be referring to a young German boy called Georg Lutov. His family owns a factory in Braunschweig and he is doing his degree here specifically to put a revolutionary concept of IDCs on the market. We are taking particular interest in his work, because of its application to the world economy. There are some fascinating options coming out of Lutov's research."

"Very interesting, Professor, would there be any chance of inviting this young man to Number 10. I would really like to hear his views on certain aspects of the identification process. We are presently evaluating various alternatives in this field."

"Well, Prime Minister, I will have a word with him. I imagine that he would be only too pleased to be able to give you a presentation. It is not very often that young students get to meet Prime Ministers."

"Thank you very much, Professor. Let me know what he thinks and I will make a plan. Goodbye."

"Goodbye, Prime Minister."

Chapter 14

Igor Lutov was contemplating expansion. The business had grown fast and now employed over one hundred people in ten branches throughout the city. 'Arches' stationery had become a household name in Braunschweig and this had not gone unnoticed in the secretive corridors of the Kremlin. What the company needed was investment and President Belnikov seized the opportunity to offer it. The first approach was made through the Braunschweig Chamber of Commerce.

Horst Meyer, an old banking friend, who had assisted Lutov with his finances over the years and had given him free advice on certain tax matters, discussed the planned expansion with him. In these days of credit squeeze and belt tightening, it was difficult to raise funds at less than extortionate rates of interest. Old Meyer asked around and the sensors of the SVR picked up his inquiries. It did not take long for funds to become available. Ost Deutsche Bank came up with the finance. They had made their fortune by exchanging their Ostmarks for Deutschmarks, one for one, upon the collapse of the Berlin Wall. Suddenly, due to Helmut Kohl's generosity, the bank's assets went from being a joke to being massive, almost overnight. The financial situation in the old East Germany did not change so fast, however. In fact there was an exodus of people and money to the West. Investment opportunities in the old East Germany were sparse so, when the Russian Government suggested a soft loan to Arches Stationery to facilitate their expansion, Ost Deutsche Bank jumped at the chance to use Russian finance in order to make Deutschmarks in interest for the bank.

The offer to finance the Arches Expansion Programme was made through Horst Meyer. Igor Lutov saw his trusted friend's advice as a blessing, something for which he should be grateful, not an offer to be treated with suspicion. The terms were very favourable and he forecast that, even at present production rates, the loan would be paid back within two years. What he could not have foreseen was that the invisible Russian backers would take control of his company, his family and his life in the same time frame.

Igor's son Georg was in his fourth year at Loughborough University. His thesis had been published and widely praised. It was almost as though a new religion had burst upon the free world.

Tarnbeck Market was a small market town in the old West Riding of Yorkshire in northern England. Previously it had been a centre of the wool trade and had become wealthy from the woolly denizens of the wild hills and dales that surrounded it. The town had a solid well-established feel to it. The grey millstone grit walls gave the buildings a timeless quality, as though they had grown out of the ground upon which they were built. During the wealthy years, the inhabitants had benefitted from the presence of the big five banks, each of which maintained a branch in the town. They were competing with each other to lend money to the wool-rich local population.

As the wool trade contracted in the face of competition from man-made fibres, the wealth of the town withered away until Tarnbeck Market itself, which had brought shouting traders to the square from all over the surrounding countryside for centuries, ceased to function.

The branch line, linking Tarnbeck with Settle was withdrawn and the town became a dormitory for retired doctors, lawyers and stockbrokers. As a result, the Land Rover and BMW agents in neighbouring Settle thrived.

Interest rates at the banks were brought down by competition as they vied with each other for the attention of the dwindling clientele. Finally the smallest of the Big Five decided to cut its losses. It did not take long for the rest to see the sense in closing their offices and realising the capital value of the real estate they were occupying.

The sudden dearth of banking services led the inhabitants of Tarnbeck to complain to their local Member of Parliament. He, in turn brought the subject to the attention of the Chancellor of the Exchequer who held the Government's purse strings.

The Prime Minister had read Georg Lutov's thesis. It provided solutions to many of the obstacles to the introduction of enforced identification. Harry Crighton called the young graduate for a meeting at Number 11 Downing Street, the residence of the Chancellor of the Exchequer. He wanted to pick Lutov's brains. For his part, Georg Lutov urgently wanted an opportunity to put his theories into practice. In effect, he needed to carry out a working experiment to see at first hand, the practical application of the new system.

It was at that point that the problems of Tarnbeck were brought to the Chancellor's attention and he had a brilliant idea. Why not offer the citizens of Tarnbeck an opportunity to be the first in Britain to garner the benefits of the revolutionary new technology for free? They would be the first people in Britain truly to live on Credits. They would be the advance guard in a campaign to root out the one thing which had been the cause of most of the world's troubles, namely money. 'The love of money is the root of all evil'. Everybody knew that. Remove money from the equation of life and you remove much of the evil in the world. The Credits system would eliminate the need for banks. Unlike in the old capitalist world, prices would remain stable once a value had been established. A governing board would run the Credit Authority of Britain and Northern Ireland, otherwise known as the CABNI. Not only would the Chancellor eliminate money with the new authority, he would also eliminate the 'Great' from Great Britain in its name. This was a passionate desire of the Chancellor whose father had been a renowned anti-imperialist. The next thing to go, if he had his way, would be the monarchy.

Lutov was very excited by this new development. He felt he was on the brink of something that would change the way human beings behaved. A new era of peace would infuse the world and the name of Georg Lutov would go down in history as the inventor of the new world order. Now a member of the Aryan race which had been responsible for so much violence in European history, would be responsible for bringing peace and stability to a world exhausted by turmoil. He was immensely proud.

Later, upon reflection, when he realised the significance of his invention to the course of human history, he felt nervous. If he had known the horrors which awaited the capitalist world in the coming months and years, he would, very possibly, have decided that his life was not worth living at all. For the time being, however, he was not conscious of the looming threat over the horizon.

His presentation to the Prime Minister was brimming with enthusiastic optimism. Part of his degree course had been the design and construction of a working set of the new generation IDCs. They were patented and manufactured by Arches Stationery. The new contract would bring in handsome profits for the company and Igor Lutov contemplated carrying on the business expansion without taking out the Ost Deutsche Bank loan. Horst Meyer pointed out to his old friend that, without the loan, he would not be able to build the facility for producing the IDCs. If he invested the profits from the cards, he would make more than was demanded in interest on the loan. So it would be silly not to take the loan. Igor Lutov followed old Horst's advice, a decision he would come to regret.

Along with the cards, Georg Lutov had designed a machine that could read the new IDCs and perform the functions offered by them as part of his thesis. The prototype was constructed by a German manufacturer who had built the ticketing machines for the Deutsche Bundesbahn, the German national railway system. They had a reputation for efficiency and user-friendliness.

The machine was capable of identifying the holder of the card, based on some four hundred relevant parameters, including the validity of the Implanted Interface Chip, the holder's DNA and blood group. It would also include the driving license number, criminal record, allergies, next of kin and even details of the holder's income group and financial status. The list went on and on. Never in the history of humankind had so much information been available about each individual. As promised, the machines also performed several of the functions currently carried out by government offices. Social security, council tax, income tax would now be known as 'Credit Tax' and traffic fines with a tranche of other administrative costs were all to be deducted automatically. The construction of the machines was sponsored by the British Ministry of

Science and Technology as their contribution to the advancement of the identification programme.

In Tarnbeck Market, the town Council held a meeting chaired by the Mayor. All members on the electoral roll were invited to attend. The proposal to try out the new Credit system in Tarnbeck was presented as a considerable privilege for the people of the town. There was no mention of enforced identification, of course. Enforcement would be insinuated at a later date, after the cards had become an essential part of being British. Enforcement would be seen as non-essential, since everybody appreciated the benefits of the new system and were blind to its potential for disaster.

The boundaries of the experiment were cleverly drawn up to exclude wealthy neighbouring villages, so their residents felt as though they were being discriminated against. The residents of Tarnbeck, on the other hand, felt that they were being offered something which raised their social standing, eased the pressures of government administration and reduced their costs. In other words something very desirable, indeed.

The experiment was initiated just before Christmas. The local shops, including the Tarnbeck branch of Spenders Supermarket were all equipped with the appropriate machinery. Bar code readers replaced check-out counters. The purchasers simply offered the bar codes of the items they were buying to the reader and the red light would turn to amber. The buyer would then offer the card to the implanted verification chip to activate it and then swipe it through the slot at the side of the machine. The light would turn to green, indicating that the transaction was complete and the anti-theft device on the product had been deactivated. The post office and the larger shops were equipped with 'Accounts' machines, where IDCs could be topped up with outstanding salary credits.

Money ceased to play a part in daily life. Currency became something which interested collectors, in the same way as postage stamps or coins.

Residents of the neighbouring villages were excluded from the experiment, with a promise from the Prime Minister that they would part of the scheme as soon as its practicality had been verified. To some extent this promise mollified them but they were still tied to the old monetary system and could not use the facilities of Tarnbeck, which were now exclusively linked to the ID card. This involved them in further expense, since they had to drive greater distances in order to do their shopping with the old money.

Tarnbeck was transformed. The Tarnbeck Experiment was closely watched by the whole nation. Could this indeed be a remedy for the financial chaos into which the world had plunged? Was this the beacon by which the world would be able to find its way out of the chasm?

Georg Lutov became the darling of the media. He was interviewed as the young star who would rescue the West from years of living on tick. The stern features and powerful build which had characterised his student years, had softened. It became a media competition to see who would be first to snap a smiling Gluto. The society magazines, like 'Cheers!' and 'Hi Society', urgently followed the Gluto everywhere. His social life was dogged at every turn by hoards of paparazzi. Finally they lined him up with Olga, a Russian girl who was also studying at Loughborough University. The relationship was simply based on Georg's command of Russian. Finding that they could communicate in a language which was rarely understood by their fellow students, drew them together. The desperate efforts of the socialite press to turn the relationship into a romance failed dismally, which infuriated them, so they reverted to sexual innuendo to try and force their victims into indiscretion. This also failed when the young Georg started dating Miriam Itaili, a petite little student from Tanzania, who was studying for a degree in Physical Education with a view to taking up physiotherapy. Funnily enough, in spite of the disingenuous attentions of the press, Olga remained a close friend to both of them.

The Tarnbeck Experiment continued for one complete year and was seen as a resounding success by its residents and a large proportion of the country. Larger towns now demanded to join the scheme. In Scotland and Northern Ireland there was some resistance from individuals but, generally speaking, the IDC was seen as the new way to go. Only London withstood the pressure. The financial sector was still very powerful indeed, in spite of the thrashing it had taken in recent weeks. Abandoning Sterling, abandoning the Euro, abandoning the Dollar and the Yen was anathema to the entrenched capitalists who worked in 'The Square Mile'. It would take generations for the age-old traditions of borrowing and lending to be extinguished. It was far more difficult to satiate man's innate greed with the new system in place. There would always be a need for the Stock Exchange, where fortunes could be made and lost overnight simply by buying and selling commodities. Gambling was an essential element of the human make up. Being born was a gamble, so why try and stop it?

Meanwhile the banks continued their slide into insolvency. The reason why the process was taking so long was because of the traditional confidentiality maintained between a banker and his client. This relationship was, in fact, a myth. For some years now, banks had been forced by law to release details of their clients' accounts to government investigators, upon demand. Confidentiality was a thing of the past but there was still an aura of silence which surrounded senior bankers. Employing this misconception to the full, they managed to hide their own debts behind a wall of confidentiality. The size of the sums owed to the banks was kept away from the prying eyes of government, so the financial disaster was, in actual fact, far greater than it first appeared. Like an iceberg, only ten percent of it was visible and the world was unwittingly careering towards a largely unseen but inevitable, fiscal collapse of gargantuan proportions.

Dick Tarrant was more aware of this than many of his colleagues because it was he who had discovered it in the first place. Even he was loath to broadcast the extent of the problem. However, the more he researched, the more concerned he became. Sam Jackson had never seen such devastation in the world of finance. Even the most level-headed and experienced financial gurus seemed to be at a loss.

Once again they were sitting in the Library Bar.

"The one thread that consistently surfaces is the Russian link. So many people connected with the debacle seem to be terminated after failing to recover loans from ex-Soviet bloc organisations." Sam raised a finger to emphasise his point. "Melvyn Strand, Freddie Barnes and Mr Petrov have all died and that Frenchman, Baccarat, too. It's getting to be too much of a coincidence. Then Alex gets mown down in a hit-and-run. This is being orchestrated by someone behind the scenes and we need to find out who it is before they achieve their aim, whatever that may be."

"Did you hear the news this morning?" Dick looked up. "Apparently, the nephew of the two old ladies who owned Harry Crighton's place in Warningham was pulled out of the Thames last night. He had a blunt instrument wound over a fracture of his skull. The police are treating it as a murder inquiry. A search of his room in Battersea revealed the presence of two mortars of the same type and manufacture as the one which caused the PM's house to burn. It looks like the lad had a grudge to settle. He had also been involved in that fire up at Barry Makepeace's place on Primrose Hill. Maybe we should take a closer look at that."

"Yes, it does look more and more as though somebody is trying to destabilise the country." Sam rubbed his chin thoughtfully. "Maybe we could source the two mortars. There can't be that many distributors of big fireworks like those around, surely."

"I imagine Scotland Yard will be following that one up," said Sam. "According to one of the thugs involved in the Primrose Hill affair, they were paid to carry out the attack. He reckoned that a fellow with a foreign accent tipped them and then offered to top them up upon completion.

"A man with a foreign accent? Maybe we should talk to this gentleman."

"How can we find out who he is?"

"Get Jack Wise to talk to his mates at the Yard. The Deputy Commissioner of the Met was in the Paras with him."

"Right then, do you want me to call him?"

"Yeah, give him a call. Maybe he's thirsty." Sam chuckled.

Dick took out his phone, pressed some buttons on the keyboard and held the phone to his ear.

"Hello Jack, It's me, Dick Tarrant. Any chance you could join us briefly at Aunties?" He paused. "We have some updates and a request for you. Ok, we'll see you when you have put the puppies to bed. Thanks Jack." He replaced the phone in his pocket. "He'll be here shortly. He just loves those dogs."

It was twenty minutes later when Jack appeared at the door of the Library Bar accompanied by little Jock, the barman.

"Will it be the KWV for you, Mr Wise?" he asked.

"That would be perfect, Jock. Many thanks." Jack took a seat in the middle, facing the fire. "Now, Gentlemen, who wants to fire the first shots?"

"Well, Jack," Dick leaned forward, "We were wondering if you could use your influence at Scotland Yard to get us an interview with one of the thugs who burned down the Makepeace property the other night. Apparently he said that they were paid to do it."

"I'll contact John Jason. We served together in the Falklands. He is quite a useful contact. He should be able to get us an interview."

"That would be great, Jack. The other thing was that the nephew of the twin sisters, the previous owners of the Prime Minister's country retreat, was found, dead, in the Thames last night. Drowning was not the cause of death. It appears that he may be linked to the arson attack on the PM's house. Pyrotechnics, identical to the one used in the attack, were found in his room by the police. We would like to find out whether his death was linked to that attack."

"I cannot for the life of me work out the motivation for the attacks" Sam scratched the grey cloud and reset his spectacles, "but, from all the evidence, it seems that these are coordinated and carefully targetted. It almost looks as though somebody is having a go at the whole fabric of British society, what with the banks and insurance companies falling over like trees in a hurricane. I'm trying to find a link between all these events. I think we can rule out coincidence completely at this stage. So, having accepted the fact that a campaign of terror is being mounted, it is just a matter of finding out who the attacker is and what is motivating him. His tactics involve the use of surprise. At the moment I don't think he believes we know that he is after us. He is hoping we will only realise when it is too late. What we have got to do is to work out the target, only then can we counter-attack. So, gentlemen, can you think of anything unusual which is going on in this country which might cause the collapse of British society?"

They all sat, deep in thought for some moments and then Jack raised his hand.

"The PM lost four of his ministers in a single cabinet meeting the other day. That would indicate that there is some friction at the top. I could talk to Duncan Hughes. He's on the door of the cabinet room. He might be able to enlighten us."

"Do you have his number, Jack?"

"Indeed I do, Sam. Hang on, I'll give him a call now."

Jack stood up taking his phone out of his pocket and went to the far corner of the Library. Minutes later he returned.

"He said that he'd be round here in ten minutes. He was going to drop in for a cold one anyway."

Jock the barman came through and stoked up the fire.

"Can I get any of you gentlemen a drink?"
"Thanks, Jock." Jack looked inquiringly around the group. "Would you make that a round please?"

When Jock returned with a tray of drinks, he was closely followed by Duncan Hughes.

"Duncan, what can I get you?"

"I'll have a dram with you, Jack."

"On my tab please Jock." He looked up at the barman, who nodded acknowledgement.

"Now, Duncan, the reason why I wanted you to join us is that we believe there is a serious situation developing which could threaten the security of the country. We just can't work out what the villains are trying to do."

Duncan pulled up an armchair and sat down.

"And how can I help?"

"You remember you told me that four cabinet ministers resigned at an extraordinary cabinet meeting, a couple of days back." Duncan nodded. "Can you remember what that was all about?"

"Well, Jack, and this had better stay strictly between the four of us," The other three heads nodded their agreement. "It was about the PM's policy for putting the spine back into Britain. He wants to re-introduce National Service. He also wants to bring in a compulsory Identity Card system, to control the illegal immigrants and the criminal fraternity. Both these policies ran up against the consciences of the more liberal-minded members of the cabinet. Mark Dewhurst, Secretary of State for Education, Paul Strong, Health Secretary and Charles Macullum, Defence Secretary, have all tendered their resignations and even Jimmie Price seemed pretty unhappy with the PM's plan. It seems as though Crighton has lost the plot a bit. Anyway, since the start of the Tarnbeck Experiment, there seems to be a lot of interest in cashless living, with the new IDCs taking the place of the old currency and this has raised the hackles of the city. So they will also be baying for the PM's blood. They've even come up with a new name for him. In the City, they call him 'Crisis Crighton'."

"Well, if Tarnbeck works, then they won't have much to bay about, will they?"

Dick Tarrant was seriously worried that the Experiment would indeed work and its effects on his existing capital were as yet unknown. Who, for example, would decide on the rate when exchanging the old money to the new 'Credit' system? Would it be the CABNI? And if it was, who controlled that authority? Dick suddenly saw a whole new vista of bureaucratic corruption and political hegemony opening up. It was vastly intimidating in its scope and breadth if you had a lot to lose, which Dick had. Most of the population of the United Kingdom were not as concerned as people in the higher income brackets. Many of them had lived on credit for most of their lives. To transfer debt from a bank to an authority was not life threatening. Life would go on and, just possibly, some of the benefits would filter down to the masses. It also seemed possible that money that had previously been squirreled away by the fat cats would come into the pockets of the workers who had earned it.

The people of Tarnbeck were, for the most part, comfortable, reactionary and retired. They were not restive youths, eager to rise up in revolt and man the barricades against an oppressive regime. They were not going to incite their fellow citizens to armed insurrection. The Tarnbeck system suited them down to the ground. They could totter off down to the supermarket with no need to take the handbag, just the card. No need to go to the bank to get money. No need to take credit cards, or cheque books, car keys or house keys. They were all there, hanging round your neck embedded in the card of convenience. The card gave new life, a new identity, to the people. Thank God for the card!

Chapter 15

Norwich Cathedral, which appeared on the logo of one of the biggest insurance companies in the United Kingdom, was among the most beautiful and venerated architectural structures in Europe. Its spire had dominated the landscape of low-lying Norfolk, built to draw men's minds to the Heavens. For hundreds of years it had inspired its congregations with Christian devotion. The leaping stone vaults of its nave and transepts had echoed to the swelling Gregorian chants of its monks and the peerless harmonies of its choristers for hundreds of years, from the Middle Ages right up to the present day. Where some religious edifices intimidated, Norwich Cathedral inspired confidence and hope in the visitor. Comfortable ecclesiastical housing in warm, ancient brick and tile, basked peacefully around it in the reflected personality of the great Cathedral. There was a feeling of continuation and permanence in its ancient stonework and the thrusting spiritual uplift of its towering pinnacles and buttresses. The doors and window frames of the houses in the Close had recently been painted and there was evidence of new tiles replacing broken ones on the old roofs. The low hedges bordering the pathways had been neatly pruned before winter set in. Somebody cared. The visitor was irresistibly struck with awe and wonder and a kind of inner peace on the first encounter. So the world's reaction was similar to 9/11 when the structure fell.

It happened on a peaceful Sunday morning, during the service of Matins. It was a cold, bright winter's day. The sky was clear and blue. The trees and grass covered with a delicate, lacy frosting of infinitely detailed white crystals. The air was frozen in stillness. A cold mist rose from the still unfrozen water of the River Nene. The local doctor walked his small terrier along the towpath on the opposite bank to the cathedral. The water was calm, with the reflection of the Cathedral spire moving gently as the sluggish current swirled the river's surface. A thin skin if ice was starting to form in the still backwaters where willow trees draped frosty tendrils into the icy water. The silence was only broken by the steamy breathing of the dog and the crunch of boot on frosty meadow.

Suddenly an elemental rumble shook frost from the trees. The treasured reflection in the river of soaring pinnacles and graceful tracery dissolved in a thunderous eruption of smoke and dust. For a split second the doctor could not tell where the noise was coming from. It was like an earthquake. Then he was conscious of movement on the other side of the river and his bewildered gaze took in the moment when the great spire descended vertically into the boiling thunder of rubble and dust. A part of old England which had adorned the City of Norwich for a thousand years had, seemingly impossibly, disappeared in less than five seconds, leaving a massive grey-brown stain hanging in the cold air where it had just stood. It took measurable seconds for the reality to sink in and for the good doctor to realise that his services would immediately be required. He started to run. The dog raced in his footsteps, tail firmly clamped down for fear of impending Armageddon.

The congregation was mercifully small. It consisted mainly of people over fifty years of age. All in all, there were some sixty-two dead and twenty-one injured when the casualties were counted. The injuries, mainly from collateral damage, occurred among the surrounding houses in the Cathedral Close. The clatter of falling debris and clouds of dust finally petered out leaving a silence which seemed to be waiting for the world to believe what had just come to pass. After some minutes, the silence was broken

163

by distant sirens. Obviously emergency services knew that some cataclysmic event had taken place but none of the rescue crews could have been prepared for the scene that greeted their horrified eyes as they approached the scene.

Once again the British Government proved to be unprepared as the medieval masonry succumbed to the irresistible power of expertly placed modern explosives.

The press and media worldwide reeled in horror at this heartless act of cold-blooded murder and mindless destruction. The police and security services were baffled until an illegal immigrant, of Belarusian origin fell off his motorbike on the way from Norwich to Bury St Edmunds. He had decided to route through Thetford because of the icy roads. It was between Wymondham and the air base of Mildenhall that he and his bike left the road having skidded on a small patch of black ice, colliding with a Scots Pine. The bike ended up with bent front forks and a severely distorted front wheel rim. The Belarusian, whose helmet was not securely fastened, was rather more extensively damaged, suffering severe concussion, a fractured pelvis and a compound fracture of the right femur. The accident was witnessed by a farmer who was harrowing frost into a field on the opposite side of the road to the pine forest. He immediately alerted the emergency services and they arrived from Thetford, very commendably, in less than eight minutes. The police were quick to establish the boy's illegal status. Hidden in the lining of his jacket, he carried an Identity Card from the French Government illegal immigrants' detention centre at Sangatte in northern France.

It was almost as though the French had placed the camp close to the Channel Tunnel in order to give the immigrants access to the trucks which transited to the

United Kingdom. Security at the camp was minimal since the authorities wanted nothing more than to see the illegals leave French soil as expeditiously as possible. They were not picky about where they went, as long as they ceased to be a problem for the French authorities. Frequently trucks were conveniently left open for hours awaiting customs inspection in the holding area, before loading on the trains. At this time of year the immigrants concealed themselves as best they could, preferably inside the trucks among the cargo and some truck drivers were not averse to a small financial inducement to facilitate the transfer, on the strict understanding that they knew nothing of their illegal cargo.

In Britain the flood of illegal immigrants was not taken seriously until their numbers swelled to swallow up many local employment opportunities. These newcomers were prepared to accept pay and conditions outlawed for decades in the UK. The local 'Scrooges' were keen to satisfy these labourers' simple financial requirements, while turning a blind eye to the outcry among the newly unemployed residents. The influx of cheap labour eventually caused a backlash in local communities and the government had to appear to be doing something to confront the burgeoning number of central and eastern Europeans who saw the United Kingdom as a soft touch. At last, the police were authorised to make unannounced sweeps through known immigrant refuges.

Hundreds were arrested and detained, which provoked an outraged outcry from human rights activists. The BBC and various liberal-minded newspapers initiated a campaign for immigrant rights, condemning the 'draconian' government's immigration policy. Then there was a leak from the Home Office, which confirmed that that nobody actually knew how many illegal immigrants there were in the country. In desperation, the government tried to blame previous administrations for the lapse in security but the opposition was having none of that and quickly placed full responsibility on the ruling party. Government incompetence rose like a tide of sewage, drowning any hope of the party's re-election. The party in opposition had a field day, portraying Her Majesty's Government as players in a farce. Independent television could hardly contain their hilarity. The electorate began by giggling and then became more and more angered by the dismissive approach of the Prime Minister. 'Fightin' Crighton reacted by intensifying the campaign against the illegals, giving the Kremlin a fertile nursery for the propagation of the seeds of revolution.

Many of these Europeans were adherents of the resurgent Catholic Church. Popes, after all, could now come from Poland or even Germany. The Church of England was founded by a king whose divorce was forbidden by the Pope. Henry VIII's response was to establish his own church and steal all the land owned by the monasteries and convents belonging to the Catholic Church and consequently, the Pope. The Pope was not amused and proceeded to excommunicate Henry, labelling him a pariah and a justifiable target for any of the faithful who wanted to rid the world of this loose cannon.

It was a simple task for Mr Novgorod to approach a Russian-speaking Catholic illegal with a plan to redress the wrongs committed by the Church of England against the faithful catechists of Rome. It was thus that the plan to demolish Norwich Cathedral was hatched. The target was chosen simply because of its association with big insurance. A team of young Belarusians was chosen because of their familiarity with the Russian language and legal vulnerability. Being illegal immigrants made them far more susceptible to coercion and the Russians were happy to take advantage of that situation.

Three young Belarusians were selected, one female and two male, and an inducement offered to be supplemented significantly upon completion of the mission. They received intensive training in the use of explosives at the safe house in Abbey Road. The same range officer, who had trained Kevin, took on the new recruits and revealed to them the astounding possibilities offered by a doughy bun made out of a substance called Semtex. When placed carefully and accurately it could bring down the most massive of structures. In the case of Norwich Cathedral it was effected by the simple expedient of removing the main support for the largely un-cemented building blocks. The whole pile would then tumble to destruction, like a house of cards.

In their typically unobtrusive, English way, the vergers at Norwich Cathedral did not like to be nosey. The sanctity of the holy building was deeply respected. Those who needed time for prayer and contemplation could always find a quiet place in which to allow their inner thoughts to rise to the surface. 'The peace of God, which passes all understanding', was here in ample supply. So vast was this holy auditorium that daily services could very often continue without disturbing the normal run-of-the-mill tourism. Visitors were encouraged to explore each nook and cranny. A detailed guidebook revealed all manner of secrets hidden away in dark corners. Norwich, with its ancient castle and cathedral, had many stories to tell and the thrilling thing for the visitor was that the evidence was there for all to see. The dressed stones that formed the building's structure had not moved for hundreds of years. The masonry, the intricately sculpted tributes to past dignitaries, the primeval brass memorials which formed part of the floor upon which the visitor's eyes now rested, was exactly the same as that which King Edward II's eyes had seen seven hundred years before. The stone stairways had been worn by centuries of reverent feet and the sounds, the smells and the atmosphere were exactly the same. The visitor was a part of the Cathedral's history. This was no Hollywood set. This was the real thing.

The three young foreign students assured their welcome by depositing contributions to the 'Upkeep of the Fabric Fund' in the collection box as they entered the cathedral. The Door Verger noticed, with a quiet smile of gratitude, that the offerings had been made in paper money, exhibiting a generosity unusual amongst British students.

There had never been any security issues at Norwich, even during Henry VIII's dissolution of the monasteries. So powerful was the Duke of Norfolk at the time that he remained staunchly Catholic right the way through, as does his family to the present day, down in Arundel. The three Belarusians, each wearing a backpack, were able to carry out their mission completely undisturbed. They laid their charges exactly as instructed. Each charge contained a tiny radio receiver, attached to a small detonator. The only concern for the three was that the charges might be detonated by some stray microwave signal before they could be set. In fact, the plot went precisely according to plan and the charges went off at exactly 11:15 local time, fifteen minutes into the service of Matins.

The cataclysm that befell the assembled congregation, though horrific, was brief. The building, which had provided sanctuary from death for hundreds of years, was merciful when it came to dealing it out. This was what the doctor witnessed from across the river, that cold quiet Sunday morning.

The desperate search for survivors was obstructed by the tortured piles of ancient masonry. As with many medieval buildings, the finely dressed stonework hid tons of rough conglomerates which filled the gaps between the precisely chiselled work of the ancient masons. When the walls collapsed, the interior of the cathedral filled with the rubble released as they burst apart. It was hard to identify what kind of building had once stood on the site, so complete was the devastation.

What worried the security services more than anything else was the fact that, during the Second World War, it had taken the Nazi Luftwaffe several very expensive raids on Coventry to achieve what had happened in Norwich in seconds. The difference was that every citizen of Coventry knew who had destroyed their Cathedral, but no-one in Norwich knew who had performed this particular atrocity. Nobody connected the young Belarusian and his two compatriots with the cathedral. Later, they were found in the boy's room in bed & breakfast accommodation out at Yaxham Broad, having overdosed on an exotic cocktail of ecstasy, crack, heroin and the final killer, amphetamines. Both eventually died of heart failure. The initial verdict on the cause was a love pact suicide. A young girl had been visiting them the evening before and it appeared there had been some kind of heated discussion before she left in tears. The only available description of her was that she was petite and very young with blonde hair which came to a point at the nape of her neck.

Unbeknown to the young Belarusian who hit the Scots Pine on his motorbike, the accident had actually saved his life.

"Mr Speaker, Honourable Friends, Honourable Members of the House," the Prime Minister stood up and moved to the Dispatch Box, for a speech to a crammed House of Commons. "Great Britain..." the use of the word 'Great' was a word that had not recently been associated with Britain in Crighton's speeches. Ears pricked up and there was the squeak of pin-striped suiting on leather on the benches of the great debating chamber, as Members of the House leaned forward in anticipation "Great Britain is facing a challenge not seen since the dark days of World War II."

Even the older members now stirred themselves and searched for their spectacles and hearing aids, to witness what looked like being history in the making.

"We have in our midst a human virus, which appears to be intent on consuming the very entrails of our society." There was a murmur of surprise among the backbenches, a shuffling of shoes and paperwork, as Members prepared themselves to receive this momentous news. "As you will all be aware, at eleven fifteen yesterday morning, one of our most revered and ancient, sanctuaries was destroyed in an act so evil that it is difficult for me to find strong enough words of condemnation. The innocence of the victims and the structure of the buildings involved is without question. Norwich Cathedral has been a symbol of peace and serenity for hundreds of years to all British people, be they from whatever religious or political persuasion. Its destruction is the destruction of something we all hold sacred. It is the destruction of a part of our heritage, a part of being British."

There was a rumble of agreement that grew until cries of "Hear! Hear!" drowned out the Prime Minister. The

Speaker allowed the shouts of support to continue until, once again, she took control.

"Order... Order!" Her voice was amplified by her position in the House and microphones that had ushered Parliamentary debate into the modern era. Beryl Barker had been chosen as the 'Speaker of the House', not simply because of her imposing size and intellect, but also the commanding quality of her voice, as indicated by her name. The hubbub subsided.

"Prime Minister, please continue."

"Thank you, Madam Speaker." Suddenly, there was total silence in the House.

On the Sky News TV channel a 'BREAKING NEWS' flash interrupted their broadcast about world recession. The newsreader looked into the eyes of the viewers, pressing a hand into his right ear. He glanced at his producer, for confirmation and then nodded.

"We interrupt our news bulletin here, to take you, live, to the House of Commons, where the Prime Minister is delivering a speech of national importance."

There was a confused series of abbreviated commercials, then the screen connected with the debating chamber. There was uproar. Members were standing, waving their order cards for attention. There were signs that the debate in the Mother of Parliaments might even degenerate to the physical. Some of the Honourable Members were caught on camera reaching to grab a neighbour's clothing for attention.

Beryl Barker rose to the occasion. Standing up and grasping the microphone, which hung from the beams above her head, she uttered a word not been from the Speaker's chair before.

"SILENCE!" she shouted. The word echoed around the ancient timbers of the roof like thunder.

A stunned pause descended upon the proceedings and all heads turned to the imperious figure of the Speaker. Beryl Barker held the respect of every Member and what she said, went.

"Honourable Members are reminded that all debate in this house is directed through this chair. If I, the Speaker get the impression that any honourable Members are unfamiliar with this fundamental rule, I will have them barred from this house until they learn the way we work here. If they persist in their unparliamentary behaviour, I will have the House cleared until we can re-assemble in the civilised manner for which this chamber was founded. You represent the citizens of Great Britain, Ladies and Gentlemen, not a rabble."

It was as though teacher had wielded a very big stick. Embarrassed parliamentarians looked around in an effort to find their rightful seats.

"And until you earn the title of Honourable Members, I will refer to you as Ladies and Gentlemen, titles which you are also in danger of losing, if you continue in the disgraceful manner which I and the country have just witnessed."

Silence reigned, as each Member absorbed the gravity of their situation, each suddenly aware of the cameras, which had recorded their every move. The proposal which had raised the temperature of the debate to near boiling point, had come from the Prime Minister. It was 'Compulsory Identification'.

Chapter 16

Jack Wise arranged a meeting at New Scotland Yard, the headquarters of the Metropolitan Police Service on Victoria Street, close to Parliament. His appointment was with an old friend with whom he had served in 2 Para during the Falklands campaign. Coming home, after the islands had been recaptured John Jason had left the army and joined the Met. He completed his training at Hendon and went on the beat in East London. His rise through the ranks had been deservedly meteoric and he had attained his goal before reaching the age of fifty. He now held the rank of Deputy Commissioner and that was exactly where he wanted to be for the rest of his career. He had no ambition to take the Commissioner's job as he felt that his main contribution could best be made from below. He was a man's man and was respected throughout the force as the person to see if there was a problem. His respect was inspired by a Sergeant Major who, during the privations, danger and exhaustion experienced in the Falklands campaign, had enabled him to find reserves of energy and fortitude he had never dared expect. The Sergeant Major's name was Jack Wise.

"Come in, Jack. Take a pew." The severity of the Deputy Commissioner's black uniform with all its regalia, including medals earned on active service, was removed by the fact that John Jason had loosened his tie and undone the top button of his shirt when Jack walked in.

"Thanks Johnnie." Jack pulled up a chair at the D/Comm's desk.

"Now, Jack, what did you want to see me about?"

"First of all, thank you for seeing me at such short notice." Jack smiled and the D/Comm nodded his acknowledgement.

"You know me, Jack. If you give me a call, it's going to be interesting. I would even postpone a meeting with the First Anglers of the River Thames Society to hear what you have to say, so shoot."

Jack hid his smile at remembering the acronym. There was indeed something 'interesting' which he wanted to share with his friend.

"Listen, Johnnie, I and some friends of mine believe that we have stumbled on something which could threaten the social and political structure of the UK. It is so big that we will need..." He buried his head in his hands and the D/Comm suddenly paid full attention. He had never seen Sergeant Major Jack Wise flummoxed before.

"Go on Jack. I'm all ears."

"Okay, Johnnie, here we go," and Jack recited the chronology of the previous days' events, including the plunge in the world economy and the, possibly associated, deaths in the banking industry. He mentioned Alex's hit-and-run, as part of that. Then he moved on to the recent destruction of property.

"It's as though there is somebody out there, maybe a single entity behind all these things, who appears to be hell-bent on destroying the way we carry out our daily lives. We, my friends and I, have come to the conclusion that there is somebody trying to kill the Britain we know and to put something else in its place. The whole world seems to be falling around our ears and there's nothing we can do about it. Are we being paranoid, or what?"

Jason winced and swept a hand through his hair.

"Wow!" he said. "If I had heard this from anybody else, I would have thrown them out of the door, but coming from you... " He looked Jack in the eye. "Who is 'we'?"

"You know Dick Tarrant, the heli pilot in Helmand with Alex. You remember? Alex was Air Ops there."

"Oh yes. We didn't get our medals, did we?"

"No. I don't think we will, either! I suspect that a certain Squadron Leader in Oman got them, didn't he?"

They both laughed at the memory of a man who was now of very senior rank. He had a chest full of medals earned by his men in the field who he'd been unable to visit 'due to pressing administrative obligations'. They both grinned at the inside information which they shared. "So what do you want me to do, Jack?"

"Firstly, Johnnie," Jack, caught the eyes of his trusted friend and confidante and held them "I want you to meet my partners in crime." The D/Comm nodded. "And then we want to interview that Belarusian fellow who drove his motorcycle into a tree between Wymondham and Thetford, a couple of days back."

"What's his significance then?"

"Well, he's an illegal immigrant for a start and he was travelling between Norwich and Thetford on a motorbike on a day when travel had been officially discouraged

176

because of the icy conditions on the roads. This would indicate that there was some urgent reason why he needed to travel. It just so happened that two of his countrymen, who were staying in the same B&B as him, died of drug overdoses on the same day. Forensics discovered traces of an explosive material, similar to Semtex, under their fingernails. Then, of course, Norwich Cathedral came tumbling down just before that. Call me an old conspiracy theorist, Johnnie but, just at the moment, I think we need to follow up every hunch we get."

"I see what you mean, Jack. Let me see if I can get you access to the secure hospital wing at Norwich. You say that the couple who died were living in the same B&B as our friend, is that correct?"

"That's right, yes."

"Then we should advise East Anglian Police about this and get them to double up security on the boy. We don't want anything to happen to him, do we?"

"Not before we've had a chat with him, Johnnie, no."

Jason picked up the phone. "Morning, Betty." He was speaking to a Woman Police Constable who acted as his personal assistant. "Could you put me through to Dennis Turler, Chief Constable of the East Anglia Police? I'll need a secure line for this one, please. Thanks Betty."

Moments later his green phone chimed and he picked it up. "Morning, Dennis, John Jason here." Greetings were exchanged. "Listen, I gather that you have a young Belarusian illegal in the secure wing at Norwich Hospital. Is that right?"

"That's quite correct, Johnnie. He had a nasty accident. Hit a tree on his motorbike. Actually, it wasn't his bike, he had 'borrowed' it. The owner was not best pleased when he got the news!"

"Oh, I see. So the bike was stolen?"

"So it appears."

"OK, Dennis. What I'm calling about is that we have received info that this lad may be mixed up in something in which we are extremely interested. Would there be any chance of us having a chat with the him?"

"Do you want this official, Johnnie?"

"At this stage, I would like to keep it under wraps. We are not quite sure who is playing for which team at the moment and it would be a pity to show our hand before we do. In fact, Dennis, we are very concerned about the safety of this young man, particularly since his two room-mates have both become deceased since his accident. Are you stepping up security at all?"

"We have doubled the watch and one officer will stay in the private ward with the detainee at all times. There will also be an officer on the door. Both officers are armed. All food will be tested prior to delivery and his medicines checked by the Crime Lab before administration. I don't think there's much else we can do really. Do you?"

"We could always move him."

"Where to? "

"A clinic, with a secure wing?" Jason raised his eyebrows.

"You're talking about The Wellesley, aren't you, Johnnie."

"Well, that's a possibility, yes."

"When would you want to move him?"

"How about tonight?"

"Air, or ground?"

"Ground would probably be best, don't you think? Less of a fuss, more discreet, as long as they don't ram him into a tree, of course, with all this ice around."

"Well there are always unforeseen risks, Johnnie but these boys know their job... unless, of course, you want my mother-in-law to drive?"

Jason laughed. "I'm sure she would do an excellent job, Dennis, but let's stick with the devils we know, shall we?"

"How about enquiries? What do we tell interested parties who might be searching for their long lost boyfriend?"

"Oh, I think we just tell them that he was deported as an illegal immigrant. I can get paperwork sorted out for that. We'll need to convince the Home Office of course but, with the PM stoking the fires at the moment, I don't think we'll have too much problem with that. Oh no! Wait a moment! Maybe we should leave him in the hospital. You never know, we might catch one of the opposing team doing a recce."
"Well we could always pretend that he's still there. We just have to prime Reception about the rules of the game and they can welcome the fly into the web."

"Fine, Johnnie. I'll get the ball rolling. Will you do The Wellesley end of things?"

"Will do, Dennis. Thanks for your help. I don't suppose we could get photos of the two deceased Belarusians sharing digs with our friend, could we?"

"Not a problem, I'll e-mail them right away."

"Thanks Johnnie. Much appreciated." Jason put the phone down and pressed the intercom. "Betty, could you get me the Commissioner?" He then turned back to Jack Wise. "So, Jack, when am I going to meet the team?"

Just then the green phone rang and Jason apologised with a raised hand and put the phone to his ear.

"Good morning Commissioner. Yes. I just wanted to update you on progress with the Norwich incident." He then ran through all the plans made in the previous minutes, including the transfer of the Belarusian. "Does this meet with your approval, Commissioner?" After a short silence, Jason smiled and nodded his head. "So we can go ahead along those lines then, Sir? Excellent. Thank you very much." He returned to Jack Wise. "Sorry Jack, go ahead, when do we meet up."

Jack grinned. "I don't believe I heard that!" He said. "You asked permission to do something which you have already done! Incredible!"

"One of the privileges of rank, Jack. The Commissioner doesn't want to get his hands dirty, so he lets us do it. I'm good with the soap! Now, what about the team?"

"We could meet at Aunties this evening, if you were available. Have you got a large black beard and dark glasses?" Now it was Jason's turn to laugh.

"Deputy Commissioners are invisible until the manure hits the fan. Then all you have to do is look for something brown on two feet. Normally it will be a Deputy Commissioner." He laughed. "I will try and remember not to wear this kit, of course."

The transfer went smoothly and now the Belarusian was well placed for his own safety and also for interviews. The very next morning, there was a visitor asking for him at the Norfolk & Norwich Hospital. She was small, blonde and looked very young and rather lost. The receptionist had not been advised about the transfer and assumed that the young Belarusian man was still in the hospital's secure wing. She asked the girl for identification and she produced a Belarusian passport. The receptionist took it, compared the face with the photo and put it in a small safe on her desk. The girl tried to object but the receptionist was adamant. "You can pick it up on your way out." She said. "It's regulations for visitors to the Secure Wing. You will pass through a security check as you go in. Nothing to worry about, it's just like the airports."

The girl appeared uncertain. The mention of a security check seemed to have made her change her mind.

"Off you go." said the receptionist. "It's that door over there. Just follow the signs to D Wing."

The girl turned hesitantly and left the reception area. She walked along white-painted corridors, the floors covered with easily-cleaned seamless vinyl which smelled of disinfectant. She walked until she was out of sight of the reception area and then abruptly changed course, following signs to C Wing. Finally she reached a ward full of convalescents. French windows opened on to a grass lawn which was covered with frost. The girl waited in the passageway leading through to the toilets until she was alone. Then she reached up and took the small hammer from the nearest fire alarm and broke its glass. Immediately the fire bells began their urgent clanging and suddenly all was movement. The nursing staff was well versed in the procedures and immediately started to evacuate the patients from 'C' wing. The Belarusian girl grabbed an old man in a wheelchair and asked one of the passing nurses where to go.

"Straight down there, love." she said. "Follow the signs to 'Reception' and 'Main Exit'. Thanks for your help."

When she reached reception it was crowded with people. She left her patient and shouted at the receptionist for her passport. There was no reaction. The general scuffle of people around the reception desk swamped any form of communication. Suddenly she felt a strong arm grasp her and propel her firmly towards the main door. When she got outside there were more members of the emergency services directing people to holding areas for a head count. There was no smoke in evidence.

"Looks like a false alarm." said a fireman as he unreeled a large fire hose.

"You can never be too sure," said his mate as he secured the hose to a fire hydrant. "Better safe than sorry, eh?"

Ludmilla decided it was time to make herself scarce and faded into the crowd of onlookers on the other side of the police cordon.

One detail of events discussed during the initial post-mortem and in the aftermath of the false alarm, was the fact that it was not a false alarm at all. The alarm glass had been deliberately broken. It was after this discovery that investigators, while looking for possible perpetrators of this incident, checked for high risk patients in D Wing. There were only two and one of those had been transferred in some secrecy, the night before. When the receptionist was questioned she said that the transfer had been made without her knowledge. She had been off duty at the time. There had been only one visitor to 'D' wing all week that she was aware of and that was a young girl. She would be in the Visitors' Register. Her passport ... "

Oh Lord!" the receptionist's hand leapt to cover her mouth. "How could I forget? Her passport must still be in the safe," she said, letting her hand drop back into the handbag in her lap to retrieve the safe keys. It was still in there when she went to get it so she brought it back to the meeting.

"I'd better get that to the police." said Mrs Dawkins, the HR Manager, who was chairing the meeting.

"They'll be needing that. We may have CCTV footage as well. Mr Roberts, can you sort that out and get it to me as quickly as possible?"

"Certainly can." said the Security Officer. "I'll get copies sent down to the police station right away. I'd better take that passport too.
"Oh no. I'll sort that out. Mr Roberts. Passports are on HR's broad shoulders." The Human Resources Manager heaved her shoulders in a theatrical assumption of the burden of responsibility.

Dan didn't like the Doris Dawkins. He didn't like her bottle-black hair. He didn't like her low-cut blouse which revealed too much of her over generous top hamper. His fertile imagination gave Doris's ample bosom a good crop of dark hair to go with the free-range armpits. Her voice was commanding and condescending in equal proportion. She ran way outside her lane on the hierarchy racetrack and tended to bully her way into undeserved positions of authority. Who had asked her to convene this post-mortem, anyway? Would it not have been more appropriate for the Health, Safety and Environment people to handle it? Why did she feel that it was the job of HR to hand the passport to the Police? After all, what did a security issue have to do with Human Resources?

"Sorry Mrs Dawkins." He could immediately feel the temperature rising, "but I'll have to have the passport. I need it for my report."

"And what report would that be, Mr Roberts?"

"Security Report, Mrs Dawkins. There has been a breach in the hospital's security cordon and we have to take a look at how we can best fix it."

"A breach Mr Roberts? How so? Nothing was stolen and nobody was injured. Surely this comes under the aegis of the 'H' part of my department. I would remind you that 'H' stands for 'Human'. The young lady on the CCTV and in the passport is a Human Resource issue, Mr Roberts." She looked down at her notes as though seeking further ammunition against the rebellious Mr Roberts.

"Oh, and as for the CCTV coverage. I'll take care of that too."

"Very well Mrs Dawkins. So be it. I shall adjust my report accordingly."

"Good, Mr Roberts." It was almost as though she had meant to say 'Good Boy, Mr Roberts, I'm so glad that you see it my way.'

"Quite, the contrary, Mrs Dawkins. I would like it recorded in the minutes of this meeting that I specifically do NOT see it your way. My report will record as much."

"And to whom will you be reporting, Mr Roberts?"

"My report will be made to the Hospital Management Committee with copies to the Chief Constable of East Anglia Police."

"And why to the police, Mr Roberts? Surely this is an internal matter."

"Excuse me, Ladies and Gentlemen. Duty calls." One of the younger doctors stood up and made to leave.

Doris Dawkins sat up straight and applied herself with some vehemence to this interruption in her argument. Some of the younger generation just did not seem to know the rules of etiquette any more. "And don't you think that your duty lies in this room, Doctor?" Mrs Dawkins was annoyed that someone should leave while she was making a perfectly justifiable and important point. The doctor continued his departure. "Doctor, don't you think," She raised a finger and pointed accusingly at the offender, "that it is rather impolite to leave a meeting, without the agreement of the chairperson when important matters remain to be discussed?"

"Madam Chairman, I have three patients on the critical list in ICU. If one of them died while I was listening to a discussion about who is to receive copies of some report or other, I would never forgive myself." He turned to a colleague. "Steve, are you coming?"

Another doctor, sitting on the opposite side of the table, rose to his feet, shuffled some papers into a file and made his way to the door, squeezing past the backs of other committee members. Mrs Dawkins addressed her full attention to this second departure, assuming by his apparent silence, that he was embarrassed by his colleague's forthrightness.

"So, Doctor, I assume that you are also abandoning this meeting without so much as a 'by-your-leave' from the chairperson. Just because your colleague appears to need some enlightenment on the rules and responsibilities of committee does not mean that you have to follow his example, you know."

"In reply to your question, madam, I would ask the Lady Chairperson whether my patients require her permission to live or to die. If so, then I would suggest that she curtail this meeting as quickly as she possibly can and accompany us to ICU, before the Almighty pre-empts her."

The other eight members of the committee barely succeeded in containing their mirth. The woman was incensed and stood up and, visibly shaking with fury, she gathered her papers. Her voice quivered with anger as she closed the unfinished meeting. "Very well, Ladies and Gentlemen, if we have no further business to cover, I have far more important things to do than to continue in this ill-disciplined company. I declare the meeting closed." and she stormed out of the room.

By the time she reached the door, there were only two people remaining seated in the conference room. The one turned to the other and grinned from ear to ear.

"I have been longing for someone to do that to Doris!" and the other replied. "What an honour to have been here to see it happen!"

So Ludmilla's features would remain hidden in her passport and on the CCTV footage until Mr Roberts' report landed on the desk of the Chief Constable of the East Anglia Police.

Chapter 17

Dick and Jack arrived at The Wellesley Clinic with an hour to spare. They met at reception and were directed to the fourth floor. Alex was in a single room, with a window looking out on Lord's Cricket Ground. The pitch was covered in a white coating of frost. High cloud had slipped in from the north-east overnight and fog was forecast for the evening. The temperature was not expected to rise above freezing all day, nor the following day or the day after that.

The nursing sister showed Jack and Dick to Alex's room. She knocked on the door and went in. Margie was sitting at the head of the bed holding her husband's right hand.

"A couple of your friends, here to visit you Mr Stewart. Will you see them now?"

"Oh yes please Sister. Margie is already getting bored of my company!" The nurse ushered the two men in and closed the door as she left. Jack went over to Margie and took her hand.

"Well, Margie, he's done it again!" He leaned down and gave her a peck on the cheek. He had always thought that if Alex had not won her, he could very easily have settled for Margie, rather than his little Dachshund and her three puppies.

Alex's right leg was in traction. His left shoulder was strapped up and a cage kept the weight of the bedclothes off his left leg. He wore something which looked like a wire crash helmet on his closely shaven head. There was a dressing over the small hole where the surgeon had performed the craniotomy. When Alex's head hit the ground, the impact had fractured his skull, causing the lining of the brain to bleed internally. The surgeon had to relieve the pressure from the haemorrhage, which threatened to compress the brain and would quickly have led to Alex's death if left untreated.

"Any bloody excuse to stay in bed!" Dick Tarrant enjoyed ribbing his friend, a kind of payback for the whipping he had received all those years before at school. "So, how are we?"

"Getting along just fine thanks Dick. Margie likes the nurses. They are all over forty and the prettiest one resembles the north end of a south-bound London bus."

Jack and Dick both giggled and Margie raised an admonitory finger.

"Now Alex," said Jack, "We didn't just come here to see how you are, although I'm pleased to see we should not have worried. What we were really interested in was whether you think you would recognise the lady who was driving the car which put you in here?"

"She was small and blonde and looked very young; too young to be holding a driving licence." Alex winced as he moved to change his position in the bed. "Shortish hair. I have to say, I only saw her fleetingly as the streetlights fell on her face. I couldn't swear but I would say that she was quite a pretty little thing, when she wasn't trying to kill someone, of course."

"Okay. We are trying to get hold of some CCTV footage and we were wondering whether you could fit a bit of viewing into your busy schedule while you are in here. Maybe you might recognise somebody?"

"Well, I'll have to speak to my physio, of course. She's not a member of staff here and she's under thirty. The nurses hate her. Margie hasn't met her yet and I need to keep it that way. Anyway, I'll see if we can fit you into the programme at some stage. Meanwhile, please knock before entering!"

They all laughed, Jack and Dick with some relief at seeing their friend in such good spirits and Margie, because her husband appeared to be on the mend. It was the first time that Dick Tarrant had met Margie and, although he thoroughly approved, he was as yet unaware of her other qualities, until Jack spoke to her.

"Margie, we may have something to exercise your computer enhancement talents again. Would you be keen to have a go? It would be a great help for us."
"Oh yes," she replied, "I have my laptop with me and I have just downloaded 'Picasa Gallery 10'. Fantastic! What have you got for me?"

"Well we are hoping that there will be some CCTV coverage to sift through and, if Alex finds the girl, we would very much like you to enhance her features to the point where she could be picked out in a crowd."

"Great," said Margie, "this kit I have downloaded will be perfect for that."

It wasn't until nine o'clock the next morning that the report from the Hospital Security Officer's report arrived on the Chief Constable's desk. It was only then that the police became aware of the new evidence. The Chief

Constable called Roberts at the hospital. "What's with the CCTV footage then, Mr Roberts? Don't tell me you wiped it."

"No Chief, The Human Resources Manager has it and she also has the passport of a young lady who came to the hospital to see our Belarusian friend. You know, the lad they moved to London a couple of nights ago?"

"And why does Human Resources feel it necessary to deal with security issues now, Mr Roberts?"

"Why don't you ask her yourself, Chief? She can't fire you."

"Do you have her number with you?"

" 'Matter of fact, I do. Hang on a minute. I have it here on my mobile." A couple of minutes later, he read a number back to the Chief Constable.

"Thank you Mr Roberts. I'll get right on to her." Dan Roberts grinned.

He knew that the Chief Constable did not suffer fools kindly. He had a feeling that Doris would be regretting her high-handed approach and he was right.

"Good morning, madam. I wish to speak to the Human Resources Manager please."

"You are speaking to Mrs Doris Dawkins, Human Resources Manager of Norfolk & Norwich Hospital. Who am I speaking to?"

"Good morning, Chief Constable, Dennis Turler, here. I understand that you are in possession of items that may be relevant to some of our on-going investigations. I specifically refer to a passport, belonging to a young Belarusian lady who visited your D Wing the day before yesterday. We need that down here at Police Head Quarters immediately. There is also some CCTV footage in your possession. We need that as well."

Doris Dawkins detected the handiwork of Dan Roberts and swore that she would sort him out when the chance came, which they always did in HR.

"Good morning, Chief Constable." Doris Dawkins could adopt a deep syrupy voice when she wanted something. "So who's been telling tales to teacher then, Mr Turler? It wouldn't be a Mr Dan Roberts, by any chance, would it?"

"I am simply trying to prevent you from being charged with withholding evidence and information, Mrs Dawkins. Please send the passport and the CCTV tapes down here as quickly as possible. Minutes count."

"I have never been so insulted in all my life!" Doris Dawkins instantly assumed her affronted tone.
"Charged? How can you charge somebody in my position with these unfounded accusations?"

"Very easily, Mrs Dawkins, very easily indeed and if I have to come up to the hospital to get these items, you will most certainly see what I mean. We might be forced to start with 'Obstructing the Police in their inquiries'."

"You shall have the video and the passport, Chief Constable." Mrs Dawkins' voice now adopted the tone of a wounded martyr. "I do not need to be threatened, in order to do my duty. The Independent Police Complaints Committee will, however, be hearing from me, concerning your cavalier attitude. I don't know what's come over the general public these days. No respect for authority!"

The Chief Constable managed to prevent himself from asking what authority Mrs Dawkins thought she had. Instead he just smiled and said, "I look forward to receiving those items, Mrs Dawkins. If I have received nothing within half an hour, I will come and check that everything is going according to plan. The warning remains in place." There was no answer from the other end of the line, only a resigned click.

Dick Tarrant and Jack Wise returned to The Wellesley Clinic reception. Johnnie Jason had just arrived and he was dressed in casual civvies. Jack could not help noticing how anonymous he looked when out of uniform.

"Johnnie, this is Dick Tarrant." They shook hands. "He is the person who first spotted the conspiracy which we are interested in. I would also like you to meet Sam, our computer guru. We'll do that when we've finished here. He is busy in a seminar at the Stock Exchange as we speak, but he will catch up with us at Aunties later. He has a lot of ideas and I think that you will be interested to meet him."

"Okay then, Jack, let's go and meet this young man who likes to attack trees with his motorbike."

They followed a stocky man in a white hospital jacket. Its tailor had not taken into account the build of ex-members of Her Majesty's Royal Marines. Jack instantly recognised the ex-marine and they exchanged glances. When they reached the secure wing, they checked through security.

Even the D/Comm had to submit himself to the check even though the screen operator recognised him. He actually thanked him after he had passed through the system.

The white-coated guide stopped outside the door of a private room. There were two other people in white coats on duty in the corridor. They were obviously taking the Belarusian lad very seriously indeed. Jack wondered idly whether weapons were concealed beneath those coats. He would have put money on the fact that these 'medical staff' carried considerably more than the stethoscopes hanging around their necks. He was fairly certain also that the stethoscopes performed communication functions other than listening to the beating of a human heart or the air passing in and out of the human lungs.

The door was opened and the guide indicated that the visitors should enter. The Belarusian was reclining on a bed with his torso raised on a frame with pillows. A drip fed into his left arm and his head was bandaged and the bedding cage protected his legs. When he saw the three large men enter the room, he shrank away. Such colour as there was, drained from his face and fear spread in a white mask across his features.

"Speak English?" Jack's voice was avuncular, quiet and soothing. "Your name is Vulko Yugov?"

The young man hesitated and then, very slowly, nodded his head.

"You are an illegal immigrant," Jack's voice rose and the Belarusian shrivelled as the volume increased. "What were you doing in Norwich?"

The boy shook his head.

"Are you aware that your two friends have been murdered? Are you?" Jack's face was now inches away from the terrified Belarusian's. He was not quite shouting but Jack's voice was parade ground trained.

"Why murdered? How you know? You speak bad words."

"You, Mr Yugov, will be the next to die if we do not protect you."

The young Belarusian's gaze dropped to the hospital cover on his bed as the significance of Jack's words sank in.

"We will protect you as best we can but, without your help, we will not know who is trying to kill you, so we will not know from whom we should protect you. We need to know who it is as soon as possible, before they find out where you are. If they find this out, it is only a matter of time before they kill you."

The young Belarusian shrank into a shell of silent panic. He realised that, whatever he did in this situation, the risks were potentially lethal. His very status in the country was illegal and the destruction of Norwich Cathedral had caused the deaths of some sixty-two people, an atrocity which would be taken extremely seriously by the British authorities. He would be sent away to prison for a long sentence and then, probably deported. He suddenly understood the Russian strategy. They promised riches and, after delivering a part payment, they delivered a death sentence. This solution saved money and eliminated the leakage of information. It was watertight but only if all the participants could reliably be removed from the stage. For Vulko Yugov the future looked very insecure indeed. If he were to be imprisoned, the chances of the Russians getting to him were almost inevitable. If he were deported, the tentacles of the SVR would find him in Belarus. Wherever he went now, there were very limited prospects of a future for him. John Jason recognised the symptoms. He was high risk for suicide.

As he left the wing, with Jack and Dick, he caught the brawny arm of their white-coated escort.

"You need to keep an eye on this lad. Looks like he has seen light at the end of the tunnel and this time it's a train coming in the opposite direction. He will be studying his options and one of them will be to top himself. We don't want to lose this one. He could be the person who holds the key."

"Got you, sir. We'll take good care of him, don't you worry."
Jason nodded solemnly. "And if he wants to talk to somebody, give me a shout. We are on the edge of something very big here and we still don't know what it is." He handed a visiting card to the ex-Royal Marine.

"Very Good, Mr Jason. I'll let you know if the little guy wants to spill the beans."

"Thanks." said the D/Comm and he and his two colleagues left the clinic.

The D/Comm had transport and offered it to the others.

"You said that you were meeting another player at Aunties, Jack. Do you want to come with me?"

"Thanks Johnnie. Much appreciated." He opened one of the back doors of the black, Five Series BMW. "Jump in, Dick."

They reached Aunties about twenty minutes later and Jack led the way straight to the Library Bar. Sam was sitting in an armchair by the fire and stood up to greet Jason.

"Nice to meet you, Deputy Commissioner." he shook Jason's hand warmly.

"And the same for me, Mr Jackson. I have been a secret admirer of yours for many years and much you have achieved has been of immeasurable assistance to us in the fight against crime."

"Unfortunately it has been invaluable to the criminal fraternity as well, Deputy Commissioner." He shrugged in self-effacement. Jason already warmed to this modest icon of the computer industry.

"I have known you for a long time simply as 'Hacker Jack' or 'Jack the Hack'. Would you be comfortable if I addressed you simply as 'Sam'."

"Most assuredly Deputy Commissioner. Would you, by the same token allow me to call you 'Johnnie' instead of your full title? It would make conversation a lot easier for me!"

Jason laughed and held his hand out to the Trinidadian. "So what do you think is going on, Sam? An awful lot of people seem to be dying of late. Too many to be sheer co-incidence in my view."

"I agree, Johnnie and then there is the terrible destruction of property; the Makepeace residence in London, the Prime Minister's place in Sussex and now the big one, Norwich Cathedral with the tragic deaths involved. What sticks out in my mind is the number of people closely related to these incidents, who have died in unusual circumstances. The one common thread that weaves its way through each one of them is the trail of death which scythes through the perpetrators. It is almost as if the whole thing is being planned, the deaths as well. The Makepeace attack is a case in point. One of the thugs arrested actually stated that he was assured that the house was empty, even though the housekeeper's car was parked out at the side of the house and was destroyed intentionally, during the fire."

"And then we have the financial collapse." Dick Tarrant massaged his forehead. "Here we are, with a whole bunch of financial institutions that have gone bust, with a trail of fatalities in their aftermath. Interesting, or mere co-incidence?"

"Not interesting... Fascinating." said Sam. "I am tempted to see a link. We discussed the possibility of a Russian connection, but what possible reason could there be for all the violence?"

"It makes the government look pretty incompetent." Jack raised a contemplative finger to his lip.
"Could there be a plan to topple them, do you think?"

"What would Russia stand to gain from toppling the government of the UK?" Dick Tarrant introduced the financial aspect. "It's not as though the United Kingdom is the world leader it once was. The British economy and particularly its financial services industry are still players on the world market, but not really big enough to merit toppling. It must be part of something bigger."

"Well the world is suffering from the financial crash, not just the British. Maybe there is a really big plan behind all this. Or am I allowing my conspiracy theories to run away with me?" Sam grinned.

"As you said before, Sam, we are going to look like real dummies if we laugh your conspiracy theories off the stage and they turn out to be right." Jack remembered a previous conversation he and Sam had shared.

"Oh! There you are, Gentlemen." Jock the barman put his head round the door. "I'm so sorry, I got called away. What can I get you?"

"I think it's drams all round, except for a little of that KWV Fleur du Cap for me, Jock, if you have any left."
"Certainly, Mr Wise" said Jock and hurried away.

While the three men mulled over the gloomy future facing the capitalist world, the Prime Minister wrestled with his own thoughts. He had rapidly replaced the four rebel ministers in his cabinet with younger faces who reflected the honour of their appointments with canine loyalty to their leader. It was time to bring the two main issues of the day before the House again, National Military Service and Compulsory Identification. The new Defence Secretary, Roger Pastern, saw the re-introduction of military service as an expansion of his defence empire and was all in favour.

The replacement for Mark Dewhurst, the liberal-minded former Education Secretary, was a bit of a rarity in the ranks of modern political parties. Ted Farquahar had been to Eton College and had studied Social Psychology at Oxford. He was treated as a bit of a pariah, both by his conservative peers, for his socialist political views and by his political colleagues, for his privileged private education. For him this added a certain spice to his quest for power and influence. He was the ideal person to support Harry Crighton in the effort to shock Britain back into shape.

Stan Mumford's replacement at Trade and Industry was a young technocrat who came to the Ministry through the corridors of the Civil Service. Donald Fletch had worked his way up through the Inland Revenue. His father had been a leading light in old party politics. His view that private education should be banned in the UK, along with the House of Lords and the monarchy had proved too radical for Harold Wilson, the then British Prime Minister. His elevation to the peerage effectively silenced the heckling which had seen him physically removed from the Lower House of Parliament on more than one occasion.

Young Don could scarcely contain his excitement at being appointed Minister at the tender age of thirty-one. Heavily influenced by his father, he harboured deeply ingrained but well-disguised beliefs that nationalisation was truly the way ahead. He was convinced that compulsory identification would be a requirement of the new era. Gone were the days when the working man could be held economic hostage by a gang of mindless capitalist thugs. Government of the people, by the people and for the people was now readily attainable. The technology was in place and compulsory identification was an essential ingredient of the way ahead.

Chapter 18

The Tarnbeck experiment was turning out to be a resounding success. The ID card had proved instantly popular. It was particularly so among the more mature residents of a town with more than its fair share of senior citizens. At its introduction there had been reservations about the discomfort associated with the subcutaneous implant of the verification chip. The implant, however, was so small and its installation so pain and trouble free that it was enthusiastically accepted. There had been worries about card theft but the verification chip appeared to rule that out. Some sceptics had even raised alarms that potential thieves would remove the verification chip by killing its owner and amputating the host limb. The chip, however, had a host specific pulse sensor installed in it. If it sensed a lack of pulse, or even an unfamiliar one, it would be permanently de-activated. It could only be re-activated by a visit to the appropriate Authority, namely the 'IDC Board'. Security was therefore assured.

Its user-friendliness made shopping easier. It took the complication of tax returns away. It did away with the need to cart mountains of money around. Gone were the days when the bus driver had no change. Old Mrs Tomlinson was not the only pensioner to lose her card and have it returned by 'that nice young man from the Authority'. It had dropped out of her purse as she left Spenders. Immediately Molly Tomlinson reported it lost, its location was picked up by the ever-watchful satellite, which advised the Authority of its precise whereabouts. They quickly retrieved it and returned it to its owner.

The success of Tarnbeck attracted keen interest from surrounding towns and villages, leading them to put pressure on central government to allow the experiment to be expanded. The publicity generated by also provided a fertile seedbed for the pro compulsory identification lobby in parliament and finally, at a meeting of the Cabinet, it was agreed to bring forward the expansion. Being merely an expansion of an already existing scheme, there was no need to bring it before parliament.

It escaped public notice that the Compulsory Identification Card scheme was taking shape without any public debate whatsoever. It appeared that the IDC would not only replace money but that even the Mother of Parliaments was beginning to look increasingly obsolete. Voting with your card would cut out one more layer of potential corruption in the democratic process. The strange thing was that any discussion of this potential role of the card was strongly contested by the Members of Parliament. It did not take the public long to deduce the reason for the parliamentary objections. Members stood to lose massive credit allowances if the talking shop were to be replaced by a voting machine. Only recently the Prime Minister had found himself with a lot of explaining to do when the press revealed that the taxpayer had spent £25,000 on the redecoration of a house in Notting Hill Gate. The house did not actually even belong to the Prime Minister. It belonged to his brother. Harry Crighton squirmed his way out of that one by claiming that he frequently used his brother's address for convenience after meetings in West London, instead of going all the way back to Number 10. It was a 'security issue', he said. Privately, his security detail disagreed with him but, luckily, they had only had to provide security at that address once in the previous three years. Suffice it to say that 'Vote With Your Card' did not become a slogan in the campaign for the introduction of the IDC.

The expansion scheme increased the demand for cards from the Braunschweig factory. Old Igor Lutov had retired at the age of seventy, leaving Georg to run the shops and the factory. Georg's Tanzanian wife was enormously popular with the staff at the factory. She had completed her Physical Education course, gaining a one/one honours degree. Her doctorate was in Physiotherapy, specialising in sports injuries and she set up a very successful clinic in the town. She also became a physiotherapist to the German National Football Team.

Secretly she was worried about the implications of her husband's creation. She felt uncomfortable with the 'nanny state'. Having experienced the failure of African Socialism in her own country, she was sensitive to the invasive nature of communist government but she never raised her concerns with Georg. She was happy to see him so absorbed in his work.

Something which did cause concern to them both, was the incessant rise in the bank rate. The loan that old Horst Meyer had so strongly recommended to Igor was proving to be a millstone around the company's neck. Georg was finding it more and more difficult to keep up with the increasingly harsh demands of the Ost Deutsche Bank.

Finally, when the British Government put in a massive order for new IDCs for the expansion of the Tarnbeck experiment, it required equivalent expansion of the Arches production facilities. This, in turn, demanded a renegotiation of the loan agreement and it was inevitable that the bank would have to become involved in the ownership of the company. They took a fifty-one per cent share in the Arches Holding Company, in order to finance the new premises. As before, the hard cash for this came from the Russians. Almost imperceptibly, they were levering themselves into a position where they could control an organisation that could end up as an extremely influential part of Western life.

The success of the Tarnbeck Experiment had not gone unnoticed in other parts of the world either. The United States government watched with keen interest as its economy slipped deeper and deeper into the red. The crime rate was forced up by rising unemployment and politicians throughout the land cast about for some kind of medication for this malaise.

The British had been the forerunners in so many human fields. The industrial revolution, antiseptic surgery, parliamentary democracy, the postage stamp, the free National Health Service, railways, the iron ship, the automatic gearbox; all these things stemmed from this tiny island, and now the Tarnbeck Experiment was, once again, showing the way forward.

The US government went for it. Secretary of State Chasemore-Browne put out a request for volunteers for a pilot scheme to test the efficacy of the system. Several cities offered suburbs, most of them quiet and middle class. Hartford, Connecticut, after consulting the residents, offered West Hartford, but Mayor Levinson had a hidden agenda. In Hartford's North End you don't want to lose a tyre. If you do have a puncture and you appear to be carrying cash or valuables, your chances of survival are limited.

Hartford's North End was virtually destroyed on the 3rd of April 1968, following the assassination of Martin Luther King. The mainly Afro-Caribbean-Hispanic population ran riot and razed the commercial district to the ground. Ever since then Hartford North End had been most well known for its crime rate. It was Mayor Simon Levinson first noticed the Tarnbeck Experiment. It was not the middle class acceptance of the scheme that made it so attractive as they had all fled Hartford's North End with the riots. No, it was the complete absence of money and the compulsory registration of each member of the community, which attracted his attention. Hartford North End had become a 'no-go' area, so nothing worked.

The main problem with the project was its implementation with what he saw as the turbulent, lawless inhabitants of this human sewer. The Mayor hit upon a plan. The success of the Hartford North Project depended upon its acceptance by the people. He decided to seek the assistance of one of the strongest of human drives, namely jealousy. He would make the inhabitants so jealous that they would clamour to be given access to the system. They would, in fact, demand it.

West Hartford is all middle class and it has a large Jewish community. Drunkenness is rare because of tight state controls on the sale of alcohol as well as the reluctance of the community to be seen in an inebriated condition. The crime rate is low, the antithesis of Hartford North End. The only problem with West Hartfordians was that they were good with money so what could they possibly find attractive about an absence of it?

Mayor Levinson had an idea. Everyone likes a bargain. He himself was of Jewish descent and he frequently discussed with friends just how well he'd done on some deal or other. One such friend was Gato Petrie, the CEO of a large supermarket chain. Spacey's Supermarts had branches all over the US. They had one large Supermart in West Hartford and another in North End, which was suffering from the Credit Crunch and the rise in crime. The North

End branch had been raided twice in the last month and this week, lost around $20,000 in a single robbery. The insurance companies were squealing and premiums were becoming prohibitive. The police were reluctant to interfere since two Law Enforcement Officers had been bludgeoned to death by a crowd at the scene of a gangland killing some months before. To say that Hartford North End was a 'no-go' area would be a gross understatement. It was out of control. It was not only an acute embarrassment to the capital city of Connecticut. It was an embarrassment to the nation. Petrie was going to be the man to call.

"Just imagine if there had been no money around," said Levinson to the CEO of Spacey's, "then you wouldn't have lost it. Thieves can't steal something which is not there, can they?" Mr Petrie had to agree. "That is the secret of the ID card system. It removes money completely."

Simon Levinson and Gato Petrie went on the internet and worked their way through the IDC system. It looked very attractive indeed. Swipe your IDC and there was no way there could be defaults on payment. Everything was guaranteed and all the administration would be handled by the Authority, or the 'IDC Board'. They would guarantee credits to the Spacey's account and prices would beat all the competitors' because there were virtually no administration costs involved. Bullet-proof! Spacey's went for the new system, big time.

The problem was that Arches Stationery had patented the IDC system worldwide and the factory's capacity was now stretched to breaking point with the burgeoning demand for IDC technology. It was essential that the facility be expanded to cope with the demand and this would involve further negotiations with Ost Deutsche Bank.

Arches Stationery was slipping out of the Lutov family's hands. Igor had long since retired and lived in a small, comfortable apartment with Glacier on the western outskirts of town. Georg was finding that financial control of the company was being wrested away from him by the bank and the bank now, effectively, belonged to the Russians. It was important for each of them to retain Georg's services because he knew, better than anybody else, the potential and pitfalls of the system. His international connections, particularly in the UK and the States, were another asset which kept him in the game as far as the Russians were concerned, otherwise he would have been disposed of much earlier.

Meanwhile, the IDC system was offered to the residents of West Hartford and, after some initial scepticism, it was decided to start a pilot scheme with Spacey's Supermart. People wishing to take part in the scheme would register with the IDC Board and be issued with IDCs and implants. This would give them acccss to the facilities of the supermarket. Initially Credits would be bought in exchange for dollars and added to the card. At first there was some reluctance to receiving the implanted verification chip but as in England, when the first recipients revealed how painless and quick was the procedure, it soon evaporated.

Ford introduced a new middle-market saloon model, known as the 'Identycar', which was based on a very well tried and tested European design, the 'Focus'. The only way to get into it was with the owner's IDC. Swipe the card through the reader on the door and it would open. It was the same for the ignition. The only way to steal the car was to reduce it to spare parts on site and sell them. There had been none stolen in West Hartford since the model had first been sold there. Ford sales rose sharply in that town.

Soon the IDC system was accepted and fully implemented and, by a bit of judicious publicity, news of its success spread to surrounding local communities. It wasn't long before the people of Hartford North End started to question why the rich and affluent in West Hartford should be offered the benefits of the new system when the poor residents of the ghetto area were not. Here was yet another example of discrimination against the Afro-Caribbean and Hispanic communities. It was disgraceful. The Mayor and the City Council should be ashamed of themselves! An effigy of Mayor Levinson was burned in the street in front of a jeering crowd.

In response to the demonstrations, the Mayor appeared on television. He apologised to the people of Hartford's North End and promised that the IDC scheme would be made available to them as soon as the infrastructure could be put in place. A pilot scheme was introduced at the Spacey's Supermart in Hartford North End, with great celebrations led by Gato Petrie. He was euphoric about the benefits offered by the new system. Nobody else was optimistic about its success, except for Mayor Levinson. He had jealousy on his side. He knew that it would work which is why he, personally, invested in the installation of the machinery, which converted Spacey's Supermart North End from the Dollar to the Credit Economy.

It was extraordinary. Suddenly everybody wanted an IDC. The implant became a symbol of the 'I've arrived' society. Shoppers visited Spacey's from far and wide because their prices were so absurdly low. North End was besieged by the middle classes from West Hartford and house prices rocketed. The gangs evaporated in the face of local pressure. How do you pay for a snort of cocaine with Credits? Mary Jane doesn't perform for Credits. The dealers moved to greener pastures where green leaves were paid for with greenbacks. Robbery figures tumbled as the thieves found that their fences no longer had money to pay for stolen goods. A gold watch is a gold watch. Why would I want to steal your gold watch when I can't sell it? You cannot buy stolen property with Credits, everything has to go through the Authority.

An unaccustomed calm spread through streets which previously had been home only to suspicion and squalor, failure and fear. Tiny shoots of optimism began to sprout. Doors that had been locked and barred for decades, began to open as the properties were sold to new entrepreneurs. Somehow the threatening cloud of the years since 1968 seemed, miraculously, to be lifting. People smiled at each other in the street, instead of avoiding eye contact. Even the police began to appear on the beat again, welcomed by the new inhabitants.

Mayor Levinson was in great demand to expound on the success of his policy. It seemed that a solution to the nation's ailments was just around the corner. The 'all mighty Dollar' was no longer all mighty. It was simply an emblem of an out-dated economic regime, decorated with symbols of an order that had failed the world. Humble carvers of stone had formed a club that, over centuries, had become so powerful that they could rule the world. Now they were a thing of the past. The ancient financial cartels were irrelevant. Money was irrelevant. Now things would change. A new era had been born. Hope was right here.

This message was read loud and clear right across the nation. President Kearns was even interested, in spite of the implications for the dollar and Wall Street. For Mayor Levinson to be able to turn Hartford North End around and make it a respectable, even a desirable address, in so short a space of time was truly remarkable, almost miraculous.

The system he had implemented must have applications in deprived areas all over the country. Maybe the day of the dollar was really over. Maybe the IDC was the solution that everyone had been waiting for.

Soon other cities started to make inquiries. Levinson had to employ more staff to handle the flood of questions being asked of his office. It was quite obvious to senior politicians that this revolution was demanded by the people. If they wanted to retain office, they needed to take it seriously. Either prove it or disprove it. The IDC was here to stay. Unless, of course, it could be discredited in some way, and there were vested interests that were determined to find a way of doing just that. The problem for them was that a massive groundswell of support for the system was sweeping the country. Levinson's office was swamped with calls from the mayors of East St. Louis and of Opa-locka in Florida as well as, among many others, Memphis, Nashville Tennessee, Clarksville, Rockport Kansas and New Orleans. The list went on and on and they were desperate for information on the scheme. Suddenly the President became aware of the extent of the lawlessness that had built up over the years. The current slide into economic decline was accelerating the relentless advance of crime and it was quite obvious that, without drastic action, the world's only superpower would be super no longer.

As far as the President of the Russian Federation was concerned, things could hardly be going better. Capitalism was on the run and its proponents were unwittingly playing straight in to the Russians' hands.

It was at the time when the Tarnbeck project was entering its commissioning stage, that the first flaw was discovered. The Russians, fully conversant with the status of its development, decided to try out a feature of the system that was exclusively in their control. By feeding a heavily protected secret code up to the IDC satellites it should be possible, effectively, to turn the population of Tarnbeck off and disable their ID cards. This feature was an adaptation of the function which disabled the card's ability to open a car door and start the engine in the event that the authorities wished to deny access to a vehicle. In effect, it made all the implanted verification chips think that the user's pulse had stopped.

This disabled the card permanently unless the user could re-verify it with the IDC Board. It was designed and implemented by a team of Russian technicians without the knowledge of the Lutovs, or anybody else in fact other than Boris Belnikov, Ivan Ilyich and of course the sinister head of the SVR, Vladimir Chernorgin. The problem was, how to reactivate the system again after the trial. The team had been working on this but there was no way of knowing if it worked without trying it out and the trial would have to be for real.

The decision was made that it would take place at night in order to keep as low a profile as possible. A date and time was chosen. It would take place on a Sunday night at a quarter to midnight, local time. Belnikov sent authorisation to the laboratory and, at precisely the appointed hour, the cut-out was activated. There were some tense minutes of silence while they waited for something to happen. Time passed slowly until, suddenly, the BBC midnight newscaster made an announcement that, according to the IDC system satellites, the entire population of Tarnbeck had passed away at 23.45 that night. The police were in the process of confirming whether there were survivors.
After they discovered the fault, the CABNI instigated an in-depth investigation. It was essential to get the system up

211

and running as quickly as possible in order to restore public confidence. The shut-down was dismissed as a small glitch in a new system. 'There are bound to get a few teething problems in anything as state-of-the-art as the Tarnbeck Experiment' was the official line.

The Police toured residential areas ensuring that the people of Tarnbeck were alive and assuring them that all services would be resumed within twenty-four hours. The Board sent a re-verification team round the area with equipment to reactivate the pulse sensors and, as promised, everything was operating normally again within twenty-four hours.

What interested Georg Lutov was the fact that the pulse sensors had all fallen off line at the same moment. Georg had designed the IDC specifically to make mass shut-down of any part of the system impossible and this applied to the pulse sensors, for the precise reason that it might be used as it had b the Russians. Georg was convinced that his design could only fail if it was intentionally circumnavigated. Also, he was becoming more and more suspicious of the Ost Deutsche Bank's involvement in Arches Holdings. He was not aware of direct Russian connections but there was an uncomfortable feeling in the marrow of his bones. The Russians had shown an inordinate amount of interest in the IDCs and specifically the technical side which had sowed a seed of suspicion in his mind.

When he attempted to draw the attention of the IDC Board in the UK to this major issue, he was dismissed as a mad professor, an eccentric academic. So he went public. Sky News picked up the story and that was when Jack Wise was asked to get involved. Harry Crighton contacted the Home Secretary who, in turn, contacted John Jason at New

Scotland Yard. The D/Comm had a reputation for dealing behind the scenes. If you wanted some discreet information gathered or passed, Jason was your man. He had connections in both high and low society and one of his most important and reliable contacts was his friend, Jack Wise.

"Good afternoon, on a foul day, Jack."

"Good Afternoon Johnnie. Yes, they say that there's more snow on the way. I've just watched the News."

"Did you see the bit about the Tarnbeck shutdown. That Georg Lutov, the lad who invented the thing, says that it was designed so that no one specific failure could close down the whole system. He said it was physically impossible. He reckoned that the only way to achieve a comprehensive shut-down was to circumvent the back-ups which could only be done intentionally. That means that someone turned off Tarnbeck on purpose."

"Yes, Johnnie, I saw that. Who would want to do that then?"

"Who indeed, Jack? Who, indeed?"

"Are you free this evening, Johnnie? I might call a gathering of the clan at the usual place. This thing looks a bit naughty to me."

"Right, Jack around, six-ish?"

"See you then."

Chapter 19

Jack Wise strode into the pub, handed his coat to Jock and walked straight through to the Library Bar. Jason, Tarrant and Sam Jackson were sitting in a huddle by the fire.

"When did you hear this Sam?" Tarrant's face was a study in shock.

"I heard it on the news, on my way over here. Apparently the attacker was on a motorbike. Hit him in the head. He is now in intensive care. They didn't say where."

"What's this all about, gentlemen?" Jason had been on the road in a taxi for the last half hour.

"What's happened now?"

"It looks like someone tried to top Georg Lutov." Sam looked up at Jason.

"When was this?"

"I heard it on the news about ten minutes ago. It happened as he was coming out of the Sky News offices. A girl who was with him was hit in the shoulder by a second bullet. She is an employee of Sky News. Nobody has claimed responsibility."

"Looks like, we have another candidate for The Wellesley Clinic. Did they say how badly hurt Lutov is?"

"No, they didn't say."

"Hang on a minute, I'll call the Yard. We'd better contact The Wellesley too." Jason stood up and moved to the other side of the room to make his calls and returned minutes later, slipping his mobile into his jacket pocket. "I smell conspiracy here." He said. "Georg Lutov spouts his mouth off about the Tarnbeck Experiment problem and immediately after that, somebody tries to slot him. What do you think, Gentlemen?"

"I may be a suspicious old trout but don't I detect the distinct aroma of Russian influence around here?" Dick Tarrant sniffed the air theatrically. "First, all the banks fall over because of loans to ex-Soviet bloc countries. This is followed by a series of unusual deaths. Then Freddie Barnes gets involved in an enormous loan to a company in the Black Sea. That's revealed as a scam and Freddie gets a dose of cyanide in his chocolates. Then a small blonde joyrider in a new Mini Cooper, rams Alex with intent. How is he, by the way?"

"I went to see him yesterday." said Sam. "He's very chirpy but that left leg will take a bit of work to be back to normal. He'll probably walk with a stutter. That girl tried her damnedest to kill him. He's very lucky to be alive."

"Yes, I agree with you," Jason resumed the thread started by Dick. "I found it highly suspicious that the rent-a-thug who we caught at the Makepeace fire said that he was paid by a man with a foreign accent. Maybe we should investigate that a bit deeper. See if the kid would recognise the accent."

"And what about that Kevin kid with the fireworks in his room." It was all falling into place in Sam's head. "Have they linked him with the PM's cottage fire? He was at the Makepeace job as well. I wonder if he was paid for the

215

PM's job by the same gent who bankrolled the Makepeace affair."

The evening broke up when Jason rose to his feet and announced that he had to rush. He wanted to contact Georg's folks but Scotland Yard had not traced them as yet and their son was still in theatre. He would have to try again in the morning.

The announcement of the death of Georg Lutov hit Igor and Glacier like a sledgehammer. His sister, Irina, left Graz immediately and hurried back to Braunschweig to comfort her parents.

The D/Comm contacted them and asked them to attend an interview in London as soon as possible.

"It is extremely important that we see you, Mr Lutov. The British Government will cover your expenses." The tone of Jason's voice added a compelling note of urgency.

"When?" said Igor, his command of English had improved over the years of doing business with the computer industry, but it was still clipped and guttural.

"Could you make it tomorrow?"

"I can come today, if you require. Is this something to do with the death of my son?"

"Indeed it is, Mr Lutov. I have some very important news for you. I suggest that you bring your wife with you. It concerns her as well."

"My daughter is also with us here. Maybe she could help us with the journey?"

"She would be most welcome, Mr Lutov. This matter involves you all."

"We come today. I call you when bookings are complete."

Irina booked e-tickets with British Midland from Hannover Langenhagen Airport to London Heathrow and Igor called Jason with the details.

"Thank you Mr Lutov. You will be met by one of my officers on your arrival so don't worry about travel arrangements this side. You will be staying at the Sofitel Saint James Hotel in central London. The officer who meets you will drop you there and I will come over to meet you at six o'clock this evening."

The journey went smoothly and the hotel was pleasantly light and airy. Igor and Glacier's room was next to Irina's on the second floor. They could not help allowing their minds to drift back to the years of hardship in the post-war rubble of Europe. Luxury on the scale of this modern hotel would have been unthinkable in those days. It was just sad that they had to experience it in such tragic circumstances. What had they done to deserve to lose their only son? To have come through all this and then to have his life snuffed out was beyond comprehension. How could God expect their loyalty, when He had deprived them of one of their two most valued possessions? It was baffling.

The telephone rang. It was Jason. He said that he would meet them at reception. His first impression of the Lutov family was of a father whose deeply lined features had seen the harder side of what the world had to offer, a mother whom age had given dignity and a kind of serenity and a daughter who very obviously carried her mother's genes. The difference between the parents and the

217

daughter was that her eyes had seen more humour during her journey through the years.

"Good evening, Mr Lutov." Jason was in civilian clothes. The old Russian grasped his hand in a surprisingly powerful grip. He then turned to the ladies and introduced himself. "John Jason. I am the Deputy Commissioner of the Metropolitan Police here in London. Perhaps I could suggest that we go to your room as it will be more private?"

They returned to the elevator and, after Igor had closed the door to their bedroom, Jason started the conversation by asking him whether his son had any known enemies.

"He had problem with manager of Ost Deutsche Bank, but I don't think this man would kill him."

"Anybody else you can think of?"

"He was suspicious that there was some kind of Russian involvement. The Russians have spent a lot of time at the factory and they seem to be very interested in the technical side of the IDCs."

"And what do you think about these suspicions, Mr Lutov?"

"I agree with my son." There was a look akin to defiance in the old man's eyes. "The bank has stolen the company from us. They insisted on taking some of the company when I borrowed money in order to expand. Now they want their money back with interest, which we cannot afford, so they take share in the company, more and more, until they own more than fifty per cent. Now the company belong to them. Where does the Ost Deutsche Bank get its money? There is little business in former East Germany, so where does it come from? The Russian Mafia, maybe? Georg is certain that there is a connection. He even mentioned it on the television."

The Russian connection was beginning to turn up regularly now. Maybe there was some substance to Georg and Igor Lutov's suspicions.

"Now, I would like you all to take a seat. You may find what I am going to tell you a bit shocking." Jason remained standing.

The two parents sat on the bed and Irina took the dressing table stool. A pregnant silence hung in the air. Each Lutov's face appeared to be expecting even worse news to be coming from the D/Comm.

"Your son is not dead. He is alive, in hospital. His injury is not life-threatening. The bullet passed through his skull and may have damaged one of his frontal lobes but he is expected to make a full recovery."

Glacier's eyes closed and she sank her head into Igor's shoulder. Igor hugged her to him and stroked her hair. Irina just stared at Jason, as though in a trance. Her lips moved, but no sound came out.

"We thought it better to keep the perpetrators under the impression that their attack had been successful. This would make things a lot safer for your son Georg until we can identify the killers and deal with them." Jason looked around the stunned little group. "If you agree with this plan, we will go ahead with funeral arrangements and it would add authenticity if you would attend the cremation. Forensics will have finished up by Thursday so we could have the funeral on Friday. Can you spare yourselves until then?"

The three Lutovs nodded their heads in silence.

"I am so sorry to have put you through this terrible grief and now this but I think that we are following the right path if we are to trap the villains. I think that you will agree that they must be stopped. It appears more and more likely that the attempt on your son's life was a part of a much wider plot and we desperately need to get to the bottom of it before it or something far worse happens again." The three Lutovs nodded their heads vigorously. "Your son has, as you know, been interviewed on television about the unexplained close-down of the Tarnbeck Experiment. Basically, he said that it was physically impossible for the complete system to close down because of the failure of one of its components. He said that there are too many back-ups and, for all the verification implants to fail at one specific time, just could not happen by chance. It would take so many millions of permutations to coincide in the computer that it was inconceivable. He said that it could only happen if there was intentional intervention. Therefore, he implied that someone had deliberately turned off the verification chips. He also suggested the identity of some possibly interested parties and it was after that interview that the assassination attempt was made." He paused for a moment, to give his theory time to sink in. "I believe that the 'someone' we are talking about is closely connected to the failure of the Tarnbeck IDCs. Either they don't like them or, maybe they don't like the suspicions raised by Georg during his interview. Either way, they are prepared to be completely ruthless in the execution of their plans so we need to keep Georg out of sight, until we catch up with the bad boys." Jason glanced at each one of the newly not bereaved group. "So now I will leave you to get settled in. I will get in touch again tomorrow morning at around nine o'clock. Is there anything else we need to talk about?"

"Mr Jason," Igor Lutov looked up solemnly, "I wish to thank you for your help, from the bottom of my heart. It is extraordinary to have our son back. Thank you. Thank you, Mr Jason."

"That is what I do for a living, Mr Lutov. Sometimes it all ends in tragedy but in this particular instance we have been lucky so far. I would ask you to contain your joy at having Georg back. Mourners don't usually smile a lot."

"We know how to mourn, Mr Jason. We learned the hard way, during these last days."

"Very good," he stood up. "Mr Lutov, Ladies, I will see you tomorrow then. Good evening to you, and remember that this evening comes with the generosity of the British taxpayer, so enjoy yourselves." Jason left the room.

Georg Lutov had come round from the anaesthetic during the night. The surgeons had discovered that the small calibre bullet had grazed the left frontal lobe of his brain and, although there might be some damage, the lobe itself looked as though it would recover completely. Whether the shock would change his character was something which only time would tell.

The first recorded frontal lobotomy had been carried out on one of Napoleon Bonaparte's soldiers during the battle of Austerlitz. During the battle, the first experimental patient jumped into a trench, for cover and received a bayonet thrust up under his chin, through the nasal cavity and out of the top of his head. The blade severed the two frontal lobes of his brain. Prior to this event the soldier had exhibited such lack of discipline and disrespect for his officers that he was due to stand before a court martial. After the wound had healed, his character was seen to have changed radically. He became a model of good discipline and respect. It was one of the first times that the effects of a frontal lobotomy on human character had been observed and it later became a not entirely predictable surgical procedure. As far as Georg was concerned, the world would have to sit and wait for the effects of his injury to manifest themselves. For now, he appeared perfectly normal.

The significance of the shooting was not, however, lost on the minds of Tarrant, Jason and Sam.

"It seems that the Russian connection grows stronger by the day." said Jason, as the three sat by the fire in the Library Bar at Aunties. "Lutov vents his spleen full frontal, on the Tarnbeck experts and the Russians on TV and is rewarded with a bullet in the head. What is the connection between Lutov and the other recent events? What could be the possible link between the destruction of property and what has happened here?"

"Well," Sam pushed his glasses back up his nose, "in my mind and in my work, I like things to follow patterns. The pattern I begin to make out here is an attack on the three things which represent English life."

"Go on Sam." Tarrant and Jason leaned forward in rapt attention.

"The Prime Minister represents law and order, Makepeace stands for wealth and Norwich Cathedral represents the innate sense of morality which the majority of the English think is their birthright. If you were to destroy the people's faith in these three principles, you destroy the English way of life."

"And what about the financial crash, Sam?" Dick Tarrant had his own ideas about that but they were focussed solely on the Stock Market and the banking system. Maybe Sam's lateral thinking had identified some link which had escaped him.

"If I were mounting an attack on the UK, I would go about it very much in the same way as we are seeing. Firstly I would destroy the banks, which, as you can see, is easy enough to do in times of Bull markets. All the banks were falling over themselves to lend money. 'You want a loan of 100% at 8% interest, over ten years? Why not be sure to cover any unforeseen costs and make it 125%? It'll be the same rate of interest and I'll even give you another couple more years to pay off the loan."

"That is exactly what is happening, Sam, but, what then?"

"Well, when the banks and the building societies fall over and die, money comes in short supply because the people who used to dole it out have all jumped out of the window. Nobody can get loans to finance new industries or regenerate old ones. So, the old ones start to deteriorate. Overseas competition has newer production facilities and can afford to undercut the old stagers. Pretty soon, the older players start to throw in their cards. Unemployment rises. The government tries to step in, to staunch the haemorrhage but they themselves have to borrow heavily to finance the recovery. Soon the International Monetary Fund has to draw the line somewhere, basically because they too are running out of money. The British economy goes into negative inflation, which sounds great. Prices will, for the first time in living memory, actually decrease. The problem is that negative inflation is just a pretty way of saying 'recession' and recession means that the economy is dying. When the economy dies, factories and offices close and people lose their jobs. No job, no money, equals despair, equals desperation, equals revolution."

John Jason was taking notes in a case notebook and he looked up at Sam.

"Where is this all leading to, Sam?" he said.

"It could be the biggest upset we've seen since World War II. Or it could just be a series of co-incidences. Whichever it is, it is going to affect one hell of a lot of people. What is your feeling, Deputy Commissioner?"

"'Johnnie', please Sam. I'm really a soldier, not a genuine policeman!" Jason's smile was conspiratorial and Sam suddenly felt more relaxed with one of the most senior police officers in the land.

"Listening to you folks talking, I cannot escape a certain feeling of apprehension. It certainly looks as though somebody has the UK in his sights. Anyone who has missed that point just didn't come to the party. The thing that worries me is that we still don't know what the plan is. What is the aim of all these incidents? If indeed they are all part of a coordinated attack upon the fabric of our society, why? Why are they doing it?" He opened his clenched fists in an expression of frustrated confusion. "If we knew that, we could take action to pre-empt them. At the moment, all we have is a series of incidents which may, or may not be related."
"Why don't we assume, for a moment, that there is, in fact, a co-ordinated attack, in progress? Why is someone trying

to undermine the system? What could anybody gain by destroying British society?" Sam was an Anglophile to his roots, despite his Caribbean background. "It just doesn't make sense."

It was not until that point in the conversation that they noticed their company had expanded by one. Jack Wise had been standing there listening, unnoticed, for some minutes now. "Supposing it's not just the UK, that is being targeted." He held a glass of red wine to his lips and sipped thoughtfully. "Suppose it is democracy as a whole. Think back a bit. The Russkies feature strongly in the vast majority of these stories. Suppose they are having a go at re-establishing themselves as a dominant world power again? It is a well-known fact that Comrade Belnikov is pissed off that Mister Citizen-of-the-world doesn't buy anything from Russia except gas and oil and, with the prices as they are today, it is going to be difficult for him to keep the oligarchs financially viable. Of course, if he can't do that, his tenure in office might be curtailed by a funeral announcement. It would not be the first time. Mind you, Belnikov doesn't go down easily. Many people have had a go and many are not here to tell the tale."

"You're making me nervous, Jack!" Sam was laughing, as he said this.

There had been three serious attempts on Jack's life, two of them in action in Iraq and one IRA-related in Northern Ireland. It was quite obvious that none of them had come close to being successful. This did not breed a sense of indifference, it merely meant that Jack possibly appreciated every moment of his life more than his next-door-neighbour. Every extra day was a bonus.
"So where do we go from here, Sam?"

Sam took the floor again. He peered over his glasses them professorially and his 'students' paid attention.

"We know what has happened and we know that the Russians are involved in at least some of the events. The thing that we do not know is, why are they doing this? As I said earlier, I have a gut feeling that there is some master plan behind all these little pinpricks. The Russkies are up to something much bigger."

"Well, if we knew that, Sam, we would be ahead of the game, wouldn't we, but how can we read their minds? We can't predict their next move because we couldn't predict their last one." Jack held an empty hand out to indicate the extent of his qualifications as a prophet.

"Yes, but we have an idea that they are trying to break down the British way of life. They have torched the property of a tycoon and probably killed him. The police could not control the mob at his house. They have attacked the Prime Minister's house in Warningham and the police were unable to stop them. One of our greatest monuments has been reduced to rubble killing dozens and the police were completely at a loss to prevent it. There is somebody out there trying to prove that the government is losing its grip."

Dick Tarrant leaned forward. "... and the whole thing is being exacerbated by the collapse of the financial world. That is going to create unemployment on a massive scale and we all know what that does to the crime figures."

"We can see that happening already." Jason looked up from his notepad.

"So, Gentlemen, let's see if we can't predict what they will do next." Sam's analytical mind was guiding three of the most experienced brains in the country to try and penetrate the psyche of an unknown enemy bent on their downfall.

"Well," Jack steepled his fingers in front of his face, as though trying to make the future fit into the evidence which was before them. "If I were to take a leaf out of Al-Qaeda's book, I think I would go for transport" and in this, Jack's prophetic credentials were proved to be horrifyingly correct.

Chapter 20

Isambard Kingdom Brunel was small in stature, controversial by nature and an engineer of giant dimensions. His father spent time in a debtor's prison, which was an unprepossessing start for one of Britain's greatest national figures. No engineering obstacle was too big for little Brunel. Presented with the challenge of building a ship five times larger than any contemplated to date, he didn't throw his hands in the air and yell "You must be joking!" He simply sat down and scratched his head. The problem for him was not if it could be done, but how. He smoked many a cigar while his mental processes duelled with the impossible. The cigars have now been politically correctly airbrushed from photographic records of the era, in order to prevent present generations from seeking relaxation from the same source. Finally, he proved that a boat does not need to be made of wood in order to float after all, his iron basin floated nicely in the big stone washbasin.

One of the first problems he ran up against was that an iron structure of that size would have to be built facing north/south. This was not for reasons of mysticism or magnetism but simply because, if the ship was built facing east/west, the sun would warm the southern side more than the northern side during its construction. So, when the ship was launched into the cold water, the southern side would shrink more than the northern and he would end up with a banana-shaped boat, which might go round corners nicely but would be a devil to keep straight. That is fact.

Most British shipbuilders' yards were based on rivers and most rivers in the UK flow east/west, or the other way around. Brunel chose the Medway, as that river flows north into the Thames estuary. Brunel, being Brunel, decided to build 'The Great Eastern' on the eastern bank of the river and launch her sideways.

Set against this background, Brunel was given the contract to build a railway from London to the West, over the Avon gorge, with onward connections, by land and sea, to Ireland. The potential market was enormous and the investors needed a cutting edge engineer to do the job. There was really only one person with the guts to take it on and Brunel produced some of the most radical and innovative solutions to an engineering brief which many had turned down as impossible. The Clifton Suspension Bridge was one such challenge.

At the time, suspension bridges were something out of pre-history. Vines could be stretched across a river and it was possible to cobble together a swaying, fragile link from one side of a stream to the other but, to build the same structure capable of carrying masses of people and transport couldn't be done. Then the tiny man came up with the idea of a chain. It was heavy and did not stretch and the carriageway was rigid and did not have the load-bearing strength to support one hundred and eighty tons. That is where the chains took over. The whole concept, like so many of the engineer's designs, was so simple that people could not understand why nobody had thought of it before. But there was a crack in the design's armour and Sergei Novgorod spotted it.

The bridge needed constant maintenance. It was a continuous schedule to repair by chipping off rust, applying anti-rust, painting red lead, checking the track alignment as well as the electrical continuity of the signalling system. Then there were the telltale trip wires which would reveal unauthorised entry onto the bridge.

These had been installed because of earlier terrorist activities in country.

The shear bolts, which held the links of the suspension chains together, came from a small engineering foundry in Solihull. It specialised in the manufacture of unusual alloys for specific applications. The bolts were checked every six months and changed every five years. The company had been hit badly by the recession and their prices had risen considerably.

The Clifton Bridge Authority received a quote from Pollimetal, a Polish manufacturer, for the same specification of bolts at almost half the price and that is what attracted Sergei Novgorod's attention. Most of the Polish company's production was concentrated in support of the Gdansk shipbuilding industry but export orders were welcomed and prices were very competitive because of the low labour costs.

After some discreet research, Novgorod established the dimensions of the required bolts and ordered five hundred of them from Pollimetal. They were milled from ingots of an alloy made from copper, zinc and tin, known in the trade as 'light metal'. It was extremely resistant to weathering and corrosion but had very little intrinsic strength, either in shear or tension. It was normally employed for roofing and cladding purposes. Pollimetal had never before received an order for bolts, made from this material. This was a first, for them.

Novgorod organised a Ford half-ton van to be painted in the livery of Express Mail Transit, a well-known courier service with a reputation for backing up its slightly inflated prices with impeccable reliability. With EMT, there was no need to take out insurance on the packages to be moved. The company covered the insurance themselves.

On the appointed day, a similar van appeared at the factory to pick up the consignment of genuine bolts ordered by the Clifton Bridge Authority. Soon after it had left, Novgorod's van arrived at the Pollimetal foundry. It took charge of the five hundred 'light metal' bolts which he had ordered in the name of Tallinn Construkt, a fictitious Estonian construction company.

Around two kilometres before the border at Szczecin, the genuine EMT van approached an official-looking roadblock. The border officers appeared to be in the uniforms of German Grenz Polizei and they directed the EMT van into a lay-by on the right hand side of the road. The Polish Border Police had been advised of the joint German/Polish exercise, which they were told was being mounted in response to a marked increase in illegal immigrants to Germany from Turkey. The unexpected road block had already caught a number of them. After their scanty paperwork had been perfunctorily examined by another officer in civilian clothes, they were released from the security trailer parked well out of sight at the far end of the lay-by.

The other EMT van was also ordered to pull into the lay-by and one of the officers asked the driver to take all his documentation to the officer in the trailer at the far end of the parking lot. The driver willingly complied with the instructions. These random police and customs checks were not uncommon and, in fact, had even revealed parts of a massive gun which was being delivered to Saddam Hussein some years before, as well as the usual craftily hidden shipments of narcotics. Only recently a consignment of heroin had been processed and compressed

231

into the shapes of a crockery tea service. It was a dog that spotted that one, although it took some time for the drugs squad officers to discover where the consignment was hidden. The EMT driver was not at all concerned at being delayed. If anything, he approved of it. He was pleased that the police were fighting on the front line of the narcotics war and protecting his children from the evils of drug addiction.

What he would not have approved of, however, was the busy substitution of his cargo with the cargo from another, almost indistinguishable EMT van which had been parked, back to back with his van, soon after he had disappeared into the trailer. The switch had been skilfully carried out and the evidence of tampering almost undetectable. The false bolts weighed almost precisely the same as the genuine ones and, to the casual observer they were indistinguishable.

The crowds attracted by the Ashton Court Festival and the Bristol International Balloon Fiesta were enormous. The great snake of happy humanity threaded its way up out of the city of Bristol by motor car, bicycle and on foot. There were hundreds, even thousands, on the move, gathering altitude for the great leap across the Avon Gorge at Clifton. Soon the two noble stone towers of the bridge stood out against the sky like sentinels, guarding the access to the city. The river, below, was wide enough to have accommodated the very first ocean-going ship completely constructed from iron. The Great Britain was another product of the Brunel studio. The height of the carriageway, at two hundred and forty-five feet above the highest water level in the river, was easily enough to allow the ship, with its high funnel and masts, to pass beneath, on its way to the sea. It had also allowed it to return, many years later, for a comfortable retirement in the very dock where it had been built. Tragically, the bridge had also provided the venue for many a suicide, although it was said that one lady taking the plunge was saved from death by her voluminous undergarments creating a parachute,.

The crowd reached the bridge and was held at a barrier. Engineering work was in progress and had to be completed before access could be given. The reason for the delay was that one of the riggers working on the southern chain had run into a problem. When, he and his rig hand went to tighten one of the replacement bolts that they had fitted, the threads stripped and the nut rotated uselessly. The rigger removed the useless bolt and replaced it with another. This time the nut held but he decided to report the faulty bolt to his foreman as soon as he reasonably could, without holding up the schedule. Later he called the foreman on his handheld radio and told him that he had to report an abnormality. The foreman told him to proceed to the refuge at the western end of the carriageway, which he did. He showed the stripped bolt to his boss, who took it and examined it.

"That looks like a crap bolt to me, Tommy. Did you replace it with a new one?"

"That's right, Chief. I put a brand new one in and it torqued up fine, without stripping the thread."

"Okay then. Let's have another look when the crowd's gone through"

The foreman waved a green flag and spoke on his handset and the workers at the other end moved the barriers to clear the way for the holidaymakers who streamed on to the bridge. Cars and buses inched their way out over the river until the carriageway and walkways were chock-a-block. Then, one of the new bolts decided to give up. It had never been designed for the job that it was now required to perform. If it had been able to speak, it would have told them that, in the face of impossible demands, it could only do its best. That was not enough, in the circumstances.

The southern chain gave way to the inevitable, as the bolt submitted to the overload. Initially it stretched, splitting the link which it was supposed to be holding. The resulting stress imposed an impossible task on all the other bolts that had been so recently installed. Ironically, the old bolts on the northern chain could easily still handle the job, which they proved as the new ones gave up the struggle. The southern chain collapsed. The wrought iron rods that had stoutly supported the carriageway since 1864 were now released from service and became mindless weapons, bludgeoning the human confetti which tumbled down from the twisted girders.

The horror of the fall was almost instantly quenched by water. Suddenly the violence ceased and everything was calm, forty feet below the disturbed surface of the river. A previously vociferous politician hung, open-mouthed, suspended in a state that stifled his rhetoric. The blank stare of the blue eyes failed to appreciate the breasts of the secretary with whom he had made plans for that evening. She had not intended to expose them so early but unbridled water pressure and broken iron are no respecters of garments or romance. The unblinking blue eyes were rapidly filling with silt, stirred up by the unannounced arrival of the tumbling traffic upon the bed of the River Avon.

The silence was only broken by the thunderous ripping of metallic wreckage as it gave up its tenuous contribution to Brunel's masterpiece and plummeted into the water above them.

Chapter 21

"CLIFTON DISASTER - Hundreds Believed Dead" shouted the front pages of the tabloids the following morning. The broadsheets had obtained camera phone footage of the last moments of the bridge's dramatic dive, taken by one of the riggers who had been calling home to find out what was for dinner. At the first screech of tearing metal, he cut his wife off and recorded the disaster, catching the cries of horror from the surrounding onlookers as ironwork and bodies hurtled towards the water. Eventually, the bridge collapsed, twisting in its final death throes.

The initial reaction from witnesses of the disaster on terra firma was one of stunned disbelief. It was perfectly obvious for all to see there were going to be few survivors. Then fingers started pointing among the horrified spectators. There were still people hanging on to the shattered structure. As they watched, one pathetic survivor's grip gave way and she fell for what seemed like full seconds, before hitting the water. The bloodstain around the fallen body demonstrated that the impact was not survivable. The mud thrown up from the deep collected under the tattered remains of the bridge and drifted downstream.

As the first tumult of churning water began to subside, a little dinghy pushed off urgently from the Bristol shore, downstream of the hanging remnants of the once-proud bridge. Then there was a shout, which rapidly built into a chorus. Fingers pointed urgently. "OVER THERE!" they yelled. What had, at first, appeared to be a large blue garbage bag floating in the water not far from the riverbank, began to move. A hand appeared above the water, then a face. There was a survivor. The dinghy reached the swimmer. He was one of the engineering team who had been replacing the bolts. Stan Belcher had miraculously ridden a broken girder that had broken the surface of the water before he entered it, disappearing to the depths below.

His sudden introduction into the cold water must have activated some primal instinct and he survived the impact. Stan had been a good swimmer all his life, a skill bequeathed to him by generations of his fisher-folk ancestors. His ingrained instinct, on finding himself submerged in cold water, was to fight for the surface. He was completely unaware of his actions as his unconscious brain took over, inside the fractured skull, driving him to follow the bubbles upwards.

His first realisation that he was alive was when a large circle of lights and a masked face appeared, looking down at him. The hidden face was speaking.

"You're going to be okay, Mr Belcher. We are going to put you back to sleep, while we fix your head. Don't worry. Everything is going to get better now."

Then the face slipped away and the frenzy of journalists outside the hospital could only sit and wait.

The Cabinet Room was curiously tense. This was the fourth terrorist attack within ten days. Already the cause of the Clifton Disaster had been established as the failure of the bolts. No-one had claimed responsibility. Pollimetal had revealed their books and the double order had been revealed. There was complete silence over the false bolts.

237

Nobody was able to cast light on how the Light Metal bolts had been substituted. It was a mystery how Tallinn Konstruct had managed to slip through the security net, with their false specifications. The order had come in, and been confirmed by Ost Deutsche Bank in Braunschweig. Braunschweig was the centre of research in Europe. They spent more than seven per cent of their income on research so they had to be solid. In these days of fiscal constraint, any order was a good order, particularly if it was prepaid through the bank. Ost Deutsche Bank, effectively, belonged to a company in Russia. All the oil and gas came from Russia so Ost Deutsche Bank had to be solid.

Duncan Hughes closed the doors of the Cabinet Room, as Members took their seats. He took up his customary position close to the door, hands folded in front of his grey suit. He had been for the fitting of a new prosthesis for his left leg that morning and, as with a new pair of shoes, it was uncomfortable standing on the stump for long periods.

"Good morning all." Harry Crighton looked tired. "We have another disaster on our hands and, once again, it looks like terrorism. The difference, this time, is that these people are way ahead, technically. You will all have read the MI5 brief?" He looked round the table for confirmation. Heads nodded. "This disaster was put on especially to cause death. The fact that there were any survivors was not part of the plan. The plotters were intending to kill every person on that bridge. This kind of crime screams for the reinstatement of capital punishment!" His voice rose, in anger and he thumped the table, causing Marilyn Walters, the Home Secretary, to falter in her note-taking. "These bestial criminals must be stopped at all costs. I have consulted with you all and you have recommended a course of action, which I feel offers one of the few options left open to us. We must introduce compulsory identification as a matter of extreme urgency. We have to isolate our enemy, before we can deal with him." He thumped the table once more and the glasses jingled. "The time for the wringing of hands is over. Now is the time to slap wrists!" His fist bumped the table one final time and he sat down. The Home Secretary let out a long sigh of relief then raised her hand. Harry Crighton nodded his head for her to take the floor. "Marilyn, please." She stood up and surveyed her audience.

"Excuse me Prime Minister, but may I suggest that we bring forward the Tarnbeck Experiment and open it to the whole country? Most people are shouting to be able to join it. It is only the old-school financial blimps that object now and, of course, the fundamentalist and criminal elements."

"For too long now, this country has been a haven for these so-called exiles of conscience."

It was extraordinary. Suddenly it was as though a fire had been lit behind this mild-mannered housewife's eyes. The lady whom the nation had welcomed into their homes as 'Their Home Secretary', a pillar of traditional values, a shoulder to lean on, an icon of good housekeeping and common sense, was expressing the guilty gut feelings of ninety percent of middle Britain.

"It is time that they were brought out into the open, to take responsibility for their views and to fulfil their proper roles in society, instead of hiding behind a legal system which the vast majority of the public feel, favours the criminal against the innocent victim of crime."

The heat from those fiery eyes swept around the Cabinet, searching for anyone who dared challenge her message.

"Now is the time to stand up and be counted. Now is far enough. Now we, who know in our souls what Great Britain stands for, must send a clear message to the wicked, that we are on the attack. They must be made to realise that we are strong in our resolve. We will not accept the blackmail of terror. We will build our society, as we have for thousands of years, on the wisdom and experience of our forebears. This is where we are today and future generations must not see us as the weak authors of Britain's downfall."

There was a stunned silence in the room as Marilyn Walters took a sip of water. It was as though the seasoned politicians around the table were waiting to see where this Churchillian speech was taking them.

"The first step on this road to social responsibility must be to identify ourselves, to stand up and say 'Here I am! Count me in'. We, the British people, are here to stay. We will not sacrifice our values on the altar of political correctness. We are who we are and we should be proud of our identity, not skulk behind the excuse of the right to privacy. Only those who have something to hide have anything to fear. If they don't like it, they should face the consequences of their views and we should make the message clear, that we will not accept being threatened by lawless foreigners who are bent on the destruction of the this great country we all know and love." The silence continued and the Home Secretary took another sip from her glass. "Thank you, Prime Minister," she said, looking at him as she sat down.

The Prime Minister looked up at his Home Secretary with awe and, completely involuntarily, began to clap. A current of enthusiasm rippled round the table. The clapping spread as though the current was turning on some strange circuit as it went and soon the whole room rang to clapping and cries of "Hear! Hear!" Nothing like this had been seen in the Cabinet Room of 10 Downing Street in living memory. The only person in the room who restrained himself was Duncan Hughes whose ache from his new prosthesis seemed, magically, to have disappeared.

Had Boris Belnikov been there, he would have swigged a whole bottle of Pshenichnaya to celebrate.

"Hello Jack, Duncan here."

"Duncan, my friend, what can I do for you?"

"Would you, be available this evening?"

"Certainly. What's the score?"

"If we don't do anything in the very immediate future, I think it will be 'Game Over', and we will not be on the winning team. We still don't know who we are up against, do we?"

"No, Duncan, but we have our suspicions. I'll gather the family at the usual place."

"Sounds good to me, Jack. See you there."

It was now coming up to ten days since Alex had done the round with the blood-curdling blonde. He was still on crutches and would be for the next month or more, but at least he was out of bed for most of the daylight hours and Margie was pleased with his progress. As for Margie, she was about to be offered one of the most challenging and exciting assignments of her career. She received an invitation to join Jack Wise and some friends at an address in Eaton Square.

"Could you make it by six, Margie? I'll tell the others."

When the company had all assembled in the Library Bar and Jock had dispensed drinks, Jack introduced Margie to the rest of his friends. In fact, the only ones she had not met before were Duncan and Johnnie. She had heard of Jason because he was once invited out to Kenya to take part in the investigation of a particularly grisly political murder. His report had come so close to the truth that it had been conveniently lost forever. It had not even made it as far as the proverbial garbage bin on Hampstead Heath.

Jack filled in Duncan's details and the fact that they had both served with Alex. From the way she was included in the conversation, Margie got the feeling that there were no secrets between them and she felt duly honoured to have been welcomed into this family.

"So, Duncan, what have you got for us?"

"Well, Jack, I was on duty at an Extraordinary Meeting of the Cabinet this afternoon and, after a frankly impressive speech by the Home Secretary, it appears that she believes the IDC system should be extended to cover the whole country. This is the government's reaction to the attack on the Clifton Bridge which cost a hundred and thirty-nine lives. It could also be linked to the Norwich Cathedral disaster. The reason why I thought we should discuss this development is because the expansion will be carried out without it being presented to Parliament and, consequently, without debate. Effectively, the IDC system

242

will be imposed on the nation by decree. I would stress that the only experiment we have seen to prove the efficacy of the system is Tarnbeck and we have already seen one complete unauthorised shut-down of that, if, in fact, it was unscheduled."

Dick Tarrant had watched the Lutov interview on Sky News that had preceded his shooting.

"Lutov, who, after all, designed the system, seems to believe that what happened in Tarnbeck could only have been achieved by human intervention. That, I find more alarming than if it had simply been a malfunction."

Sam removed his glasses and rubbed his eyes. "The possibility of handing over such an immense source of political power to somebody who can manipulate it is very frightening indeed. Effectively you hand the country over to whoever holds the key to the on/off switch of these IDCs. Which, if you are to believe young Lutov, is the Russians."

Dick, for the first time in his life, felt a qualm of panic clutch at his stomach. This scenario would not just mean the end of Bishop's Avenue but it could even mean the end of life as Britons had lived through wars and pestilence, since the very beginning of its history. This represented the biggest upheaval in ever.

"If Lutov is correct, it means that the Russians will be able to influence every single aspect of life contained in the IDC. That will include all financial transactions. They can switch off our cars. They will even be able to deny us access to our homes when the system is fully in active."

"And our own government is leading the stampede." Sam dragged his fingers through the thick mop of hair, his trademark way of expressing frustration. The fact that he referred to "our own government", confirmed his Anglophile sympathies. "What is to be done?"

"Well, maybe we should talk to Mr Lutov and find out exactly what he thinks we ought to do with his invention, Sam. Perhaps we could come up with some way of discovering who, exactly, is behind this whole thing? He has his suspicions, of course. He made that rather obvious on television, didn't he?"

"Well, let's get down to The Wellesley and have a chat with him and we had better make it snappy" he added looking at his watch.

"I won't come with you," said Hughes, "I've got to go to the physio." He pointed at his new leg.

"Okay Duncan. Thanks for the gen. I have a feeling that things are beginning to speed up a little."

Jack stood up and removed a phone from his jacket pocket. He scrolled down through the list of numbers and pressed the call key.

"Good evening Sister, Jack Wise here. I was wondering whether we could have a quick word with fifty-six. It is rather urgent. Could you check up for me. Thank you so much. Yes, I'll hang on." Jack had referred to Lutov by his security code, in case there was anybody eavesdropping on the conversation. "Yes, Sister. Very good. We'll be there in about half an hour. There will be four of us. Thanks for your help." He folded his phone and returned it to his pocket.

"I'll call a taxi," he said, as he walked to the door. He opened it and called Jock.

"It's on its way," he said, returning to his seat. Almost immediately the door opened again and Jock poked his head around it.

"Taxi's here, Mr Wise." he said.

They all left and climbed into the black cab waiting for them.

"So what are we going to talk to Lutov about, Jack?" Tarrant was kneading his knuckles, a nervous reaction to the pressure he felt as his world began to reveal its fragility in the face of the IDC scenario.

"Something occurred to me the other day when we were chatting, Margie." Sam looked across the taxi at the woman sitting opposite. "You said that you could clone almost anything with the aid of a computer programme you are working on for your enhancement project. I believe it's called 'Quantom' or something isn't it?" Margie nodded her head, not wishing to interrupt the flow. "Even chips can now be cloned, if I understood you correctly." Margie nodded again. "So, I was wondering if Lutov would be prepared to work with you to produce something to counter the Russian plan, if indeed there is a Russian plan."

"How would that work?"

"Well, let's discuss it with him first." Jack took his mobile and called The Wellesley to confirm that they were expected and they assured him that the patient was conscious and ready to speak to them.

Upon arrival at the clinic, Jack led the way to reception and presented the nurse behind the counter with his Home Office pass. She glanced briefly at his face to verify the likeness.

"You are here for fifty-six, Mr Wise?"

"That is correct, Sister. I believe we spoke earlier."

"Indeed we did, Mr Wise," she confirmed raising the phone to her ear.

"Mr Wise is here for fifty-six," she spoke into the receiver. "Yes, there are four altogether." She replaced the handset and looked up at Jack. "Security will be down with your passes right away, Mr Wise," she said returning to the paperwork she had been working on. Minutes later, a stocky man appeared. His hair was shaven and it appeared that the hospital stores did not have white coats for people as well muscled as the man from security. He had had to squeeze himself into the biggest one they had and it did not look comfortable.

"Hello Bob." Jack greeted him as he approached.

"Good evening Mr Wise" the newcomer replied, handing out visitors' passes. "If you would just sign in over here." He indicated a high counter, the other side of the reception area and each of them filled their details in the visitors' book.

The security man led the way to the elevators, which were large enough to accommodate stretcher trolleys and smelled of disinfectant. The lighting was obtrusively bright.

Patient Fifty-six was in a private room on the fourth floor. Another man in a white coat, of similar build to the security man, sat on a chair by the door. He rose to his feet as they approached and checked the visitors' passes before unlocking the door to allow them access to the top security patient.

Georg was sitting in a hospital bed, supported by a frame and pillows. The evidence of his encounter with the assassin's bullet was surprisingly modest. His hair had been shaved and the entry and exit wounds covered with small dressings. Otherwise, he looked in fairly normal shape. Margie had always thought that 'Gluto' was a good looking man, ever since she had seen his picture in 'Cheers!' magazine at the start of the Tarnbeck Experiment. To see him now, in a hospital bed, was somehow a bit of an anti-climax. The star quality that had been bestowed on him by his fans seemed to have been removed with clinical efficiency by the hospital staff. He looked almost vulnerable.

"Good evening, Mr Lutov." Jack introduced himself, "Jack Wise." He introduced the members of the company.

Georg Lutov seemed to relax. "Please." he said, "How can I help?"

"Well, maybe I should tell you a bit more about us first." Jack sat down on the only chair in the room.

"I am Jack Wise and I have connections fairly high up in the Civil Service here. This lady is Margie Stewart." He waved his hand towards her. "She is the wife of a friend who was badly hurt by the people we think were going after you. The reason why you are still here in The Wellesley is because you have, officially, died. In fact

247

your parents actually came to your cremation. Your sister Irina wept for hours but they were acting. They know that you are still alive. We told them." Jack allowed the ghost of a smile to play at the corners of his mouth.

"This is Sam Jackson, a computer guru and, finally, here is John Jason, a senior police officer. Each acknowledged the introduction with a small bow, as their turn came. "We have come to ask you for some advice. They noticed Lutov's eyes flick over to Jason's face at the mention of his profession but there was no fear, only interest.

"Margie's husband, Alex Stewart, also 'died' but he is now up and about on crutches. We have to keep him 'dead' because that is what the opposition thinks they have achieved. At the moment, it is much safer that he doesn't exist any more. Neither do you. Are you happy with that, until we can find out who is the perpetrator?"

"I am grateful for the protection, Mr Wise. Now what advice were you looking for?"

"Having seen you on television the other night, we find ourselves broadly in sympathy with your views. Our problem is that we do not know who is behind all these incidents. We would agree with you, there are strong indications that there is a Russian factor involved but what, precisely, are they trying to do? Then, of course, how can we counter the threat?" Jack indicated Margie with his hand.

"Margie here is a also computer expert whose speciality is enhancement. She is working on a programme that might interest you. Margie, why don't you tell Mr Lutov about this programme."

She turned to Georg Lutov. "I am actually involved in the design of this programme. We named it 'Quantom' and it has a host of applications that could be useful if ever one needed to tinker with a computer network. The programme is still under development so there are hidden applications which we have not, as yet, identified. We keep bumping into new ones. It is fascinating. The potential of the finished article will be immense. Everything, from computer-aided design in engineering, to cloning DNA and artificial intelligence. The problem which we have run into is that the programme itself requires a larger hard drive than is currently available on laptops or even mainframes, so we may have to wait for the next generation of computers before we can go commercial."

"This sounds very interesting indeed, Mrs Stewart." Enthusiasm lit up Lutov's face. "You say that cloning is just one of the programme's capabilities?"

"Oh yes, that is one of its primary functions to enable it to generate artificial intelligence. But you can use it for any application that you wish. Basically it works by synchrophasing the frequencies of individual cells to receptors in the programme where they are analysed and re-transmitted to a matrix. There the cell is reproduced as a precise clone of the target cell. Since the technique is based on cell frequency analysis, you can apply it to any frequency you wish."

"That is fascinating, Mrs Stewart. Would this apply to an identity card, for example?"

"Oh yes." Margie nodded eagerly. "As long as you have the matrix cards, the programme will clone from the original onto the matrix. No problem."

"... and a chip? Could your programme clone a chip?"

"Absolutely." Margie was enthusiastic. "You give me the raw materials and I will clone anything electronic you want.

"Then why don't we make identical clones of one of the Arches' IDCs? If we manufactured enough of them, we could drown the system and cause a meltdown." Georg Lutov's brain capacity showed no signs of having been reduced by the bullet.

"What about the pulse sensitivity of the verification chip?"

"Well we could set up a black market in IDCs, which would give a team of chosen, unregistered people access to the IDC facilities. They would have identical verification chips implanted. They could shop in Spenders Supermarket using Credits added by the accounts machine. The machine would not know that the cards were clones, so it would think that it was dealing with a single card, when, in fact it was dealing with dozens." Gluto very soon devised a method of adapting an Accounts Machine. By cheating the system, it could add salary credits to a certain specific IDCs and, since they were all identical, each would be credited with identical sums. The bar code readers would deduct the appropriate Credits from the card and the Credit Authority would be none the wiser. That is, until the Spenders management noticed that their account was not being credited for the goods sold. Then the fun would start!

"How soon could we give this a try?" Jack glanced from Lutov to Margie.

"How soon could you give me one of the cards and a verification chip and the matrices? I could do the cloning in minutes."

"My father could probably do something. He still goes to the factory twice a week and he is still involved with developments of the IDC, particularly on the security side. He might be able to get us the originals and some blanks. The problem is that the cards are only made at our facility. They are not made to standard credit card specifications. The GPS transceiver with its battery, makes the cards thicker, for a start. Then the solar re-charger adds more girth to it. All these features are manufactured under stringent security, at our facility. Can you contact my father?"

"Yes," said Jason, "I could probably get him on a secure line, via Interpol. How far is he from a police station?"

Lutov squeezed his eyes shut, in concentration. "It is down by the river, about one kilometre away from his house. It's about a fifteen minute walk."

"Do you know the name of the station?"

"I can get it from Father."

Jason handed Lutov his phone leaving him to dial the number and Jason took the call.

"Mr Lutov, Good evening. It's John Jason here. I was just wondering what the name of your nearest police station is. I have something for you and a friend will drop it at the there for you to collect."

"It is known as the Linden Creuz Precinct." The elder Lutov's voice sounded tired.

"Okay. Is there any way you could get yourself down there tomorrow morning at around nine o'clock, your time?"

"I will be there." The phone went dead.

Chapter 22

The following morning, Jason had a call placed on a secure line to Linden Creuz police station. The Polizeirat in charge was a certain Captain Horst Wenzel. He had heard of John Jason, although they had not spoken. The fact that he was using the secure line was confirmation of his identity. The plan Jason laid out was for old Igor Lutov to bring one of the IDCs and give it to him for onward shipment.

"But where do the police come into it, if I may ask, Deputy Commissioner?" Wenzel was interested because a similar experiment to Tarnbeck was about to be put in place in a small town called Saltzgitter, not far from Braunschweig.

"We just want to make sure that the system cannot be manipulated by criminals, Captain. I will keep you fully informed of any information which comes out of our research."

"You say that Mr Lutov will be here at nine o'clock. That is right now. Let me inform the charge officer. I will get back to you."

"Thank you Captain. I will wait for your call. I would need to speak to Mr Lutov on this secure line, if that would be at all possible."

"I will call you, immediately he arrives, Commissioner" said Wenzel and hung up.

It was only five minutes later that Igor Lutov walked in through the main entrance of the police station. The

Polizeihauptmeister on the desk looked up and recognised the old man.

"Good morning, Mr Lutov" he said. Old Igor was well known in Braunschweig, "The captain is expecting you. Let me show you the way."

They passed along a corridor lined with glass windows giving views of patrolmen and women, buried in paperwork which had become the bane of every modern policeman's life. At the far end there was an office door and the Polizeihauptmeister knocked.

"Ja, Komm." came a voice from the office. The captain stood up and shook Lutov's hand with a slight formal nod of the head, out of respect for this man who had been one of the first people to provide job opportunities in Braunschweig, after the war. "Mr Lutov, there is an Englischer police officer who wishes to speak with you on the secure telephone."

"I believe that you are referring to the Deputy Commissioner of the Metropolitan Police?"

"You are quite correct, Mr Lutov."

"I would be happy to speak to Mr Jason, Captain."

The captain looked up, "So you know the Deputy Commissioner?"

"Oh yes, I know John Jason, Captain. He was very helpful over Georg's death." This old man was full of surprises.

The captain dabbed in a number on the phone and waited, holding the phone to his ear. "Good morning, again,

Commissioner. I have Mr Lutov here with me." There was a pause and then the captain held the phone out.

"Good morning Mr Jason. How can I help you?"

"Good morning. Listen, we have a plan we wish to try out which requires the use of an IDC with a verification chip. Do you happen to have any blank ones available?"

"I have plenty at home. I need them for developing the security regime and keeping it up to date. How many do you need?"

"Well, as many as you can spare, Mr Lutov."

"Okay, Mr Jason. Would fifty be enough?"

"That would be great."

"And will you require the GPS transceiver and the Lithium Ion battery? I will put a card reader in with the blanks too. Oh, and you will need the kinetic charger, for the transceiver. It's very simple, you wear it on your belt like a mobile phone pouch. It charges the transceiver batteries and you can connect it to the main power supply too. It can handle 110 or 240 volt supplies."

"Mr Jason. How is he?"

"Georg is fine and sends you and your wife his love. You are a lucky man, Mr Lutov."

Igor Lutov handed the phone back to the captain. "I have to return home and then I will bring a parcel for delivery to Mr Jason. I believe that you know about this?"

"That is correct. I will ensure that the parcel is safely delivered."

The parcel, with true Teutonic efficiency, arrived on Jason's desk in New Scotland Yard less than twenty-four hours later. He called Jack Wise and suggested a meeting of the family at their usual haunt. Jack contacted Margie and Sam and they met at six with Jason arriving a little later.

"What are you having Margie?" The niceties were covered before Jack started.

"Okay, Margie, this is where you come in." Jack produced Igor's parcel from his old satchel and handed it to her. "There should be fifty of the new IDCs in there with the verification chips. I have contacted Sergeant Lusk, a police officer in Tarnbeck and he is sending me his own personal IDC. What I am asking you is whether you can clone his IDC on to one of the blank ones."

"Sure Johnnie, it is really easy to do. We've got the reader here so I simply have to download the details on to my hard drive and transfer those, through Quantom, on to the card. The clever part is breaking the PIN code number. That's where Quantom comes into its own."

Sam leaned forward, "I used algorithmic synchrophasing, to crack access codes, in my hacking days."

"They still use it on the Quantom programme." Margie smiled at Sam. "Your hacking days must have been more recent than you let on!"

Sam returned the smile enigmatically. In truth, his hacking days were not over. Jason unwrapped the parcel and removed the card reader.

"We'll have to get an adapter for that."

"Oh, I've got loads of adapters at home, Johnnie I'm sure I'll find one."

"Now how long will it take to do, say, ten clones?"

"It depends a little on how hard the code is, but once I've done the first, the others should come pretty easily. Being clones, the PINs will be all the same. I would imagine that I'll have them ready for you by lunchtime tomorrow. Then we will have to clone the verification chip. That will be a little tricky, because we have to do it without removing it from the wearer. The pulse sensor will deactivate the card if the pulse stops and the only way to re-activate it is to visit the CABNI which would rather give the game away, wouldn't it?"

"So we will need to get Sergeant Lusk down here then. I will get on to that right now." Jason got up and moved to the other side of the room. When he came back, he nodded, "Sergeant Lusk will be here tomorrow morning. He's coming down on the overnight."

"I may need to keep him for a short time to see whether the clone works with his verification chip. Then we need to talk to Georg about activating the new chips."

"Jack rose from his chair. "I'll go and have a chat with Georg about getting the chips activated. Then we should be in business to start stirring the dung with the enemy. At some stage, if we get him annoyed enough, he will show his hand. Then we must be ready to grab it and find out to whom it is attached. Let's reconvene tomorrow."

Jason went home via The Wellesley. He wanted to check that the verification cards could be activated without any input from the CABNI. If there was some kind of master plan behind the IDCs then the people at the CABNI could possibly be involved in one way or another so it was imperative that the planned introduction of the clones should be done without their knowledge.

At the hospital he presented his warrant card and was shown to a waiting room. Minutes later the same stocky man who had accompanied them before, led the way to No 56. There was a security guard on the door again and he scanned Jason's warrant card before opening the door. Georg Lutov was sitting in a chair, reading. He looked up as Jason came in and attempted to stand.

"No, no, please don't get up!" Jason waved him to sit down, "My apologies for interrupting your evening but I just wanted a moment to ask about the activation of the IDCs. Your father has sent us a batch of blanks and we are going to try and clone them. The only problem is activating them once they are cloned."
"It's not a problem!" said the patient. "When you peel off the covering of the verification chip, that activates it and it will adopt the first pulse it receives after that. If that pulse ceases, it will deactivate the chip and the card will not function."

"Excellent. I would like to run our plan by you to see whether you think would work."

258

Jason launched into the intended plan to confuse the IDC system, by swamping it with clones. Georg Lutov listened intently and then pointed out some of the pitfalls.

"It sounds feasible but the Credit Authority would be able to introduce further codes to the system to exclude the clones. This could be done by calling in all the cards and comparing the details with the central database. Each card could be fed with extra coding in order to exclude the clones at which point, cloned cards would cease to operate. The cloned cardholders would then be identified and the CABNI would take punitive action against them. If the Russians are involved, I would not like to be a 'cloney'." He smiled and pointed to the hole in his head. "The other problem would be that, while the system was down, nobody could function normally which could prove fatal for some of the older generation who rely on the IDCs for their food and health needs."

"How can we discover whether it's the Russians? It seems they hold all the cards and, the way things are going, capitalism will be finished."

"That does appear to be the case." Georg fingered the dressing on his forehead. "You know about Hertford North End, of course? Hartford is not the only city in the US to have adopted the IDCs. We have been swamped by demand from the US where the system is being seen as the answer to a multitude of social problems. I hardly need emphasise that, if the world goes over to the system, if someone wants to take control they will, effectively, be running the world's economy."

The significance of Lutov's words hit Jason like a chill wind blasting open a window. Suddenly the plan was becoming clear. The numbing violence of the events of

259

recent weeks, the attacks on the fabric of society, the rising death toll with its intimidation of the general public, damaged their faith in the democratic institutions. This all fell into place with a plan to discredit the democratic infrastructure of the country. It also made sense that it was part of a global master plan. The possibilities were incalculable and, for that reason, all the more alarming. Jason sat for a moment, while the full weight of Lutov's words sank in. Becoming a Deputy Commissioner did not depend on family background or political connections. Deputy Commissioners were normally where the buck stopped unless the Commissioner himself had invited it to continue further up the ladder. This meant that the Deputies were chosen from a hardened cadre of people who were familiar with both sides of the story. Drawing on his wide experience and battle-enhanced lateral vision, Jason was ideally placed to appreciate the problem and look for the wider picture. There was a plus side to the gloom-filled news. With each attack, the enemy was becoming more clearly defined and, as its character appeared, the weaknesses would begin to show. Jason was well practiced in the art of finding cracks in human armour.

"So, perhaps we are looking at an attack on the capitalist system as a whole. Maybe this is much simpler than we all thought." Jason studied the floor, as though its aseptic polyurethane surface might reveal the true secret behind the events that were plunging the whole system into chaos. Maybe 'they' are trying to destabilise the so-called 'Free World' with a view to installing some new system in its place. But how could they possibly benefit from its collapse? Even China has admitted that their economy cannot survive without a strong capitalist market to buy their goods. What new system could there possibly be? Democracy and capitalism are so ingrained in the psyche of the free world. It has taken centuries of war and injustice to work out how to run human society and decide what kind of behaviour is acceptable and what is not. We still get it wrong. You cannot just throw the millennia of development out of the window and start with a clean sheet."

"You can, if the Free World demands it." Lutov raised a finger to emphasise his point. "There are many recognised techniques to convince them. Speaking as a half-Russian I can quote 'Intimidation' as one of them. Speaking as a half-German, I can confirm that this is a valid method by which to impose a system on a submissive people. Speaking from a hospital in a country to which I owe so much, including my life, I can see that intimidation has had little success in the UK."

"So, what are you saying, Georg?" The use of Lutov's first name had slipped out unexpectedly and apparently unnoticed. Jason had unwittingly adopted the young Lutov as a colleague.

"What I am suggesting is that whoever is behind this master plan has studied the British mentality and worked out that coercion doesn't work too well. As in a marriage, you must make the partner want, no, even demand the changes you wish to make. This is the brilliance of the IDC concept. The benefits are so patently obvious and the pitfalls so cleverly disguised. Previously I was enormously proud of the IDC system. Tarnbeck and the resulting adulation of the media made my head swell to bursting. Then along came a .22 bullet and lanced the bubble before it burst of its own accord. Amazing how there is something good in even the worst situations. How do you say in English? 'Every cloud has a silver lining?'"

Jason sat contemplating the polyurethane floor, then looked up. This young man had a stoical sense of humour that the bullet had failed to extinguish. He was grateful for Lutov's clarity of mind. The bullet that had so nearly killed him, had focussed his already impressive mind on the problem. His experience in the field of identification technology was unrivalled. It was almost as though he had been predestined to survive and Jason was well aware of how lucky they had been to be able to recruit this young man to their team.

"Georg, I want to thank you for this conversation. You have straightened out a lot of things in my mind. At last we have something to go on. We know there is an enemy. Now we have to put a face to him."

"Well you could do worse than to start with the Russian Embassy." Lutov was smiling. "Cultural Attaches are notoriously adept at multi-tasking. Ask the SVR!"

Jason rose to his feet and reached out his hand.

"I had better be getting along" he said. "I'll be back to pick your brains again very shortly. Thanks again for stirring up mine. Keep working on it!"

They shook hands and Jason went out through the same strict security. His name was checked off on a computer and the lady on the desk wished him a good evening. He found the level and efficiency of the system impressive. There was a sense of keenness about the staff that implied they were not just doing it for the salary. These people were actually trying to prevent the entry of undesirables and protect the integrity of the establishment. He wondered idly why he did not come across this kind of attitude in his daily life. Surely the police force should be at least as security conscious as a medical facility. There was a courteous rigorousness about the staff at The Wellesley was not apparent in the run-of-the-mill police station. Was it the pay? No, Police pay was almost respectable nowadays. Was it the workload? Yes, thought Jason, the ridiculous and ever-increasing mountains of paperwork were stifling the innovation expected of the normal 'bobby'. The bureaucrats now spent their working days off-loading administrative responsibilities on to the men and women who should be out meeting people in the street. The work of policemen had now been wrapped in a mask of paper, designed to hide the shortcomings of civil servants justifying their salaries.

The staff at The Wellesley had a different work ethic. Most had served together in the armed forces where they had been in a few scrapes. They trusted each other and were members of a family who knew their jobs better than most and how to get it done. First and foremost, they ran their own show. If something went wrong, the solution lay with them and they were proud of their record. Being 'up at The Wellesley' was something they didn't exactly boast about. In fact, to a large extent, they kept their jobs quiet but they had that 4confidence about them which spoke volumes for the quality of their leadership. Jason made a mental note that he would make every effort to try and nurture the same spirit in his environment. There were a lot of good people in the Met. There were some rotten apples too and it was more difficult to weed them out. If you didn't fit in with The Wellesley bunch, you didn't last and that was it. The civil service was more of a cradle-to-grave set up, where incompetence was often rewarded with promotion to a level which required that particular type of ineptitude.

Jason decided to take the Number 28 bus back to Notting Hill Gate and walk through Holland Park, to his apartment. There were not many passengers at this time of the evening. The rush hour had petered out and those making their way to the fleshpots of the West End were travelling in the opposite direction.

Jason had always appreciated a pretty girl and there was one sitting at the back of his bus. She had just managed to jump aboard before the doors closed. She was petite and very young. Her blonde hair was trimmed attractively into a point at the nape of her neck.

Chapter 23

The first indication that made Ludmilla sense her time was nearly up, came to her as she prepared for what was scheduled to be her last assignment before her transfer to the States.

Jason was scratching the surface and, with typical Metropolitan Police persistence, he was beginning to become a nuisance. It was time for his retirement; his permanent retirement. The girl was given the job, a last chance to redeem herself. Her commitment had shown signs of flagging of late. She had missed the man Wise, a simple shot, as with the Lutov boy. She had flatly turned down the mission to kill the black man. She said that disposing of him would raise questions in the United Nations and she didn't want anything to do with that. It was almost as though she was telling the bosses what she would and would not do. No-one did that with the SVR, not even the bosses.

She checked with her handler at the embassy through the normal drop-off point, which lay between pages 62 and 63 of a reference book, in the National Gallery library. It was a book on early pre-Raphaelite egg tempera paintings written in 1903 by Sir Claude Daneforth-Everard. The last time it had been taken out was on the 23rd of August, 1904, so the chances of the drop ever being discovered were slim. The reply came the following day. Her American assignment was cancelled. The news was followed by the strange near-death experience she encountered on the far side of Trafalgar Square, just after she had left the Gallery. As she waited to cross the road to Whitehall, two large men appeared on either side of her, one carrying a furled umbrella. A double-decker tourist bus was approaching from the direction of the Cenotaph.

A split second before it reached them, the umbrella slid between the girl's ankles and she felt herself propelled forward, as if by a surge in the crowd. She tripped as the umbrella locked her feet and she tumbled into the path of the oncoming bus. Had she not been so alert to potential threat, she would certainly have been crushed, but a sixth sense caused her to roll between the screeching tyres as the monster shuddered to a halt right above the young girl. For a pregnant moment, the scene was wreathed in blue smoke and the stench of scorched rubber.

There was pandemonium as the shocked crowd rushed to help and the two men, after showing initial concern, followed police instructions to make way for the emergency services, melting away into the crowd of ghoulish onlookers. They both glanced back as they left. The observers' heads were shaking in disbelief as it appeared that no-one expected there to be a survivor. A job well done thought the two Belarusians who would soon collect their reward from a grateful Mother Russia.

By the time Ludmilla crawled out from under the bus with a just graze on her forehead, they were gone. Despite her protestations, it looked to the police as though this was just another of the dozens of incidents involving tourists looking in the wrong direction. After a friendly check over by a female police constable, which included an inquiry as to whether she required further medical attention, she went on her way. This suited Ludmilla perfectly, since she knew exactly what had been the intentions of the two men and, with this knowledge, came the certainty that her life expectancy was now severely limited. When the SVR no longer required your services, their gratitude was normally expressed by a discreet death warrant. The sentence, as in this case, was frequently carried out concurrently with the delivery of that warrant. She needed protection and fast.

The tentacles of the SVR were everywhere, as she knew from experience. She had administered the poison delivered by those tentacles too often not to appreciate their all-pervading presence.

One of the benefits of her knowledge was that, during the past few days, she had been shadowing the movements of several people who were players on the opposing team to her masters. The evening before, she had maintained close surveillance on Jason. He had become the next target on the list and the girl had been tasked to be his executioner. To fulfill the requirements of the SVR, she had to complete the task on time, to the minute. If she failed, there were plenty of other volunteers to undertake the job for that kind of money. Failure was not a word in the SVR vocabulary and, when it was, the consequences were normally fatal. The girl had now missed the opportunity to terminate the D/Comm for the second time. To miss once was forgivable. To miss twice could be terminal.

When he left the clinic and caught the number 28 bus, so did she, choosing a seat at the back. It was after he had disembarked at Notting Hill Gate, that she approached him.
Another asset attributable to her wealth of experience in covert intelligence was that it was easily saleable, if she could convince the buyers of its value.

"Excuse me, sir." The girl's timid voice elicited an almost paternal reaction from the D/Comm. He turned and looked down at her.

"Yes, Miss. How can I help you?"

"Are you Mr Jason?" The girl's question surprised him. Very few people recognised him when he was in civvies and he liked it that way.

"And who might 'Mr Jason' be, when he's at home?"

"He is a Deputy Commissioner of the Metropolitan Police Service and I need to speak to him urgently. It is a matter of great importance and I may not have much time left to speak to him."

"Do you know where Mr Jason lives?" the D/Comm was playing hard to get.

"He lives in a penthouse apartment at number 138, Holland Park."

"You had better come with me, young lady." He pushed her in front of him, in an instinctively protective manner, a hangover from his years spent in the close protection of high profile clients. Something was familiar about this girl; something vaguely not good. His memory suddenly cleared, jolted by the sight of her hair that seemed to grow naturally into a point at the nape of her neck. This feature shone out at him from a computer enhancement picture by Alex's wife, Margie. This was the girl who had left her passport behind at Norwich Hospital. This was the girl who may have been driving the car that hit Alex. Already she had proved that she knew too much about him. He would have to tread extremely carefully until he reached the apartment and his personal handgun. The D/Comm put a call through to the apartment's concierge on his mobile and the door opened as they approached it. "Thanks Jimmy, said Jason, as they scuttled into the foyer and the door closed solidly behind them.

"Keep an eye out for disciples." said Jason. "This little lady may have been followed."

"Will do, sir." He held out the card to Jason's apartment and he and the girl entered the lift. Jason inserted the card into a reader on the wall of the lift and pressed the 'door close' button. The doors closed silently and the floor pressed into the soles of their feet. The ascent was rapid and within seconds, the doors swept open and Jason led the way down a short corridor to a heavy-looking green door. He swiped the card and entered a PIN number. The door opened and he ushered the girl inside.

The apartment was luxurious, in a homely kind of way. The hall was more like a wide corridor, with English watercolours on the walls, welcoming the visitor to rural views with open skies and distant, nostalgic countryside. An antique table, half way down the left-hand wall, provided a flat surface for the mail and any other objects which could not find a home. The atmosphere was pleasantly disorganized and provided a constant challenge for the long-term female companion who had replaced his wife, who had died in childbirth almost two years previously.

"Now, come along in." the policeman shepherded the young Russian through into the large and comfortable living area. The wallpaper was interwoven with a soft lime green pattern of foliage and from the picture rail hung portraits of men and women who bore a striking family resemblance to the present owner of the flat. The small dining room contained an elegant round table that could comfortably accommodate six diners. The dining chairs of graceful English design surrounded the table with the master armchair at the end by the sideboard. Hanging on the wall behind this was a large oil painting of a handsome woman of dark complexion who looked out at the world with confidence and humour. Ludmilla studied the portrait.

"There she is" said Jason, "my better half." He looked at the picture with deep warmth. "Warda. That's Arabic for 'Rose'. Her dad was Jordanian and her Mum was Scottish. Quite a mixture." His hand rose and his fingers rubbed the stubble on his chin. "She took the best bits from both backgrounds." He looked down at the Russian girl. "Strange how God always takes the good ones first." He turned away and busied himself with plumping up the cushions and lighting the gas flames in the open fire. "Now, first of all, what can I get you, before we settle down?"

"Do you have coffee?"

"Indeed I do." Jason replied and went through to the kitchen. The sound of a coffee mill briefly broke the silence and very soon the smell of fresh coffee pervaded the room. Ludmilla was confused. Being served fresh-ground coffee by a senior police officer, who had been, until minutes previously, her target for assassination, was not something she could have expected in her country. Her own people more commonly handed out death warrants, as she had so recently experienced.

"Now, Miss ... er ...?"

"Ludmilla... Ludmilla Romanova Scharanski" the girl replied, using her correct name for the first time in many years. 'Romanova' had remained a dark secret all through the years of her induction into the Soviet Communist fold. Had they had run across that name, she would have joined the bodies of her royal relations in the cellars of Ekaterinburg. It was an indication of the conviction with which she was now changing direction, that she felt comfortable revealing the long guarded secret to this British police officer.

"So, Miss Scharanski, why do you want to see John Jason so urgently?"

"I have come to inform you that I have killed some of your operatives."
Jason initially wondered if he had heard correctly. "You say 'killed', did I hear correctly?"

"That is correct."

He felt like an amateur. This was not the way murder investigations were meant to kick off. The interviews were supposed to grind along until the perpetrator was finally crushed into submission, reluctantly admitting guilt and, with any luck, a conviction would follow. Eventually the exhausted parties in the drama would go their separate ways, before the next impossible case reared its ugly head. To have a story opened up by a beautiful little waif, without any preamble was, frankly, a bit of an anti-climax. Jason had a strange feeling that he was going to wake up to find the pretty little girl gone in a whiff of perfumed smoke.

"So who did you kill?" Disbelief was obvious in his eyes

"Mr Melvyn Strand, Jean Pierre Baccarat, Frederick Paul Barnes, Nikolai Sergei Petrov, Alex Selwyn Stewart. Do you want me to go on?"

Jason looked into the young green eyes, his brows furrowed in disbelief. "Are you bullshitting me?" The petite little head with its smooth blonde hair slowly turned from side to side and Jason suddenly caught a glimpse of fear, buried deep in those green eyes. "You killed them?" the head bowed, as though in pain, then rose again. Their eyes made contact and the head nodded slowly. "Why? Why are you telling me, all this?"

"My time is up. They will dispose of me. They tried today. I ended up under a bus" she touched the scrape on her forehead, "but I was okay."

"Who are 'they'?"

"The Sluzhba Vneshney Razvedki."

"The SVR are after you? Do you work for them?"

"I have been working for them, until today. Now they need to finish me off."

Jason sat down opposite the girl. The most bizarre thoughts were rattling around his head. Half of them were full of concern for this young person who was afraid for her life; so afraid was she that she was prepared to admit to cold-blooded murder, and not just one murder, but many. The rest were surging with excitement at the prospect of untangling the mystery of who was behind the string of recent disasters and deaths. He had not, as yet, admitted his identity to the girl and he could not be sure that she was telling the truth, whether it be about her name or the nefarious activities in which she had been involved. It was just possible that she had been planted to give the other side access to the hub of Western intelligence and counter-terrorism planning. One good thing about the girl's revelations was that she seemed unaware of the survival of Alex Stewart. So, at least that stratagem appeared to have worked, so far.

"Why did you do it?" Jason was having problems getting his head around this pretty, innocent-looking girl, planning and then committing, in cold blood, such heinous crimes.

"We are at war. The Soviet Union and Russian communism were defeated by the combined efforts of two people: Ronald Reagan and Margaret Thatcher. They took the capitalist system to war against Russia. They suffocated the Russian economy. They convinced the world that market forces should rule the world. They were ruthless in the implementation of this philosophy. In many ways, Russian technology led the West by years but Thatcher and Reagan never allowed the world to appreciate that. They relentlessly forced the non-communist world to buy products made in what they termed 'the Free World' and all the smaller countries fell for that subterfuge. Capitalism destroyed communism in just as devious and underhand a way as Nazism would have killed democracy if Mother Russia had not sacrificed millions of her sons and daughters to rescue it. And look at the thanks we got! Nothing but the destruction of a way of life which assured a livelihood for the survivors. My killings are acts of war. I am behaving just as you would have done, if you had had the opportunity to rid the world of Hitler or Goering or Goebbels."

Jason sat and scratched his head. This was an extraordinary thread, which could lead them into the maze.

"So who put you on to John Jason?"

Clearly she was not fooled by his pretence. "You are my target. Don't you see?" she pointed a finger. "I failed twice with you" she swept her hair away from her eyes, as she bowed her head. "That is why I am no longer useful to them."

273

"So do you still have to kill me? More coffee?" He had just let slip his identity.

"Yes please. That was so good!"

"What? You want to kill me, or you want more coffee?"

"Coffee first please."

"Oh, like Monsieur Baccarat?" Jason was familiar with the Baccarat file and the fact that coffee was being prepared at the time of his death. He looked into the Russian girl's eyes with a humourless smile. Ludmilla had been expecting handcuffs and a prison cell, closely followed by a 'friendly' interrogation, drugs and oblivion. 'Oh, she sadly died of an overdose. We tried everything but we lost her on the way to the hospital' would be the official line. But she was still here.

The doorbell shrilled and Jason grabbed his remote as he strode away down the corridor.

"It's ECHO-INDIA" came a metallic voice from the set.

"Send her up, Jimmy."

Minutes later, there was the sound of a card being swiped and the door suddenly swung open.

"Hi! Bunty. Come in. I have a small, no fuck it, A BIG problem right here in the flat. Get in here and I will explain."

Bunty walked in and parked her umbrella with the collection of others, in the old naval 8-inch shell case by the front door. She was a large, handsome woman who had served in the Royal Corps of Signals. She had worked with Johnnie when he was doing his time with the Military and had become great friends with his late wife. When she died, Bunty took a shattered Johnnie Jason under her wing and was, to a large extent, the reason for his meteoric ascent in the police force. Her relationship with him was now platonic but, a few years back, she could definitely have considered an alternative arrangement.

"So who is she?"

"Yes, precisely. Come and meet her. This is the most extraordinary thing that has ever happened to me, Bunty. She is tasked to kill me."

Bunty's eyes widened. "Oh, I see. Are you armed?"

"Yes I am, but I have a feeling I won't need it."

"Well, I'm glad to hear it, Johnnie." She laid a hand on his arm in a theatrical gesture of confidentiality. "Now, do you want me here, or are you still working out the funeral arrangements?"

"No Bunty! Come and meet her. She looks like a chick who could do with some company. Come along in."

They walked into the sitting room. At first, Bunty missed the crumpled little form of the girl, bowed down on the floor. At first glance, she thought that something terrible had happened and that the girl had decided enough was enough. Then she saw the small shoulders begin to quake and a long, soft moan escaped from the crumpled Parka. Bunty's maternal instincts took over and, before Jason could grab her, she dropped to the carpet and hugged the weeping Russian. She turned to look up at Jason and found herself staring into the business end of a short-nosed .38 special, a revolver favoured by the police in the United States.

"Bunty!" Jason shouted. "Get away from her! Get away from her now! She is here to kill me!"
Bunty withdrew from the cringing form and stood up.

"Silly of me," she murmured and the blonde head of the girl appeared from the folds of the Parka. Her eyes were blood-shot and fresh tears flowed down her cheeks. She wiped her eyes with the back of her hand and the weeping continued, the soft moans punctuated by sobs and a kind of retching in surrender to despair.

"Please kill me!" she croaked. "I cannot go on! It is you or them. Finish it now. Please finish it now! I have had enough killing!"

Bunty and Jason looked down at the pathetic little, quaking heap of broken humanity. "Ludmilla," Jason's aim never wavered "are you armed?"

"Yes" came the querulous reply.

"I want you to disarm yourself, now."

The girl unwrapped herself slowly from the floor, followed every inch of the way by the 38 Special. She removed a small emergency signal flare from a concealed pocket of her jacket, two pre-packed syringes and a strange looking knife in a slim scabbard. The blade of the knife that was revealed had a sharpened loop at its tip. "Is for cutting safety harnesses." She pointed at the blade, "But works well on the jugular." Bunty froze. This girl was serious.

276

"So, now? What do we do with you? Are you still on your mission? Or... "

The internal phone rang and Jason directed Bunty to answer it.

"Got a couple of 'Hankies" said the concierge. 'Hankies' were the surveillance team's colloquialism for 'Sniffers'.

The Met was good at looking after their officers under threat and Jason was frequently one of those. Sniffers, in this particular case, are not interested in their next fix. They are an opposition surveillance team.

"Where are they, Jimmy?" Jason had grabbed the phone.

"They are just coming in off Holland Park Avenue. It's two male Caucasians: big guys with a couple of disciples in tow."

"Are the rat catchers aware?" He referred to the team of surveillance officers who were on twenty-four hour call for just such an occasion.

"They are in place. They've just exited the underground station and are proceeding via Holland Park Mews to your location. They are ready for you."

"OK, thanks Jimmy. I am leaving right now. I will see you downstairs."

Bunty grasped the sleeve of Jason's jacket. "Do be careful, Johnnie. It would be such a pity to get chopped by strangers when you just made friends with your assassin, wouldn't it?"

"Bunty, this is terribly important. I have to find out whether these boys are coming for me, or for Ludmilla. We'll put her in the cellar and you hold the fort."

The 'cellar' was, in fact, the shaft of an old, hand propelled dumbwaiter, which had once brought meals up from the kitchens, in the days before the house had been divided into apartments. Camouflaged behind an old Dutch dresser, full of crockery, the original hatch was cleverly concealed behind a couple of boxes of Chilean Gato Negro wine.

"I am going for a pee in the park. If they are after me, then we will be one Deputy Commissioner short. If they are going for Ludmilla, we will know they suspect No 138 Holland Park of harbouring her. Then our boys will have a direct access to the maze, leading to the mastermind."

Bunty reached out. "Don't be silly, will you, Johnnie. I've got nobody else to look after."
Jason threw on a greatcoat and was just leaving when Ludmilla rushed over and whispered "Thank God I didn't kill you!"

"You get into the cellar," he said. "Get in there quickly," he pointed to the shaft. "If everything goes according to plan, I won't be long. Either way, we are soon going to know who we are up against. Now hurry, and keep absolutely silent when you are in there. My wish for you to survive has an ulterior motive, over and above my humanitarian instincts." He smiled and patted the girl's shoulder. "Now go... Go quickly!" Jason turned, twisted both the locking knobs on the door simultaneously, swung it open and left. He entered the elevator, swiped his card and descended to the lobby.

"How are the hankies, Jimmy?"

"Right here, Mr Jason" he was looking into a monitor, one of four behind the concierge's desk.

"There they are." He pressed a key on his keyboard, "and here are the disciples." He pointed at the men following the two thugs on a neighbouring screen. "The Catchers have them visual. Good luck, Mr Jason."

"Thanks Jimmy. See you in a bit."

The doorman pressed a pair of keys on his computer screen and a buzzer sounded by the main front entrance. Jason pulled the heavy door open and went out into the night. There was a thin mist clinging around the streetlights and drips of condensation fell from the bare branches of the trees forming an avenue down the road. A hint of coal smoke perfumed the cold night air. He was glad of the old Trilby hat he had grabbed as he left the apartment. The cold was raw and the damp seemed to penetrate the threads of his tweed coat.

Not a soul was to be seen on the street. Jason turned left out of the apartment block and trudged down the pavement, the toes of his suede shoes soaking up water from the damp pavement. He reached Abbotsbury Road and turned left, as if to go to the park. He pulled in close to the wrought iron fence and hid himself in the shadows. Tugging down the brim of his hat to hide his face from the light, he crept back to the corner. He kept low, allowing his outline to be broken by the heavy fencing. He watched as the two strangers, checking carefully in both directions, crossed the road and approached the entrance of Number 138.

"The hankies are with you, Jimmy" he murmured into the microphone which doubled as a Rotary Club lapel pin "and the disciples are just entering Holland Park from Pembridge Villas."

"Very good, Mr Jason."

"Are the catchers on stage?"

"They are, all two of them."

"OK, Jimmy. We'll wait until we find out what the hankies are planning then we'll swing into action."

"Very good, sir." Jimmy keyed the door opener on his computer. "They are coming in right now." As the two large men entered, the totally unexpected exploded onto the quietness of the street. The front entrance of the apartment block burst open and the two 'hankies' barrelled out into the street to join their two disciples just as a black cab pulled up in front of the building. The four men yanked open the doors and jumped aboard, slamming them closed as the cab sped away trailing clouds of exhaust in its wake. The sound of its retreating tyres receded to merge with the traffic on Holland Park Avenue.

The cab's number, Q308 RYF, was engraved in the policeman's memory. That was one thing that Jason had not lost from his Hendon training.

The flicker of flames reflected off the windowpanes of the main entrance of No 138. Jason ran for all he was worth. Flames were now licking up under the doors. He shouted into his microphone. There was no answer from the concierge. The door was locked with access denied by the unconscious form of Jimmy lying on the floor, halfway between the front desk and the entrance. Smoke was billowing up towards the stairwell. He had obviously been aware that there was a threat and had managed to get the fire doors closed before he was attacked. Jason produced the 38 Special and tried the glass panel above the door handle. It was reinforced and the weight of the snub nose of the revolver's barrel couldn't break it. Jason took aim and pulled the trigger. The handgun barked and the pane splintered. Using the barrel to clear the shards of glass, he reached in and released the locking mechanism. The door eased inwards and Jason barged through grabbing Jimmy by the shoulders of his jacket and hauling him outside. There was blood on the side of his head. The roar of the fire spoke of more than simple kindling. This fire was set to consume the building and if they could not control it, apart from its other residents, they would lose one who was crucial to the identification and detention of the arsonists

"Control: Mobile Three!" Jason was shouting in spite of his own strict instructions on radio discipline.

"Fire service, Ambulance and back up, Pembridge Mansions, immediate. I say again Immediate! suspected serious arson attack."

"Roger, Three. On our way."

"Also, code red on Q308 RYF, black cab."

Even Jason was impressed by the speed of the reaction. It seemed that only seconds had elapsed before he heard the distant sirens approaching from Old Court Place in Kensington. Smoke was now billowing from the heat-shattered windows on the ground floor.

Jason was on his mobile. "Listen carefully, Bunty. Arsonists have set fire to our building. The Fire service is here and so far the fire is confined to the ground floor. I want you to take Ludmilla down to the third floor and use the Lyles' fire escape. This is important because whoever did this probably did it to flush out Ludmilla and they will, in all likelihood, be marking ours. Am I making sense so far?"

"You are, Johnnie. I will get on with it. See you below. What's our RV?"

"Let's meet up at Verbanella's."

"See you there, Johnnie. Look after yourself!"

"That's good coming from you! I am still in the frying pan. You are just about to jump into the fire! Let me get on to the Lyles quickly."

"Good evening, sir." It was the fire chief who had been directed to him by the rat catchers. "Any residents you know about?"

"Yes chief but they are evacuating as we speak. Just give me a second" and he went back to his phone.

"Hello Belinda, Johnnie here."

"Yes Johnnie. What on earth is going on? Is this another drill? We only had one last Thursday. This new man really is taking things a bit far, don't you think?"

"Well, as a matter of fact, Bins, he has very likely saved your life. The fire is so far contained in the ground floor but you had better get out, just in case. Bunty is coming

282

down to you because she has a problem with our fire escape."

He omitted to mention the fact that 'the problem' was possibly carrying a high-powered sniper's rifle. That would only make her anxious.

"Okay Johnnie. I'll wait for her... Oh, here she is already. We'll see you later."

"Thanks Bins. I am meeting Bunty up at Verbanella's. You are very welcome to join us, if you have time."

"Very kind of you, Johnnie but I had better stick around."

"Right you are. I will catch you later. Many thanks again."

He closed his telephone as he entered Holland Park Avenue and started up the hill towards Notting Hill Gate. The streetlights were brighter on this main thoroughfare but they did not take the rawness out of the night. Jason's stomach lurched in apprehension as each black cab passed. Near the top of the hill where the buildings huddled closer to the road, a discreet sign projecting from above a recessed doorway, announced the availability of top quality Italian cuisine. Jason glanced behind him and went in. Verbanella's lived up to its reputation for great value and friendly service. His phone buzzed as he pushed the door open and he put it to his ear as he returned to the street. "Jason here."

"Two' requests you contact. Cab was found, safe and sound, with contents."

"Excellent, thanks."

This was the best bit of news they had received in a week. Jason plugged a small earpiece into his ear and spoke into the Rotary pin. Calls from the small transmitter in his top pocket were encrypted and secure. 'Two' was the code used by Jack Wise when he was wearing his policeman's hat. "Hello Jack." said Jason.

"Hello Johnnie. We have detained four Belarusians and they are held at 'X-ray'." This was Vauxhall Cross, the headquarters of MI5. "They are claiming diplomatic immunity. We contacted their consular section and they have no records of any missing persons tonight. They claim that the people we have our hands on are not among the Belarusian diplomatic mission but may be seeking refuge in British courts for a crime which carries the death sentence in their own country. The thing which makes me most suspicious is that the Russians have already put out a press release, disclaiming responsibility for the attack on 138 Holland Park. It seems that we are getting closer to the entrance to the maze. Should we have a meeting? I can call the family?"

"Go for it, Jack. I have one or two loose ends to tie up here, including my assassin. Shall I bring her along? She is very pretty! I have to wait for her though as she and Bunty climbed out of the frying pan, through the fire and should be joining me shortly."

Chapter 24

Jock welcomed Jack Wise as he threw off his Tweed coat.

"Do you have any of that 'Fleur du Cap' left, Jock?"

"I do indeed, Mr Wise." he smiled. "I turned a blind eye when Food & Beverage tried to cancel the order." He tapped the eye patch, over his missing eye.

"Jock, you are a star! And you can tell Betty that I said so!"

"I'm so sorry, Mr Wise but Betty passed away these twenty-two months back. Did I not tell you?"
Jack grabbed the little Scotsman and bowed his head. "How could I have been so thoughtless, Jock!" he gasped. "I am so sorry!"

"You have other things on your mind, Mr Wise. You will be in the Library, I presume?"

"Is Johnnie there?"

"Indeed he is."

"Thanks so much, Jock. I'm so sorry about Betty."

Jack Wise passed through the Drawing Room Bar on his way to the Library. Major Frank Dawlish was sitting by the bar and nodded as he made eye contact with the large ex-Regimental Sergeant Major.

"Anything for us, Jack?"

"Come and join us Frank. There is fun on the horizon. Is Mac with you?"

Jack was referring to RSM 'Mac' Macawley who had been intimately linked with some previous 'Family outings' and was a close confidant of the Major's. They were both involved with an extremely discreet military unit known as Special Operations Task Force or 'The Softies', a well-deserved antonym for their true nature.

"Mac should be landing just now. He's been away for this big summit in The Hague. I am actually waiting for him. He has never missed a free Aberlour!"

"Come and join us. We could use your input."

He followed in Jack's wake to the other bar where there was quite a gathering around the low coffee table by the fire. Margie Stewart, Alex's wife had brought along the cloned IDCs.

Jack ushered Frank into the group. "We all know each other don't we?" Sam stood up and offered his hand to Frank. "I don't believe we've met." The deep gravel of the Caribbean voice resonated from the bloom of grey African hair. "Samuel Jackson. I am usually known as 'Sam'."

Frank grasped the proffered hand NS reminded him that they had met briefly before. "I was looking after the Mews when you were there. A great pleasure to meet you properly Sam." The smile was warm and genuine. "You have a lot of friends, where I come from. One of them should be joining us any minute. He knows you too, although I don't believe you ever met." The two of them sat down.

"So, children," Jack took the floor, standing opposite the fire, "let me bring you up to date." All eyes focused on him. "Johnnie Jason's apartment block has just been the

286

subject of an arson attack. The rescue services are still at the scene but, as far as we are aware, the fire was contained on the ground floor. The only casualty reported is the concierge, who received what appears to be a bullet wound to the head. He is currently receiving treatment at a clinic where his condition is described as 'stable'. He is conscious and has made a verbal report of the incident to Special Branch officers who accompanied him to the clinic. He is expected to make a full recovery. Any questions, so far?"

Frank Dawlish raised his hand. "Do we know who the perpetrators were?"

"Yes, I think we do. They left the scene in a black cab and Jason got the number. They were pulled over by a police car in Earls Court. There was a confrontation involving some drunken rugby fans who were initially hostile to the officers but when the suspects in the black cab produced evidence that they were armed the fans weighed in with the police to disarm them. The teams were - Police officers – 2, rugby fans – 9 versus Belarusians - 4. The Belarusians lost as the fearless and inebriated opposition laid into them, wresting the guns from their hands. One police officer had to be taken for treatment and the other nearly drowned when one of the fans vomited an estimated four litres of lager over him. Nothing that a good hot shower won't sort out! At this stage, the cavalry arrived and carted the suspects away."

"So, we have four Belarusians, and...?"

"The taxi driver left the scene. We have the number plates he discarded during the fracas. They are on their way to forensics, as I speak."

"So, where do we go from here then, Jack?"

"I'll leave that up to Johnnie, Frank. He should be here at any moment and he told me that he could be bringing with him a secret weapon' which he reckons could open up some very interesting avenues."

The door of the Library Bar was pushed open tentatively and Mac's head poked round it.

"Come along in, Mac. Sit yourself down."

"Major Dawlish will bring you up to speed on events so far Mac, suffice it to say, we may be needing your particular expertise in the near future."

Jack's words were more prophetic than he would probably have liked. As Mac took his seat, the door opened again but this time abruptly. Jock entered and signaled for Jack Wise to join him.

"Excuse me, Mr Wise", he said, with quiet urgency, "Mr Jason would like a word." Jack stood up and strode briskly to the door. "He's in the Pantry, sir."

The Pantry was a room behind the bar where light snacks were prepared and the washing up done. It was spotlessly clean and well-ordered; evidence of Jock's meticulous attention to detail. The D/Comm was standing behind the door as Jack walked in with a broad smile on his face.

"We are going to have to stop meeting like this, Johnnie. Bad for the lads' morale you know!" Jason was not smiling. He looked extremely tense, almost distracted.

"The bastards got my driver!"

"Who are you referring to, Johnnie?" It was the first time that Jack had noticed the figure of a petite blonde girl, hiding behind the D/Comm, as though he were protecting her. "... and who have we here?"

"This is Ludmilla Scharanski, Jack, the secret weapon I was telling you about. The trouble is that she's not secret any more. The sniffers are on to her. They must have followed us from Verbanella's."

"And what about your driver, Johnnie? Is he okay?"

"Yes, He got one in the upper arm and kept driving. He's a good lad, PC Dutton." Jack had never detected fear in the eyes of his friend before even though they had been through some life-threatening situations together. Both had experienced fright and shock but had always controlled their expressions instantly as a result of training and lateral thinking, both of which are essential for people involved in this kind of business.

"These guys mean business, Jack." Johnnie looked into his friend's eyes, as though looking for help. Jason had run out of ideas.

"Did you spot any sniffers when you came in through the front entrance?"

"We were running, Jack! No time!"

"Okay, Johnnie, all is not lost. We have a couple of people here who may be able to turn this whole thing around. You know Frank Dawlish and Mac Macawley?"

"The Softies? Yes, of course I am."

"Well they are waiting to see you in the Library. May I suggest you get Jock to close the front door to strangers and get back-up while we work out a cunning plan?"

"What about the secret weapon?"

"Ludmilla," Jason looked down into the surprisingly powerful gaze of the young girl, "are you with us or are you with them? I have to point out that you are considerably more valuable to us than you are to them. They want to kill you and we don't. We really do want to keep you alive."

"I must be with you in order to stay alive, but the war continues. I consider that the people who are trying to kill me are traitors to the cause of releasing humanity from the crime of capitalism as taught by Marx and Engels

"Right! So are you trying to kill me any more?" The D/Comm smiled at his erstwhile assassin.

"You were my target. I failed. You have helped me when I came to you for help. You have now saved my life again but my life is nothing, when compared to my beliefs."

"OK, can I trust you not to kill me while we try and catch your traitors?"

The girl looked up at him, with the hint of a smile creasing the corners of her young green eyes. "You have saved my life so I will not take yours, unless we both have to sacrifice ourselves in the war to save the human race."

"Just a thought, Ludmilla," Jack put a finger to his lips, "Romanova? Any connections?"

"My great-great-aunt was a daughter of your Queen Victoria. Yes, I am a Romanov."

"Wow!" Jack's eyes widened and his large jaw dropped. "So if we save you, maybe we will be beneficiaries of the Romanov billions! I'm just joking, Ludmilla. I am beginning to like you already. At least you haven't tried to assassinate me yet. That must be a plus?"

Ludmilla became quiet as her head bowed in confusion. She really didn't understand all the jocularity and why they seemed to kind to her.

"OK, Children, let's get on with it then. Ludmilla, I suggest that you stay here, under Jock's protection. He's only got one eye but the other has twenty twenty vision."

Jack strode out of the pantry. He noticed that the bar was empty which was a bit unusual at this time of on a Friday evening. There were one or two regulars chatting at the tables but no-one was at the bar. Then Jack noticed that patrons were being turned away at the door. Jock was there, full of apologies. The bar had been hired for a reception and he was 'so sorry but due to security...'

The crowd outside grew dramatically as the minutes ticked by and soon there were paparazzi present, whose lenses were not always trained on the entrance of the pub. Other photographers hastened to the scene as the news spread through the media. They were there to capture pictures of the Deputy Commissioner leaving a pub with Margie, the wife of a public hero who had been killed in a hit-and-run incident. Would she find solace in the arms of a police officer of the force that had failed her husband? This was good stuff! Maybe if Hi Society got in on the kick, there would be megacolumns to sell about the first tryst, a

291

romance between the young, widowed mother and the recently bereaved D/Comm? There were bucks to be had here!

The crowd began to press around the entrance. A police van arrived and officers deployed quickly, forming a human cordon around the entrance. It was all quite friendly. Many of the photographers were familiar to the officers. "Come on Harry! Get your shots and bugger off! Let me get back to my missus!"

Most of the media players were enjoying the game, as were the cops, but Mac, observing the scene through a night-vision monocular from an upstairs window of the pub, spotted some anomalies among the media-hungry crowd. Certain photographers appeared to be capturing the scene on their telephones. There were four of them who Mac spotted immediately. Another two 'disciples' with hearing aids stood in the darkness near the taxis that had drawn up with the prospect of new fares.

"Right, Mac, what we do is this situation. Do you have any pyrotechnics with you?" Frank grabbed the ex-RSM's arm.

"I have a flare gun and a knife given to me by the D/Comm when we picked him up earlier."

"Right," Frank smacked his knee. "Bomb scare!" He said as he wiped his hand over his face to conceal the smile. "We've got the bastards." He pointed at Mac. "You're just going home, at the request of the cops, a regular being asked to leave because of a security alert, okay? Wave to the crowd and play embarrassed as you leave the door. Then you sneak away into the darkness, armed with your firework? Are you with me?"

"I'm with you, sir."

"Drop the banger into the litter bin out behind the taxis, followed by some burning paper. Meanwhile, the boys in blue will spread alarm about a bomb scare. The naughty boys will guess that it is a ruse but will not be able to leave the scene for fear of losing Ludmilla. Everyone else will evacuate, however, leaving the bad boys in a bit of a quandary. We will round them up and cart them off for a spot of friendly Q and A. How does that sound?"

Jock had just reappeared, anxious to know the plan. "If I may make a suggestion, sir?" Jack threw out his hand, theatrically, towards Jock. "And a word from our barman."

"Forgive me, sir, but I overheard some of your conversations and I just wanted to mention that 'greeners' are here, in a moment or two, to collect the empties. Do you not have anything you need to dispose of? I can have a word with the refuse boys."

"Jock you are amazing! Do they do Hamilton Terrace?"

"No problem, there, sir. I will pick up anything you want 'disposed of' at the depot and deliver her, sorry 'it', to No 289."

"So, Ludmilla, are you happy with that?"

"I am a prisoner of the capitalists. How can I argue?"

"Well, the accommodation at Hamilton Terrace is about three star and you won't die of starvation. You are now a member of the 'family', whether you like it or not, so, don't kill me yet!."

Ludmilla was having a problem to hate these new people. She had no friends but they were, at least, trying to keep her alive. She nodded her head.

"Right, then. Action! Mac, off you go and make as much noise as you can with that banger."

Mac stood up, feeling in the pocket of his coat, to confirm that the incendiary was still in place before leaving. The crowd outside craned their necks as he emerged.

"What's up, Mister? Who's throwing a party? Anybody we know? Come on, Gov, let us in on the secret!"

Mac smiled and waved cheerily to the crowd.

"The boss just asked me to leave, for reasons of security," he said, "whatever that means". Maybe they've got a bomb scare or something." He shrugged his shoulders and hauled on his overcoat as he passed through them.

The bomb scare murmured its way back and, when a police officer announced that they had a security alert, most of the hacks withdrew to a safe distance as a cordon was extended around the entrance. The four sniffers and their two disciples appeared confused and reluctant to follow police instructions. They were suspicious and knew there was a subterfuge in progress. Suddenly a muffled explosion on the other side of the square sent everybody ducking and running for cover. That is, with the exception of the sniffers. They knew Ludmilla was within their grasp and they did not want to lose her. Not only would that cause them a lot of embarrassment, it would probably cost them their lives. They had to stay and watch out for her escape as their lives depended on it. So, as the cordon tape was unwrapped around them, they were easy to pick out allowing three of the four, under the guidance of Mac, to be arrested. The fourth high-tailed it into the crowd.

The greeners' disposal truck entered the mews at the rear of Aunties and reversed up to the tradesman's entrance. There was a crescendo of engine noise and the groaning of heavy metal as the crusher compressed the garbage in the machine's churning interior. No casual observer would have noticed the small girl who was hurried into the lorry's cab, before it left the mews and went on round the square, to perform the same rubbish collection service at the Farendon Hotel. By the time they reached the depot, Mac and Jock were waiting for them. Jock had arranged for Mac to be admitted to the yard to pick up Ludmilla who lay on the floor in the back of his Ford Focus, as it swept out of the gate.

Mac frequently checked his rear-view mirror for suspicious vehicles showing an unwelcome interest in their progress but, by the time they left Warwick Avenue, none had caught his eye. They entered Hamilton Terrace and dropped down into the steep entrance to No 289. The garage door lifted as they approached and closed immediately they had entered. Surveillance cameras kept a vigilant watch for strangers during the well-practiced manoeuvre.

Ludmilla was delivered into the hands of a woman police inspector who briefed her, in Russian, on the facilities available to her. She was shown to a surprisingly comfortable, even attractive, living-cum-bed room. The only indication that it was not for use by a normal guest, were the bars on the windows and the multiple locks on the door. There was even a copy of yesterday's Pravda newspaper, on the coffee table. Ludmilla, for the first time in many weeks, felt safe and able to relax. She sat on the bed and then lay back, surrendering herself to deep and dreamless sleep.

The four sniffers and their one disciple were not so lucky. Interrogation techniques vary widely in the world of intelligence gathering but, generally speaking in Britain, physical violence is discouraged, particularly if it is by the detainee. In which case, various forms of restraint and discouragement are available.

Lamber Priory hides its secular activities behind an ecclesiastical exterior. The retired Colonel and his wife who live there appear to have a heavy business and social calendar and there is a constant stream of visitors attending courses and other functions run at the Priory. What is not so obvious is that most of the visitors have close connections with Vauxhall Cross or GCHQ at Cheltenham. Some of them are not there of their own free will, the four sniffers and their one disciple from outside Aunties, plus the two and their two disciples in the black cab were a case in point. Their accommodation, when compared to that of the young Russian girl, was bare. It was designed to support life and prevent death. The term 'padded cell' had faded into history as an outdated mode of containment for the violently mentally disturbed but they survived and even thrived, in the cellars of Lamber Priory. The 'Aunties five' would join the Belarusians in experiencing a return to the bygone days of old-fashioned interrogation in these facilities.

Although physical violence was avoided as much as possible, psychological abuse was not. The use of sleep deprivation, humiliation, disorientation and fear were all employed to maximum effect. Upon arrival, the new inmates were stripped naked and subjected to an intimate body search carried out by female medical personnel as an

296

introduction to the humiliation programme. No toilet facilities were provided in the cells so bodily functions were carried out on the floor, for all to see. This, elicited angry comments from both fellow inmates and staff and the miscreant was further humiliated by having to clean up after himself using a bowl of water, an empty bucket and his bare hands, in that way which increased the degradation.

Lights were turned on and off at irregular intervals and meals served on no particular schedule. This, together with the administration of ice-cold water jettisoned from a bucket, prevented the new arrivals from sleeping, leading to unbearable fatigue and severe disorientation. Alarm bells were rung randomly and the prisoners taken, undressed, to be questioned by a fully clothed board of interrogators. Implied death penalties hung, like swords of Damocles, over their heads. Execution of the death sentence could be carried out without warning at any time, they were told, so the inmate never knew whether he would return to his cell. The degradation led to anger and the loss of self-respect and the inability to resolve the situation led to feelings of despair and guilt. Jealousy reared its ugly head when one of the prisoners was allowed to don underpants and given a cigarette to smoke on his return from an interview. He was treated with deference by the escorting guards, creating suspicions that bubbled to the surface among his compatriots. What secrets had he revealed? Which of his companions had he betrayed? His denials were only to be expected.

Now things turned nasty. Fights broke out and were suppressed with a practiced and proficiently administered system of contained violence which inflicted maximum pain, with minimum visible damage. As a last resort, extremely high voltage combined with low amperage, electricity was used to control the combatants. One of the disciples exhibited an irritating tendency to use his teeth as weapons during these contrived confrontations. On the third occasion, he was extracted from the scene, anaesthetised and had all his teeth painlessly removed. His post-operative appearance was allowed to raise new terrors among his fellow inmates until he was fitted with a set of false teeth. The new teeth were comfortable, efficient and a considerable improvement on the originals but had the desired effect upon his fellow inmates. It seemed impossible for a prisoner to do anything right. When he performed a task demanded by the authorities, he was punished. The next person to be given the task, performed it half as well and was praised or even rewarded. There was no logical way to earn the warders' respect. Nothing made sense any more. Morale ceased to exist. Each suffered a complete breakdown of personal identity. No-one could be trusted. Conversations became stilted; silences prolonged, as the psychological poison ran its course.

Soon conversation ceased altogether and the keepers watched the moment arrive when the restorative process could begin. Some of the subjects would never fully recover. Their faith in themselves and their fellow human beings was irreparably damaged and could never be fully restored. For the rest of their lives they would remain reclusive, the fragile fabric of their egos permanently torn by the launderers who knew the art of draining the human psyche.

Chapter 25

By and large, most animals react well to good treatment from humans. A dog, which has suffered mind-chilling cruelty at the hands of a thoughtless owner, will reward a new owner's kindness with boundless affection and loyalty. Mammals are not the only genus in the animal world to react in this way. Birds, snakes, even fish, display signs of loyalty and it was upon this theory that the treatment of the Belarusians and their disciples was based. The interrogators sowed seeds of renewed trust in the fertile ground of the detainees' minds and assiduously cultivated them. Tiny concessions were made over several days. Gradually sleep patterns were restored. Twelve hours of light were followed by two hours of twilight, then eight hours of darkness and two hours of dawn. Toilet buckets and paper were introduced. Mealtimes were regularised. The ice-cold buckets of water became warmer until they were simply placed inside the door of the cell to be used for washing.

Constant reminders of the improvements were delivered. The mode of delivery was quite simple. The slightest deviation from regulations would incur the severest of responses. The victim would be subjected to withering reprimands for minor oversights and relegated to former conditions, with no explanation and no prospect of reprieve. He would be kept in this limbo until signs of serious mental regression made themselves evident, then he would gradually be restored to the conditions enjoyed by his colleagues. It was a delicate balancing act between rationality and insanity.

As conditions improved, tentative conversations began to be heard again. Pairs of detainees were tasked with small jobs around the estate. They were always accompanied by a warder, armed with a Taser electrical stun weapon as well as a firearm. There is nothing like working together under an oppressive regime, to build up camaraderie. Very soon, trust began to reappear and, with trust, came communication with the increasingly benevolent authorities. Maybe they weren't such bad guys after all.

It was less than two weeks after the imposition of the regime that all the internees were called to assemble upstairs in the conference room. There would be a meeting to discuss their future.

It was during this time that the young Ludmilla Romanova Scharanski requested diplomatic asylum. Her captors almost treated her as a respected prisoner of war and she had come to the conclusion that there was a better chance of survival with them than with her masters in Moscow. As far as they were concerned, she was surplus to requirements and, as with most garbage, she would be disposed of, preferably by incineration, in a crematorium. This would, indeed, have been the end result, had the tourist bus in Whitehall done its job. Because Ludmilla could carry no identification papers, a minute digital chip, implanted beneath a gold filling in a left upper molar, contained all her details. It was unlikely that even the most sophisticated surveillance equipment in the West would have spotted it before her body, defying identification, had been released for cremation.

She felt deeply betrayed by her masters. Not only had they cold-bloodedly attempted to take her life but, from what information she had gleaned while on operations, the reason for her missions had little to do with the triumph of communism over capitalism, and everything to do with the selfish jealousy and greed among the upper echelons of modern Russia's political hierarchy. She was disgusted that the socialist ideals, for which millions upon millions of her countrymen had sacrificed their lives, had been cast to the four winds in favour of a grasping oligarchy whose riches rivalled those of the old Czars, her antecedents. The stories of pogroms after the Great Patriotic War should have alerted the population to the coming nightmare but the Stalinist propaganda had been absorbed by an exhausted proletariat. Having survived the horrors of recent years, they had come to accept anything, rather than the continuous brutality. They had beaten an enemy who, for years, appeared invincible. They were heroes. Those who disappeared into the gulags and died in their millions, were portrayed as the traitors who needed to be cleansed from the Rodina. The rest would benefit from the wisdom of the Great Leader and the magnificent efforts of those who had sacrificed themselves.

She had lost her family in the revolution and followed 'the new way'. Marx and Engels had offered the world a new future and Ludmilla had grasped it with heart and soul. She was proud to be one of the 'ants' who were the core of the new order. She would play her part in saving the human race from the decadence into which the Western world had slipped; a decadence that would lead to the end of mankind.

After Lenin's brave experiment, the ordinary man in the street was no better off than he had been under the monarchy. 'It is disgusting!' they people would say 'These parasites have to be eradicated! They are more useless than termites. Termites do at least build themselves magnificent cities in which to live. Each termite lives for the public good. Each has its place in society with its specific duties and they fulfill those duties to the best of their ability. Fear of death does not limit their total commitment to the community. They are true communists.'

Ludmilla suddenly realized that she was talking aloud.

"What you forget, Ludmilla is that they all serve a queen." Frank's avuncular figure was hunched in an armchair opposite. "That's the only reason why they build that city in the first place. So, in fact, they are true monarchists, just like bees"

"What are you trying to tell me?"

"We also have our Queen to whom I owe my commission; not to the Prime Minister; not to the Defence Secretary; not to a Field Marshal in the army. My commission comes from Her Majesty. She signed it personally. I am her man."

Ludmilla, who herself came from royal blood, listened intently.

"I would agree with you that capitalism frequently hovers on the edge of criminality," Frank continued, "but then I would also say that communism, by its crushing of individuality and rule by fear, is immoral as well as criminal. Capitalism contains and controls greed. Communism rules by hunger alone."

"What are we going to do?" Ludmilla's dejected voice was almost a whisper. "Whichever way we go seems to end in disaster."

"If you look back through British history you will see that we have blundered from one disaster into another." Frank's eyes rolled upwards towards the ceiling, as if in despair. "The only thing we can do as ants in the capitalist system, is fight for the rights of the individual under a strong and wise rule of law. This does not guarantee success, of course. Look at us. How many of our greatest men lost their reputations and even their lives in defence of their beliefs. Some of our greatest people died violent deaths for their beliefs. Take Sir Walter Raleigh, knighted for his heroic discovery of major parts of the globe and a favourite of Queen Elizabeth the First. He lost his head when 'Good Queen Bess' saw him as a threat to her all-pervasive egotism. Look at Winston Churchill. You know about him?"

"The great British leader, who led the nation through the war?"

"The very man... and what reward did he get for his heroic leadership?"

"Peace and the respect of his nation."

"Well, you could say that. But how did the Great British public express their gratitude?"

"They bestowed on him honours appropriate to his magnificent efforts."

"Well, not exactly. In fact they threw him out of office." Ludmilla frowned. "But why?"

"Clement Attlee, the leader of the socialists in the coalition government during the War, was offering enormous benefits to the British people as a reward for their efforts against the Nazis. He delivered free national health, free education, a national pension scheme and help for those out of work. He offered the people who had suffered for more than five years under the threat of Nazism, a future. 'The sunlit uplands' were there for all to see. Churchill, by comparison, rested on the laurels of victory and lost the election. Can you imagine Stalin losing an election? However unpopular he was at the end of the war, the population was just too exhausted to stomach more violence and brutality. Much better just to keep your head down and do as you are told. Am I right?" Frank leaned forward, as though looking for the girl's advice. "What are your thoughts? Tell me."

Once again, Ludmilla was deeply confused. Here were her enemies, behaving like trusted friends. Was this a part of the Secret Service's brainwashing technique? Were all these disparate people; a Deputy Commissioner of Police, an army Major, an self-confessed member of the security elite, a young lady, the bereaved wife of one of her successful hits, and a black computer specialist from Trinidad... were they all part of the scheme? True, they presented a threat to her life but they did not seem to be hiding their identities. They had the motive to get rid of her, but they had actually expressed their determination to keep her alive. Her own people represented a bigger threat. It was like an affair. The ardour of her devotion to Communism had been terminated by what had happened. She could no longer place her faith in her fickle, previous lover. Maybe now was the time, with the bitter experience of the past under her young belt, to search for another.

"What do you want of me?" she said, fastening her green-eyed gaze on Frank's craggy features.

"You know who we are, almost better than my late wife did. You know that we are gathered together against a threat which, we feel, is aimed at our very survival, as a functioning society. Our problem is that we do not know

304

what the perceived enemy is aiming at. Is it individuals? Is it our people? Do you guys want to get rid of our way of life? What are your bosses looking for?"

"All I can say is that my targets have been concerned with the success of capitalism." She looked up.

"Go on." Frank nudged further forward.

"We will destabilise the capitalist system and replace it with another."

It was at that moment that the door burst open and a large mass of grey afro hair stopped the conversation.

"I've got it!" Sam shattered the quietness of the room as he grasped Ludmilla's slender white fingers in his dark skinned knuckles. "They want to take over the world!"

There was a stunned silence.

"Who does?" Frank frowned at the intrusion.

"The Russkies!"

"What are you talking about, Sam? How can they take over the world with a couple of assassinations?"

"It's the ID cards!"

"How do you propose to take over the world with IDCs? Slap people on the head with them? Chop them up finely and put them in their Muesli? How, Sam?" Jason looked at Sam with playful incredulity.

"Who invented these new, high-tech IDCs which are being used at Tarnbeck, Johnnie?"

"Well, I think it was old Igor Lutov, wasn't it?"

"And who financed the factory in Braunschweig?"

"According to Georg, it was the Ost Deutsche Bank in former East Germany. Am I correct?"

"Correct, Johnnie and who finances them?"

"According to Georg, it's the Russkies."

"That's also correct Johnnie. Don't you think it a bit strange that, immediately after his interview, he got shot by an assassin on the back of a motorbike?"

"Indeed I do but I still don't see any direct link between his assassination attempt and the Russkies."

There was a moment's pause as each considered the implications.

"It was I who shot Georg Lutov." Ludmilla's voice cut the conversation dead. The three of them sat looking aghast at each other. The girl was serious business.

"Oh, I see" said Jason slowly, closing his eyes and rubbing his fingers over his forehead. "You have been a busy girl, haven't you!" He suddenly realized the urgency of keeping Lutov's survival secret from his assassin. He turned to Sam. How was he going to get the message across at such close quarters, without letting the cat out of the bag? "When is his memorial service, Sam?"

"But, but I thought that..." Sam's voice trailed off as he saw the D/Comm's fierce glare. "Have they completed the autopsy report?" Jason's eyes closed momentarily, with relief.

"Yes that was all finished before the cremation. His parents came over for that but the memorial service is to be held in Braunschweig. I think it is tomorrow. Frank is sending Mac Macawley, to see if he recognises anybody."

Ludmilla was fully aware of the cremation and the attendance of Georg's parents. She had watched the broken-hearted couple following the cortege. As far as she was concerned, that was one of her professional successes.

"Listen, Ludmilla," Jason stood up, "as you will appreciate, we have to keep you under lock and key for a bit, not so much to stop you running away as to stop your previous masters from getting to you. As you have already seen, we are keen to keep you safe and on our side, so no nightmares please and if you need anything, just shout. The phone is there and you will be put in contact with any one of us if you need anything." He sat down again. "I have one favour to ask you."

"Tell me." She looked up, suspicious.

"We have a meeting this evening with the heavier members of your team. Their detention has been rigorous because they are violent men and they appear to have seen the error of their ways. We now wish to return them to their families with minimum embarrassment to us and to themselves. This is quite a difficult message to get through to them, considering the level of their intellect and their imprisonment. We need someone who can get our message to them in a language they will understand. We do have translators, obviously, but I am not sure that they could convey our good intentions as you could. Would you be prepared to do that for us?"

A look of fear jolted crossed Ludmilla's young face. "They will recognise me. If they are released, it would be certain death for me!"

"You will not be in the room, young lady. You will be behind a TV screen."

"But, my voice. They will know it is me."

"Don't worry. We have ways of disguising your voice. They will not even know if you are male or female. Amazing what they can do with digital sound these days." Jason smiled, fully aware of his own awe at the abilities of the geeks in the back rooms of Priory. "I think it is only fair to tell you that you will be monitored by our translators, so just bear that in mind."

"I will do it but I have one favour to ask in return."

"Go for it. I will tell you if we can accommodate you."

"In order to make these men fully aware of the danger which our people have put us in, I may have to... how do you say? Soliloquise?"

"Wow! Soliloquise? You even have me scratching my head!" he laughed, "But there's no problem there. It might be an idea if you just run through it first with the translator. She will be right there with you. Then if we don't like it, we'll tell you first and if you insist, we can always turn you off. But I suspect that that will probably not be necessary." Jason, as happens with so many policemen, felt a tie growing between himself and the criminal, even though she had been so close to costing him his life.

"I agree." Ludmilla was nodding her head enthusiastically. "Let us proceed."

There were three different conference rooms in Lamber Priory, two laid out in a single floor configuration with chairs arranged around a large 'I' shaped table. A display stand was positioned at one end for small demonstrations but the main purpose of the rooms was discussion, rather than lecture. The last was like a theatre, built into the old chapel of the former Priory, with tiers of seats, ranked up into the auditorium and arranged to give each visitor a clear view of the speaker and their presentation board. A podium with a lectern and a sophisticated panel that could control digital sound and visual aids for the lecturer's delivery had replaced the altar. The one common factor in each of the rooms was the extraordinarily high level of security. Closed circuit TV covered each and every seat from above and below making the passing of secret messages under the table impossible. Also, each seat had its own sound monitor that could listen to the breathing and even the heartbeat of each person attending the 'conference'. This was the venue chosen for the meeting of the nine Belarusians, who were, for the first time in two weeks, fully clothed. The clothing, though issued by the Quarter Master, was a considerable improvement on those in which the prisoners had been detained.

They were led, handcuffed, into the auditorium and seated apart from each other, separated by gaps wide enough to prevent any physical contact between them. Armed guards were positioned to give adequate crossfire in the event of a disturbance but that was a palpable impossibility, given the situation.

They were nervous sitting there, handcuffed and in unfamiliar clothing. The seats were the most comfortable things on which they had parked their backsides during the last two weeks. Was this a film show? Was this the announcement of their sentence? Would they leave this place for some remote, distant woodland, to be 'disappeared'? Would their families ever be compensated if that were the case? Most likely not. How do the British 'disappear' people? They were intimately familiar with the techniques employed in Russia. Despair was a common companion to each one of them. Even release was a desolate alternative. Two of them had been involved in the assassination of the young Russian girl. Neither realised that she had survived but the message was clear. Failure was not an option. Even this petite heroine of the SVR had passed her sell-by date and she had to be disposed of.

The lighting was excellent. Everybody had a clear view of the stage and each member of the audience. There were four chairs facing the inmates arranged on the platform. The tension mounted. Then four men entered the stage from the wings and took their seats. One was very tall and lean. He took one of the centre seats. Another was solidly built, no fat, all muscle, his face deeply lined, his head covered in greying gingery hair. He was obviously his own barber, ably assisted by an electric trimmer. The third was of similar build but with close-cropped grey hair and very little evidence of a neck. The last player to appear sported a massive cloud of grey afro hair. His skin was dark and wrinkled, like the bark of some ancient tropical tree. They took their seats and the tall, lean member of the cast took the stage. He approached the lectern and blew into the microphone. A soft explosion echoed round the hall from speakers mounted along the side walls. "Good morning Gentlemen. My name is Deputy Commissioner John Jason of the Metropolitan Police Service."

There was a moment's pause and then a deep voice came over the sound system, in a language full of rumbling vowels and guttural consonants. For this sound to have issued from the mouth of a petite blonde girl took Jason's breath away, as though he was momentarily shocked by a suspicion that the show had been stolen by the enemy. Then he remembered Ludmilla's fear of recognition and the amazing camouflage of the voice almost brought a smile to his face.

"You have been detained by Her Majesty's Government, partly to prevent you from committing further criminal acts and partly to protect you from the wrath of your masters." He paused and allowed the translation to rumble through the speakers. Some of the inmates looked curiously around the room, searching for the source of the translation. The CCTV cameras were virtually impossible to see, tiny pin-pricks in the joints of the wall panelling around the auditorium. Every sound each prisoner made was recorded by minute transceivers, cleverly concealed in the identity tags they wore on their right wrists.

"We do not want to keep you from your loved ones," the translation once again boomed out. "We wish to return you to your families as soon as we possibly can. That is our aim." Ludmilla once again fed the words into her microphone, listening almost with disbelief, as they came out in the accents of a roughneck oil worker from Siberia. Even she could scarcely contain the smile that teased the corners of her mouth. "Some of you may face your return to your homes with apprehension but we are determined

311

that you will not suffer at the hands of the people who have put you through this experience."

The widely separated audience looked at one another, but without the chance of communication, their expressions were their only link. Some were buried deep in thoughts been numbed by their recent ordeal. Others looked to their colleagues for a reaction.

"Our intention is to teach you how to survive after your release." This announcement focused all eyes on the speaker. "We have experience in how to do this and my colleagues are here to share this expertise. All of them have had to go through it at one time or another and all have survived." Jason smiled and introduced the other members of the team on the stage. "It is not easy! My friends here have looked death in the face, sometimes at the hands of your masters, but they survived and they are determined to give you their knowledge developed through years of hard experience."

Jason left the lectern and moved to the front of the stage, catching the eye of each member of his congregation. It was almost like an evangelical meeting. Jason was summoning the children to the fold. 'This is the way to go. Hallelujah! Follow us! We are the 'Saved'! We have the answer. It's going to be a rough road, but these Brothers here have already made it!' Mac, Sam and Jack were smiling enthusiastically. Jason almost imagined himself as a large black preacher in a Southern Baptist Church, stirring the happy clappers 'They have seen the promised land! They are living in it! Look at them! Are they sad? Are they afraid? NO! ... Join us!'

Ludmilla's deep tones penetrated each tired ear into the battered minds of these people who had lost all self-respect, all pride, all hope of a future.

"If you cannot take our offer, there will be no death sentence, there will be no physical or mental torture. You will simply stay here until we can work out what to do with you." There was silence, broken only by the soft jingle of handcuffs. "The food's quite good, too, isn't it?" Jason smiled as he looked from face to face. "So what do you want to do?"

A hand went up. It was one of the larger Belarusians. His voice did not echo round the chamber but was captured by his transceiver and beamed into the discreet head set in Jason's left ear. The translation followed, from Ludmilla. It was a clear "I want to join you."

"Okay, young man. You can go back to your quarters. Fred, can you do the honours?" Fred was an ex-Corporal in the Royal Marines who was very familiar with John Jason's history. He guided the young Belarusian out of the hall. "Anybody else?"

Four hands rose among the remaining prisoners and, after a brief conversation with the Siberian roughneck, they left under escort. As they left, the others raised their hands and were escorted out of the hall after their colleagues.

"Well, that's a start", said Jack, as he entered the sound room and sat next to Ludmilla. "How did it go?"

Ludmilla removed her headset and smiled. "Amazing!" she said. "I sounded like an old Siberian!"

"Well, luckily, you don't look like one!" Jack laughed out loud. "What do you think, Ludmilla?"

"These men will follow you, but they need training."

"That is what Mac and I intend to give them, Ludmilla." Frank tapped her on the shoulder. "We are off to Scotland for a bit of rambling and, when they come back, they will be as tough as Rolex watches and they will even be able to tell the time. Well, maybe that's a little optimistic. The instructors are mostly Jocks, but they will be able to talk Scots."

Chapter 26

The training course at Achnadhu was intense. English was the sole language used on the base. This reduced some of the Belarusians to the monastic silence they had exhibited towards the end of the Priory experience. The accommodation had none of the luxuries the Belarusians had experienced while they were in detention. Bivouacs take getting used to. Also, they were now wearing a uniform they had been trained to hate. But the food was great, if you could find some way of preparing it on a windswept mountainside far from anywhere with no fire, no phone, no roof over your head and it's raining. On top of that, you have to be at the Loch Arnich lodge, by 1200 Zulu on Thursday, otherwise you return to the Priory. Don't try and escape, by the way. 'We know where you are. We can see you when you go for a crap in the morning. Oh, and another thing. You have to take that with you as we've got dogs looking for you. Dogs love crap'.

"Okay, you two made it! What happened to the other eight? I thought you Belarusians were supposed to be tough. Your instructors have been waiting for you in the pub for the last hour and they went through exactly the same routine as you guys. Do you want to know how they did that? Let's go and find out."

To say that the first three days were an education would be a gross understatement. The physical demands made of these so-called 'hard' men from Belarus forced them to find reserves which most of them had been unaware of, until that point. Living continuously on the edge of their endurance, knocked out of them any residue of cockiness, which might have survived the course at the Priory. Frequently the prisoners had to swallow their pride and ask for help and advice from their companions and instructors. It was a very leveling experience.

Once the standard of fitness began to reach acceptable levels, English language began to creep into their conversation. First of all, shyly, then with self-conscious humour and, finally as an increasingly usable communication tool.

The training followed a strict format: Fitness, Survival, Self-defence Intelligence gathering, Offense, Escape & Evasion. The first three days combined fitness and survival. The previously hard-nosed hit men had been uncooperative on their introduction to Lamber Priory. The ruthless severity of the regime there knocked all ten men into involuntary cooperation. There was simply no option.

At Achnadhu, the initial training drained them physically before they began to learn the secrets of the trade, from low faecal discharge diets to self-help first aid for both trauma and sickness. They were taught about the dressing and treatment of wounds using the standard first-aid field kit, strong tea with sugar and salt for the treatment of diarrhoea and willow leaf tea for the treatment of pain. Long distance walking, known as 'tabbing', and the importance of rhythm, both in pacing, breathing and resting, increased their endurance and range. They were introduced to wild animals, fruit and plants which could be used safely to support self-sufficiency in diet. Simple, but effective fishing techniques, including the tickling of trout, expanded their horizons like nothing they had learned before. Having been dragged up in the back streets of Minsk or Vitsyebk, Homyel or Mahilyow, none of them had come across a course of this nature in their lives before. It was fascinating for them and they absorbed the information like dry sponges. The instructors at Achnadhu began to warm to their strange new charges. They were pleasantly surprised by the lack of complaint.

All the instructors were intimately familiar with close quarters combat and they all stressed the importance of avoiding it. Much better to defeat your opponent before he had a chance to react than to become involved in a contest which relied on familiarity with martial arts or sheer physical strength for a win. Surprise could disable the strongest combatant and the detainees to were introduced to various techniques for gaining the upper hand in that way. From there it was a natural progression to Offense, involving many of the same techniques.

It does not necessarily take an explosion to disable a city's power supply. Short circuits are powerful tools when it comes to overloading the grid. A strategic fire door, padlocked with a key now at the bottom of the river, can cause the deaths of hundreds. The surreptitious opening of seacocks can sink an entire battle fleet as it did the German Grand Fleet in Scapa Flow at the end of the First World War. With not a shot fired, the British eliminated a fleet of warships that had very nearly beaten them at the Battle of Jutland. A small group of men employing offensive techniques by subterfuge and sabotage can be more effective than an army, using bullets and bombs.

The Belarusians' thirst for knowledge increased their hunger for the language. It was truly amazing. Eight of the ten were conversing with each other in English by the end of the second week.

"They're not a bad bunch, these lads, Sarge. We could do with a few like that ourselves." The corporal had known and worked with Mac for many years and Mac respected the younger man's opinion.

"Well, you never know, Tom, we might even see some of them back here after they have done what they have to."

What they had to do was at that moment being discussed between Ludmilla and the Family at the safe house in Hamilton Terrace.

"So, Ludmilla, have you any idea what's behind the offensive you have been on?" Jack was standing behind Frank's chair. "Have you any idea whom we might contact, in order to find out?"

"All I know is that my controller's contact code was '1914'. All my instructions came through him. I do not know where he is based but I was instructed that, without that code, I was forbidden to accept any task."

"1914? Okay. Isn't that around the time they were planning the Communist revolution?" He shook his head "No, that can't be the clue. Anyway, the Russkies don't do crosswords like we Poms do. Johnnie, do we have access to a list of the accredited diplomatic staff at the Embassy?"

"Yes we do. The Foreign Office releases those names to us so we can provide security. Also, they have certain privileges accorded them in order to avoid diplomatic incidents. You wouldn't want the Ambassador's car to be clamped for parking illegally outside Borodin's, would you now!" This raised a murmur of laughter from the group.

"So, Johnnie, are any accredited members born in 1914? He must come from Georgia, if he's that old!" Another wave of laughter rippled through the group.

"Well, I'd have to ask." said Jason. "Give me a moment." He rose from his chair and moved over to the other side of the room. Producing a small radio from his jacket pocket he began to speak softly, into the Rotarians' badge pinned to his jacket lapel. Three minutes later he returned to the group.

"They don't have anyone over the age of sixty-two and that's the Ambassador himself."

Sam bowed his head, his eyes tight shut while he stirred the grey cloud with a finger. "This has to be easier than that!" he exclaimed, between clenched teeth. He kept scratching. "There's a code as old as the hills," he said, looking up "which I have used on occasion. 'Numbers for letters'. One... nine... one... four. 'One' equals 'A', 'Nine' equals 'I', 'One' equals 'A', 'Four' equals 'D'... 'AIAD'. Anybody in the Embassy with those initials?"

"I told you before, Sam, you are not just a pretty face." Frank grinned.

"Some people tell me I'm not even a pretty face!"

"Hang on a minute, guys, let me just check." Jason retreated to the far corner of the room again and produced his encrypted radio. Minutes later, he returned. "Anatole Andrev is the nearest they could find. Close enough?"

"What does he do?"

"He's in consular services? Unlikely. Controllers are usually on the Cultural desk, in my experience," and Jack Wise spoke from intimate experience.

Sam was still scratching the grey cloud. "How many letters in the alphabet?"

"Twenty-six, in the Latin alphabet. The cyrillic alphabet varies with where you are and which alphabet you are using." Ludmilla looked up at Sam and he put his thumb in the air.

"Thank you, Ludmilla. So, since you are Russian, why don't we start with cyrillic?" he raised a finger for attention. "In my very limited experience of the security world, I have found that name codes are almost always two letters, unless there are two names the same. Am I right?"

"I agree with that," said Jack and Jason nodded his head.

"So, if it's just the two letters, that gives us '19' and '14', what would the nineteenth letter in the Russian alphabet be, Ludmilla?"

Ludmilla counted off the letters on her fingers. "Er... 'C', which is, approximately, like your 'S'."

"And, the fourteenth letter?"

"That would be an 'M' "

"So, Johnnie, would you like to phone a friend?"

Jason stood up and retired to the other side of the room with his encrypted radio. "CM' you said, did you, Sam?"

"That's what the lady said, yes."

Jason spoke quietly into his Rotarians lapel pin. "No. Nobody with those initials at the Embassy."

"Okay, Ludmilla, let's try it backwards. You start with the last letter and count back nineteen letters. What do you get?"

Ludmilla smiled as she struggled with the inverted alphabet. "First you get 'H' and then 'T'."

"What about that Johnnie? 'H' and 'T." Jason once again addressed his lapel pin, then he shook his head. "No, that doesn't work either."

"Right you are then, let's try the Latin alphabet. Let's see. A, B, C. That looks like 'S' is the nineteenth letter and... er... 'N' is the fourteenth."

Jason retired to the corner to check the information. He smiled and raised a thumb in the air. "That's better. 'Sergei Novgorod' and, guess what, he's a Second Secretary on the Cultural desk. Very promising. So, Jack, what's the plan?"

"Well, speaking for myself, I would very much like to have a few words with Mr Novgorod. In fact, I think we all would. Do you agree, Ludmilla?"

"I do agree, very much. I wish to find out why they want to kill me."

"Well that seems to be as good a reason as any. What do you think, Frank. You're good at these things. Could you see any way that we might be able to contact Mr Novgorod?"

"Let us scratch our heads a little and see if we can't come up with something." he looked meaningfully at Sam.

Two days later a report appeared in the Wessex Argus, a local newspaper based in the small neat little town of Dorchester, not far from the south coast of Dorset. Locally, the paper was called the Wargus. According to the paper, Whychcombe, a large old farmhouse in the rolling hills near Puppispuddle, just to the north of the town, had come up for sale on the death of James Deverelle, the last in the line of an old Wessex family. Deverelle had studied Russian, obtaining a First in Russian and Political Science at Martyr's College, Oxford. During his time at there, the Argus reported, he had spent his holidays visiting members of the Russian 'diaspora', who had fled the country during the Communist revolution.

The new owners planned to modernise the house and, according to the article, this included the installation of central heating, a luxury spurned by the Deverelles. For this, the cellars had to be cleared to make room for the boilers and pipework. During the clearance, a hoard of Russian treasures had been found in a wooden chest, behind a brick wall in one of the vaults. There were thought to be some priceless icons amongst the artefacts.

The Wargus piece had attracted little attention in the national press but caught the eye of the Russian Cultural Attaché. On February 15th, the treasures were to be revealed to an invited selection of the general public at 'Brassroots', a small gallery, off the Edgware Road in London. The Russian Cultural Attaché was to be among the guests.

The timing of the event was carefully chosen to coincide with the opening of a meeting of European Union

Ministers of Culture, aimed at founding a Centre for the Study of the European Cultural Experience. This would be the first step on the road to creating a new and controversial European Ministry of Culture under whose aegis all national galleries and museums in the Union would be required to operate. Although they were not part of the Union, the Russians were considered to be a significant part of the European Cultural Experience and the Attaché felt he had to attend with a couple of his staff to take notes. This left his second in command, Sergei Novgorod, free to go to Brassroots for the exhibition of the Whychcombe treasure.

Brassroots was not only known for the quality of its exhibits but also for the fact that their cellars were devoted more to bottles than to bullion. An evening at Brassroots, although undeniably educational, was always entertaining. Novgorod was looking forward to the event with undisguised enthusiasm.

Billy, the owner of the gallery, was well known to the Family having served in the Islanders prior to entering the art world. His gallery had been pooh-poohed by the establishment for his insistence on figurative art. Not for him the dead baby seal in a bath of formalin. That was for the Hunterian Museum. Not for him the tyre-marks of a bicycle ridden by a chimpanzee, over an expensive piece of freshly primed canvas. That was chimpanzee art which should be exhibited at the zoo or, perhaps the Royal Academy, don't even think of looking in Brassroots. Billy did not accommodate such philistinism. He liked the way some inspired people, failing language, managed to express an atmosphere, an emotion, a smell, a noise, even speed, on a flat piece of canvas. He did not limit himself to two dimensions. He also loved the sculpture of the blind Swede, Carl Milles, who could create a small person, in awe of the future, standing in the protection of a massive hand of God, none of which Milles could see. He enjoyed going through customs, at Zurich Airport, wearing a 'Bangkok Special' costing US$50 (the salesman saw you coming) Rolex Sea Mariner on his wrist. The watch was patently fake but, in a way, it was a work of figurative art.

If the Swiss customs caught you, they placed your $50 replica on a steel plate and smashed it right in front of you with an impressive-looking 5 kilo hammer. However, he always kept the real one in his suitcase for these little japes. Billy was the man who was arranging the unveiling of the Whychcombe Hoard. He was asked by the Family to assemble the exhibits.

Frank was amazed by the collection of seemingly priceless riches available on the shelves of the 'Effects' departments of the two film studios. Everything was there, from medieval cooking equipment to extraordinary replicas of royal headgear and decorative orders, to appropriately well-worn furniture. There were shelves laden with glittering jewellery. Familiar impressionist paintings peered out from heavily gilded frames on the walls. Some had been damaged, with intricate care, to fulfil their parts in long gone films. It was mind-blowing! Frank could have spent a week feasting his eyes on this repository of counterfeit treasure. He remembered, as a child, searching hungrily at his mother's invitation, through the jewellery drawer in her dressing table. Wine-coloured, multi-faceted glass 'rubies' reflected candlelight almost as well as the real thing. The fact that it was all what his Mother called paste or 'dress' jewellery almost increased its value in his eyes. Russian icons had a shelf of their own at the studios. The curator of this collection was keen to introduce him to some of the rarer ones, which had caused, not just murders, but wars.

With Billy's guidance on the mobile, the collection was eventually made and Frank left Elstree with a brass-bound pirate's chest, full of the 'discoveries'. Billy, with the panache of an established gallery owner, assembled the displays.

Security was rather more obvious than was normal, in fact almost too obvious. The guests were checked, both electronically and physically, by a team of unsmiling actors from Vauxhall Cross, as they entered the quiet reverence of the gallery. Their uniforms were a clever imitation of the security officers in the classic Elstree production 'Bank on It!'

Among the 'actors' was a young intern at Vauxhall Cross who bore a striking resemblance to a certain Second Secretary on the cultural desk at the Russian Embassy. Within an hour of the opening of the exhibition, the two were wearing identical clothes including a gold hammer & sickle emblem on a chain around his neck. Novgorod also wore an Old Etonian tie with the stripes going the right way, ironically an expression of his life-time wish but also in honour of 'Sir' Anthony Blunt, who was Master of the Queen's Pictures as well as a very senior Soviet spy.

The Exhibition started in typical Billy style. There were no three-quarters-naked, purple-pubed celebrities, just a collection of boring suits, male and female, most of whom came from the security services, with a promise of free booze and the proviso that they would be ejected if they misbehaved. Programmes were handed out at the main entrance with the ubiquitous private view glass of wine.

Initially the reception was a restrained affair. The drab dress seemed to have a dampening influence on the party. Then three waiters appeared and started to distribute more drinks and canapés. Tongues began to loosen and conversations bubbled. People stooped to examine the displays. Hushed gasps of praise and wonder were heard as the spectators wandered between the exhibits. Novgorod headed for the icons. Even he had to admit that they were breathtaking. They were obviously valuable too, judging by the thickness of the glass protecting them. The intricacy of the feather-light applications of gold leaf, elaborately burnished into the designs with infinite care, was totally convincing. Not for one second did Novgorod suspect that he was being awed by forgeries.

Chairs were conveniently placed around the gallery and he chose the middle one of three to sit down with his glass. Almost immediately, he was joined on his left by a man, followed on his right by an attractive female in blue. Novgorod smiled at each of them before he collapsed into their surprisingly powerful embrace. With practiced ease, the two agents lifted their newly acquired guest and escorted him through the swing doors into the kitchen. The other Novgorod, known for operational purposes as 'Novgorod minor', took his place on the chair. So seamless had been the changeover that even those in on the operation failed to see it.

Novgorod minor continued to drink the white wine until it was time for him to make his exit. He made his farewells, including some well-lubricated expressions of praise for the icons, narrowly missing a lady who was returning from the washroom. He apologised profusely and noisily as he departed. The members of the press could not have missed it and Novgorod was not unknown to the gentlemen of the Press. He hailed a taxi and proceeded to Claudio's Nightclub in Soho, where he made a fool of himself by offering one of the bouncers the chance to arm wrestle him on the stage. The management was relieved when he left. They all knew Sergei Novgorod and diplomatic incidents were always an embarrassment in the nightclubs. He left, staggering down the street, and that was the last occasion that anybody recorded seeing the Second Secretary. The CCTVs lost contact with him as he entered Leicester Square. One moment he was waiting to cross the road, the next, he was gone.

The genuine Novgorod was quickly and anonymously transferred to No 289 Hamilton Terrace, where he was accommodated in a small room on the third floor. His disappearance was soon noticed by the Embassy's security staff and the Met immediately contacted and a strong protest lodged. The Second Secretary had to be found immediately. There was almost a note of panic in the demand.

Jason invited Vladimir Valenkev, Head of Security at the Embassy, to come for a briefing at New Scotland Yard. There he was introduced to the night manager of Claudio's, who confirmed that Novgorod had visited them. CCTV footage, darkened by the dim lighting prevalent in the club, showed the unmistakable image of the Second Secretary during his arm-wrestling challenge to the bouncer. Further coverage saw him proceed to Leicester Square and his subsequent disappearance. Witnesses all confirmed that Novgorod had left the Brassroots Gallery on his own, evidently having taken full advantage of the available liquid refreshment. The taxi driver was also contacted and confirmed that Novgorod had left the club 'three sheets to the wind'.

"You had no evidence that Novgorod intended to defect did you? Money problems?... women?... that sort of thing?" Jason looked at Valenkev searchingly, as though trying to lay his twelve years' running a serious police force at his disposal. Valenkev stood up abruptly and, thanking Jason briefly, he left.

Chapter 27

Scopolamine is not a recent addition to the arsenal of drugs available to the intelligence services. It has been around for many years. It has the effect of dissecting the sensory and motor systems of the brain from the intellect. Criminals have also been known to employ its unique properties. On one occasion, a female victim was approached in the street by someone, purportedly renewing a long-lost acquaintance. At the time, the handshake seemed innocent enough but it was, in fact, the method of administration of the drug. The victim was invited to drink coffee with the smartly dressed criminal and the coffee had been further spiked with the drug. Within minutes, she had lost control of her intellect. Her sensory and motor neurone systems continued to function normally and the lady was led to a cash machine by the robbers, where, she was instructed to present her credit card and handed over the maximum one thousand dollars she was permitted to withdraw. She was later discovered by a policeman, sitting on the ground by the cash machine, 'in a very confused state.' The money was never recovered and since the transaction had been carried out 'voluntarily', the bank was loath to reimburse the funds.

Novgorod's case was rather different. The drug was first given to him, mixed with his wine, at the gallery. By the time he came round from that, he was under the influence of a second dose of Scopolamine. Then he was introduced to little Ludmilla, who had ample motivation to drain the Secret Intelligence databank of the Novgorod brain.

It was all over within half an hour. A ransom note was delivered to the newsroom of the Evening Standard, demanding payment of $10,000,000 for the release of the

Second Secretary. The destination of the ransom money was a numbered account in the Cayman Islands. Failure to deliver would result in the return of the Second Secretary to the Embassy, piece by piece. The caller said that he represented the Lost Generations of the Rodina.

There was genuine panic, not so much at the Embassy, as by a Mr Boris Belnikov at the office of the President of the Commonwealth of Independent States.

"Ilyich, come. Come now!" The Prime Minister of Russia felt a ripple of fear wrench at his guts as the call blared on his intercom. He hurried through to Belnikov's cramped office.

"Ilyich, what happened to this Cultural Secretary in London? Get, Chernorgin."

The sinister rat-like figure of the head of the SVR materialised in the doorway. He did not say a word. He did not need to. There is no respect deeper than that generated by fear.

"What are we doing about this ransom note, Chernorgin?"

"The ransom will be paid, then the paper trail will start. We will remove this Lost Generation. They will cease to exist. Have no fear, Belnikov, the SVR does not fail."

What neither Chernorgin, Belnikov nor Ivan Ilyich had taken into account, was that the Lost Generations of the Rodina could not cease to exist, since it never existed in the first place. So it would be impossible to destroy. The transfer went through.

The CaribbBank was one of a number of small financial institutions that had been set up some years previously and registered in the Cayman Islands by the British Government, specifically to handle covert payments of illicit monies. The account into which the ransom was paid was listed in the bank's files, contained in a computer folder in an office in Cheltenham, England. The account was configured in such a way that the receipt of funds triggered an acknowledgment of the transfer back to the sender and automatically closed the account, putting the bank into liquidation. The bank, however, retained details of the sources of the ransom money in order that experts in GCHQ could identify who had made the transaction. News of the bank's demise was delayed for several days, in order to allay suspicion.

Sergei Novgorod were discovered by workers repairing a set of points on the underground track near Hampstead Station. He had been tightly bound with duct tape and, although deeply confused when released from his bondage, he was otherwise in good health. On his return to the Russian Embassy, his future ceased or at least it did as far as British records were concerned. After some wild speculation in the press and some behind-the-scenes prodding by the government, the story died quietly away.

Upon further research, the specialists in Cheltenham discovered that the ransom money had been paid by a bank based in former East Germany. Apparently from nowhere, this small nationalised institution had blossomed after re-unification, to the point where it became the major shareholder in Igor and Glacier Lutov's brainchild, the Arches Stationery Corporation. Anonymously, the bank belonged to two very senior politicians in Russia.

When the two Germanys combined and Ostmarks became Deutschmarks, one of the requirements laid down was that all previously parastatal companies in East Germany, valued at more than one million Deutschmarks, would have to register on the Frankfurt Stock Exchange in order to continue trading. Ost Deutsche Bank was one such establishment and arrangements were duly made to float its shares on the market.

The Northern Provident Mutual Alliance Bank, known as the NorProv, had started by making loans to destitute miners in the north of England after the PM, Margaret Thatcher, had put them out of work, according to popular perception. Its offices had previously been occupied by Tyne and Wear Shipbuilders, another major British industry which had fallen by the wayside, throttled by cheap competition from the Far East. The bank had a reputation for solid service to its investors. Their staff salary bills were higher than most modern banking institutions, because they liked personal contact with their clients. The Chief Executive, Donald Cullinan, referred to his account holders as 'Our Members'. This expressed his philosophy, which was that he was simply the guardian of the Society's wellbeing. Open an account with NorProv and you joined a family, with all the benefits, as well the responsibilities that it implied. Because of this close-knit relationship with the account holders, they had not suffered so badly from the debacle experienced by their speculative bigger brothers. They were one of the few smaller banks that did not collapse under the weight of the recession. Through entrepreneurial investment in local communities and with the advice and cooperation of their clients they had actually expanded and this drew them to the attention of Jack Wise.

"Hello Dick, it's Jack Wise here." Jack could never get used to the fact that his name popped up on Dick's phone, when he rang. "Listen, we have a golden opportunity which has risen over the horizon."

"What can you possibly have found in this morass of disaster, Jack? I am in the process of trying to sell off half of Bishop's Avenue, including my own property, before everybody jumps out of high windows!"

"Don't jump Dick! We have a cunning plan! Meet me at Aunties now. And I mean now. I am here."

"I'll be there in twenty, Jack."

"Make it ten, Dick. This opportunity is golden and you know how fickle the price of gold is!"

"On my way."

Dick Tarrant, having been one of the first people to spot the coming implosion of the financial world, felt almost guilty. He would normally have been skeptical about golden opportunities had they not come from the mouth of one of his most respected friends. He hurriedly took a seat by the fire in the Library Bar opposite his friend.

"Go for it, Jack, before I jump."

Jack then launched into the plan. It was machiavellian in its concept. "We will use the opposition's finances to beat them. The $10,000,000 paid to the... er... CaribbBank, for the release of Mr Sergei Novgorod, has become 'available', since the bank failed to find an organization called the Lost Generations of the Rodina, to make the payment. The bank is now in liquidation and the liquidators have asked us confidentially, whether we know of a good cause which might benefit from an injection of this sort of sum." He folded his arms and studied the floor as he rubbed his chin, searching for inspiration.

"Then I thought of an eminently deserving group of good hearted people who need a bit of a pat on the back for weathering the recession through simple, old-fashioned fiscal restraint and good manners." He looked up and Dick waited for the firework to pop. "You are familiar with the board of directors of the NorProv aren't you Dick?"

"I most certainly am, Jack. In fact my account with them is probably the thing that will pull me through, in the end. There are some very level heads living north of the Humber and I am grateful for the strength of their support. Good people, the NorProv lot."

"So I have heard, Dick." Jack raised his eyebrows and stared into Dick's eyes. "There is a little bank which surfaced from the rubble of East Germany after the Wall came down. They were promised that their Ostmarks would become Deutschmarks, if they were prepared to offer shares in the company to the general public, on the Frankfurt Stock Exchange. This they readily agreed to do." He paused, to make sure that Dick was still with him.

Dick nodded with enthusiasm.

"Go on Jack, Sounds interesting."

"Well, given that this windfall $10,000,000 has nowhere obvious to go, I thought we might 'appropriate' it. What do you think, Dick?"

"Do you have evidence of the source of the funds?"

"The source is a numbered account at Ost Deutsche Bank in Frankfurt an der Oder, in former East Germany. We have evidence to suggest that this bank has been used, on occasion to carry out transactions on behalf of the Russian Government."

"So, what's the plan then, Jack?"

"Well, I thought, knowing your connections with NorProv and with your agreement, of course, we might be able to persuade them to buy a controlling interest in Ost Deutsche Bank. Does that sound like a possibility, Dick?"

"Well, I'm not sure whether the board would be that interested in investing money in a run-down ex-East German bank, Jack, but I could always give it a try. What are the benefits of ownership?"

"They would replace the Russians as the financiers of the bank and they would therefore become the new owners of the Arches Stationery Group, the exclusive manufacturers of the IDCs."

"My God! So they would!"

"And it would not cost them a penny. Her generous Majesty's Government would cover the purchase of the shares from funds unwittingly supplied by the Russians themselves."

"Nice one, Jack! That is a peach, if it comes off."

"I cannot see why it shouldn't. I have even done a little bit of speculative investment myself. To, test the possibilities of course."

"You naughty boy Jack! Insider trading, eh?"

"I'll buy the next round, then, promise!"

"Okay, then, I will have a word with Don Cullinan. He's the present Chairman. Do you want me to explain the finer details to him, or would you prefer to keep those under wraps?"

"I don't know Cullinan personally. I always imagine him buried in some dark Dickensian office, surrounded by piles of dusty folders, loosely bound with red tape and covered in sealing wax,"

"Oh no, Jack! Don is exactly the opposite. His office is rather spartan and filled with high-tech electronic equipment. He is hardly ever there. He's always out seeing clients and account holders. He is a very hands-on CEO. He has two rules in life. First, you should never borrow more money than you've got and second, you should never lend money to a friend. If your friend wants to borrow money, you should charge him interest, in which case, he might as well go to the bank. If he is genuinely on the bones of his bum and is a close friend, you should give him the money, if you can spare it. Lend money to a friend and you will lose the friend. That's what Don says and I have to agree with him. I like Don very much. He has saved me many times from jumping into a financial bucket with no bottom. He has also given me advice on some quite humble-looking investments that have yielded enormous rewards. He is not just a banker, he is a confessor and counsellor."

"Well in that case, I think it would be better to let him in on the secret. Then he can't come back and say we never told him."

"If I tell him everything, he would need to sign the Official Secrets Act, wouldn't he?"

"Yes, but you say that he is a man of his word. If we make him sign the Official Secrets Act, we are, in effect, saying that we don't trust him to keep his mouth shut. I think, having heard your opinion of him, we should make him aware of the depth of the enterprise he is embarking on and the risks attached to making the more intimate details public knowledge. He is not receiving stolen goods. The money has passed through well-known legal channels and is clean. All we are doing is asking him to invest it wisely for us. Is he a church-goer?"

"Yes I think he is

"Okay, then. Will you have a chat with him, Dick?"

"Yes, I will, but technically, Jack, whose money is it then, at the moment?"

"Technically it is in the hands of the Liquidator and the Government is one of the creditors of CaribbBank, which has declared insolvency. I think that it is highly unlikely that the Russians are going to admit that they paid a ransom of $10,000,000 to a dissident organisation which, to all intents and purposes, never existed. Do you agree?"

"It's clever, Jack. Yes, it's very clever, but would $10,000,000 be enough to take over a bank?"

"Well, obviously, that depends on the share value of Ost Deutsche Bank. The financial wizards in Frankfurt will have that worked out before they float the shares. Considering the worldwide repercussions of the deal, I feel that HMG would be prepared discretely to back NorProv, to the point that the offer could not be refused. The important thing is that NorProv should get in there before the Russkies can pour in their billions. If they do, we can slip away with the IDCs. If they don't, then we have an auction of global proportions and Sam will be there to tell us what to do. Am I right?"

"Very good, Jack, I will get on to Don Cullinan right away, to keep him awake through tonight!"

"Go for it Dick! I know you can do it!"

The two parted company and Don Cullinan spent a sleepless night. The purchasing of Ost Deutsche Bank shares went ahead quietly over the next weeks. No one organization appeared to be buying suspiciously large tranches of shares. Smaller parcels were bought by minor investment portfolios as well as a number of individuals. What was carefully obscured from other players in the marketplace was the fact that all these buyers were linked by an almost invisible thread through Northern Provident Mutual Alliance Bank of Newcastle upon Tyne. One of the more old-fashioned characteristics of NorProv was that its clients became shareholders in the bank when they opened an account there. So, as each account holder invested money in Ost Deutsche Bank, they were, in effect, increasing the proportion of the bank owned by the Mutual Alliance of NorProv.

When Cullinan established that his customers collectively controlled around eighty percent of Ost Deutsche Bank's shares he made a quiet announcement at a closed door meeting of senior account holders, to the effect that Norprov now held a controlling interest in Ost Deutsche Bank. He stressed to his listeners the importance that all matters discussed should remain private for the time being

338

and must not enter the public domain until the deal had been finalised. He rounded off his announcement by advising those seated around the table that Norprov, by owning Ost Deutsche Bank, had become the new financiers of the Arches Stationery Group.

Many of those present had never heard of Arches and it came as something of a shock, when it was revealed that they were the inspiration behind the Tarnbeck Experiment and the exclusive manufacturers and suppliers of the revolutionary new IDCs, which were now taking parts of the United States by storm.

"I will be advising all of our members of the significance of their investment and the importance of keeping our cards, if you will excuse the pun, extremely close to our chests, until the full significance of this investment breaks in the financial world."

Murmurings of 'Wow!' and 'Good old Don' and 'Bit of a dark horse, our Don!' came from the floor, as the implications of the Ost Deutsche Bank deal filtered through. The Cullinan genes came through tough, wily cattle rustling stock, from the Scottish Borders and Don was no less astute. The Roman Emperor Hadrian had erected a massive wall, right across the country, in an effort to control their activities, but the trade went on. Don Cullinan was proud of his roots and the members felt that their monies were safe in his hands.

Financial whizz-kids in the City were derisory when they heard about the Ost Deutsche Bank deal. 'Old Don Cullinan must be losing his marbles!' they jeered. 'Why would you want to buy a little bank, in a part of the world whose economy is shrinking almost as fast as its population? He must be nuts! Or maybe he's got a bit of

East German stuff on the side and he wants to give her a nice Christmas present.' Little did they know.

The purchase of the shares had been handled so discreetly that it went unnoticed in the Kremlin. The hijacking and subsequent release of Sergei Novgorod had commanded such urgent attention from the prime movers of Russian politics, that the Ost Deutsche Bank deal paled into insignificance. It was only when Norprov announced that the Chief Executive of the Arches Stationery Group was to be removed from office that feathers started to fly in the Kremlin.

Ivan Ilyich retired to his dacha. There he remained, surrounded by fading memories of the great figures of the communist revolution. Lenin, Beria, Trotsky, Stalin, Marx, Engels and the disgraced architect of Russian victory in the Great Patriotic War, Marshal Zukov, had all enjoyed the quietness of the room in which he was now sitting. Now they watched him as he slipped into the lonely gloom of old age. His wife had gone. He had failed in his mission. The wind heaved another layer of driven snow against the timbers of the house, as if chanting a requiem to the life of Ivan Ilyich and the lost cause of world Communism. He rose, unsteadily to his feet and made his

way to the familiar front door, through which had passed each one of the heroes who stared down at him. He felt their deep contempt as he opened the door and stumbled out into the storm, leaving it open. Why bother to close it? He wasn't coming back.

Chapter 28

"This is BBC World News at nine o'clock. Good morning. I am John Steen."

"Reports are coming in that the Russian Prime Minister, Ivan Ilyich, may be unwell. His absence at Moscow Scheremetyevo Airport to welcome President Mpendapombe of the African Peoples' Republic of Danganya, raised concerns as to his health. Ilyich is seventy-nine. Russian President Boris Belnikov apologised to President Mpendapombe, but quoted 'pressing matters of State' as his reason for not welcoming him, further raising concerns as to the health of Prime Minister Ilyich."

There followed reports of massive flooding, after twelve inches of rain in the previous twenty-four hours hit the southern Chinese city of Guangzhou. More than five hundred bodies had been recovered but the death toll was expected to rise. Appeals had been sent out by the Chinese Government for search and rescue teams to assist in the recovery of victims. The Chinese Government declared Guangzhou a disaster area.

Boris Belnikov sat on an uncomfortable office chair in the spartan confines of his office in the Kremlin. The walls were adorned with hand-written notes, reminding him of up-coming appointments and duties which seemed to be closing in on him. He was suffocating under the weight of insurmountable problems. Ilyich, his mentor, had taken the easy way out. Security had found his frozen corpse, three hundred metres from his Dacha, shrouded in fresh snow and curled around the gravestone of his beloved Babushka, in a last, pitiful appeal for deliverance.

Chernorgin had not been seen since the discovery that the 'Lost Generations of the Rodina' was a scam. He was was gone. He would dissolve himself comfortably into the realms of the Russian Mafia. There were rumours of a coup d'état being planned by the Russian diaspora. Their special forces had received a drubbing at the hands of Chechen rebels in Grozny. Twenty-two of the best trained soldiers now lay in blood-spattered disgrace, at the hands of a bunch of Chechen hillbillies. The price of oil remained below $80 a barrel, thus choking the Russian economy. An Air force Ilyushin 76 had crashed on take-off, into a block of flats in Minsk the capital of Belarus, killing all eighty-one on board and thirty-two on the ground.

Convincing evidence of sabotage hovered menacingly around the circumstances of the disaster. Belnikov felt compelled to visit the scene to bolster flagging faith in his administration and demonstrate strong Russian support for the people of Belarus, one of the few staunch allies of Russia.

It was the quantity of caramelised sugar found in the burned-out tanks of the Ilyushin that raised the suspicions of investigators sent from Moscow to the scene of the Minsk accident. Sugar is not one of the normal constituents of the kerosene pumped into the tanks of jet aircraft and the last place where the Ilyushin had taken in fuel was Minsk.

The Russian investigators ran into a wall of old-style Communist bureaucracy, in their efforts to establish the cause of the accident. The first target of their suspicions was the supplier of the fuel uplifted at Minsk and it took a week for the investigators to reach the appropriate authority that could give them clearance to begin their investigation. The Civil Aviation Department of the Ministry of Transport asserted vehemently that the refueling facilities at Minsk Airport had been audited only the day before the accident. The team of six auditors had been specifically chosen externally, in order to exclude any risk of Government involvement in the reliability of the supply of fuel stocks. The Minsk facilities had been explored in depth and, after exhaustive inspection, declared exemplary by the auditors. All the paperwork involved was presented to the investigators, along with the auditors' report.

The investigators studied the fuel quality inspection procedures, right down from the airport tank farm, to the vehicles that delivered the fuel to the aircraft. Each member of staff was rigorously interrogated; there could be no doubt as to the qualifications and abilities of any one of them. To get a job with these boys, you had to know your stuff. There were plenty of other qualified people to take your uniform off you, if you did not come up to scratch.

The auditors had even insisted that the old Russian final filters on the fuel bowser trucks should be changed. They provided new ones from an impeccable German manufacturer of high quality spares for old Soviet machinery. It was not until the crash of President Belnikov's helicopter, on his way to the scene of the Ilyushin disaster, that the true content of the filters was discovered. Sugar.

"Good evening. This is the BBC. I'm John Steen. Reports are coming in of an accident involving President Boris

Belnikov of the Commonwealth of Independent States, the President of Russia."

"Go to Sky News! Quick, Jack! Quickly!"

Frank had dragged the meeting upstairs to the TV lounge, a room designated for those who wished to watch 'The Box'. "Quick, Jack, this is breaking news!"

After some confusion with the TV remote, Jack brought up Sky News on a screen with 'BREAKING NEWS' streaming across the lower portion. 'Russian President, Boris Belnikov, involved in helicopter accident' it screamed, in red. The newsreader appeared on screen, assailed by conflicting instructions from the producer, through his earphone. He clutched his ear and stared, expectantly, at the camera. His eyebrows twitched, in an expression of imminent contact. His finger rose in the air and the eyes focused back on to the camera. "Yes, I can hear you, Maria. Go ahead."

There followed flickering groups of almost-identifiable pictures. First a handbag, a Reebok trainer and then a helicopter. It was unmistakably a Russian Mi-17 with the tail rotor on the left side, descending and descending fast, almost falling. Then there was the high building, The initial, nearly survivable impact followed by the sudden lurch forwards and the scatter of rotor blades, knifing into surrounding structures, some escaping to reap a harvest far away from the site of the initial impact. Then came the fireball. Nobody could survive that holocaust as it littered its fiery way down the side of the building. The camera phone followed each impact, each, explosive dismemberment of the thrashing vehicle that contained the leader of one of the world's most powerful nations. Surprisingly, the fire extinguished itself, assisted by the fountains of water that rained down from the ruptured water tanks on the rooftop on which the helicopter had initially attempted to alight. There was a stunned silence from the newsreader, as the camera phone of the witness stuttered back to her face.

"Maria? Are you still with us? Hello... Maria?... are you there?" There was no reply. Only the shocked features of the girl continued to fill the screen, then the Newsroom took over and a new reader appeared.

"While we try to re-establish communications with Minsk, here is Lisa with the weather."

Nadya Petrovotski, an ancient incumbent of the block that had been the initial target for a landing by the desperate pilot, was shaken awake by the impact and the waterfall which cascaded in torrents past her small balcony. Her washing would be soaked. There was fire too. Nadia was terrified of fire.

Living on the seventh floor of a block with no working elevator, she relied on neighbours to supply her frugal needs. For an octogenarian to scale fourteen flights of stairs was impossible. In the event of a fire, she would jump. Much better the microsecond of impact than the roasting; rare, medium rare, well done or charred. No. She would go to the balcony and... She stopped short. There was somebody out there on the balcony. Her eyesight was not that good any more, but she thought that it looked like a man. Was he jumping as well? Or maybe he was the rescue services? Then she saw that her rescuer appeared to be asleep and on closer inspection, she saw he had no legs.

She reached down and asked the head if he wanted to jump with her. "It won't hurt," she said comfortingly. "Only the last bit, but that won't take long. Come! Let's go together." Then her eyes focused with the imminence of death. This man bore a striking resemblance to the cartoons she had seen in the press. The shock of iron-grey hair, the boxer's nose, the long upper lip. The face was unmistakable. These were the thuggish features of President Belnikov of Russia, on her balcony, with no legs.

There was nothing she could do. This man was busy dying and she would be blamed. "Come with me" she said, as a grandmother would speak to a child. The dormant body heaved, as though trying to sit up. It was trying to speak. Old Nadya leaned closer to catch the words.

"Ludmilla Scharanski is the one..." The whisper petered out in an exhausted sigh. The President of Russia was dead.

The death of Boris Belnikov electrified the world. For years to come, people would remember what they were doing at the precise moment they heard the news. A strange silence descended on the corridors of power in the Kremlin, as if everybody had stood back to see what would happen next. Who would be the next to go? What strange malaise had suddenly caused the chicken to lose its head? Mortality was something that did not apply to people at the top of the pile, only to the little men and women in the street, surely. And now that the two most powerful people in the country had been removed, who would fill the vacuum?

In the western media, rumours of a major security blunder were rife, orchestrated by members of the Russian

346

diaspora. The SVR had been exposed carrying out some covert operations in the United Kingdom. According to unnamed sources close to MI6, the British security services had scored a major victory against units of the Russian Secret Service, and a number of them had been detained for questioning, before being deported back to their country. The names of the deportees were withheld, for security reasons and the Russian Embassy remained stolidly silent, when approached by members of the media. Pravda announced that the British Government had been implicated in a series of recent incidents which threatened the security of the Russian State, and an unspecified number of diplomatic staff at the British Embassy in Moscow had been declared Persona Non Grata. The press was treating this as a normal tit-for-tat spat, between two governments who had never really seen eye to eye since the end of the Second World War.

Then Pravda published a preliminary report on the Ilyushin helicopter crash and subsequent death of the Russian President. Investigators at the scene implied that both accidents appeared to have been caused by fuel contamination and that there were increasing suspicions that the contamination could only have been intentional. Sabotage could not, at this stage, be ruled out and it was darkly hinted at that foreign powers could have been involved. Putting two and two together, several investigative journalists drew the conclusion that Russia, in a round about way, was accusing Britain of being part of a plot to overthrow the Russian Government. The Russian Ambassador to the Court of St James in London was recalled to Moscow for 'consultations' while the British Ambassador remained in Moscow, protesting the complete lack of justification in the Russian accusations. The British Prime Minister called an urgent extraordinary meeting of his cabinet. They met at 10 Downing Street and the scuffle of activity around the hallowed black door did not fail to raise interest among the doyens of the international press. News hacks poured in on every side to catch what were perceived to be, potentially, some of the most exciting headlines to have hit the front pages for months.

"Good afternoon, all of you." Crighton hurried in and thumped a pile of papers on the table, before taking his seat. He poured some water from a jug and took a sip from his glass before looking up and addressing his colleagues. "Please make yourselves comfortable." Duncan Hughes was on duty at the door and closed it quietly, before assuming his position as guardian of the security of the Cabinet Room.

"This could take some time." There was a shuffling of papers and the squeaking of seats as the highest members of the government waited attentively for the news. "We have received a communication from Marshal Kharkov, head of the caretaker government of the Commonwealth of Independent States, the Acting President of the Russian Federation,"

Crighton looked around the assembled company of ministers. Every eye was fixed on the Prime Minister. There was no sound in the room to interrupt his speech. Even the pictures on the walls hung on his words. He reached down and lifted a sheet of paper from the top of the pile in front of him.

"They have reason to believe that the British Government may be held responsible for the deaths of one hundred and twenty-three victims of an Ilyushin military transport accident in Minsk, three days ago. Since the cause of that accident is being blamed on fuel contamination, investigators concentrated on this as the cause of the fatal crash of the Russian Presidential helicopter, causing the death of the President. Russian security services had previously reported the illegal arrest and detention in London of six Belarusian citizens, and the disappearance of a female Russian citizen, a dissident, wanted for acts of espionage against the Russian State." Crighton turned a leaf of his notes.

"Upon making inquiries through diplomatic channels as to the whereabouts and condition of these persons, the Embassy, which represents the interests of Belorussia, as well as the Commonwealth of Independent States, met with a wall of silence. The only information released by the British Government was an admission that the aforementioned had indeed been detained and, subsequently, released and deported. None of this information had been handed over to the Russian Embassy at the time;, only after persistent inquiries had been made. This indicated that the British Government, while fully aware of the existence of the aforementioned, was not prepared to share this information with representatives from the Russian Embassy. In the circumstances, this reticence was taken to be an admission of collusion on the part of the British Government and, unless a satisfactory explanation of its stance was forthcoming, the Government of the Russian Federation would break off Diplomatic relations with Great Britain and any further consequences of their action laid at the door of the British Government." The document was signed 'Kharkov'. The signature was quite legible. The communication arrived on paper and bore the familiar twin headed eagle crest of the Russian Federation. It was embossed in colour and had been delivered to Number 10 by an official Russian Embassy Mercedes. This was the real thing.

"So, Ladies and Gentlemen, there you have it. This is our subject for discussion and I rely on your well-educated input for our reaction."

The first person to raise his hand was Roger Pastern, the Defence Secretary.

"Roger, would you please start us off."

"Thank you, Prime Minister. If, as seems to be implied, the Russians are intending some kind of action against the British Isles, I would point out to Members of the Cabinet that the total number of British citizens carrying arms for her Majesty's Armed Forces totals less than four hundred thousand in all three services, to defend a population of more than sixty million. When National Service was abolished in 1960, the population of Great Britain was around fifty million, of whom nearly a million were in uniform. It seems that, the bigger the population, the smaller the number of trained service personnel are available to defend them."

He paused to allow the significance of his words to sink in. "I would also point out to those who say that the threat to peace has disappeared since the end of the Cold War, that the threat is right here, right now, on the table in front of us." Once again, he paused to ensure that he had the full attention of the Cabinet. Every eye in the room was fixed on the Minister of Defence.

"To those who say that a couple of assassinations could not possibly constitute grounds for going to war, I would draw their attention to the assassination of Archduke Franz Ferdinand of Austria in Sarajevo on the 28th of June 1914, the prime cause of the First World War." Pastern liked to display his intricate knowledge of British history, which was a weak point in the Education Secretary's education.

"And your recommendations, Roger?"

"If Britain is to present any plausible deterrent, we will need to have a trained Army, Air Force and Navy. As we stand, the only realistic deterrent we possess is nuclear, and that threatens the whole planet. 'Mutually Assured Destruction' is not just MAD in mnemonic terms, it's mad in principle. To sacrifice the entire world in the defence of one country is patently madness."

"So, Roger, are you suggesting that surrender would be preferable?" Ted Farquahar, the Education Secretary, was a notorious hawk when it came to the defence of democracy against what he saw as the forces of evil as far as the Russians were concerned, and he was down one point already against the Defence Secretary, with his airy-fairy quotes from history.

"Anything is better than the wholesale destruction of Satellite Earth, Ted, but I would expect your department to be able to use dialogue as a primary weapon, before resorting to physical means. The problem that we have here, as I see it, is that, without palpable physical strength, we have few cards left with which to negotiate. I have never been a great poker player. Have you?"

"So, Roger," the Prime Minister broke in, "what you are saying is that our Armed Forces should be strengthened and mobilised. Am I hearing you correctly?"

"Indeed, Prime Minister. I feel that, in the face of what threatens to be a national emergency, we need to boost recruitment aggressively and, if that doesn't work, then we will have to go for the reinstatement of National Military Service before the instructor cadre becomes too depleted to set up training courses for the new intake."

The Prime Minister warmed to his appointment of Roger Pastern. Things were developing in a way that he could hardly have hoped for. He just prayed that the 'Instructor Cadre', as he called it, would be up to the job. Ted Fletch from Trade and Industry also sensed a boost for his Ministry, in the supply of war materials. The manufacturing industry would have to be revitalised to cope with demand. He felt a stirring of excitement as the possibility of war reared its head over the horizon.

"... and dialogue?" Ted Farquahar looked at the Prime Minister. "What cards do we have, Prime Minister?"

"We have evidence that there was Russian involvement in most of the attacks which have been carried out in recent weeks. We have the evidence extracted from the First Secretary on the cultural desk of the Russian Embassy as well as that of some of the other foreign agents we have detained in highly suspicious circumstances. We have further information gleaned from some of the perpetrators of the Makepeace property fire in Hampstead and the physical evidence left behind after the destruction of my own country retreat. The person linked to that attack had also been apprehended at the scene of the Makepeace affair but he has since died under mysterious circumstances." A sinister master plan appeared to be taking shape.

"The Russians will have difficulty in denying that our evidence, however obtained, has the weight of truth behind it. We even have the assassin who claims responsibility for many of the deaths, which initially, we put down to causes associated with the economic crisis. There is no doubt whatsoever, that there was a master plan behind the atrocities and that the master plan had its origins in Russia." Crighton took a sip of water from the tumbler in front of him.

"We currently have a team of experts, operating under deep cover. They have been researching Russian strategic planning in our direction and are responsible for bringing these plans to our attention. It appears that we are not the only targets. The United States is also on the list, as are a number of other sovereign states worldwide. Ladies and gentlemen, it appears that the Russians have global ambitions and I feel we should take a certain amount of pride in the fact that the international community first became aware of the threat through us."

"And who are these operatives, Prime Minister?"

"Well, I think I should leave that up to our Defence Secretary to reveal, Roger."

Pastern fidgeted momentarily with the papers on the table in front of him. "Er... for reasons of security, I am unable to divulge the identities of these assets, partly because of the depth of their cover but, I am assured by the highest authority that they have been employed on several previous excursions and have exhibited an irreproachable level of expertise and courage."

"In other words, Roger, you don't know who they are. Is that what you are saying?" Farquahar could not resist scoring a point off Pastern who had allowed his dislike of Farquahar's privileged background to show during previous debates.

"There is no requirement for the Defence Secretary to know the names of each serving officer. That would only lead to confusion and the dilution of the military chain of command. My responsibilities concern the more strategic aspects of Government military policy, using the advice of senior members of the Armed Forces. Never forget that the they are non-political. They simply action the requirements of the Government with due respect for the Geneva Conventions, the Rules of War and Treatment of Prisoners." Pastern appeared to be quoting from the Handbook for Defence Secretary, which in truth, he had been studying since his appointment.

"Gentlemen! Now is not the time for scoring points. Let's get back to business before we lose the focus of our discussions" Crighton reprimanded the two ministers like naughty schoolboys. Old Jimmy Price caught the Prime Minister's eye.

"Jimmy," Crighton nodded at the Minister for Science and Technology, readjusting his chair in an involuntary expression of relief, "what have you got for us?"

"Prime Minister," Jimmy Price, although a lot older and more experienced than Crighton, came from a generation who did not feel comfortable with first name terms when discussing matters of State. He spoke with the softer accent of the old West Riding of Yorkshire, rather than the more aggressive tones of the eastern side of that county. "From my experience in the Trade Union movement..." Many speeches that started this way drew yawns from the audience as, normally, they were expressions of hard times past and how the speaker won through in the end. With Jimmy Price, it was different. "...I have always felt that confrontation hinders solution. We have to build up a level of trust between the two adversaries so they can, first of all, understand both sides of the arguments and come up with a solution beneficial to both sides. This will inevitably need a bit of give and take, but the final solution should represent a victory for both sides and an advance for all concerned. Does that make sense?" Heads nodded in agreement around the table.

"In the current situation, we have an ambitious gang of people who have a plan to dominate affairs, to the exclusion of all opposition. Their plan has been spotted and a rival strategy put into action by the intended victims. The rival countermeasures threaten to disrupt the original strategy of the gang leader and he has to react appropriately by upping his stakes, in order to assert his superiority. He escalates the threat, hoping the victim will back down. When he doesn't, the only perceived course for the antagonist is physical, including threats of violence. OK Big Boy, let's see who has the bigger mouth and who has the knockout punch. This is when dialogue tends to become more difficult, when teeth start flying!" A murmur of mirth crept around the ministers.

"In my experience, once bones start to get broken, the solution is delayed. It doesn't disappear, it's just delayed, while the bones get put back together." He pointed to his broken nose eliciting more laughter.

"If we can get the Russians to realise that we know their game and are prepared to talk about it, we should be able to avoid fisticuffs. Am I right?"

A murmur of assent rose from the table with one or two cries of "Hear! Hear!"

"So, Prime Minister, what I suggest is that you call the Russian Ambassador before he leaves. Give him a piece of your mind and tell him that we are not the only target for their games and that, if the targets all club together, he doesn't stand a chance in a punch-up."

The reaction to Jimmy Prices words was almost euphoric. Suddenly the boot was on the other foot and the Russians would have to think again.

"Excellent Jimmy!" Crighton was gently rubbing his hands together. "Let's do it!"

Chapter 29

The sudden deaths of the President and the Prime Minister of Russia raised a seething turmoil of speculation, not only among the media but also the silent Russian population. The man in the street relayed what was unfolding, even though the Russian media was tightly muzzled. Now it seemed that the dark curtains which had, for so long, cloaked the Kremlin in secrecy, were being dragged reluctantly back a fraction. Tiny cameos of human activity, within those impenetrable walls, leaked out over the internet. The world, meanwhile, stood by on tenterhooks waiting for the curtains to part enough for them to see the next act in the Russian drama. In typical Russian fashion, there wasn't one; not one to satisfy the demands of the media, that is. The Kremlin closed in on itself, like some enormous snail, retracting into its grey, impregnable shell. Tiny snippets of rumours came from exiled members of the diaspora. One of those whispers concerned a candidate for the post of Prime Minister. The reason why it was not taken seriously was because the prospective candidate was female. No name had been mentioned, although the hungry hacks were told that she was supposed to come from the diaspora, and she was young. The longer they waited, the more the new candidate gathered celebrity status, until it became almost a joke. Cartoons appeared in the press. One was of a line-up of bathing beauties portrayed from the rear. The central figure had a gorgeous figure and a beautiful mane of blonde hair. The five on each side were of more ample proportions and conspicuously less skilled at displaying them.

'AND THE WINNER IS...!' the caption trumpeted.

The reverse of the picture showed the faces of the five more voluptuous figures, revealing the features of various well-known members of the Politburo, while the statuesque lady in the centre, turned out to be none other than the late Boris Belnikov, complete with goatee beard, disguised in female form. The message was obvious, 'More of the same.'

Ludmilla Scharanski, on seeing this, had difficulty hiding a smile. With the assistance of Jack Wise, she had been contacted by several influential Russian exiles, who maintained close but covert contact with sympathetic ears in the Motherland. They saw in her a person, unique in her relationship with many in the Russian political spectrum. Her proven loyalty to true Communist ideals was, without doubt, although the full details would be veiled for the present. Her aristocratic roots, though hidden for many years in order to survive under the Soviet regime, now appealed as a panacea to the many Royalists who had fled the horrors of the revolution.

Ludmilla Romanova Scharanski, given a bit of grey hair, would make a very good figurehead for the new post-Soviet Russia. She would bring back much of the old money. She would give confidence to a nation whose brains had been transplanted to the decadent capitalist world, through oppression. Who invented the first commercially certified helicopter? Sikorski of course, a Russian. Where did he develop it? In America. Who made the biggest aircraft in the world? Antanov. Was he an American? No! Did they export them? Yes. Well, OK, Only two of them, but they were bulging with ideas which the West had not even dreamed of. Why did they not sell more? Well, the workmanship was a bit agricultural because the Russian computers were a bit agricultural and their metallurgists were motivated more by getting a loaf of bread and a bottle of vodka, than by finding the right alloy for the right job. True or false? That will be argued for many years.

The fact was that Ludmilla, having found motivation among people whom she was now tempted to call her friends, suddenly found that her life had developed a completely new horizon. When the chips were down, where did Karl Marx go and live and eventually, die? In London.

The approaches came from old names who had been on Ludmilla's list of possible targets during her violent sojourn of survival with the SVR. Some of the old faces, from Russia's distant past, appeared at Hamilton Terrace. Ludmilla was astonished that so many were still alive. Others were the new generation of exiles, children and grandchildren of an aristocracy which had, as far as Ludmilla was aware, been wiped from the face of the earth by two world wars and successive vicious pogroms that had swept through the Russian population like a forest fire. To see them now gave her a visceral thrill. She suddenly realised that here was a fertile seedbed from which to cultivate a new team to lead the country out of the grinding, mindless poverty of post-Stalinist Russia. Here was a new layer of citizens, motivated, not just by the potential for riches, but by a deep reverence for the Russia which had not only thrown back the massed armies of Napoleon Bonaparte, but also those of Hindenburg and Hitler.

Having suffered the indignity of being punished for her dedicated service to the Rodina, Ludmilla turned her considerable strength to wresting the nation from the hands of the present self-seeking rulers and calling on the people to rule themselves. It sounded like the preaching of

Karl Marx but, as Margaret Thatcher was quoted as having said "The trouble with socialism is that you run out of other peoples' money to run it," Ludmilla's goal was to motivate the 'Lost Generations'. She wanted them to see the New Russia as a place where their old money could grow, to the benefit of a people, which had been so frequently cheated and massacred by successions of ill-educated, greedy megalomaniacs.

As Jack pulled in more and more of the characters from Russia's imperial past, Ludmilla began to get a feel for the deeply daunting task of turning the old Russian Bear into a Bull. But there was always the mouth-watering potential that opened up with each introduction, as she met the progeny of those who had held the reins of this massive beast, in years gone by. She began to see the Russian Revolution as an uncontrolled explosion, which had vapourised a civilisation, leaving in place only the essential ingredients, vastly reduced and without a matrix to bind them together. It was as though the vast body of the Russian Empire had been dissected into millions of individual corpuscles and the serum which had previously held it all together and allowed it to flow, had frozen solid into blind, uncompromising ice. All the remaining corpuscles were held in place, but now they were almost immovable. Progress was glacial.

With the introduction of capital, it was warmed back to health over the years, by the entrepreneurial hands of those who had been dispossessed and had to start all over again. In friendly climes, the economy would unfreeze. The new generation of investors would open up access to the immense resources of the largest country in the world. Oil, gas, timber, coal, fresh water and, above all, a population of world-beating intellect. Russian culture was a secret cornucopia, a hidden treasure chest, unopened for a

360

hundred years. It had the potential to invert the world's distrust of an indolent, vodka-soaked pariah state, and open up a hoard of such rich enticements that the country would become the new world of opportunity. America had exploded into world leadership, by cultivating a stable culture for human enlightenment and challenge. The rewards for the dispossessed who sailed in past the Statue of Liberty as she welcomed the down-trodden masses, were enormous. Coming from all over the world, they had built a multi-ethnic state with financial and military clout, which the world had never before experienced. Having said all that, they had little 'American' history. They had brought with them the histories of Britain, Greece, Vietnam, of Ireland and Germany and of Russia and China. They were marked as 'Irish American' or 'Hispanic American', or 'African American'. The Jewish people and the Italians did not even have to declare their 'Americanship'. They just ran the place.

'American History' went all the way back to the 'Declaration of Independence' and, if you looked any further, it was peopled by a few pilgrims and a bunch of natives according to the writers of the time. They called the indiginous people 'Red' Indians, because they thought they were from the India on the other side of the world. These guys couldn't even write, so they obviously didn't do 'history'.

Russia was different. True enough, Lenin had virtually banned any positive pre-revolutionary history, along with anything closely linked to God, without the intervening assistance of the Politburo. But Russia had history. The Bolshoi and Nuryev, Tchaikovsky, where would the world be without Tchaikovsky? As for he Czars, well, they did add some impressive architecture, though they did not have much rapport with the hoi polloi. Life simply 'continued' under the Czars.

Under the Soviets, twenty-four million corpses had reason to believe that life under the Politburo did not continue and, if their mouths had still worked, they would have told them so. That's a lot of people not criticising what you are doing to kill a country.

The more Russians she met, the more Ludmilla felt the stirring of a visceral yearning to restore the self-respect of a people stunned by war and unspeakable atrocity. The more the exiles got to know of the young girl who showed such interest in their stories, the more intrigued they were with her aims. She talked freely with them, as though her plans were no secret, but such openness was something so foreign that it allowed suspicion to cloud their trust in her. It was only when they became aware of her past, including her attempted assassination at the hands of the SVR, that trust tentatively returned.

The exiles began to see Scharanski as a possible figurehead. With the political scene in such turmoil in the Motherland, opportunities for change began to appear. Great cracks of uncertainty split the fabric of fear that had for so long ruled political life under Stalin and his successors. Shafts of free expression pierced the impenetrable gloom behind the walls of the Kremlin. According to some old biddy living in the block where Belnikov's helicopter had crashed, the name Scharanski was among the last words to have come from the dying President's lips. Kremlin staffers swapped stories in whispers, drowned out from inquisitive monitors, by the flushing of a toilet or the running of a tap. They now knew that Scharanski was no amateur when it came to extreme solutions. Her reputation gathered momentum with each passing day and soon her name could be heard in the hushed exchanges on the streets of Moscow, Saint Petersburg and as far away as the Ukraine.

Her privacy was tightly guarded, at her own request. Visitors were brought on roundabout routes by windowless transports, in order to confuse them and any followers. The escorts carried out frequent vehicle changes for the same reason during the trip to Hamilton Terrace.

Then SVR agents observed a young woman of diminutive stature, with a curl of long blonde hair escaping from her fur bonnet, disembarking from a Lufthansa flight at Moscow's Scheremetyevo Airport. The flight was inbound from Berlin Tegel. The name on the manifest was Leonora Schrader. What attracted the attention of the security agents was her similarity to Ludmilla Scharanski and the fact that her initials and, indeed, the first three letters of her given name were the same as those of their target. In spite of her teutonic-sounding surname, she carried a Russian passport. She was met by representatives of an organisation that had recently given the government some cause for concern. They had been issuing well-informed criticism of the Russian environmental programme and its seeming disregard for issues affecting government policy in the so-called 'Free World'. They were environmentalists and they enjoyed considerable support, both moral and financial, from the West. Passport Control drew L. Schrader to one side and told her to wait in a small office while her details were verified. Her ID card was checked against the computer.

According to the records, the original Leonora's grandfather had been a weapons expert with the German Army. He was captured by the Russians at the fall of Stalingrad and was one of the very few German survivors to be sent to a gulag and survive. His son, Alexei had been born out of wedlock, after a short relationship with a Russian peasant woman who had provided meagre nourishment to the German prisoners in Siberia. The grandfather was held prisoner for four years until his expertise in ballistics and weaponry was recognised and he was offered a place at a manufacturing facility in Omsk. It was there that he was spotted by the legendary designer of the AK47 assault rifle, Kalashnikov. He was moved to a research bureau involved in the development of explosives for specialised applications. Alexei and Leonora followed him and, according to the limited records of the time, they were all declared missing when the factory was destroyed in a massive and uncontained explosion. The official death toll was two hundred and sixty-one, though the actual figure was reported locally to have been far higher. Grandfather, son and granddaughter effectively disappeared, but Leonora's identity papers mysteriously ended up in the hands of MI6, where they were stored against some future need. The subsequent forged paperwork for the new Leonora were of such high quality that even the Russian experts could not fault them, but this did not allay the suspicions of the SVR on the look-out for Ludmilla Scharanski.

Rumours spread like wildfire among the tiny dissident population. Obsessively, they kept themselves unobtrusive to the point that even the SVR was unaware of the identity of many of their members. Even so, news of the rumoured arrival of 'The Scharanski' spread like wildfire through the population. Only the very old remembered the true Russian way of life that existed under the Czars. The younger generation had never experienced the thrill of the Cossacks charging through a village. The magnificent cavalry would come leaping out of the darkness with flashing sabres, pennants flying from glittering lances and their riders' fierce, warlike cries punctuating the thunderous sound of hooves. Children scattered in fear. Even grown men flinched at the sight of the rushing tide of horsemen. Was it possible that these same warriors could end up as dancers? Yes it was, because Cossack dancing displayed all the excitement and heroic vigour of the original charge. The performers were well-versed in their true valour, though nowadays, all that warlike heroism had been forgotten. These representational performances were now only laid on in a Moscow stadium for visiting dignitaries. This was what The Scharanski felt she urgently needed to revitalise. This was the essence of being Russian. For The Scharanski, the past was also the future.

Chapter 30

The British, through their experiences in a long colonial past have become experts at putting people into power, without anybody noticing. Several Middle Eastern, Indian, African and Far Eastern rulers owe their positions to the quiet behind-the-scenes manoeuvring of British diplomats. Sometimes a discreet injection of British military personnel was required to push things in the right direction, but the numbers were normally so small that nobody noticed them. 'The Family' was a very good example of such influence. The 'Softies' were past masters of the techniques involved and Jack Wise was typical of the movers and shakers who wound the various loose ends into a workable plan. Ludmilla benefitted from this expertise and her short visit to her homeland was engineered as the first move in a game that was to have the highest stakes imaginable.

On her return to Hamilton Terrace, Jack Wise approached her with news that sent a shock through her system. "We have been approached by a Mr Yuri Gorshkov who says that you will know who he is, although you have never met each other. He called via Vauxhall Cross. He wants to meet you."

Ludmilla Scharanski's mouth involuntarily dropped open and her head snapped round as if to make sure that Jack had not suddenly changed sides and become a serious threat. "Gorshkov? Yuri Gorshkov?" She raised a hand to her lips. "When did he contact you?"

"This morning at about... when would it have been? At around ten past nine, I suppose. He said that he would prefer not to speak on the telephone and we arranged to communicate via a drop you have apparently been using in some library or other. Does that ring a bell?"

"It does, yes. It most certainly does! It was just after that drop that they pushed me under the bus. I am not prepared to meet this man. He was my controller when I absconded and came under the protection of Mr Jason. I would suspect that, having failed to get me with a bus, he may have made some rather more sophisticated plans." She smiled at Jack and he could not help admiring her attitude. Without losing the smile, she added, "Now, with your assistance, I have seen what I have to do in order to serve my country best. I am extremely grateful for your help, particularly since we had a rather inauspicious start to our relationship. Mr Jason is an extraordinary man. I still do not understand why he did not kill me when he discovered who I was and my orders."

"It is easy to kill someone you do not know. Just point, shoot and leave," said Jack. "Much more difficult to kill someone you like. I think Johnnie Jason liked you from the word go. I know that I myself have seldom been as intrigued by anyone. It is a fascinating anomaly to have an assassin in your midst, especially one you like. To be honest, I hope your plans work. I see an enormous leap forward in international relations if they do. Having said tha,t the three main protagonists of the First World War were all related to you. They were all grandchildren of our Queen Victoria, but that didn't stop them trying to kill each other. Maybe, if you can get it right, we can all come to our senses."

"Let's hope so."

"Now what are we going to do about this Mr Yuri Gorshkov? If you don't want to meet him, maybe we could send someone else, in your place. Regimental Sergeant Major Mac Macawley springs to mind. He's big enough and stupid enough. The only problem is that his hair is grey, his face resembles the north end of a south-bound bus and he doesn't have bumps in the right places." Ludmilla laughed out loud. It was the first time that Jack had seen her do that and it transformed her. "The hair we could probably fix, but for the rest, I think even I would be a better candidate!" The Scharanski continued to laugh, as though some dam wall had broken, allowing it to pour out for the first time in many long and silent years. Her face lit up, the grey tiredness dissolved from around her eyes, leaving tiny creases of pure pleasure in their place. It was a joy to watch the life coming back to features that had been weighed down by the ruthless violence of her job, with the ever-present fear of death lurking behind the eyes. This Scharanski could win the hearts of the people. Then, suddenly, she was back to business.

"Maybe you could send somebody with the bumps in the right places?" the smile was still there.

"Yes, maybe we could. Let me just consult with a colleague." He reached for his phone and scrolled down through his contacts. "Alex? Jack here. Have you got a moment? We are just down the road. Yes, that's right. I'll tell the footman to let you in. Good, then we'll see you in a minute. Don't rush. We wouldn't want you breaking a leg or anything, would we!"

Alex now inhabited a safe apartment, just down the road from The Wellesley. He shared it with two of the white-coated security officials from the clinic. He had served with one of them in Afghanistan and the other had been his personal close protection during his stay at the hospital. Margie was still playing the part of the tragically bereaved widow, so meetings between her and Alex had to be organized with the utmost discretion, either at Hamilton Terrace or at The Wellesley, which she could visit on the pretext of receiving counselling. Alex still walked with the aid of a stick because of his injuries, so determinedly delivered to him by Ludmilla Scharanski. Ironically, his route to Hamilton Terrace led him, unwittingly, past the Russian safe house in Abbey Road, where Kevin Brundy had learned the subtle art of pyrotechnic mortar delivery that led to the destruction of the Prime Minister's country retreat and Kevin's untimely death.

The cameras picked up the limping figure as Alex approached No 289. Security advised the 'footman' and the front door swung open as he reached the top of the steps. The door closed smartly after he had entered.

"Good evening, Mr Stewart. Mr Wise is waiting for you in Number 24."

Alex went to the elevator and pressed 2. In typical convoluted fashion, the powers that be had labelled the floors in reverse order and the elevator travelled up and down the lift shaft several times before stopping at the floor corresponding to the request. This complicated ruse was designed to confuse any malevolent intruder, but malfunctions were frequent and caused endless frustration. However, everyone lived with the inconvenience, rather than trying to change it.

Room 24 was an office on what was actually the third floor. It was where Jack kept his files and a secretary called Peggy who was attached to MI6. Ludmilla Scharanski had also been provided with a desk and chair in the same office and had struck up a good relationship with Peggy. The MI6 girl was fascinated by the arrival of the

Russian. She was aware that Ludmilla must be someone special to warrant such treatment and the trickle of visitors who came to see her included some eminent figures who were familiar faces to MI6. Slowly, she began to understand that the Russian was not just anyone, but was being groomed for a role of greater significance than anybody she had previously encountered.

"Good morning, Mr Stewart." she greeted Alex as he entered the office. "Mr Wise will be with you just now. Can I get you a coffee?" Alex accepted graciously.

It suddenly dawned on him that he was looking at a face he recognized; the neatly cut blonde hair, the determined chin, an attractive face, unless it was behind the wheel of a charging red Mini with a black roof.

He reached out a hand to her. "Hello." he said, trying to conceal his amazement, "Alex Stewart."

"Oh my God!" the colour drained from Ludmilla Scharanski's face. "I thought you were..."

"Dead? So did I for a moment." He took the girl's hand and held the gaze of the green eyes, mesmerised like those of a rabbit in the headlights of the charging car. "In fact, it was quite a close call. My wife very nearly claimed on the insurance." Alex found himself smiling, in spite of the gravity of the subject.

"I am most terribly sorry, Mr Stewart. I was under orders. They came from the very highest levels. There was nothing personal. I was acting as your executioner, not your murderer."

"Well, Miss Scharanski, that makes me feel a lot better. So much nicer to be executed, rather than murdered, don't you agree?" He released the girl's hand, slowly reconciling himself to the fact that this person had very nearly deprived Margie of a husband and Robbie and Jessie of a father.

Alex had lost his own father when had fallen to North Korean guns, during the Korean War. He had never set eyes on the soldier who had fired the fatal shot but felt that, were the two to meet, his father's death would bond them, rather than create an impassable gulf between them. He had to search deep into the dark crevices of his psyche to find the mind-set, which would allow him to treat this young lady as a combatant rather than a terrorist. It was a fascinating dilemma, particularly when the assailant, whose hand he had been holding and into whose eyes he was still looking, was as attractive as this one. "Having been your target on one occasion, I am obviously a bit nervous about trusting you not to try again," he said. "It will probably take me a little time to adjust to the new lie of the land, but I expect, when I get to know more about you, I shall be able to rationalise our relationship."

She still held his gaze as she replied, "I am now totally in your hands," before turning to Jack Wise. "I am in your debt for saving me from my previous masters and my future is at your disposal. I can only serve my country and correct the wrongs of the past decades with your assistance. For this, I am deeply grateful and I hope to be able to justify your trust in my good intentions over the coming weeks and months."

"And Yuri Gorschkov?"

"Do you want me to talk to Margie? She may have an idea. Perhaps she will know someone who could fill in for Mac?" Alex suggested.

The idea of Mac, dressed like a pantomime dame, going into the lion's den brought a smile to Jack Wise's face. "How are we going to do this?" Jack did not, under any circumstances, want to reveal Ludmilla Scharanski's whereabouts at the present time and he imagined that Mr Gorschkov was of a similar disposition. They would have to arrange a mutually acceptable remote venue they could all reveal themselves in safety.

"We will need someone who is familiar with the story and who can be relied on for discretion."

"Let me call Margie," said Alex, "she is staying with her sister, Penny's in Holland Park. It's not far from here and Penny would look after Robbie and Jessie, if you want her to pop over."

"That would be great, Alex. Get the taxi to drop her in Kilburn and I will send a driver. Tell her to wait at the No 28 bus stop."

Alex passed on the message and Jack went to organise the driver. It was of critical importance that they gave the opposition as little opportunity as possible to link Margie with Hamilton Terrace, hence the circuitous route. She arrived in Room 24 just over half an hour later.

"Good evening all," she said brightly, as she was shown in. "Hello Darling Boy." Alex stood up haltingly to kiss his wife. It was obvious by the closed eyes and the soft touch of her hand to his face that Margie was missing her husband. Ludmilla felt a pang of remorse, when she

372

remembered how close she had been to terminating this loving relationship. Now, she realised she would find it almost impossible to assassinate Alexander Selwyn Stewart. Jack Wise had been right about that when he explained Jason's reluctance to end Ludmilla's life. Emotional involvement was a sentiment so heavily discouraged in her training that she had never let it feature in her life. It came as a shock for her to find that people whom she had, until recently, treated simply as enemy operatives, had now become 'people'. Up until this point in her life, she had never contemplated 'friendship' but somehow she felt that towards these people. Her comrades had not been friends; they were fellow operatives. Each one of them, while representing a link in the chain or a cog in the machine, was also a threat. The conspiracy of fear, which regulated the SVR excluded friendship. That involved trust land trust demanded commitment. Commitment was frequently partnered by emotion and emotion could not be a part of an SVR agent's psychological make-up. In fact, lack of emotion was one of the strongest weapons in the agent's armoury and was actively encouraged. Any display of emotion was such anathema to the murky upper echelons of the organization that it could easily prove fatal.

For Ludmilla Scharansky to find this extraordinary new family was so unexpected that she went into a kind of culture shock. She had to remodel her concept of life and its opportunities as she nudged her twenty-ninth birthday feeling that her lateral horizons were almost unlimited. Now was the time. She was entering through a gate which had previously been barred and which would now open into a garden full of beauty and challenge and, not least of all, danger. An almost euphoric thrill of anticipation infused her being. Honour was tempered by an unexpected injection of humility. She found it difficult to assimilate

Ludmilla Scharanski, the hard-nosed, emotionless SVR assassin, with Ludmilla Romanova Scharanski, the messenger of the new age. Ahead of her was a task of enormous proportions; no less than the restoration of the Russian people as members of a team with the daunting task of nurturing 'Satellite Earth' back from the brink of oblivion. Never in human history had a job of such far-reaching proportions been laid on the shoulders of one so young, particularly a female. She would need nerves of titanium, the Wisdom of Solomon and the luck of the Irish, if she was going to pull it off.

"Why don't you send me?" It was Margie who broke the spell. "They don't know me from Adam or should that be Eve?" Her remark raised smiles around the room.

"I don't know whether that would really be appropriate, Margie." Jack raised his hands defensively. "We have already put Alex at risk so I don't think we should ask your family to put its neck on the line again. That's not the first time for Alex either."

"Well okay," said Margie, "but if you are looking for a volunteer who knows the story so far and is, to a certain extent, part of the family, my hand is in the air." Alex was resting his forehead in his hand and raised his head in some surprise.

"You Darling? What about Robbie and Jessie?"

"Well, they are quite happy with Penny and I don't see this meeting as particularly dangerous or likely to take long. I would enjoy the outing. I could even bring back some snaps for the family album so that I can show you who I met. It might make a better evening's viewing than watching Eastenders!

This reference to a famous British soap opera raised a smile from her audience.

"That's not a bad idea, Girl!" Alex smacked his knee enthusiastically and, almost immediately regretted it, as a shaft of pain lanced up his leg. He winced before returning to the conversation and both Ludmilla and Margie flinched in sympathy. "If we could get pictures, that would be a bonus," he said, managing to return his pained face to normal.

"I have a camera in my mobile," Ludmilla held up her phone. "We'll have to get a new SIM card for it, otherwise if you use it, my people will be able to track you. Even if you don't actually transmit, they can pick you up. Just turning it on is enough. It looks like a normal Nokia N73 but it has been modified so they can interrogate it through the mobile network. They will be looking out for it, now that I am away, so to speak."

"So how do I use it then?" To her surprise, Margie was speaking as though she had already been selected for the Gorschkov interview. It also intrigued her that she was speaking to the appointed assassin of her husband, without any antagonism. She actually found herself attracted to this forceful young woman. Guiltily, she tucked away her feelings of admiration towards this feisty young woman.

"To activate just the camera, you switch it on and scroll down to 'call barring' on the 'security settings' tab of the main menu to bar all incoming calls. This will deny interrogation by my people and they will not be able to identify the phone when you switch it on. You should do this somewhere outside the mobile footprint, otherwise they may pick you up as you turn it on. I suspect they will probably have a twenty-four hour vigil on that phone."

"I'm not too happy with that, Ludmilla." Jack Wise raised a hand. "If they have some other way of identifying your phone, then Margie here would not only be walking into the lion's den, she would be climbing into his mouth. We have camera equipment here, which would fill the bill quite adequately. Peggy, would you call comms and ask Mr Taylor to pop up for a moment?"

Grant Taylor was an invaluable part of the Hamilton Terrace set-up. Having served with the Royal Corps of Signals, he had been selected for the Special Boat Service as a communications specialist. In this role he had operated under deep cover in some of the more sensitive areas of the globe. He had accumulated an encyclopaedic knowledge of the possibilities of secure communications and ways to circumvent the firewalls and filters the opposition put in place to prevent access to their secrets. He had worked extensively with Jack the Hack, when Trinidadian had been 'doing some computer work for the MOD' based in Alborough Mews.

When he arrived from his workshop in the basement, Taylor looked an unlikely candidate for his demanding job. His physical fitness was disguised by a lean, almost spindly frame, topped by a mop of unruly ginger hair, giving him his inevitable nickname. His slight build had astonished his fellow soldiers when he took the British Army record for the marathon, by a full six minutes.

"Good afternoon, Mr Wise," he smiled as he came into the office. "What are you up to with all these pretty ladies?"

Jack returned the smile. That was another of Grant Taylor's qualities, the envy of his colleagues. His diminutive stature seemed to bring out motherly instincts in the opposite sex and he was never short of female

376

company. "Hello Ginger, we need a very discreet camera for Margie here. She has to interview a member of the opposition and we would like her to bring back some pictures of the interviewee. Have you anything?"

"Well, Mr Wise. She has pretty eyes, so, might I suggest the Zircon brooch for her scarf? It is a zero-emissions unit and can store up to fifty twelve mega-pixel images. I think it would look very attractive on the lady in question, don't you?"

Alex was now smiling at his wife's amusement. The Taylor magic was working already! "So, Margie, you are going on this escapade regardless of your husband's concerns?"

"Oh, come along Alex. You're not the only one who needs a bit of excitement. Now it's my turn."

Alex shrugged his shoulders and looked at Jack. "Well Jack, what do you think? She'll have to sign up, I suppose." Alex was referring to the Official Secrets Act, which they all signed before embarking on any mission involving the MOD.

"Well Margie? Are you happy with that?"

"Sure," said Margie.

"Okay," Jack turned to his secretary, "Peggy, could you do the honours?"

"Certainly, Mr Wise. Here we go." and she presented the relevant document to Margie. "You sign here and down there. Mr Wise will witness it for you."

"... and Miss Scharanski?"

"Miss Scharanski is not a citizen of GB, Mr Wise."

"Oh well, Ludmilla, I suppose we will just have to trust you. We're working in your favour, so we are not at cross purposes." Ludmilla nodded her head in acceptance. "So we had better organise the drop and get the ball rolling. Ludmilla, can you and Margie get your heads together and you can brief her on the drop. I suggest that replies to the drop should come via an advert in the newspapers. See if you can work something out. You can use No 23. I don't think anyone's in there."

The two women stood up and left the room. The Gorshkov Connection was rolling. Its significance to the future could hardly be exaggerated.

That afternoon, Margie went to the hairdressers and came out with nicotine blonde hair, high gloss lipstick and enormous black eyelashes. She looked so different that Robbie and Jessie did not recognise their mother when she went round to her sister's apartment to get changed. Penny howled with laughter when she worked out who was standing at her door as she opened it. "Margie! You little tart! That's fantastic!" Then the two children saw their mother hiding behind the disguise. Robbie burst out laughing and Jessie started crying but, when she saw that everyone else was laughing, she ran and clung to Margie's skirts, burying her embarrassment in their folds.

"Now come along children. Mummy has to go out." Once again she started to cry.

"Why do you have to go out all the time?" she whimpered.

"Don't cry Darling. Mummy will be back soon and then she will stay with you for the rest of the day. All right?" The two children looked at her and Robbie went back to his book about ships. He loved ships. In fact, he loved any big machines driven by tiny human beings. "Jessie, come and help Mummy get ready. She has to go and meet a very important man, so she has to look her best. Come and give me a hand." Jessie took her mother's hand and allowed herself to be led through to Penny's dressing room. Margie would be borrowing the wardrobe from her sister for this particular performance.

Soon she was ready. She wore a dark pink shirt under a sober navy suit. Her shoes were comfortable light tan brogues with one-inch heels. The soft mauve silk scarf wound around her neck was fastened with a small brooch set with three large zircons separated by two small diamonds. One did not glitter with quite the same sparkle as the other as, beneath the surface of the central plane of one diamond was a lens. The digital mechanism and battery were stored behind the two right hand stones. It was a work of such minute ingenuity that it took Margie's breath away. The craft of a watchmaker combined with the cunning of a magician. To activate the camera, there was a minute pressure switch under the left hand zircon. Storage on the camera's minuscule memory cell was sixty-four gigabytes, enough capacity to hold six hours of video. It was a very clever piece of kit and it gave off no radiation to betray its position to sensors.

Margie left Hamilton Terrace in an anonymous little Peugeot, which took her to Trafalgar Square. It was dark and a light drizzle caused the traffic to swish as it passed through the streets of the West End.

By arrangement with the National Gallery library, Margie entered the National Portrait Gallery, through a door at the rear of the main building. Security escorted her to the library where she successfully found the title 'Early Pre-Raphaelite Egg Tempura Paintings' by Sir Claude Daneforth-Everard. She slipped a note in between pages 62 and 63 and returned the book to its proper place among the erudite, though hardly opened, volumes that lined the shelves at the far corner of the library. The note was addressed to YG and instructed him to meet a representative of LS at the Cow Bell Milk Bar in Warwick Avenue at 10 a.m. on the 17th February, the day after tomorrow. Acknowledgment of these instructions would be made by entering the following message in the personal column of the Evening Standard: "Please come home L. We miss you." YG must carry a copy of the paper and a blue file, wear gloves and sit at the counter as close as possible to the window. He should be drinking a banana milk shake.

The following day, Margie caught her breath as her eyes lighted on the familiar words in the newspaper. "Please come home L. We miss you." The game was on.

On the morning of the 17th, it was cold and clear as Margie set out from Penny's flat. She took the Bakerloo underground to Warwick Avenue and walked from the station to the milk bar. It took her less than ten minutes. She entered the little cafe as the minute hand passed the twelve on her watch. There were two young students sitting on bar stools by the window. They were both girls in their late teens or early twenties. Next to them sat a grey-haired lady in a gabardine mac, reading a paper. There was a party of middle-aged housewives obviously out for a morning's shopping. They were at a table the other side of the room. They all appeared to be talking at the same time and not listening to a word anybody else was saying. There were no men in the bar.

Margie took a seat at a table next to the talkative shoppers and waited. Five past ten. Ten past ten. It was at ten fifteen that Margie noticed the blue file. The reason why she looked up was because the grey-haired lady, next to the two students ordered a banana milk shake. She waved a blue cardboard file to gain the attention of the girl who was serving behind the bar. She wore blue woollen gloves.

Margie rose to her feet, pressed the left hand Zirkon, as though adjusting her scarf and went over to where the woman was sitting. She took a stool by the bar, leaving one empty place between her and the lady. There was a paper place mat on the counter in front of her. She took a ballpoint pen from her bag and, in large letters, she wrote 'YG' then allowed it to fall on the floor. She reached down and picked it up, glancing at the lady as she moved the sheet up to the bar, in full sight of her unexpected target. The lady nodded. "Good morning." she said.

"Good morning," Margie replied, "couldn't he make it?"

"We can sit over there. Is better."

"Okay, lead the way."

They went back to the table where Margie had been sitting. "So what's with Yuri then?"

"I am Yuri Gorschkov." A twinkle of humour flickered momentarily at the corners of her eyes.

"Well I'm blowed!" Margie gasped in a suppressed whisperk. "My apologies, I was expecting a rather

381

different person. But anyway, what do you want to talk about? I'm all ears."

"Are you accompanied?"

"No, they let me out on my own now. I'm old enough."

Yuri Gorschkov smiled broadly. "You are in contact with Miss Ludmilla Scharanski?"

"I know people who know people who are in contact with Ludmilla Scharanski, yes. What do you want with her?"

"I bring a message from certain members of the Sluzhba Vneshney Razvedki."

"I can get it to her, if you are happy with that. Where is your message?"

"It is in this blue file, but first, I cannot emphasise strongly enough the extreme discretion required in these negotiations. If any of this becomes known to parties with vested interests in the old system, then the future of Russia, the future of the whole world will be under threat. Do I make myself clear?"

"Indeed you do, Miss Gorschkov, indeed you do and, rest assured, I am fully aware of the importance of discretion in all our dealings. We all are." Margie leaned forward to lay stress on her words. "May I ask why you are trying to contact Miss Scharanski?"

"As you may have already heard, Miss Scharanski is well known to me. I have been her controller at the SVR these last four years. Of course, we have never met, so she will be unaware of my identity. She will not be pleased to be contacted by me as she will see me as the instrument behind the attempt on her life. I can, however, assure you and her that I was not involved in the decision to terminate her services, in the same way that she was not involved in the decision to terminate Mr Barnes, Mr Baccarat, Mr Strand, Mr Borden, Mr Lutov or, for that matter, Mr Stewart. She was simply the tool used to effect the terminations. When she failed in two attempts on D/Comm Jason, it was decided that she had become a threat to SVR operations in this country and following SVR procedures, she had to be removed."

"I understand that, Miss Gorschkov, but why the sudden interest in renewing contact now?"

"I am sure that you will be familiar with developments on the political stage in Moscow."

Margie nodded. "With the departure of the President and the Prime Minister, there must be a bit of a power vacuum in the Kremlin."

"Precisely," Gorschkov nodded in return. "As you may also know, Russia is ruled by a tiny group of extremely competitive individuals who are at each other's throats on a minute by minute basis. With the departure of Belnikov and Ilyich, Chernorgin, the head of the SVR disappeared. Some believe that he is in hiding, others believe that he has been disposed of by the oligarchs. He has many deadly enemies. Whatever the truth, the SVR currently has no leader and is, therefore, in a state of acute vacillation. Many members of the government, in the absence of leadership, are even expressing a desire for a return to the old monarchy."

"Ludmilla Romanova Scharanski." Margie's voice was flat as the realisation dawned on her that this woman was presenting what amounted to a direct invitation from senior members of the Russian security services. The full weight of what little Ludmilla was taking on suddenly dawned and, for a moment, she had a problem believing that she was not dreaming this whole thing up.

"Are you serious?"

"In that file you will find a document, signed by many of the most senior officers in the SVR. This is not a forgery. This is a proposal of the utmost importance. When we discovered that Miss Scharansky had defected, we also found out her family links with the Romanovs. As a symbolic leader there could hardly be a better choice. She has direct ties with the old Royal Family but also with the Soviet Communist era. She also has good looks and a brain. What more could our country hope for?"

"That would seem to be a pretty unbeatable combination. The only thing going against her is her age and experience. Do you think that a twenty-nine-year-old has the experience to be able to rule such an unruly collection of self-seekers?"

"Well, your Queen took the throne of what was then the largest empire that the world had ever seen, when she was younger than Miss Scharanski and look at her great-great-aunt, Victoria, who took over when she was only twenty-three and stayed there for more than sixty years. With a pedigree like that, I cannot see a problem for Miss Scharanski."

"You have a good point there. The major problems in your plan are to protect Miss Scharanski from what you term 'the vested interests' and to introduce her to the people of Russia as a credible alternative to the present holders of power."

"That is where this document comes in." Gorschkov held up the blue file. "When she sees this, I believe Miss Scharanski will come to accept that even those whom she may have perceived as a threat are now rallying round her. Would you be prepared to deliver it to her?"

"With great pleasure, Miss Gorschkov," Margie took the folder, "and, if we need to contact you?"

"I think the drop system is best at the moment, although we should change the venue, since this one is well known to the SVR. What about Camden Public Library? Let me just call them." The Russian went over to the counter and asked for a phone book. After looking through it, she tapped a number into her mobile and pressed the call button.

"Do you by any chance have a copy of 'The Heraldry of Butterflies' by Francis Lacorte." There was a slight pause while the librarian checked her computer. "You have? Oh, thank you very much." She turned to Margie. "Between pages 61 and 62, 'The Heraldry of Butterflies' by Francis Lacorte, at the Camden Public Library. Will you remember that?"

"Yes, I've got that."

"Then I must be on my way before I am missed." As she stood, she held her hand out to Margie. "I hope that this will be the first of many meetings, Mrs Stewart."

Once again, Margie was dumbfounded. How on Earth, could Gorschkov have known her identity? "How did you know?" She blurted.

"Our mutual friend, Ludmilla Scharanski took these photos of you when you came over from Africa for your husband's funeral, after his tragic accident." Gorschkov showed a small sheaf of pictures, taken at Heathrow, as Margie, looking distraught, led her two children through the press of photographers at Arrivals. "The hair is quite good, but your face is a difficult one to disguise. I hope you will take that as a compliment, Mrs Stewart. Good day to you." She was smiling broadly as she left the milk bar.

Chapter 31

The revelations concerning the IDC scandal had a resounding effect on the American economy. Hartford's Mayor Levinson became the target of an FBI investigation. Suspicions surrounded his acquisition of large tracts of land at knock down prices in Hartford North End, prior to the introduction of the IDC system to the impoverished area. The subsequent skyrocketing value of the properties, made Levinson one of the richest men in the American Civil Service and the envy of those who had missed out on the bandwagon. Envy is a dangerous enemy and Levinson discovered that his previous popularity evaporated overnight, as soon as his new-found riches made the headlines. The irony was that the public was still strongly in favour of the IDC system. They were just deeply envious of the man who had introduced it to the States.

Similarly, the Tarnbeck Experiment was considered a great success and the IDC system spread rapidly throughout the UK because of irresistible popular demand, in spite of the fact that it had, on one occasion, completely failed. Everyone wanted to be part of the new moneyless economy.

Soon physical mountains of money began to pile up in the IDC Board offices. As more and more people swung away from the expensive use of cash, exchanging it for the cheap and simple use of the IDC, banks began to lose their function. They relied on money therefore, no money, no banks.

More and more persuasive advertising attempted to lure the fickle public back to the loan sharks who had fleeced them for millennia. The bankers suddenly saw the empty future yawning before them. If nobody wanted money, then how were the bankers going to receive their grotesque salaries and bonus payments. Up until now, they had held the world to ransom. Governments tripped over themselves in order to prevent financial disasters. They bailed out banks with taxpayers' money. They happily rescued bankrupt financial institutions, to the tune of, not millions, but billions, some even spoke of trillions of dollars, in order to keep the economy going. They even continued to finance obscene bonuses. The bankers said that, without the enormous bonuses, they could not keep the people who knew how to run the old capitalist system. Initially the government had to agree and so, grossly overblown salaries and bonuses were being paid to the staff and CEOs. There was a desperate rush amongst the mega-earners, to grab as much as they could, before the IDC Board tripped in and money became worth just Credits. Now it looked as though money was rapidly becoming irrelevant.

To obtain a loan from the Credit Authority was simple and interest free. Each individual had a fixed credit limit, calculated on salary plus stored capital. It was impossible for a 'member' to borrow more than he or she owned. The Authority would simply not allow that to happen. Information on the financial status of each person was instantly available from the computer.

People who were prudent with their credits could live very comfortably. People who were not, ended up in front of the Dole Tribunal who, in the right circumstances, could re-activate an IDC which had failed, due to excessive withdrawals on a card which had insufficient funds to support them. An application for re-activation would be studied on individual merits and the members concerned would probably be required to perform some tasks for the

Authority for free, to restore their credit rating. Clearing blocked field drains or sewers or cutting back unruly brambles were normal tasks for the indebted and the company involved would be pleased to have their free labour. Persistent debtors might have their cards completely de-activated, which meant that they would rely totally on the Authority for life support.

Those who made grotesque demands for 'Credits' on their 'bonuses' would also be assessed as to their overall contribution to the general wellbeing of the national economy. This would be calculated on how much they had actually contributed to keeping their employees in work. A recent case, where an old-established and well-loved chocolate making company, who had guaranteed work to their employees through the difficult years of the Second World War, was wiped out by a hostile bid from an American company who made mainly tinned cheese. The chocolate factory had built a town to support its employees with kindergartens, schools and quality housing. Now the housing concept had collapsed. Security for the employees had collapsed and it was too late to yearn for the past. The world had been changed by greed. Under the IDC system, that could never have happened.

Big Brother had arrived at the noisy demand of the public, and they were happy. They were not just happy but were demanding the new system under which all the previous employees of the old chocolate company would be guaranteed their houses and pensions, if the management agreed to the new IDC. "Life WILL go on as normal, but you will not need money. We will handle that for you."

It was at this point that the sinister presence of Vladimir Chernorgin arose from the turmoil of Russian politics.

Rumours of Ludmilla Scharanski's defection and her emergence as a figurehead for the new Russia were rife.

Chernorgin's one hope of survival among the oligarchs was to threaten the capitalist world which was backing her and Chernorgin had the precise tool to effect this apocalypse. He alone, among the highest ranks of the old regime, had access to the IDC. The team who had secretly been developing the technology to close down the complete system was still in place and he was the only survivor of the three who could activate it to kill the verification chips. All he needed to do was to give them the go-ahead.

The message came through signals transmitted via channels with which Ludmilla was already familiar, and intercepted by the Government Communications HQ in Cheltenham, England. The SVR was following lines of communication established during the cold war and their message was clear and unequivocal. "In order to prevent a global catastrophe, MI6 must hand over Scharanski to officers who will be in contact. Receipt of this message can be acknowledged by placing a large Tesco shopping bag in the window of the office of Deputy Commissioner of the Metropolitan Police in New Scotland Yard. If no acknowledgment is observed in the next seventy-two hours, the process will be initiated."

"So, now what, Jack?" Jason had called Jack Wise.

"Why don't we try a Harrods bag and see what they do? They sent the message over ancient code equipment and they might think that we are not up to speed."

"Okay, let's try it."

The SVR are not noted for their sense of humour and Vladimir Chernorgin was a prime example. When the Harrods bag appeared in Jason's window, Chernorgin, far from appreciating the joke, seethed with rage. These British fools would see how their sense of humour would affect the world. The last laugh would be on them. They would see. He called the concealed unit responsible for de-activating the verification chips and ordered them to proceed with the process that led the West Riding of Yorkshire Police to believe that the entire population of Tarnbeck had expired.

By now, there were rather more people involved. The populations of Hartford West and Hartford North End, East St Louis, Opa-locka, in Florida, Memphis Tennessee, Nashville, Clarksville, Rockport and even New Orleans, Los Angeles and San Francisco, Baltimore and Seattle and, further afield, Buenos Aires, Argentina, Kyoto in Japan joined the expansion. The list went on and on. They were all locked into Georg Lutov's IDC system and they were loving it.

Even Singapore was looking at it and, in Hong Kong, the shops and department stores were setting up their computers in preparation for a system, which would be introduced by public demand, not imposed by an intrusive government. The whole country was shouting to escape the monetary system and the corrupt bankers which had leached preposterous profits, throwing thousands into bankruptcy and homelessness, divorce and even suicide. The IDC system was the new dawn. For the first time since the introduction of coinage, mankind would escape being held to ransom by bankers, and Vladimir Chernorgin held the key. Now he had power over more people than any man had ever possessed in the history of the world. He turned the IDC off. He de-activated all the verification chips, worldwide.

In one instant the commercial world came to a halt. The population of the developed world was suddenly denied access to homes, cars, food, anything which required the use of the IDC. Since money was no longer available, and with no substitute around, trading, effectively, ceased and along with it, normal life.

"Did you see the papers this morning, sir?" Freddie Kinyanjui was delivering the night's batch of diplomatic signals to Christopher Odihambo.

"There weren't any, were there?"

"No, sir, well I haven't seen any. I believe there has been a complete news blackout. Apparently the IDCs have failed. Even the BBC is off the air."

"What's going on Freddie? This happened once before, didn't it? They had to get that young German to come and fix things."

"Yes, sir. He reckoned that it was done deliberately. He said that there were so many back-ups and fail-safe devices installed that it would be impossible for the system to go down completely. The irony is that all our signals from Kenya have come through."

"Yes," The High Commissioner smiled, "the country is apparently operating as normal. The Kenya Shilling is still in circulation and commercial life continues as before. Funny, really, when you think about it. Everybody was shouting about how stupid the government was not to jump at the chance to join the system, and now our government looks like a group of wise old birds who won the day by dragging their feet." Kinyanjui liked this High Commissioner's directness. Even though they were from politically opposing tribes, he enjoyed working for this man. It could be something to do with his British upbringing, or maybe the fact that his father had been a diplomat before him. His outlook was broad-minded and cosmopolitan. "You couldn't get the kitchen to rustle up some tea could you, Freddie, before they cut off the power."

"Certainly, sir."

"Come and join me, if you've got a moment. I wouldn't mind chewing over some of the security implications with you."

"I'll be right with you, sir."

Freddie Kinyanjui returned to the High Commissioner's office after speaking to an orderly. The office reflected the urbanity of its incumbent. Pictures of Kenyan scenes hung from the walls. They were originals. A line of bronze sable antelope sculpted by a white Kenyan, leapt gracefully along the top of an old Mvuli wood bookcase. Its contents reflected the High Commissioner's wide taste in reading material. The books were not there simply for decoration.

There was a warm greenness to the room which reminded the Major of the light which came from the forest close to his own house the side of Mount Kenya. A silver-framed photograph of the High Commissioner presenting his credentials to Her Majesty, was signed by her 'With Best Wishes.' Christopher Odihambo had been a guest at

Balmoral, on more than one occasion and his son, Tom, had studied in the same class as the heir apparent. They had even played squash together. Tom was an excellent player. Their friendship had continued through university and there had been a certain amount of friendly rivalry for the attentions of one particular member of the opposite sex. The Prince finally conceded defeat but their friendship survived intact. On several occasions the Prince had paid visits to the Odihambos in Kenya.

Christopher Odihambo moved over to a pair of comfortable armchairs near a window looking out onto the High Commission gardens. "So, Freddie, come and sit down here and let's get things straightened out. First of all, security."

"If we get a prolonged power cut, we have two generators, so that should not affect the integrity of the security system. Communications locally could be affected if our credit runs out with the phone company. I imagine that the CABNI will have to come up with a contingency plan to tide everyone over until they get things up and running again, otherwise the whole country will come to a grinding halt."

"Judging by what's happened so far, it looks as though it already has." Odihambo was smiling, unphased by the emergency. He almost seemed to be enjoying it. It was interesting watching how a country as sophisticated as the UK could be brought to its knees so quickly by the breakdown of a man-made machine.

"Long-range comms should be okay. We have satellite links with Nairobi and we even have an old Paktor set."

"What's a Paktor set when it's at home, Freddie?"

"It's like the old telex, but it is transmitted over the HF radio. It works quite well actually. The trouble is, I think we are running out of people to talk to. It is a bit of a museum piece."

"Okay. Let's get in contact with Nairobi and let them know what's up." He massaged his forehead. "Now, have we got supplies in to see us through? How's the fuel situation for the generators and cars?"

"I'll check on that sir."

"Then we ought to have somebody checking on how things are developing. Simon Olempatu's doing UK Foreign Office liaison isn't he? He may need a good pair of shoes, if the fuel runs out." The High Commissioner was smiling again.

In Downing Street, Bryan Jones, the Chancellor of the Exchequer had been called urgently to Number 10. The Prime Minister had assembled his cabinet around him. He could sense that there was a general feeling that his insistence on the adoption of the IDCs was at the bottom of this disaster. The media would doubtless let their feelings be known in no uncertain terms. It was of immediate importance to his political future that the system should be up and running as soon as possible. "Where is that Lutov character?" He was almost shouting at the Home Secretary and she flinched before replying.

"I believe he returned to Germany, when news of the Russian involvement came to light, Prime Minister."

"We need him over here. We need him here right now. Send a 'plane to Hanover, if necessary. He invented the damn things. He must know how to fix them."

"Will you be wanting to re-activate the monetary system, Prime Minster, in case the IDCs stay down for a while?" The Chancellor had always been nervous about the sudden change away from the time-honoured method of trading.

"No Johnnie that will not be necessary. It would move us back to the bad old days. I am not prepared to allow that. I want access to the CABNI. We cannot afford to have central government interrupted by a little system malfunction. It is ridiculous not having anyone here who can fix these things." Crighton thumped a fist on the table. "GET LUTOV" he shouted in the general direction of everyone in the room.

Throughout the day the true scale of the catastrophe unfolded. Messages started to filter in from all over the world. Widespread rioting broke out in many parts of the United States as people were refused service without a working IDC. In desperation, members of the public broke into food stores and looted them. The looting quickly spread to other shops. Soon there was a general free-for-all. The police were no match for the rampaging crowds.

National Guard units were called out to restore order when the Legislative Assembly building of Connecticut was trashed and set alight. Two firemen were beaten to death by the mob. Twenty-two in the crowd were killed in the armed response of the National Guard. Some of the dead were killed by their uniformed and well-armed sons.

The same scenes erupted in Sao Paulo, Brazil and Buenos Aires in Argentina. The Singapore Dollar leapt in value against the dying Japanese yen. The American dollar had ceased to trade on the international money market, so powerful had been the takeover of the IDC. Some developing countries still used the dollar, in the absence of a workable alternative.

The Pound Sterling had become a collector's piece, no longer legal tender, after the 31st of March. Of course I promise to pay the bearer on demand the sum of twenty pounds' had, since the introduction of the IDC, reverted to the lie, which it had always been since the termination of the Sterling Silver Standard. Since that date a ten pound note had simply been a piece of paper with a promise, which the banks had consistently failed to honour over the years, right up to the present day. Now they were gone, because the new system had arrived, and failed.

Georg Lutov arrived at Northolt aboard a Royal Air Force Jetstream 31. He was met by Jack Wise who drove him straight to the central directory of the IDCs in Milton Keynes. Specialists had been working through the night, trying to isolate the malfunction disabling the verification chips, without success. From their point of view there was no malfunction. The satellites were working correctly but they were receiving an instruction from somewhere, which stubbornly forbade them from acknowledging the synchronization of the verification chips with the appropriate IDCs.

Every time the experts managed to get the chips to communicate with the cards, an instruction popped up from nowhere and changed the coding of the chip and this denied any transaction the card was trying to perform. It was as though somebody had jumbled up all the numbers, and Lutov had his suspicions as to who might be involved. Then he had an idea. If the IDC malfunction was intentional then, whoever was doing it must be using the same galaxy of satellites as the IDC Board. Changing to an alternative galaxy should cure the problem or at least until the hacker discovered which satellites the authority had moved to.

After Georg Lutov had been filtered through tight security at Central Directory, he logged on to the main computer terminal and extracted the coding for the satellites, currently being used by the Authority. In order to test his theory, he wanted access to a separate satellite system. Several commercial operators were available, but none of them was prepared to offer their services for free. Only after repeated assurances of the Director of the CABNI himself, did they finally agree and released the access codes and dish orientation for the experiment.

Very soon after that, Lutov managed to open up an avenue of communication between the verification chips and the IDCs, and the whole system came back on line. It continued to function for almost twenty-four hours before the hackers zeroed in on the new satellites and blocked them. Georg Lutov scratched his head again. It was obvious that some form of encryption would be necessary in order to preserve the integrity of the IDCs. By employing a similar signal to the GPS pseudorandom code, he could continuously change the coding and defeat the hackers. He called Sam Jackson while the IDCs were still functioning and the Trinidadian made his way round to the Central Directory with his familiar, pleasant tingling feeling, in anticipation of the challenge ahead.

Employing techniques similar to those which had enabled him to break into the Pentagon and Langley computer networks, he intended to find out just who was fiddling around with the IDCs. If he could do that, then he could introduce them to a virus. It was a new one, known as 'the Dog' because of its voracious appetite for hard drives, the difficulty in getting rid of it and the mess it leaves behind when it has finished.

Once Sam got his teeth into a project of this nature, he would go without sleep until he had achieved his target. To see Sam in action was an eye-opener for Georg Lutov. His meticulous attention to the logic employed by the hackers eventually led him to their geographical location, and finally to the actual computer they were using. Luckily their internet provider was not connected to Western links. The SVR closely controlled and monitored ROL in much the same way the CIA kept a sharp eye on such providers as Aol, Facebook and Myspace. Sam's aim was to give ROL a pet. He would give them a little 'Dog' to play with.

While Sam and Georg worked on getting the IDCs back on line, Jack and Johnnie Jason concentrated on finding the source of the problem.

Ludmilla Scharanski was pivotal in their investigations. She urgently needed to find out who was on which side in the chaotic political mayhem running Russia in the absence of its two leaders. Yuri Gorschkov would eventually lead her to Vladimir Chernorgin. Gorschkov was still a fully paid-up member of the SVR and, with the turmoil currently reigning in Moscow, her name was rapidly rising to the top of the pile.

Suspicion was one of the main motivations of the SVR and this driver of ambition was so ingrained among its staff that it tended to dull their senses to things that should arouse genuine suspicion. None of them spotted the fact that Yuri Gorschkov had changed sides. In truth most members of the SVR staff were unaware that Gorschkov was, in fact, female. Chernorgin was one of the cognoscenti, because it was he who had recruited her and he would never have suspected her of joining the opposing team. She had too much to lose. He knew her. She would not throw away her future in the new post-Belnikov Russia. Of this he was certain. What he did not realise was that he would be the one to lose his future and Gorschkov would be the one to take his place.

Margie found the note between pages 62 and 63 in the 'Heraldry of Butterflies' in the Camden Public Library. She took it back to Hamilton Terrace and handed it to Scharanski. It proposed a meeting at a small Italian restaurant close to the Grand Union Canal in Little Venice. Gorschkov suggested that Scharanski bring Margie with her as a guarantor of her safety. Gorschkov said that she would come unaccompanied, as before.

Margie led Ludmilla Scharanski over to the table where the now familiar grey-haired figure of Yuri Gorschkov was sitting. It was the first time the two Russians had met, in spite of their professional relationship, which stretched back over almost five years. Ludmilla was surprised that she felt unaccountably secure in the presence of her erstwhile controller. She was expecting to feel threatened, to experience a feeling of loathing, even a twinge of fear, but she didn't. Within minutes, she felt relaxed and when she heard what the SVR agent had to say, her relaxation turned to excitement.

If what Gorschkov said was correct, then the SVR was ready for change. She mentioned that there was a groundswell among top industrialists in Russia to rid themselves of the oppressive cult of secrecy encouraged by the Belnikov regime. It was time for a breath of fresh air to blow through the corridors of the Kremlin. She suggested that there was growing support for the idea of bringing Scharanski back as a young leader. Her history with the SVR and the SVR's attempt on her life enhanced her credibility on both sides of the political spectrum.

"How would you feel about meeting some of my colleagues, so that you could see that I am not operating alone?" Gorschkov was speaking in precise and colloquial English, for Margie's benefit and Scharanski had come to the point where she was even thinking in English.

"I would be very interested indeed." Ludmilla's pulse raced at the prospect of such a meeting. "How can you keep this from the all-seeing eye of the SVR?"

"One way is not to tell anybody about our meetings until the ball starts rolling. There will come a point when people will have to know and, as far as I am concerned, the sooner the better. Government by rumour is not a good way to rule a country. The only thing delaying me from revealing the whole story is that there are still many old school communists around and we need to have something positive to offer them before we break the news."

"How much support do you have back in Russia?" Margie was fascinated to have come in on the ground floor, so to speak. She was watching history in the making.

"It is hard to tell right now, because the conspiracy of silence is a very strong legacy of a century of communism. But when you (Gorschkov turned and nodded at Ludmilla) paid a visit to Russia, as Miss Leonora Schrader, a lot of people suspected that it was really you. They called you 'The Scharanski.' Even Belnikov knew you were a threat. Your name was among the last words he uttered as he died. Mrs Petrovotsky, the old lady who watched him die, told the police, after they took him away to lie in state."

This news left Ludmilla even more confused than before. It seemed that here was confirmation of her status as a possible successor to the old regime, but the closing down of the IDCs meant that there was substantial intervention possible from the old guard.

"Could we not offer the regime the IDC? As you can see, it would have been a grand success in the capitalist world, were it not for the intervention of 'certain parties'."

"I think that sounds like a very sound plan. What we need to do is to study how susceptible the IDC's are to corruption. It is very obvious from what has just occurred, that the system is vulnerable and we need to monitor that continuously in order to prevent it falling into the wrong hands. The answer would probably be to hand back the Arches Stationery Group to the original owners and let them work on that."

Margie was not sure how far to let Gorschkov into the family, but she could hardly avoid the fact that Gorschkov knew all about the Lutovs. "Are you sure of Russian involvement in the close-down of the IDCs."

"Well, if you had spoken to Georg Lutov before he was terminated," she shot a meaningful look at Ludmilla, "he would have told you that the Russians were deeply involved through their financing of the Ost Deutsche Bank. I now regret that we had to take him out of the game. He would have been a key player in the new round." So Yuri Gorschkov was still under the impression that Georg Lutov was no longer of this world. Margie thought for a moment of letting their new friend in on the secret until she felt the unmistakable pressure of Ludmilla's boot on her toe under the table. "Oh well, maybe the old man will still remember the basics, if he is prepared to work for us."

"We can but try," said Ludmilla, "or maybe they will find somebody who can work out how to prevent the hackers from blocking the system."

"It surely cannot be beyond the realms of human ingenuity." Margie had enormous faith in Jack the Hack's brain. In fact she was confident he had already found a solution, which, of course, he had. His little 'Dog', which he had given to the Russians was romping its way through the computers of the hacking unit, set up to block the verification chips. By the time that the operators realised that the virus had side-stepped all their firewalls and filters without triggering a single alarm, it was much too late. It had sneaked in, pretending to be the very anti-virus protection which was supposed to protect them. A secondary virus protection system spotted the problem and instantly closed the primary protection down, thinking it had been infected, but the primary system was having none of that and closed down the secondary system. While the two systems fought it out, the little Dog waltzed past them and gobbled up the complete set of hard drives, along with their processing units. The whole secret unit was shredded in less time than it would take to close it down normally. The smile on Sam's face was infectious and soon spread to the stern features of Georg Lutov. The IDC system was saved.

Chapter 32

Three years later

"Hello Sam, it's Jack Wise. I was wondering whether you would like to come over for a little gathering of the clan, at His Majesty's expense, of course." Jack had taken days to get used to referring to the new monarch by the correct gender.

The Queen had been injured controlling runaway horses. The horses had bolted as a device exploded as the Royal Procession passed down the Mall during the celebrations of her sixty-five years of reign. Her act of extraordinary skill and horsemanship had, very possibly, saved the lives of her coachmen and members of the crowd for whom the horses were heading, charging in panic.

Three Metropolitan police officers, together with four members of the crowd and two troopers from the Household Cavalry were killed in the explosion and thirty-two were injured, twelve seriously. Seven horses had to be destroyed. An unknown group calling itself 'Das Kapital' claimed responsibility but the incredible bravery of the octogenarian Queen would go down in history as a symbol of British courage. It bound the nation together as nothing had done since the dark days of World War II.

The Queen's injuries would have killed a lesser person, but miraculously, she survived. She was dragged down the road behind the horses that had broken free of the limbers that attached them to the Queen's carriage. As the horseless open landau careered out of control, she climbed forward and grabbed the reins from her coachmen as they flew through the air. She hung on to them, cursing and swearing as she bounced and tumbled across the asphalt.

She knew each of the horses well, by name, and they knew her too and eventually, her furious shouting brought them to their senses. Sadly, by this time, Her Majesty was terribly injured. The rescue services were on the scene within seconds and tenderly coaxed the royal personage on to a stretcher and into an ambulance, to be rushed away to the London Clinic. The nation waited apprehensively for news of her condition.

Finally, at just after six in the evening, her Doctor, Sir Daoud Yakoub, appeared at the main entrance to the clinic. He held a written page in front of him and asked for quiet.

"Her Majesty The Queen has suffered extensive injuries as a result of her heroic action this afternoon. Her condition is now stable and she is conscious. She has thanked the rescue services that transferred her so promptly to this Clinic. She has also asked me to tell you that she will speak to the nation as soon as she is able. Meanwhile, she has asked me to say, that now is the time to demonstrate one of the renowned qualities of the British people; courage in times of adversity."

Sir David, as he was known nationally, held his hands up as questions erupted from Press in the crowded forecourt.

"I have work to do," he shouted as he turned to re-enter the clinic. Many of the assembled journalists shouted "Good luck, Dave. Look after her! Get her back in one piece!" He looked back at them and shouted, "I'll do everything I can." He held up his hand with fingers crossed and got a cheer from the hacks.

The Queen responded well to treatment. Being a horsewoman, it was not the first time that she had broken bones, but when she was given the list of fractures she had incurred in the Mall, her remark was, "David! I didn't realise I had so many bones in my body!" which raised a smile on the face of the orthopedic surgeon responsible for her recovery.

Typically, she felt obliged, in her inconvenient condition, to step down from the throne, in order to allow her son to take the reins. It seemed an apposite moment to secede.

In a characteristically humorous response to questions from the media, the Prince simply replied. "My Mother, the Queen, has asked me to 'take the reign', while she recovers. I have some experience in this field, but I shall appreciate all the assistance I can get. My thanks to you all, in advance."

News of her abdication brought a groan of sadness from the nation and many other parts of the world. Her handover speech, made from her hospital bed surrounded by all the surgical paraphernalia involved in her recovery, was so optimistic and stirring that it brought tears of admiration and patriotism to the eyes of many of her subjects. It also instilled an intense feeling of pride in being British and restored the backbone to a nation whose morale was in sore need of resuscitation.

The televised speech was introduced by Jonathan Bentham, an old newsreader friend of Her Majesty's. Bentham had introduced the Queen's Christmas Speech on many occasions and was well known to the audience.

"Good evening, everybody. Unused as I am to being the purveyor of good news, I am now sitting by the bed of Her Majesty the Queen, who has, miraculously, survived an extraordinary incident with an act of skill and heroism.

Her doctors have given us access in order that she may speak to you, her people, and I will not stand in her way."

The camera panned to a scene worthy of a science-fiction movie, with cranes and pulleys, video monitors and bandages and a bed. As the camera focussed, there was an image in the middle of all the paraphanalia that nobody could mistake. Her Majesty the Queen, with one of her eyes swollen and bruised and several cuts and grazes on her face was smiling a smile that turned, what could have been a scene of disaster, into a celebration of triumph over intimidating odds.

"Friends and fellow countrymen, as you can see, I was very lucky to be spared in this outrage. My heart goes out to the bereaved and the mourning. Our nation takes heart from your courage. Your example now will inspire us to carry on. Your dead are heroes, as are you. What I will say to you is that the perpetrators of this cowardly act will see a reaction very different to the one for which they were hoping. We, the British, will not be cowed by these evil people. What they have achieved, far better than anyone else could have done, is to bind together the people of Great Britain as members of one family under one God. It will unite the world against them. The pain I am suffering at their hands is as nothing, when compared to the enormous pride I feel at being a member of the British nation and also a part of this God-fearing human family. With His help, we will come through this together with renewed vigour. The fire of the terrorist bombs will forge new temper in the steel which is our nation. Take your courage in both hands and feed it to those who wilt under the pressure. Look after your family, look after your nation and be proud of them. God bless you all!"

The scene faded to a view of the band of the Household Cavalry, reforming after the initial shock of the explosion. They played the National Anthem as they rode into the forecourt of Buckingham Palace, missing their seven horses. It was almost as though the tragedy had never taken place, although this was the second time that an event of this nature had hit horsemen in the Mall.

"As you know, Sam, there have been some interesting developments in recent days." Jack rubbed his forehead, "and we would appreciate your input into how to get the IDCs accepted by the Russians. Could you come over? Alex and Margie will be here, together with Georg Lutov, Dick Tarrant and Johnnie Jason. It should be quite a reunion." He smiled happily at the prospect.

"Accommodation and Aberlour will be available free of charge. Alex says that the Haunted West Wing is missing you."

He was going to see if he could get Miss Scharanski over, as well, but he would have to keep that seriously under his hat. She was in a very precarious position with some of the old guard and he didn't want to expose her to more risks than he had to.

"Well, Jack, I have officially retired, so you can no longer rely on me professionally but, simply on a social basis, I can hardly resist the invitation. Thank you very much indeed."

"That's great Sam. When can you get here?"

"Well, Jack, as I say, I am retired now, so my time is my own."

"Give me a shout when you know and I'll come and meet you. Make sure that you don't have a haircut or a shave. There will be ladies present and they might not recognise you!"

"Can't wait!"

In order to contact Ludmilla, Jack had arranged a secure connection with GCHQ. Frank Dawlish and 'Mac' Macawley had provided close escort during her transition from refugee to politician. There had been two close shaves with the opposition and, on one of those, Mac had used some old tricks to dispose of the attacker. He and Ludmilla were on a train to Oxford, at the invitation of the Senior Tutor of Trinity College.

The dinner party was arranged to kick off in his rooms at eight-thirty p.m, so it was dark as they boarded the train at Paddington. There would be many of her old adversaries present, to introduce her to the way that they thought the new Russia could be reborn.

Most of the commuters had already gone home and the West End theatregoers were still being entertained, so the train was virtually empty. Mac and Ludmilla were the only occupants of their carriage on the small local train. They sat apart. Ludmilla was by herself, sitting by the window, with three empty seats around her. Mac positioned himself three rows back, so he could keep an eye on all approaches. At Reading station a large man entered the carriage and took a seat immediately behind Ludmilla. As the train pulled out of the station, he rose to his feet and his hand reached into the pocket of his overcoat. It never came out again during that agent's lifetime. Mac's chop to the neck severed the spinal column just below the skull and the man fell on to the seat. As he fell, a Glock automatic pistol tumbled on to the floor from his nerveless grasp. The next station at which the train stopped was Tilehurst.

Tilehurst is an unmanned station, so nobody witnessed the transfer of the body from the train to the waiting room on platform 3. One of the duties of the 'cleaners' who, at Mac's request, came to dispose of the evidence, was to doctor the only CCTV that had monitored the proceedings. The pistol was sent to forensics for fingerprinting to check if it had been used by anyone other than the killer. Evidence proved that it had which indicated that the asssassin was not acting alone.

This experience caused the close support team to exercise a heightened state of alert, when the future Prime Minister of the Federal Republic of Russia paid an extremely discreet visit to the Library Bar of the Antediluvian Club in London.

Jock welcomed her at the pantry door. "So, good to see you Miss Ludmilla! We have some of the Pshenichnaya here if you would like it. I know that it was to your taste in the old days."

"That would still be very much to my taste Jock!" She said, grasping Jock's hand and shaking it vigorously.

"I'll bring it to the bar, Ma'am. There are a lot of your friends there waiting for you."

"Thank you Jock." She released his hand and followed Mac and Frank through the familiar surroundings. Frank pushed open the door of the Library Bar and stuck his head through. "Ladies and Gentlemen, I have an unexpected and very welcome addition to the party!" and he pushed the door open for Ludmilla Romanova Scharanski to come past him.

There was a gasp of surprise from the assembled members of 'the Family'. They rose from their seats and Margie rushed over to her. "Ludmilla! You made it!" she shouted as she grasped the tiny Russian by the shoulders and kissed her on both cheeks. Alex was grinning as he limped across to her. "No hard feelings?" she said as she offered her cheek.

"Grrrr!" Alex bared his teeth, then closed his eyes and kissed his unsuccessful assassin.

"Ludmilla, come and join us by the fire." She took the small, comfortable Victorian chair, close to the fireplace and accepted the vodka, offered by the one-eyed barman. "Thank you so much, Jock. And you remembered the lemongrass!"

"So, Ludmilla, welcome back!" Jack had both his thumbs in the air. "So now what? "

Scharanski looked up at Jack. "You people rescued me and, for that, I am eternally grateful, considering my efforts to destroy you." She glanced at Alex and Margie. "I am now concerned about how we, and I say 'we', because this is of global concern, can introduce the IDCs to my own country. It will solve so many of our problems, but the Rouble is still the pillar of trade at the moment and the old guard is taking full advantage of that."

Dick Tarrant leaned forward, with his hand in the air. "I will, basically, lose everything, if we go over to the 'Credit Card' system. I will lose my house in Bishop's Avenue, because I have a mortgage on the property and, if the bank ceases to exist, I have no credits. So I lose the house. Correct?"

Jack the Hack pushed his glasses back up his nose and looked across at Dick. "Surely the mortgage would simply be transferred across to the Authority's books? You can't have the country full of homeless mortgage holders. That would defeat the whole object. No-one would join. No-one could afford to join. The scheme would fall flat on its face before you could get it established."

"And who is the Authority?"

"Ah, now there, if you will forgive the expression, you have the sixty-four thousand dollar question!" Sam scratched his head, digging for ideas. "I could probably throw together a programme for you, which would be impartial and not easy to corrupt. The applicant would just swipe his ID card in the Accounts machine, key in the loan requirement and answer the questions the computer asks." Sam's specs had slipped again. "The application will be authorised or denied almost immediately. All I need to know is what questions are needed, then I could churn out your programme, quick time and we could try it out."

"Well we could talk to the CABNI about that. They will have feed-back from Tarnbeck and the American experience." Jack had kept tabs on the interchange of information between the CABNI and the Americans. "Why don't I get in touch with them?"

"Sounds good."

Ludmilla stood up. "Are you people aware that the future of the world is what you are deciding right now?" She

412

stretched her hands apart, almost as though she did not believe they were taking things seriously enough.

Jack stood up beside the fire. "Ludmilla, with great respect, we have a problem here, which concerns us all. Not just 'the West', but also you in Russia. If we go into the IDC system, it will involve a massive philosophical and financial turnaround. Money, physical Money, will not exist anymore. No more 'Greenbacks', no more Pounds Sterling, no more Roubles, no more Yen and, for a capitalist, that is quite a leap in the dark. We have to get it right first time. Up until this point, everything has been on experimental. We have always had money to fall back on if the IDC system didn't work. There will be some very interesting reactions from the oligarchs, I should imagine, don't you agree Ludmilla?"

Ludmilla sat down next to Jack. "You're right there, Jack, but we can do it." She looked around the group with enthusiasm blazing out of those piercing green eyes. "In some ways our society is more adaptable to the IDCs than yours is and it seems to work over here, so it will work well in Russia."

"How will you implement it, Ludmilla?" His eyebrows rose, like two question marks. "You have a lot of enemies in your country."

"I have only one dangerous enemy in my country. It was Vladimir Chernorgin who ordered my execution after my second attempt to kill you, Mr Jason failed". She looked at the Deputy Commissioner, with an enigmatic smile.

Jason grinned and, putting his hands together, he looked up to the ceiling. "Alhamdulillah!" he murmured and the other members of the party looked upwards, with muttered expressions of relief. "I would have got you, next time, for sure, but then they tried to get me. And here I am."

"Okay Ludmilla, what do you need from us?" Frank Dawlish chipped in. "Security we can provide to a limited extent, but when you cross over, er, my Russian is not that good. I don't think that your people are very good in Glaswegian either, so Regimental Sergeant Major Macawley may have some difficulty convincing your people that he is a cute little hanger-on. He doesn't have the bumps in the right places, if you remember!"

Everybody laughed at memories of the last meeting they had, some three years before.

"No! No, my friends," she paused and stood up, beside Jack. "I had no friends before but you are now my friends and you have introduced me to others from Old Russia. They will support me. They will look after me until we bring the 'Rodina' back into the family." She looked round the 'Aunties' family. "You are wonderful people and I love you all, although I may have had a strange way of expressing it, in the past!"

She passed from one member of the party to the next, grasping hands and kissing offered cheeks. It was with considerable emotion that she left the room, escorted by Mac and Frank, for the beginning of her appointment with history.

Made in the USA
Charleston, SC
13 November 2015